Little Shadow

A Novel

By S. L. Schultz

Book one of the *Little Shadow Trilogy*

Published by

EditPros LLC
423 F Street, Suite 206
Davis, CA 95616
www.editpros.com

This is a work of fiction. Names, characters, places, and incidents either are the product of the author's imagination or are used fictitiously. Any resemblance to actual persons, living or dead, events, or locales is entirely coincidental.

ISBN: 978-1-937317-17-1

Library of Congress Control Number: 2014930873
Printed in the United States of America

To my father, Kenneth Winton Schultz
(Aug. 31, 1926–Jan. 16, 2014), one of the few, the proud.

"What is life? It is the flash of a firefly in the night. It is the breath of a buffalo in the wintertime. It is the little shadow which runs across the grass and loses itself in the sunset."

~Crowfoot

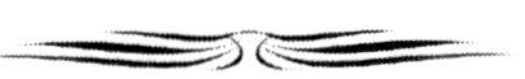

Prologue

Persian Gulf – February 1991

1
Dark Bloom

Dear Billy. Not honey, darling, sweetie, or babe. *There is something I've got to tell you.* Bagwell hopes she is writing to him about a wonderful surprise. *It's not easy. It's not easy at all.* A prickly fear crawls slowly up his back and cloaks him. Is she sick? Is something wrong with Lily? For Christ's sake, has someone dear to him died? *I don't love you anymore.* Shaking his head in disbelief, he reads these words again. *I don't love you anymore.* His eyes race over the remainder of the letter, and then he drops his head into the cup of his hands to cry. But the tears won't come.

Lifting his head, he peers into the raging sandstorm on the Arabian Desert. Visibility is reduced to silhouettes. Human forms appear like ghosts hovering above the ground, moving in and out, to and fro. More than anything, he wishes to see among the forms that of his little girl, Lily, dancing to him, her arms lifted gracefully overhead, her blue eyes, his eyes, shining like sapphires. Instead, his fellow jarheads pace as they wait for the action to grow closer and their own involvement to begin. The distant explosions of rockets punctuate their movements, missiles that echo hollow as they hit the sand, driving deep and spreading, stirring up the earth. The craters left behind become the graves where fallen Marines and soldiers lie.

Sincerely, Brenda. Fuck her and her sincerity! Bagwell wishes he had read the letter when he first received it, back in rear-rear, where a substance or two would be available to help him ease his pain. Why the hell did he wait until now? He glances up and peers again into the storm. Where is his little Lily? Why can't she be dancing to him? With just one of her smiles, reaching him through this blowing sand, the hole in his heart might heal.

How had he failed? What was it that he lacked? He could grab his combat knife, long and sharp and shiny, and plunge it deep into his belly. With a few quick cuts, delivered with the deft touch of The Ripper, watch his entrails tumble out as his lids shutter down upon his last sight. It wouldn't be his daughter, Lily. His last sight would be the sand growing thicker, obscuring all form into a surrounding box of slate gray. Bagwell balls the letter in one clenched hand and casts it into the sand. He watches as the drifting grains like a wave of ants weigh the letter down before it can slip into the wind forever.

A voice sneaks up on him from behind. "Bad news, Bagwell?"

"Fuck!" Bagwell jumps and turns from his seat in the sand to see Glover's black face, a marked contrast against the gray.

"Did I scare the piss out of ya?" Glover grins.

"Don't do that, man!" One little corner of the letter remains visible; his eye glues to it.

"Sachs wants two men out on point. Up for some target practice?"

Bagwell leans over and with two fingers snatches up the letter from its grave. He hopes that the wind and sand have somehow wiped it clean. "Oh, yeah. I'm real hungry for a head in the crosshairs."

Bagwell and Glover head out on their two-man mission, trudging their way through the knee-deep sand. The storm, one of many in this Desert Storm conflict, has calmed but it hasn't died, the visibility now broadened. Although the number of exploding rockets has dwindled, at any moment their emerging forms could be reduced to pieces, raining down in organ-and-flesh confetti, tans and black, blue and white, but mostly red. Bagwell imagines his sun-bleached hair blowing free from his head like straw after a tornado reduces a barn to splinters. The truth is he doesn't care if he dies. Now. He isn't sure he can slice open his belly. So if a Scud missile lands on him this moment, so be it. He would never have to know what it feels like when his ruptured heart awakens. But then, there's Lily.

We never planned for this to happen. We? Who the fuck was "we"? The next sentence had clinched it. *You asked him to watch over Sweet Pea and me.* Oh, him. With a burst of adrenalin only fury can feed, Bagwell begins trudging through the sand with ease.

"What the fuck, Bagwell!" Glover calls after him. "You trying to get us seen? We're out of this hellhole as soon as this shit is over. I plan on making it. How about you?"

Bagwell puts a brake on his pace and shifts the M40A1 sniper rifle over to the other shoulder. He can shoot into the eye of an enemy at a thousand meters. Do three hundred push-ups barely breaking a sweat. Run for hours with what feels like a hundred pounds strapped to his back. For what? To travel seven thousand miles into a barren land where towelheads guard their black gold, a commodity so dear that capitalist pigs are willing to sacrifice a half million of the military to steal it? He was a "lean, mean, killing machine," who enlisted to make his family proud. To make her proud! That bitch. How had he failed? What was it that he lacked?

He had been gone only a year. Was he so incidental, so easy to forget, that ten years together was forgotten in a flash? Bagwell imagines pinning her photo, the one with her dressed in that short little lace thing, up among the other photos on the Wall of Shame. The wall displays a black and white and color montage of cheating wives, lying girlfriends, and thieving whores, serving as a reminder that the only people you can ever really trust are the fraternity of Marines. You couldn't even trust your best friend back home who was with you when you jumped eleven times out of a plane, and the time the dirt bikes slid twenty-five feet and stopped with the front wheels dangling over a swamp as thick as soup. Your blood brother. The one with whom you consumed three cases of Pabst, two fifths of Wild Turkey and an ounce of weed. Okay, that took twenty-four hours, but they did it. He and Bagwell had been friends since they were boys. Maybe "his" picture should go up on that wall, too. The one of him holding the trophy he won going fastest in the quarter mile. His hair slicked back and his boots all dusty. His trademark smile, the one that seemed to make the girls go mad, lighting up his face.

"Fuck! Bagwell, stop!" Glover grabs Bagwell from the back of his vest and thrusts him down into the sand. "This is where we set up. It ain't no place to be lost in fantasy, brother. I need you here with me now." Glover leans over Bagwell lying half on his back in the sand and hooks his brown eyes to Bagwell's blue. "What the fuck is up with you? What was in that letter?"

Bagwell, holding the rifle in one hand, reaches up and pushes Glover away with the other, causing him to stumble back. "Get the fuck out of my face!"

Glover recovers his bearing and like a bulldog pushes Bagwell flat on his back and says distinctly and forcefully one inch from his face, "Be present, Marine. Be present."

Digging out their position hidden in the sand takes five hours. The sun breaks through the clearing storm; soon the thermostat reads one hundred thirteen degrees. They set up the sniper rifle pointing squarely towards enemy movement. Through the spotter's scope a few handfuls of soldiers and a scattering of officers preening like cocks can be seen. The two Americans have orders to take out the officers when the time is right. This time is determined by their superiors hidden safely away, a great distance back, in a tent city where they just might be playing poker. Glover and Bagwell lie on their bellies and watch as the storm dwindles to occasional squalls. These cyclones of sand remind Bagwell of cartoon characters spinning like tops. But he didn't feel like laughing. Though he was fighting to be present, the words of the letter hunted him down like a hound.

You asked him to watch over Sweet Pea and me. That son of a bitch. *James needs us.* James needs us! Bagwell busies himself looking through the rifle that Glover has guided through the spotter's scope. Of the two, Bagwell is the better shot. In fact, he's the best in his squad. Placing the crosshairs carefully on the head of an Iraqi in command, he bites down on a forbidden cigarette, smothering the smoke. He imagines James' head in this place and her head beside it. One shot, one kill. One shot, one kill. One shot, two kills. With one squeeze, of three to five pounds, in less than a second they would both be dead. He imagines the red mist spraying out. *We never planned it. It just happened.* Was he fucking her before I left? He spits the dead butt into the sand and feels an urge to scramble to his feet and run into the enemy line like a lion roaring. He could tear limbs away with his teeth, annihilating the entire enclave, salivating for one or two more. He could do it. Be a hero. Would he win her back?

Glover breaks the silence. "You got that glazed look again, Bagwell."

Bagwell turns to Glover and sees concern on his fellow Marine's face. Here was honest fraternity. Here was a man he could count on to catch him if he fell. Or could he? All trust was in question now.

"It's about that letter. I know it is. The one crawling out of your pocket right there." Glover points to the right breast pocket of Bagwell's vest.

Bagwell glances down to see a few words on the crumpled mass of the letter peeking from his pocket. The wind and sand had not cleaned it off after all. He pulls the letter out with two fingers of his left hand and with his right begins to tear it.

"Are you sure you want to do that, Bagwell? Maybe you didn't read all the words just right."

"Oh, I read them all right."

Glover grabs the letter from him. "You'll regret it."

Bagwell grabs it back, tearing off the lower quarter where the words *James and I are a couple now* are written on top of some damn flower. "Mother fuck! Now look what you did!"

Glover sighs. "I didn't mean for that to happen."

Bagwell answers back through clenched teeth. "That's just what she said."

Glover shakes his head. "So, it's one of those, huh?"

Bagwell turns back to his rifle and states, "I'm going to kill them."

"Kill who?" Glover asks.

A moment or two of silence passes, then Bagwell blurts out, "So are they going to tell us to do our job or what? I'm sick of lying in this shit. I've got fucking sand seeping into every hole on my body!"

Suddenly their radio comes alive with a crackle. Glover picks up the piece and speaks into it. "We cannot read, over." The crackling continues. He speaks louder, more distinctly. "We cannot read, over."

Bagwell says, "You got to be kidding me! Get off of that thing before the Iraqis triangulate! Three seconds! You know the rule!"

"Oh, you smoke a fucking cigarette, but you're worried about triangulation?"

Bagwell turns quickly into Glover's face. "Don't fuck with me!"

"I ain't your enemy, Bagwell. I'm sorry about your bad news. But, I didn't have anything to do with it."

Bagwell withdraws. "You're right. You're right. I'm just frustrated with this equipment."

Glover throws the radio aside. "I know. Nothing works in this fucking battalion."

Suddenly, a distant whistle, strong and shrill, grows louder. In seconds the two men know that a rocket is heading for them.

Glover yells, "Incoming!"

Both men shimmy on their bellies into the recess of their dugout in the sand, covering the backs of their heads with crossed arms. The rocket impacts the heart of the desert about a hundred feet away, exploding back out into something at once beautiful and grotesque. It is a gigantic flower blooming out of the earth; it is a spouting fountain from a punctured vein. Sand rains down upon them in clumps and grains.

Glover yells in precaution, "Gas! Gas! Gas!"

Glover and Bagwell scramble to place their masks over their faces, peering at each other as if under the sea, their damp sweaty cammies now wet through with piss.

One word serves as Bagwell's mantra: Lily, Lily, Lily. Her lovely little face appears in his mind haloed with curls. She holds her arms out for him to scoop her small frame into his. *You know how much Lily likes him.* How could she write those words! She's *my*

girl! She's *my* girl! Bagwell wants to cry, but he can't.

Within seconds, another whistle is heard, distant, again growing closer. Glover screams again, "Incoming!"

The second rocket impacts the sand some seventy-five feet away; the rain of sand half-buries them. The earth stirs beneath the two men, as they rock and sway and tremble.

Bagwell scrambles himself up to the rifle and frantically searches through the crosshairs for the heads. His voice is muffled through the plastic of the mask, "Spot me, Glover! Spot me!"

Glover pulls Bagwell away from the rifle. "No! We don't know what the orders were."

Bagwell turns to him wild-eyed. "I don't give a fuck! We're fucking bait! They sent us out as bait!"

The third whistle is heard approaching in what feels like slow motion. The two men, sensing strongly that this rocket is falling closer, stare for a moment into each other's eyes.

Bagwell leans in towards Glover and speaks clearly through the mask, "You're a good friend."

The light of the explosion is blinding. Bagwell feels himself flying weightless through the air, twisting and turning, caught within the eye of the funnel. After what seems to him like years, he lands roughly with a hollow thump, followed with total darkness.

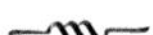

Bagwell stands in his backyard on a summer day. The blue sky towers, sloping down into the horizon that can be seen in every direction. God's cathedral. He watches as Lily runs into the house through the screen door to hit the play button on the cassette deck. The music of The Cure, his favorite, that she has learned to love, booms out through the screen door. Lily dances out in perfect time, her red shoes contrasting with the green of the grass. She leaps into Bagwell's arms. He lifts her and they spiral around the yard, their laughter rising in bubbles. Brenda stands at the screen door wiping her hands on a kitchen towel, orange and yellow checked, a smile gracing her quiet demeanor. Lily is on her feet once more; Bagwell clasps her tiny hands tightly as they continue with their twirl. A breeze whispers through blue cornflowers,

pink peonies and yellow chrysanthemums. The family's Australian shepherd, Jake, breaks the beat with occasional woofs, his tail swatting away at flies. Little Lily's face is as bright as the sun. Her eyes, which gaze upon her father's face, adore.

—m—

Bagwell's consciousness moves upward through a long dark tunnel, stony and moist. Tentatively, he opens his eyes to find himself lying on his back, half covered with sand. The gas mask is askew upon his face; he sucks in a needed breath, terrified to move. He hears a groan and knows that it is not his own. Turning his head towards the sound, he spies Glover lying on his side, ten feet away, arms flung over his head, his legs bent as if he is running. Even from here, Bagwell can see the dark bloom on Glover's chest as red as Lily's shoes. He was home. He thought he was home. A sob catches in his throat. He has to move. He has to check on Glover. As he begins to lift his upper body, the sand slipping off, he notices the heaviness of his right leg. He bends over to check it. Through the hole in his cammie he sees a tear in the flesh, six inches in length, one inch wide, where a piece of shrapnel protrudes through a small pool of coagulated blood. How fucking long has it been since that last explosion? Looking up towards the sun he figures an hour, maybe two?

Glover groans. Bagwell turns himself over with his hands. Dragging his injured leg, he crawls slowly over to Glover, peering into every direction of the rolling sand that has no end. The vast expanse is beautiful when silent. He carefully rolls Glover onto his back, a dry sob rising into his throat. Jesus, he can't cry now. He slaps Glover gently on the cheeks. "Glover. Glover, you hear me? Glover."

Glover's eyelids open partially. They drop. They open partially again. He tries to speak, his voice breathless and garbled, "Wha ... wha ... hap ..."

Bagwell opens Glover's vest, tears away the cammie to get a look at his wound. Like his own, the blood is mostly coagulated, except in this case for one small deep cavern, where red air bubbles rise out to burst. Bagwell utters a long drawn out "fuck" beneath his breath. He takes a pressure bandage out of the first-aid kit hanging on his belt and applies it to the wound. Next he punctures Glover's upper thigh with a double dose of morphine. With this done, he begins to look around for the radio and when he spies it, crawls over to find it partially destroyed, their fort in the sand now flattened. He wonders why they haven't been rescued. For Christ's sake, they know where we are. Did they leave us behind for dead? I was home. I was home, he thinks. He remembers the letter. *I don't love you anymore.* How the fuck did he fail? What was it that he lacked? The dry sobs rush up, rolling through him, doubling him over with a heave. The water breaks, the only water he can see anywhere in this God-forsaken sea of sand. Glover. He's got to take care of Glover. Dragging his leg, he crawls back to Glover as his tears, soft and salty, run into his mouth. He looks around, orienting himself, knowing that pain in his leg or not, he must carry Glover to safety. They must be looking for us, he thinks. They must be.

"Okay, Glover, we got to go." Glover groans in reply. Bagwell stands on one leg, stepping down on the injured other, the pain hot and sharp. His tears that were silent now find a voice like the moaning of a dove. He bends over, lifts Glover up over one shoulder, and begins to walk.

Bagwell drags each foot up out of the sand, watching the sun begin to drop. He no longer feels the pain in his leg and marks his own breath with the ragged breath of Glover. His friend is breathing. He is still breathing. A light wind rises and dries the last of Bagwell's tears. The sun is hot, so hot he is happy to see it drop. But he knows they must reach safety before the darkness falls. After that they probably would never be found. The desert comes alive in the night with hungry creatures and dangerous marauders. Then he hears the sound, like the hum of an insect's wings, or could it be.... He falls to his knees and drops Glover to the ground on his back, covering his friend's body with his own, and whispers in his ear to be still.

Bagwell lifts slightly to see a sudden desert squall move through. The ballet of wind pulls the two pieces of the letter from his vest and rolls them away across the sand. He wants to reach out so badly to retrieve them, but knows he mustn't move – if not to save his own life, to save Glover's. With another gust, the pieces disappear. Oh, well, he thinks, it doesn't matter now. He knows that he read the words all right. The hum of an insect's wings grows louder. Bagwell now clearly identifies the sound as an engine, but doesn't know if it is friend or foe.

Part I
Battlefield

American Midwest – June 1991

2
Safe House

Thursday 9:33 p.m.

Brenda stands, her knees growing weak, with the one-page letter in her hand. The airmail paper is thin as a butterfly's wing, but the weight of the content could knock her to the floor. Billy arrives home tomorrow. She stares out the window over the kitchen sink upon the fields stretching back behind the house. These fields contain growing hay, soybeans, and knee-high corn. The earth lies dry, the furrows between the rows rough, coarse, and crumbling. Out of the corner of one eye she registers, but just barely, Jake, trotting around the backyard with his muzzle deep into the yellowing grass. In the distance, two forms take shape in the fading light; a doe with her fawn stand on the edge of a small wood feeding. Brenda watches as the doe lifts her muzzle to the wind, tail twitching, ears making subtle shifts from side to side. The sight of the two creatures, vulnerable and alone, triggers a memory that has haunted Brenda for two decades.

Brenda, five years old, sits in the back seat of the family car wearing a pink flowered dress, trimmed in lace. On her feet are patent leather shoes that capture passing images in an ever-shifting collage. She is so small and her legs so short that they stick out just a few inches beyond where the seat ends. As she stares out the window, the glaring sun periodically blinds her when it peeks between sprawling oaks and walnuts, and sporadic farmhouses that line the road on both sides. The houses and trees cast long shadows on the earth. Lying behind the trees and in between houses are vast fields of corn, green, tall and thick, or golden wheat moving with the breath of the wind in waves.

Silence fills the car. Brenda's mother and father do not exchange a word. Even she as a small child can feel the tension that strains the air, making her afraid to breathe or even shift a leg. Brenda keeps her eyes steady on the scene outside the window, afraid that she will see her father reach quickly across the space between him and her mother, and strike her with his hand. Though she has never seen this happen, it often feels like she will. She glances for a moment at her mother to see her wavy brown hair, a string of pearls around her neck, and when she turns, the brightness of her red colored lips. Brenda turns back to the window and begins to count the houses, peering at them closely as they pass. She searches for the house she has seen in a dream. She will recognize it right away. Inside this house she will be safe.

Her father sniffs his nose and clears his throat as he always does. His bearing is absolute as he stares out the windshield, daring either her mother or her to break the silence. Brenda counts the houses longing to be outside this car. But would she get lost in the maze of corn? Would the waves of the wheat ride her away forever? Where is the house? The windows will look like open eyes, the porch that spreads across the front, a smile. The fallen leaves and branches from the trees above will be the hair. The front door painted red, the nose. Soon she will be safe.

One by one they pass the houses, but not the one she longs to see. The glare of the light grows dim now and the faces of the houses lose detail. She must find the house before the night comes!

Her mother's voice breaks the silence, starting with a word Brenda is forbidden to say, "Shit. Oh, brother."

Her father turns to look at her mother with his eyebrows raised. "Now what?"

Her mother darts a look at him and turns to stare again out front. "I forgot to take the meat out of the freezer."

Her father sighs and shakes his head emphatically. "I can't count on you for anything, can I?"

Her mother starts to cry, and Brenda turns to stare again out the window. When her father stops the car at a stop sign in the middle of the fields, Brenda pushes down on the door handle and in a moment runs free. The corn stalks stand tall as giants, and the maze they create seems to have no end. The tassels on the ears wave above her in the breeze. Field mice engaged in evening meals scatter, while crows call harshly, the sentries of a search party she keeps turning to avoid. The sky grows darker; she has no idea where she is going. She only knows that she must find the farmhouse that exists someplace, somewhere.

Brenda, now breathless, half stumbles through the stalks. She can hear her name called in the distance. Just when she thinks she has no more might, the corn ends and before her waves the wheat. The wheat, though not so tall, cuts into her bare and tender legs with fibrous grain. Through the diffused luminescence of twilight she thinks she sees the farmhouse in the distance. The very one she has longed to see. If only she can make it through this field. She is panting, her legs weak, when one foot connects with the exposed coil of a root. For a moment she feels herself flying through the air, and when she hits the ground in a painful thump everything goes black. In this darkness, she fears she will be lost forever.

"Mommy!" The voice of her own child, Lily, sweet and clear as the twinkling of a bell, startles Brenda from her haunting. Lily, running up from behind, wraps her arms around her mother's legs and squeezes them with all her might. The letter, released from Brenda's hand through this simple shock, floats to the ground in a long, slow sway. Clutching her daughter's small hands in her left hand, she sweeps the letter up in her right. Lily can read quite well now.

Lily releases her mother's legs and begins to jump up and down like a pogo stick, asking "Is it a letter from Daddy? Is he coming home, Mommy? Is he?"

Brenda wonders what the hell she is going to tell her child. Quickly she sticks the letter behind a canister full of flour, turns away from the sink, and bends over to scoop her daughter up into her arms. Not an easy task. Lily is now five, petite, but long limbed. Brenda kisses her on the cheek. "He's ... he's coming back soon, Sweet Pea."

"When?"

"Soon, Lily. Soon." Brenda glances out the picture window to see the sun quickly sinking. Long lines of purple, gold, and orange streak the horizon. The blue of the sky above deepens, creating a dark, dense field, through which the light of the stars will shine. Brenda takes Lily by the hand and speaks to her the words that were spoken to her by her mother, and her mother before that. "Let's sit in the rocker and watch the sun slip into bed." Brenda settles into the chair with Lily lying in her arms, her little head resting softly against her shoulder.

"Is Uncle James staying here tonight?" Lily asks.

"James is staying every night, Lily. He lives here now."

"But where will Daddy stay?"

"I ... I don't know. But someplace close, I'm sure." With this thought, Brenda's stomach sinks. Brenda isn't ready to see him. She has conveniently pushed him into a hidden recess and kept him there at bay. It is easier that way. Not that he deserves to be put there and forgotten. A glimpse of his face springs before her mind's eye and something in her heart stirs. They had been high school sweethearts, together since the age of fifteen. Until James, she'd never been kissed by another boy.

She remembers all the hurtful words she wrote in that letter to Billy, what was it, three months ago? *I don't love you anymore.* How could she be so cold? Telling Billy that she and James were a couple now. How will she face him? Pulling Lily in closer, Brenda gently rocks the chair and watches as the sun sets. She hopes to catch the blue flash that indicates good tidings before the light disappears into the night, an old wives' tale passed down through the centuries, covered with webs but not forgotten. Brenda needs good tidings.

"I want Daddy to stay here," Lily says in a broken voice.

"He won't be far away."

It was Billy's fault for leaving her. He knew she couldn't be alone. What made him think he had to be a part of that stinking war, anyway? He hated the desert. He hated the heat. But that was Billy for you, always ready to fight for a cause. The war was mostly over now, and they didn't even get Hussein. Brenda heard that Billy will always walk with a limp, part of the shrapnel in his leg forever. That's what Grandma Martha, Brenda's paternal grandmother, told her, even though she had not asked. Everyone was upset with her for being mad at Billy.

Brenda thinks about the letter stuffed behind the canister in the kitchen and her heart begins to beat faster. *You can't hide from me, Brenda. Don't even try. You and James should get your things in order.* What the hell does that mean? Grandma Martha had mentioned that Billy was seeking help for his head, as the deep and ragged wound on his leg healed. Was it a healthy or unhealthy head that produced the letter she had just received? She imagines him, tall and muscular, walking with a limp, perhaps a cane or crutch aiding him. She remembers Billy in all his glory. He was the town's wild boy whose courage knew no limits. Jumping off the railroad trestle on a homemade bungee cord, landing just an inch above the creek. Plunging out of a small plane into a cloud-dotted sky, to float back to the earth on a sail. Tearing around the hills on two wheels, snowmobiling across the fields of snow and sliding across the ice of a frozen lake. She had witnessed it all, and one person – James – was always at his side. Brenda's bottom lip begins to tremble. Good God, what has she done?

Lily presses her face into her mother's shoulder. Brenda can feel the tears on her daughter's lashes. "I want Daddy to stay here."

"I thought you liked James, Lily."

A few beats of silence follow, then Lily finally says, "I don't like him anymore." Lily scrambles up from Brenda's lap and runs towards her bedroom. Brenda stands up and follows, finding that her child has thrown herself face down on the bed. Brenda sits down on the edge and gently turns her child over.

Lily says, "My daddy is never mean."

Lily begins to cry harder and Brenda bends to hold her. Brenda remembers Billy running with Lily across the grass. Would she ever see him run again? He would swing his little girl around in circles as she laughed with glee. Carry her on his shoulders so together they would be more than seven feet tall. He never tired of being with his little girl.

Brenda raises her torso, while caressing her daughter's face, soft as down. She looks around her daughter's room, taking in the purple flowered wallpaper, white wood furniture and, in one corner, a pile of stuffed animals three feet high. Only one lies on her bed next to her: a yellow striped kitty with a small blue bell hanging from a purple ribbon around the neck. The kitty was a substitute toy for one that had been taken away – too ragged, too frayed, too worn, a brown bear dressed in a red plaid jumper, given to her when she was just two. Billy had won the toy for her at the town fair and, from that moment forward, the bear went everywhere with Lily. James decided three months previously that the bear would have to go. He said the stuffed animal was an eyesore, a disease-ridden thing, a rag and, besides, Lily was a big girl now. Lily wouldn't give it up, so James snuck into her room on the sly, took it, and told her that Growlie the bear had run away from home.

"I want to be with my daddy," Lily says.

Brenda whispers to her, "It's going to be okay." But Brenda doesn't feel sure.

Lily grows quiet from her crying and starts to fall asleep. She does, however, open her eyes in a slit and whisper, "Don't forget to call in Jake." Billy had asked Lily to take special care of the family dog. Then she adds, "Don't forget to call for Growlie, too."

Tears spring to Brenda's eyes as she whispers back, "I won't forget." She pulls the covers up to Lily's chin, stands quietly and tiptoes out of the room. The door remains open, for Lily tends to be as afraid of the dark as Brenda is.

Brenda walks over to the sliding glass doors and steps out onto the wooden deck, leans against the railing, draws in a deep breath, and lets it out in a sigh. He shouldn't have left her to go to that stupid war. She had felt safe with Billy. She wasn't sure she felt as safe with James. The way in which he took her daughter's toy gnawed upon her.

The darkness has fallen, and the moon rises, most of the light hidden behind clouds. Where is that damn dog? Billy's dog. Lily's dog. Her dog. But not James' dog. "Jake!" she calls. "Jake!" Then she sees him, or thinks she does, rooting around at the foot of the flagpole, in the far corner of the yard. He answers her with one loud woof. What the heck was he doing? She can just make out the long metal pole stretching up into the night. There has not been a flag flying from it since Billy left. "Growlie! Come!" Growlie? What is she thinking? No wonder the dog doesn't come when she calls. Brenda knows she should walk down the steps into the dark and drag the damn dog home. But it's so dark.

Brenda steps back into the house to grab a flashlight out of the drawer. The flashlight, long and large, casts a broad light. She feels safer now and walks down the steps and onto the lawn that stands already damp with dew. The first fireflies of the night appear, helping to guide her with their tiny twinkling lights. Aiming the beam of the flashlight towards the flagpole, she now sees the Australian shepherd frantically digging a hole. Shreds of the nasturtiums and the sweet alyssum fly to disappear into the night like missiles. "Jake! No!" she yells.

The dog's curious behavior makes her wary of what else might lie outside the light. As she approaches the dog, she peers off cautiously from side to side. When she finally reaches him, a pair of headlights suddenly arc across the yard. A pickup truck pulls into the driveway and up beside the house.

James.

Brenda watches as Jake's eyes are caught momentarily in the light. Then he turns back to the hole, pulls something out of the earth, and begins to trot back to the house, wholly excited with his prize. No doubt it was a bone that Billy buried for him there. Brenda, with her light in hand, heads back to the house as well, until remembering that James will mock her for her fear, and she turns the flashlight off.

Making her way back through the yard, her heart beating fast, she climbs the steps of the porch and walks into the kitchen and the half-light. There stands James in tight blue jeans and a short-sleeved black tee. To his left stands Lily, golden curls mussed, eyes half open, the yellow striped kitty clutched tight. In the center sits the dog, his tail swishing from side to side, his tongue hanging out in a pant. Between his front paws lies the dirty prize.

Brenda approaches the dog, reaching over to grab him by the collar. "You're a bad dog! You come when I call!"

James speaks up. "What the hell is going on here?" He sweeps away his long dark bangs with the fingers of his right hand.

"Mommy, what is it?" Lily asks.

James turns to Lily. "Why aren't you in bed?"

Lily steps back as her blue eyes widen.

Brenda says, "She's okay. Jake dug up some old bone back near the flagpole."

"He what?" James moves in closer, eyes darting towards the object on the floor.

Brenda drops to her knees, and hoping Jake doesn't feel possessive, reaches out tentatively to touch what she believes to be a bone. The dog seems content just to have found it.

James steps forward and pushes Brenda away. "I'll take that." He scoops up the object, which falls apart in his hand, one piece dropping to the floor. Obviously not a bone.

In that moment, Brenda recognizes the glimpse of a plastic eye and the rigid prongs of whiskers.

Lily cries out, "Growlie!"

Brenda softly gasps.

Before James can stuff the remnants of what once was Lily's favorite toy in the back waistband of his jeans, Brenda screams out, "No!" She scrambles up from her knees and opens her hands towards James. "Give it to me."

Lily drops her yellow kitty and emits a series of long shrill screams.

"Stop that!" James hisses through clenched teeth.

Brenda repeats, "Give it to me."

James releases the remnants of the bear into Brenda's hands and mutters under his breath, "Fucking dog."

Lily, now crying, runs up to her mother. "Where was he? Was he in the dirt? Is ... he ... dead?"

Brenda kneels down holding what is left of the bear, looking up at James with tears and a question in her eyes. "He was never alive, Lily."

James drops to his knees. "No. No. Yes, he is dead. He is dead now. He's all gone."

Lily, gently touching the remnants with her fingers asks, "Where is his jumper?"

Brenda pulls her child in to soothe her, as Lily rubs her little face into the damp decaying body of her toy.

"You're a big girl now, Lily," James says. "I told you that before. Big girls don't need their baby toys anymore." He touches Lily gently on the arm, but she pulls away.

"My daddy is coming home," Lily says, glaring at James.

James turns to look at Brenda. She avoids his eyes and thinks, *Billy is home already.*

3
Unseen Forces

Friday 6:55 a.m.

Martha wonders if the trimmers will yell, "Timber!" as the old oak falls. Will the earth shake as the girth and height of the tree make contact with her skin?

The tree was born of a seed blown to this town many years before. It grew tall with its branches spreading wide. But now the tree was partially defoliated and weakened by disease. Yet still it stands erect, anchored by the deep roots and stretched upward by the warming light of the sun. The oak's removal will leave a hole in a canopy of trees, allowing the sun to shine directly on the family farmhouse. Martha's African violets will suffer. She will have to move them, forty in all, lush, fertile, and in perpetual bloom.

Martha stands in the north window of the house beneath the canopy. She bathes herself in the slivers of early morning light. She watches the light dance as the branches and leaves shift in the breeze. Tears roll down her cheeks, catching the essence of the light in prisms. They reflect every leaf of the canopy, every branch, every twig, every small singing thing that calls this safe place home.

Martha remembers when she and her husband, Samuel, moved to this house fifty years before. The house sitting on the hill was plain and the trees surrounding this family home were small. The land was rolling and covered with tall grass and the purple flowers of nettle, the white of Queen Anne's lace, and the yellow petals and dark centers of black-eyed Susan. In the distance a creek sparkled, ambling over rocks, curving and cutting its way through the vast country fields. Martin was a babe, Sammie not yet born. Martha and Samuel dreamed of raising a barn behind the house and painting its wide wooden planks red. They would milk cows, grow crops, go to church, and make friends. Martha and Samuel would become an integral part of this small town.

Martha pulls one corner of her apron, a flowered print of red, blue, and green, up to dry her tears beneath glasses, thick and round. She reaches up to pat her long gray hair held back into a ponytail by a blue cotton ribbon.

The trees had outlived Samuel and she had been sure they would all outlive her as well.

The grandmother turns to face the room that is the heart of her home, the scene of many family gatherings: weddings in white to mourning in black, graduations and births between. If she listens hard, she can hear old cries and laughter, too. Her eyes bounce from one object to another, resting at last on the picture that hangs on the wall above the sofa. A painting brushed to life decades before by an old friend long dead. The painting depicts a local wood, silent, deep in snow, that in some strange way looks warm. There is a stream, only part of which is frozen. The murmur of the moving water can almost be heard.

Martha steps forward to move out of the room. Catching her foot in the fringe of a throw rug, she stumbles, catches herself, and watches as the painting scrapes the wall, falling to the floor behind the sofa. Peeking over the back, Martha sees the glass broken in a diagonal that splits the face. She draws a breath. On the farm there are many signs to interpret in nature and within the routines of daily life: rings around the moon, colors in the horizon, spoons and forks dropped, where and when squirrels bury their autumn nuts. This fallen picture also constitutes a sign.

Suddenly Martha hears the back door to the house open and someone calling, "Ma!" She heads towards the kitchen and meets her son Martin halfway.

"So, are they going to cut that damn tree down or what?" Martin asks.

"Good morning to you, too." Martha answers.

"I thought they were coming at seven."

"It's five to seven, Martin."

"Not on my watch. What's wrong with your eyes?"

Martha turns her face away from him.

"They're red," Martin adds.

"Now they match your brother's," Martha says, as she walks over to the kitchen sink and begins to wash her breakfast dishes.

Martin leans against the counter. "You're not crying over that tree, are you?"

"How did you get so hard-hearted?"

"I'm not hard-hearted."

"No, you're a marshmallow." She turns from the sink, wiping her hands on her apron. "The painting of the woods fell off the wall."

"You want me to put it back up?"

"It's a sign."

"Oh, a sign."

"It means death, Martin."

"Oh, brother. You got any cookies?"

"In the next few days. Someone's going to die."

"Ma, for crying out loud!"

"I know you don't believe it." Martha pulls a tin box decorated with a sleigh-ride out of the cupboard. She pulls the top off and slides it towards Martin.

Martin takes a cookie. "How old are these things?"

"They're not old! Your grandmother's heart gave out two days after the picture in the bedroom fell off the wall. You know the one. Little pink flowers made out of shells. Your dad bought them for me in Florida."

"Ma, I really don't want to hear it."

Martha takes one step closer to Martin. "My cousin Lulu got thrown off a horse three days after a picture fell. Broke her neck and died instantly."

Martin turns from his mother and starts to walk out of the room. "I'll put the picture back on the wall, Ma."

"You can't. The glass is broken." Martha follows him into the living room.

Through the north window Martin and Martha watch as the tree-removal crew arrives. Martha's heart beats faster.

"I'll get them started," Martin says as he turns to leave the room.

"You make sure they understand that they are not to touch any of the other trees."

"Yes, Ma."

As she watches the men unload their equipment from the truck, the scene begins to waver. Her face becomes flushed with a sudden heat as she stumbles back, half falling into an old rocker. One tendril alone connects her to the present: a fleeting thought that maybe she is the one to pass, as a few minutes of her life flash before her.

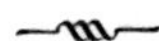

Martha rings the dinner bell and watches as Martin and Sammie come running across the field. Martin is ten, Sammie five. She can tell this by measuring the height of the boys against the flowers in the field. The word spread that angels glide above these pastures. Martha swears she has seen them a time or two. The movement of their wings brings the wind, and their voices lead the birds in chorus. Martha feels sure that they protect her boys from harm. Martin carries a stick in one hand; Sammie carries a box. No doubt there is something alive inside. Their pants are crusted with mud, their faces smudged. Sammie calls desperately to Martin, who always walks several feet ahead.

Two corn cribs are full of ears, kernels gnawed away by mice. The milk house, made of cement blocks, is surrounded by bushes of berries, red and black. One garden lies full of flowers where Martha bends and tills, and another full of growing vegetables: sour rhubarb, sweet tomatoes, long green beans, round, lush melons, and assorted roots still buried. The barn stands tall and wide behind the house. Straw protrudes from every door and window as if the barn is overstuffed. Martha can hear the cows mooing as Samuel cleans out their stalls. He may be finished by now, with one bottle of beer in hand, three more empty at his feet.

Probably he mumbles about things he refuses to express out loud. Martha rings the bell again.

—∞—

Martin the man stands beside her. "Are you napping? I've never seen you nap during the day."

Martha opens her eyes to see the wall above the sofa bare. She pushes on the arms of the rocker to stand. "I'm ... fine." In truth, she wobbles.

Martin reaches out to steady her.

Martha figures that if it is her time to go, so be it. But the butterflies in her stomach warn her that this may not be. Her head begins to swim with the faces, ages, and lifestyles of all the family members. Each of them has a story; none are immune to the process of the taking. No one is sick and dying at this time – unless someone has fallen ill overnight: stabbed by a pain, drenched in sweat, or fallen to the floor in weakness. The fallen picture offers no clues as to who it will be. Nor does the sign offer how. It could be something other than a failing body: an accident, a murder, or simply an act of God. Unseen forces are at play here.

Martha feels an urge to call everyone and warn them, but what good will it do? Most of them will only shrug it away or laugh, except for Sammie and maybe Brenda. But Martha knows; over the years she has kept a tally of the accuracy of signs. If only somehow she could convince them. Maybe they could monitor their health, curb unkind words, drive with caution, and watch for falling limbs. Maybe there exists a way to cheat the fate the fallen picture has foretold.

Martha places her hand on her son's arm. "Martin, you've got to keep an eye on your brother over the next few days."

"I've kept an eye on him all my life. Can I have a break now?"

Martha can hear the cords being pulled outside that will bring the saws alive. Their song sings tense and shrill, setting her jaw on edge, the butterflies in her stomach fluttering to be free. She imagines the saws cutting into her own skin, the red blood flowing. "No! No! Tell them to stop!" Swiftly she turns and heads out of the room towards the kitchen, her hands over her ears.

Martin follows and calls after her, "What the hell is going on with you?"

Martha says, "I don't care if the tree is sick. I don't want it cut down."

"It's just a tree, Mother."

Martha stops and turns to him. "It is not just a tree." She can hear the branches falling to the ground. Too late now to stop them. "You've got to keep an extra eye on Brenda since Billy is away."

"How about I just quit my job as county supervisor and keep an eye on everyone in the family? Besides, from what I hear, Brenda doesn't need anyone looking after her. She's already moved that little prick in."

"I don't believe it." Martha falls the short distance back against the counter.

"Well, you better believe it. I've seen his truck parked there every night."

"Maybe he's just staying there temporarily, in between moves."

"Oh, he's making some moves, all right."

Martha turns to Martin, flustered. "You never give anyone the benefit of the doubt."

"I know James Tillman. The whole town knows James Tillman!"

Martha quickly dries the dishes and places them into the oak cupboard. "And I know my granddaughter. If he's living there, it's because she is afraid to be alone. After what happened to her mother ..."

"That's not an excuse for what she is doing."

Martha hears the branches of the oak thud onto the earth one by one. "You don't know what's happening inside those four walls."

"Ma, people have seen them! Everyone knows it's true, but you."

"Well, if it is true, we're in trouble. Billy is coming home today."

"How do you know?"

"He wrote me. He's written me over the months."

"Oh, boy. Hold on to your hats."

She mutters, "It must be coming to a head. The picture ..."

"Ma, I'll buy a new piece of glass for the picture. I'll hang it back on the wall."

"That won't change anything!" Martha hears a loud whoosh and this thud shakes the house. She figures it must be the top of the tree. The sound of the saws makes her feel like screaming. She never dreamed that losing the tree would be this hard. Hard. But not this hard. She drops her head and muffs her ears with her hands.

Martin steps around the counter and guides his mother by her shoulders towards the back door. "Let's go. I'm putting you into the car, and we're leaving for a while."

Martha breaks out of Martin's clasp. "No! I'm not going anywhere." She says softly, "It's all gone."

"What's gone?"

"The farm."

"It's been gone, Ma."

"The barn, the corn cribs, the cows. Now the trees."

Martha cannot help but move back towards the living room and the north window. What remains left of the oak is shocking. The saws are screaming for her as she imagines the nests spilling out of the tree, the squirrels jumping from their holes, the creatures of many legs holding on for dear life. She covers her ears with her hands once again.

Martin follows her into the living room and says loudly, "You're making yourself sick."

Martha drops her hands with a sudden thought. "Is Petey still staying out all night?"

"I don't know what the hell he's doing."

"He's your son!"

"He's twenty years old!"

"And fragile in many ways."

"Well, that's not my fault."

"Of course it is!"

"I gave up my dream and my life for them."

"And look what they gave up having you as a father. Any sense of security. Any sense of unconditional love."

"Oh, like my father was so great. Hanging out with the cows all day drinking himself silly."

Martha turns to him wide eyed, hands on her hips. "Martin Becker! Your father gave you this home. He never told you how to live. He loved you in spite ... in spite of everything."

"Oh, I'm the ogre. How about if I just stuff a gun into my mouth. Will that make you happy? Will that satisfy your 'sign'?"

"Please, just watch over them."

Martin turns to glare out of the window, his head bobbing to the fall of the branches. "My son, the ... is on his own."

Martha falls back into the rocker, shaking her head in disbelief. "You are right. You aren't hard-hearted. You have no heart." Leaning her head back against the crocheted cushion, she rocks back and forth, and back and forth, and the rhythm unlocks the memory of Billy's levelheadedness. For a moment her face brightens. "Billy will sort it out and handle it in the right way."

Martin turns to her. "James and Brenda are living together in his house."

"Nobody knows but James and Brenda what is going on."

"I know what's going on. My daughter couldn't keep her legs closed. Just like women throughout time. The men go to war. The women can't bother to wait."

"James is watching over her for Billy."

"No, Ma. James is screwing my daughter, his best friend's wife. The crap is going to hit the fan, and it should."

Martha stands up from the chair and moves into Martin's face. "You mark what I've said, Martin." She steps over to the couch and peeks again over the back at the painting.

Martin rushes over and pulls the painting from behind the sofa. "A painting fell off the wall. It doesn't mean anything. I'll replace the glass today. I'll hang it back on the wall. Let it go, Ma. Let it go."

Martha realizes that the saws have stopped. She knows there will be one more that determines which way the tree will fall. Holding her breath, she hears her heart beat inside. The final saw screeches to life. Martha feels its bite through the bark. When the great tree falls, bald of branches, and a third less tall, the earth shakes, the house trembles, the butterflies flutter free. Martha waits for the snow to fall. She is enclosed in glass, turned upside down.

4
Dirt Road

Friday 7:53 a.m.

James backs down the driveway and pulls away from the house. He watches in the rearview mirror as the house reduces to a dot, imagining Brenda waving goodbye from the porch. But she's not.

In fact, last night in bed not one of their body parts touched. They did not spoon, arms entwined, his groin and chest tucked up against her backside, their legs pressed together like peas in a pod, his breath soft and warm on her long tanned neck. Last night not even one foot grazed another. They were opposing armies, each in a stronghold on his and her side of the bed preparing for battle.

Breakfast was silent. Lily ate her frosted corn flakes spoon by spoon, occasionally staring at him with her big blue eyes. Brenda made him French toast, but when she placed the egg-covered bread on his plate it plopped. He could tell that where she really wanted his breakfast was in his lap. He should not have taken the kid's bear, even though it was a dirty rag and she had fifty other stuffed animals besides. Billy won the toy for her at the fair and that bugged him. Her daddy. His former best friend. All that was changed now. Every time James thought about Billy coming home from the war today, he felt agitated, and he damn well didn't like feeling agitated.

James continues to feel horny. Holding the steering wheel of his pickup with his left hand, he reaches down to touch himself, but restrained within the denim of his pants, sooner rather than later the pain sets in.

This early morning he awoke, rolled over and gently touched Brenda in that special place. She closed her legs on his fingers and rolled the other way. That's when he knew he had really screwed up.

The kid carries a stuffed animal around with her like she's a toddler. For Christ's sake, she's five! James remembers all he was responsible for at five and laughs. The kid doesn't have a clue as to how good she's got it.

James has a few miles to drive to work through the fields. The roads in this part of the country are still hard-packed dirt, ridged like washboards. One layer of the silt runoff rises up in back, clouding visibility as he races through. James enjoys now, as he did at sixteen, running his way over the roads, testing the durability of his shocks and tires. The sun already shines bright and hot at this early hour. This land once open and vast is now punctuated with progress that makes his stomach turn; housing developments have popped up. Houses four times the size he grew up in, looking like fortresses, except they are so close together you could hear the neighbors next to you entangled in the night. Who are these people and how did they make so much money? He swears he's seen people of different races moving in. Where the hell are they coming from? The whole thing feels like a damn invasion.

James turns on the radio and Chris Isaak bursts from the speakers singing about love, wicked, wicked love. Shit! Not that song. That was the song he and Brenda first made love to. He turns the volume up louder.

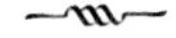

Billy came home on leave for a few days last August. Brenda was already starting to unravel. Kept talking about how she didn't like to be alone. How Billy never should have left her. Billy announced that his platoon, then stationed in Twentynine Palms, California, was being deployed to the Middle East. Brenda didn't talk much, smile, or laugh during those few days. One night, the three of them went out for beers and a couple games of pool. After Billy whipped James two out of three, they sat down at the bar on stools constructed of wooden legs and cracked vinyl seats.

"How about a shot of Jack?" Billy asked.

"Sounds good to me," James answered.

Brenda passed on the hard liquor, sticking to beer, as she stood at her husband's side.

The bartender brought the shots and Billy lifted his for a toast. James lifted his as the two men met eyes.

"Semper Fi," Billy said.

James repeated the words though he didn't really know what they meant. They tapped their glasses together, spilling out the top of the amber colored liquor, then tipped them up and swallowed. James was conscious of Brenda's breasts spilling out of a yellow tank top resting up against her husband's back. He'd had a glimpse of her breasts a couple of times over the years when they all went skinny dipping in the old mill pond. They were full and heavy with large round nipples. He wanted to touch them real bad. On top of that she had a cute little ass. How many times had he imagined taking her, from behind or any which way, alternately cupping and squeezing her dangling breasts? Shit. He had to turn away from looking at her. She was the wife of his best friend. The one woman he wanted above all others.

"How long do you think you'll be over there?" James asked.

"Six months. Maybe more. It depends on what the Iraqi army really looks like."

Brenda kissed Billy on the cheek and said, "Babe, I'm going to the bathroom."

James watched her walk away, that sweet ass swaying back and forth in a pair of faded jeans.

"She's not taking it very well," Billy said.

"A man's got to do what a man's got to do."

"Look ... I've got something to ask you." Billy moved in closer.

"Shoot."

"You're my best friend. I want you to keep an eye on her and Lily. If they need anything ..."

"Say no more. You got it." As James said those three little words, his heart began to race. Maybe watching over them wasn't such a good idea. James got hard just thinking about it. He looked up into Billy's eyes and felt shame for what he saw there. One way or another he had to keep his hands off Brenda.

Before they left that evening, everyone in the bar toasted Billy, the golden boy. They toasted to his health, his well-being, his safe return. James held his glass up the highest.

—∞—

Chris Isaak's song fades into the next. In the distance James can see a car approaching so he slows down. He doesn't want to be reported speeding. The cops know that he and a few other local boys race on the flat stretches of paved roads in the early hours. Even though his reputation as the best mechanic in town has saved his ass a few times, he knew they wouldn't mind catching him in action.

James steps on the brakes, the dust cloud diminishes. He turns down the radio, too.

Willis, no longer a burg, sure isn't a big city yet. Though the land explodes with fortresses, many of the country dwellers still know each other. When James recognizes the vehicle approaching, he wonders if maybe this might be an unlucky day. Unless his eyes are deceiving him, Molly Bagwell – Billy's mom – and his sister, Kate, are sitting inside. Oh, shit. As the vehicles pass each other, the two women turn their heads as one, looking James straight in the eyes. He swears he can read Kate's lips calling him an asshole behind the rolled-up windows of the air-conditioned car. They may be going to pick up Billy from the fucking airport now. Son of a bitch! James doesn't like being the bad guy, but he sure as hell doesn't want to give up Brenda. He watches as the car disappears into the morning. He steps on the gas and begins to whistle.

—∞—

Two months after Billy left for the Gulf, James stopped by to check on Brenda and the kid. He had checked in on them several times over the weeks. But this time he stopped over unannounced. He knew he should have called first, but some part of him wanted to catch Brenda unaware, maybe sunbathing in a bikini.

James slowed up as he approached the house, a three-bedroom ranch of red brick and blue trim. In the backyard, he could see the kid playing with another girl. James had always been fond of Lily. It wasn't until he moved in that they started butting heads. Brenda was nowhere in sight. James pulled into the driveway slowly. He climbed out of his truck as Lily called and waved to him from her place on a swing.

"Hi, Uncle James!"

James called back, "Hey, lil' darling! Where's your mom?"

"She's taking a shower."

James' heart began to beat faster as he imagined Brenda glistening wet, drops of water rolling over her breasts, falling off the cliffs of her nipples. Her long dark hair clinging to her back. He knew he should turn back to his truck and leave, but instead he walked up to the back screen door, cupped his hands to block the sun, peered in, and knocked. Chris Isaak purred out loudly from the stereo. When Brenda didn't appear, he knocked again. No answer. James started thinking about her falling in the shower, perhaps knocking herself out, lying crumpled in a corner in need of help. He decided to open the door and step in.

"Brenda?"

Suddenly she rounded the corner from the back of the house, barefoot, dressed in a flowered robe, drying her hair with a large white towel. She looked up, startled.

"Jesus, James! Give me a heart attack." She put the towel aside, shook out her hair, and clasped the robe together over her breasts, one of which had been close to dangling out.

Seeing her dressed in that flimsy little robe made his breaths grow shallow as his heart beat like mad. He watched her take him in from head to toe, and sweeping his long dark bangs back from his eyes, he flashed his trademark smile, the one that had gotten him into bed with more than one woman. Inappropriate at this moment. But, habit.

"I'm sorry, Bren. I knocked a couple of times ..."

"It's okay. You know that our house is your house. Let me just throw on some clothes." She turned towards the bedroom.

"I wish you wouldn't." He couldn't believe he'd said that.

She turned back. "What did you say?"

He spoke louder. "I just came by to see how you and Lily were doing."

What happened next surprised James. Instead of turning back towards the bedrooms, she walked past him, smelling so good. She took a stance in front of the kitchen sink, which provided a clear window view of the two little girls playing. His surprise turned to shock at what happened after that. Brenda reached up to open a cabinet on the side of the sink, which pulled one side of her robe up, exposing her ass. She grabbed a glass and turned to him halfway, her robe front falling partially open.

"Is ... is that all?" She turned back to the sink and stepped wider.

James walked up behind her in slow motion, only half convinced that he was reading the signs. She was his best friend's wife, but his lust drove him now. Placing both hands on the sink on either side of her, he stepped up closer, floating his face down into the side of her neck. When he heard her breath as shallow as his own, he completely closed the gap. When she pressed back into him, he reached up and cupped those breasts, as she kept a vigilant eye on the girls. From that point there was no turning back.

They were seconds from exploding, when she whispered, "Stop...stop."

God, he didn't want to, but he did, as they watched Lily run towards the house. James had just enough time to stuff himself back into his pants and zip up. Brenda did everything to avoid his eyes. They were feet apart, fighting to calm their breath, when Lily walked in.

"Mom, can we have popsicles?" Lily asked.

"Sure, Sweet Pea. Just be careful not to drip any on your clean clothes," Brenda answered as she reached into the freezer and pulled out two of the treats.

Lily ran back out and Brenda turned to him. "That will never happen again. What we just did. It can't."

"Don't tell me you didn't like it."

"I just needed ... I just ..." Her voice began to break.

James stepped over and caught her chin in his right hand and bent forward to kiss her.

She knocked his hand away and turned her head.

"You're right," he said. "It won't happen again." But deep inside of himself, he knew better.

As the truck rides smoothly over the ridged country road, he zips up his pants and catches his breath. Reaching up to sweep his long bangs out of his face, one eye catches the long thin horizontal scar on his right wrist. If there was any way he could, he'd erase it. Billy has one just like it.

They were ten, playing near a creek, tucked in the back of one of these pastures. Their pocket knives were out, as they cut away at snake grass and cattails. It took five hours to build a fort, and when they climbed inside, they looked at each other and smiled.

Billy said, "You know what, James? We should become blood brothers."

"How do we do that?" James asked.

"We cut ourselves and mix our blood."

"Okay. But where do we cut ourselves?"

"How about on the forearm, right here." Billy pointed to a place on his forearm, just above the wrist.

"Won't it bleed a lot?" James asked.

"We don't have to cut real deep," Billy answered.

The two boys took their knives, wiped the dirt away on their pants, and drew the blades across their skin. Billy's opened with one slice. James' took two. The blood beaded up as the wounds began to smart.

Billy said, "Now we put our arms together."

The boys placed their arms together for a few seconds. When they took them apart, both their arms were smudged red.

"What does it mean, Billy?"

"It means that we are best friends forever."

James answered, "Cool."

—ᵚ—

James doesn't feel proud of himself, even though he has gotten what he wanted, Brenda. The betrayal didn't feel so bad when Billy was roasting in the desert thousands of miles away. But he arrives home today. The town's golden boy is coming home with a Purple Heart. Sooner or later, James will have to face him. But not here, not now. He steps on the gas, turns the radio up, and watches as the dirt rises up to cloud everything that's passed.

5
Cut in Half

Friday 10:45 a.m.

Bagwell gazes out the window of the plane into the vast, endless sky. A thick gray and white mass of clouds cuts the scene in half: heaven above in blue, that thing called life shrouded by clouds below. He wishes he could strut across the mass into the horizon and become lost. Like the sky, he too is cut in half. One half, who he had been; the other, what he has become.

A voice breaks his escape. He turns to see the pretty face of an attendant leaning in towards him. "I'm sorry, what?" He asks.

"You wanted something? You rang."

"Oh, yeah." Bagwell shuffles the papers together that lie on the tray before him. "You got any Jack? Jack Daniels?"

"Yes, Sir. Would you like something with it?"

"Coke. Jack and Coke." He turns back to the window.

The old man sitting next to him clears his throat and then speaks. "I couldn't help but notice those discharge papers. Were you over there in the Persian Gulf?"

"Yes, Sir. I was."

The man takes in Bagwell's right leg in a brace stretched out before him. He asks, "Wounded?"

"Yes, Sir." The attendant arrives back with the booze and Bagwell pays her.

The old man continues. "Wounds are kind of like souvenirs. I've got a plate in my head. Pieces of shrapnel still rolling around in my knee."

"Yeah, well, I'd been happier with a postcard."

"I fought in WWII. First Infantry, 16th Regiment. We landed on Omaha Beach. It was hell."

"War's a bitch, ain't it?" Bagwell downs half his cocktail and turns back to the window. Though his eyes look out upon the sanctuary of sky, in his head, the missiles start flying.

Bagwell clamps his jaw as bombs begin exploding. He tucks his shaking hands down between his legs beneath the tray.

Bagwell didn't know how long he carried Glover through the sand. His feelings were mixed when the U.S. Humvee came upon them. He was glad they weren't Iraqis, but he felt betrayed because the Marines took their sweet ass time finding them. If they'd gotten there sooner.... Goddamn it, if they'd gotten there sooner....

"Where the fuck have you guys been?" He shouted.

"Looking for you," one of them answered.

"You knew where we were!"

"Well, you weren't there, were you?"

"We lay there for probably two hours before I came to and made a move. Where were you in all that time?"

"Just chill. We're here now."

Bagwell grabbed the jarhead by his cammie and stepped up into his face. He said through clenched teeth, "Look at him. Look at him," indicating Glover.

The Marine broke Bagwell's grip. "We're here now."

The Marines lifted Glover up into the truck, and Bagwell hobbled up beside him. By this time, Glover had a mouthful of blood and his breath was ragged as a saw. The Marines sitting around were all encouraging Glover to hang in there. Bagwell felt like shouting at them to shut up. Shut the fuck up! He watched Glover's lids periodically lift and his eyeballs roam around. Eventually they settled on him. "Bag ... Bagwell," whispered Glover.

Bagwell leaned over towards him and took his cold hand. "Don't talk, man. Save your strength."

"You ... go see my mama. Tell her ... tell her how it was...." Glover coughed blood clear of his throat.

"You can tell your own mama how it was."

"Tell ... her."

"You're going to make it, buddy."

"Promise ... me."

Bagwell dropped down close to him. "Of course I will."

The Humvee was rolling over the dunes beneath the stars. Bagwell watched Glover turn his head up to look at them. One tear ran out the far corner of his eye as his hand inside Bagwell's went limp. His mouth fell open slightly as his last breath hissed out slowly.

Bagwell couldn't help it; he started sobbing. His fellow Marines looked away. He reached up and closed Glover's eyes and with one firm jerk, pulled his dog tags free. Holding the tags in his palm, he discovered Glover's full name for the first time: James T. Glover. James. Now that, Bagwell thought, was ironic.

—m—

Bagwell polishes off the other half of his cocktail. Damn it, if the old guy next to him doesn't start talking again.

"What were you doing over there?"

"STA. Surveillance and Target Acquisition/Scout-Sniper." Bagwell, not rude by nature, wants to shout at the old man to shut up. His mind circles and circles and there's nothing he wants more than stillness.

"You must be one hell of a shot."

Bagwell grunts in reply and turns away, praying that the old man will be quiet now.

"I lost many friends over on that beach."

"Look, Sir ... I'm trying to ... "

The old man turns to look him squarely in the eyes. "Serving your country is the greatest thing a man can do."

Bagwell mutters under his breath, "If the country is worth serving." He could feel the old man turn and glare. He adds, "We weren't over there for the right reasons, Sir."

"Well, that's not your right to determine," the old man said.

Bagwell turns to him. "Oh, yes, Sir, it is my right to determine. I have a wife and child. I need to know if I'm jeopardizing my life for the right reason."

"If you don't like this country, you should get out."

"Sir, can I be still now? Because I really need to be still now."

"I don't want to talk to you anymore anyway."

The plane begins to drop down into the long descent. Pressure begins to build in Bagwell's ears. He swallows, opens his jaw wide, and chomps down harder on his gum. Nothing helps. The pain becomes excruciating.

—᠁—

By the time the Humvee reached the med tent, Bagwell's morphine was wearing thin. His leg started throbbing with a shrill pain that half-blinded him. They threw him on a stretcher and stripped him of his cammies, injecting something into his upper right arm. He was fading fast, but caught a few sporadic words, "Infection ... shrapnel embedded in bone ... possible amputation ..." His body began to shake with alarm before everything went black.

—᠁—

Bagwell still remembers the dream he had while he was under.

He and his wife, Brenda, were sixteen again, walking hand in hand across the school grounds. They were heading for their favorite tree, a maple, which stood on the outer border of the grass. Brenda leaned her back against the bark, as Bagwell moved against her in a wet, hungry kiss. Their tongues tangled, arms clung; the tender young hips cautiously aligned. And they kissed. And they kissed. When Bagwell brushed his fingers across the nipple of her right breast, Brenda gasped. He itched to touch her down there, in that other place, pink, dark, and moist. But he intended to wait until a ring was on her finger. He felt the consummation of their love should be special. The problem was he didn't know how much longer he could wait. Brenda urged him to go further each time they engaged.

Suddenly on their left a coyote appeared, sitting with a smirk; his sparkling brown eyes looked human. They were James' eyes. Not his war buddy, but his blood brother. The coyote started making promises to Brenda for all he would procure for her. These were things that Bagwell probably never would be able to afford: a five-bedroom house with a pool, a closet of clothes as big as a den, a diamond ring you had to keep in a safe, a car so luxurious you could live inside. Things that Brenda had said she never wanted, never needed, could happily live without.

In moments, Brenda and the coyote were running across the fields, the animal occasionally peering back with a sneer. Bagwell stepped out to follow them, to save his girl from the con, and he fell flat. His right leg was gone, except for twelve inches on the top dangling from his pants. He tried to crawl, his arms pulling, his left leg pushing off every few feet. After miles of this movement, he fell fatigued, watching the two forms recede fast. But he swore, even from that distance, that Brenda turned a time or two, looking back at him with large, sad eyes.

The plane was dropping through the clouds towards earth where what was left of Bagwell's life awaited. Brenda was living with James in the house that he and Brenda built. He was sleeping in his bed, touching his wife's body with his greasy callused hands, playing with his daughter, the light of his life, on the grass he grew from seed.

James has fucked close to every woman in town between seventeen and forty. Why did he have to add Brenda to the list?

Bagwell hopes that they are using condoms. The thought of James' seed in his wife's womb makes him crazy. His hands are shaking so hard, he has to tuck them between his legs again. Two legs. He still has two legs. He realizes he has to piss. Unbuckling his seatbelt, he reaches for his cane. The pretty attendant stops as she's walking by.

"Need some help?" she asks.

"Thanks, but I think I can manage."

"You'll have to hurry. We'll be landing soon."

"Gotcha." Bagwell stands and moves towards the john. He can't help but notice people looking up, taking him in from head to toe. The attention makes him wish he were invisible. Leaving the cane outside, he steps in and pisses. He notices again the light pink tinge of his urine and the burning sensation. Is he pissing blood? Glancing into the mirror he sees the fatigue lines around his mouth and eyes. He's twenty-five years old! He looks older.

Awkwardly, Bagwell makes his way back to his seat. The pressure in his ears crescendos. The old man doesn't even glance his way. What will Lily think when she sees him? What will she think of her big, strong daddy? What will his mom think? His sister? What will Brenda think and feel when she sees him? Boy, James will sure get a laugh. Not the one who is gone, whose dying face haunts him. No, the other one, with the scar on his lower right arm where they swapped blood long ago. The one he wants to kill.

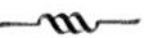

Bagwell woke up in a heavy fog, not knowing where the hell he was. He looked over to his right to see a man with half his face bandaged, the other half purple, red, and raw. A jolt of panic coursed through him as he remembered the exploding rockets, Glover's dying face, and the piece of shrapnel protruding from his leg. He tried to lift his right arm, but it was secured and punctured, a clear liquid running down through a tube. So he lifted his head, heavy as a boulder, to glance down towards where his right leg should be. The leg wouldn't move, but it was there. His head dropped back to the pillow, thin as a wafer, and he sighed.

A nurse walked over. "Welcome back. It would be best if you just lie still for now."

"I ... I was just checking on my leg."

"It's there. How are you feeling?"

"Thirsty. Really thirsty."

"Are you in any pain?"

"I don't feel a thing."

"Good. We'll be moving you out of the recovery room soon. Just rest. You're going to be fine."

Fine. He was going to be fine. A few hours after, he was moved into the big tent where two rows of beds lined the walls. A young doctor came by.

"How you feeling?"

"I don't feel a thing."

"Good." The doctor lifted the sheet and took a quick look under the bandage stained with blood and something yellow. "You're a lucky man, Bagwell."

"Oh, yeah?" He used to feel lucky.

"You had a hell of an infection setting in there. It doesn't take long in this heat and sand."

"Did you get all the shrapnel out?"

"Pretty much. But we also had to take out some of the bone."

He used to feel like he was on top of the world. "What does that mean?"

"We had to cut the bone in half. Pin it back together. You ... will probably walk with a limp."

"A ... limp?"

"You lost about an inch or so of bone."

"In length?"

"Yes, in length."

Bagwell turned his head and blinked back tears.

"You're a lucky man. You could have lost the leg."

Lucky. He was lucky. He would be discharged now to go back to Willis, where no wife awaited and a child he couldn't live without. Funny. He didn't feel fine or lucky. He felt terribly alone.

The wheels of the plane touch down and the force of the brakes pushes Bagwell deep into his seat. Part of him wants to embed into the upholstery forever, but the plane rolls to a stop outside the terminal and people start jumping up from their seats. The commotion starts swirling Bagwell's head again. He is not even sure that he can stand. So he sits and waits, letting everyone else leave.

The old man turns before he steps away. "You may feel differently about things as time goes on. It gets old looking back at things in bitterness."

"Well, Sir, I'll take that into consideration."

"You take care of yourself, Son."

"Thank you, Sir. I'll try." Bagwell feels like a jerk for being rude earlier. But, he's doing what he can to survive, to hold it together and keep his head in one place long enough.

The pretty attendant stops by one last time. "Can I help you out?"

"No. No, I can manage. But, thank you." He stands up, grabs his cane, and pulls out his bag from overhead. Slowly he makes his way out of the plane, down a hall like a tunnel and into the light; the gate waiting area appears. Children are running and laughing everywhere. He can't help but look for Lily. As lovers embrace and kiss he feels his stomach drop. He searches through the sea of faces.

"Billy!"

Suddenly his mom and sister are standing before him. His mom gathers him into a crushing hug and begins to cry. Bagwell's eyes get misty. His sister, Kate, standing beside them, steps forward and joins in on the tight embrace.

"Welcome home, Son. Praise the Lord," his mom says.

Bagwell asks, "What did you say?"

"I said, 'praise the Lord.'"

Bagwell looks over towards his sister and squints his eyes in question. Kate lifts her eyebrows and twists her mouth to the side.

"How was your flight, Son?"

"Long."

"Did they feed you?"

"Yes, Ma'am, they did."

"Ma'am?" The three laugh.

Bagwell says, "Habit. They fed us all right. But I had a problem identifying what exactly it was that we were eating."

"Well, I cooked you up a pot roast. Your favorite."

"That sounds real good."

With her arm linked in his, Bagwell's mom starts drawing him away. For a moment, his sister stands aside. He imagines her measuring his height, taking in the crippled gait. She can see his dwindling of self. She will no longer be as proud of him as she once was.

But she grabs his other arm and smiles. "You look good, Billy. Tall and handsome as ever."

And with those few words, Bagwell feels his spirit spark.

6 Real Life

Friday 12:00 noon

No one but Martin knows he has another life. This other life takes place at night, when all is calm. He lies down in bed, lets his head drop into the down, and closes his eyes. In minutes, his second life, the other season, begins to play. In this life he exists as a winner. He knows what it feels like when the champagne corks fly. She ... is still alive, standing on the sidelines, jumping up and down, even screaming for the team he coaches. At night, when all is calm, deep inside the cavern of his head, his team plays victoriously.

Petey, his son, stars as the quarterback on the team. His tall, thin frailty transforms into a well-muscled machine. Arms like tentacles, and hands like mitts, he passes the ball in perfect arcs. He runs with the speed of a cheetah and the grace of a gazelle, and somehow the ball always adheres to his side. Martin's daughter, Brenda, is not a young woman of twenty-five in his other life. She is younger than Petey, still a little girl, who was never lost in the wheat and the corn. His little girl lives unafraid of the dark and whenever she can, she holds his hand so tight that his fingers turn red. She dances on her toes in the backyard and accompanies him everywhere he goes. She is Daddy's girl.

There are times when Martin grows confused as to which life is real. One thing remains certain: in his other life there is no pain.

Sometimes in the blackness of the night, when he awakens from the cheers of people in the bleachers, he turns to see the other side of the bed bare. There has been a time or two when he swears he can hear her screams from that field. Not the field where his team has just conquered the perfect score. No, the field where she lay for hours, her flesh once supple, then mush, now stone.

On these occasions, he rolls over on his side, squeezes his eyes shut, and prays: *please tell me that it's not real.*

But morning comes shining with light and all is far from calm. He lounges in his office behind his desk, secure in his mantle as county supervisor. Catching his breath, he shakes his head and thinks about the state of his mother. What has become of this woman, virtually the backbone of the family? All she talks about now are the angels she thinks she sees gliding above the fields and the so-called signs that surround her. For crying out loud! A picture falls off a wall and suddenly someone's going to die. We're all going to die. It's a fact. Many dear to his heart have already died.

The phone rings and he jumps. "Good morning. Martin Becker."

"Good morning, Martin. This is Molly. Molly Bagwell."

The voice stuns him into momentary silence. "Molly, how have you been?"

"Billy's home. Praise the Lord."

"I'm sorry. I didn't hear you. Praise the what?"

"The Lord. Praise the Lord. I've found Jesus."

"Oh ..."

"Billy wants to see his daughter."

"Of course he does."

"Today. He wants to see her today."

"Well, I ..."

"Talk to Brenda. Make it happen. Please. My boy deserves that much."

"Of course he does. But, Molly, I ..."

Her voice grows soft. "He's ... he's not acting right. I ... I think he needs to see Lily. Please, Martin ..." Her voice becomes quiet. "Here he comes. I've got to go."

Martin hears the dial tone. Yes, it's going to be one of those days. He punches numbers on the phone.

Brenda answers, "Hello?"

"Good morning, Bren."

"Hi, Dad." Her voice sounds strained.

"How's the baby?"

"She's fine. Right now she and her friend Daisy are building a fort out of boxes in the backyard. What's up?"

"Your mother-in-law just called. Billy's back. He wants to see Lily. Today."

Silence looms.

"Bren?"

"Please stay out of it, Dad."

"He has a right ..."

"Please!"

"All right! But would you do me a favor? Would you go over and see your grandmother? She's all out of whack over that tree."

"Of course I will. Anything else, Dad?"

"No, that's all."

Again, Martin hears the dial tone.

In his dreams at night, the boys look up to him. They treat him like a God. Gathering around him at practice, they hang on his every word. If one of them cracks their gum, they swallow it. If a joke comes out bad, they run their fifteen laps. If one of them arrives late, or tries to leave early, they drop to the ground for push-ups. And when the lights go up, and the bleachers are full, the boys play with courage and precision.

Martin cannot remember a definite time when he lost control of the light. The process was slow and sure. Perhaps it started with Jeanine, before she was carried off into the night. She began to stand up to him, mouth off, and defy the parameters he drew. He tried to break her spirit again, as he did when she was seventeen. When she dressed up for an evening out, he told her she looked dowdy. In actuality, she looked like a queen, every hair in place, not a wrinkle in her dress, and that sweet soft smell drifting. When she expressed an opinion, he shook his head and laughed. She saw things differently than he did. She was more forgiving of the riffraff that run the world. Hope ran through her like a vein. The house was never clean enough for him, and the food she cooked was slop. This, too, was untrue. You could eat off the floor and he looked forward to every meal. But he had to maintain control in some way. Only when she refused to leave the house, because she couldn't bear to be seen or heard, did he feel satisfied.

Thinking back on his actions, on how he systematically broke his wife down, fills him with so much shame now, he does everything he can to avoid thinking about it. If he could, he would sleep, just sleep.

He drops his head onto his folded arms. The phone rings and shakes him. He answers, "Martin Becker."

"Hey ol' buddy. Can you break away for some golf this afternoon?"

"Don't you ever work?"

"I'm an old man."

"Well, I have a meeting at two. If it goes well, I can meet you at four."

"Sounds good. I hear young Bagwell is back in town."

"That's what I hear." Martin rubs his eyes.

"When is the showdown?"

"The showdown?"

"Between him and Jimmy boy."

"I wouldn't know. I'll give you a call after the meeting."

Martin thinks back on that Sunday sundown when Brenda was a little girl and Petey not yet born. He, Jeanine and the girl were on their way home from a visit with his folks. Suddenly, Brenda bounded from the car when they were stopped, and took off into the wheat and corn. She ran away from him. His little girl ran.

What the fuck had he done? Jesus. He'd wanted to be the one person they could all trust. The one person they could always count on. Instead he was the one they ran away from. Brenda ran into the fields. Jeanine ran into a room of her own and locked it. And Petey ... Would he ever be a man? Maybe his son so desperately wanted to avoid being like him that he chose to be ... whatever it is he is.... His son. Not the star of a football team.

Not a muscular boy bench-pressing three hundred pounds. Not a loud, obnoxious boy zooming around in a souped-up car. Not. Not. Not.

In Martin's dreams he travels with his team. Everywhere he goes he's recognized. People even ask for his autograph on a program, a scrap of paper, a felt flag with the team's logo. And when his team is triumphant, they carry him up high on their shoulders and spray him with champagne. They interview him on the evening news and make sure they spell his name just right.

In fact, the only time he has ever been interviewed on the news was the day after they found Jeanine's half-clad body lying in that field. She lay alone all night, in the blackness of the wee hours, no blanket to protect her from the frost. Her vagina penetrated, but no semen. Her arms free of bruises because she did not fight. Her neck askew, twisted in some strange way. Her eyes open towards the east where she could not see the sun rise again, ever again, never, never again. Someone took her into that field of rock and sparse trees, once upon a time tilled, but now ground as hard as lead. When she fell there was no cushion, no pillow for her head. Her flesh became a banquet where the insects fed. In the morning the vultures circled. He was away playing golf in a distant city.

They retrieved him from the fourteenth hole.

"Mr. Becker, an emergency call came in for you."

"What?"

"An emergency call."

And then later.

"Sir, we've found your wife."

"What?"

"Your wife, Sir. She's dead."

At night when all is calm, spring training jumps into full gear. He pushes the boys harder than ever so they lose their winter fat. They grunt and groan and sweat and fall and drink water from a pail. They push and pull and fly and dive, and scream out every bad word under the sun. Coach Becker wants to add another trophy to the case. He wants to break records and go down in history as the best coach there ever was. During this season, his family remains intact.

Martin looks out the window in his office and watches the early summer clouds tower. Their height climbing into heaven and dark gray and yellow color indicate a storm. Maybe he wouldn't be golfing later. They look like the clouds in the sky that formed the day after Jeanine died. He remembers how they burst, the rain running out of the sky like a river, to wash the earthly sin away. If there were footprints, they were gone. Tire marks erased. Scrape marks from where her body was dragged or dropped vanished. The area was wiped clean in a ten-minute storm that saved the killer's life, but peppered the area with scattered debris from the raging wind that accompanied it. Martin stood looking around, his jacket flapping, his face pinched. There were twigs and leaves, brittle broken branches, flower petals, and an occasional crumpled note from a sticky pad. He found one himself. It read: milk, bread, hot dog buns and beans. Jeanine's life was gone, but the life on the note danced vivid.

Ten years! Jeanine has lain stiff, wrinkled, and dusty in the ground. Ten years!

The killer has yet to be found. The kids were in bed that night, their bellies plump with popcorn. Earlier that day, Brenda had been caught kissing Billy behind her grandma's barn. Petey had been dressed up in a yellow and white checkered tablecloth tied around his neck as a cloak. On his head balanced a cardboard Burger King crown decorated with diamonds. Martin left for his golfing trip with one carry-on bag under his arm. He remembers Jeanine standing on the porch wiping her hands on an apron as he drove away. Her eyes looked hollow.

That night she stepped out into the blackness, or someone tiptoed into the house to grab her. Either way, she was gone. Neither of the children heard a sound. She was somehow transported thirteen point four miles, dead or alive, to the place she was found. Did she walk, run, or stumble to the site of her death? Was she carried, dragged, or chased? Driven in a car? Was it a beast on two legs, or a furry one on four? An escaped convict, a neighbor with a secret, a transient passing by? A bear, a wolf, a coyote left hungry in the early summer drought? His mother said regardless, whoever, whatever did it was a demon.

In the life he escapes to, Martin's team has won the state championship. He stands with his family in the center of the field. Everyone in the bleachers stands on their feet cheering madly, throwing confetti out in clouds. The stadium lights glare, punctuated with flashbulbs and questions flying at him from everywhere. Jeanine stands next to him in a blue dress he especially likes. It is slightly shorter than she normally wears, and the neckline plunges nicely. Brenda clings to his right hand, seven or so if she is a day, her eyes glistening and glued to her daddy's smile. Petey stands at his mother's side, helmet under one arm, his muscles pushing through the fabric boundaries of his uniform. His damp hair clings to his head, and his sparse whiskers sparkle. They could be voted the family of the year.

Ten years! Ten fucking years!

God, he wishes for the night.

Martin watches the clouds billow. He sees the heat wavering above the ground. There is no wind. Martin moves reluctantly into this day. Very reluctantly. The birds soar through the air with enthusiasm, chattering.

The phone rings once again. "Martin Becker."

"Dad, I have a flat tire."

"Son, I've shown you how to change a tire a half dozen times."

"I've got to get to work."

"I thought you worked early on Friday."

"I overslept."

"Where were you last night?"

"I'm twenty years old."

"When I got up to piss at 2 a.m. you still weren't home."

"If I'm old enough to join the military and kill people, I'm old enough to stay out late."

"Not while you're living under my roof."

"Believe me, Dad, as soon as I am able to get out I will."

"And how are you going to do that oversleeping?"

"I haven't overslept in a year."

"Oh, really? Your boss told me that you are half asleep all the time."

"That's bullshit."

"You make me look foolish, Petey."

"Peter. It's Peter. And I don't give a darn how I make you look."

"When the hell are you going to ..."

"Forget it, Dad. I'll call Uncle Sam."

Martin hears the third dial tone of the day. This is what it all comes down to. A son who acts more like a girl. A daughter who cringes every time she hears his voice. A mother who lives on another planet. And a brother who ducks every time he hears a sudden sound. These images hold his life captive.

Martin imagines himself driving home and locking himself inside. He will close every window and blind, and pretend that the darkness reigns. Slowly, he will remove every piece of clothing and his shoes. Even more slowly, he will climb in between the sheets and pull a pillow upon his face. He will close his eyes, take deep long breaths, and wait ... for his real life to begin.

7
Carried Away

Friday 2:15 p.m.

Brenda pulls into the driveway of the farm, the tires crackling over the gravel. She steps out of the station wagon and watches as Lily unbuckles the belt of her safety chair and jumps out of the back. Brenda walks around and grabs some fresh produce off the seat of the passenger side. As she closes the car doors, she notices the hole in the canopy of trees where the old oak used to be. Continuing to look around, she takes in the remnants of this once-vital farm. The barn, once red and sitting on a rise, is now leveled, with only the cement base remaining. Two skeletons of corn cribs lie behind, almost fallen. Two complete structures still stand beside the house: a wooden shed sitting next to the garage and a milk house constructed of cement blocks. The house is two-story red brick, with an outside stair climbing up to the second floor.

Brenda once thought the farm was a safe place for her, but it isn't. Even now her ears snap open searching for unusual sounds: distant voices, clinking glasses, tools being sharpened against the stone of a spinning wheel. She moves towards the house.

Lily runs up the four steps into the house with arms open wide. Grandma Becker bends and presses the child into her legs with one hand, softly caressing her head with the other.

Brenda steps in behind her carrying the produce: late asparagus spears still glistening with morning dew and a small green plastic basket stuffed with strawberries.

Grandma exclaims, "What a surprise!"

"Hi, Grandma."

"What do you have there?"

"Some produce from Turner's."

"How nice! You didn't have to work today?"

"I took the day off. Doctor Sheppard said it was going to be slow, people on vacations and all." Brenda cannot help but notice her grandma's red and puffy eyes. "It was hard losing that tree, wasn't it?"

"Yes, well ..." Grandma waves her hand away. "Life goes on."

Brenda walks over to her grandma and hugs her.

Lily begins her customary jumping up and down. "Nana, Nana, guess what?"

"What?"

"My daddy is coming home!"

Grandma looks at Brenda, who breaks away and turns. "I know. Isn't that wonderful!"

Lily giggles gleefully, dancing on top of the sea mist kitchen tile. A moment or two of silence hangs between Grandma and Brenda. Finally, Brenda speaks up, "The yard looks empty without that tree."

Grandma says, "It lets a lot of light in. I'm going to have to move all my violets."

"I'll help you, Grandma."

"I loved that tree. It about broke my heart to see it fall. But after they carried it away in pieces, I walked out and looked down upon the ground. It was covered with the tree's seedlings. One day, long after I'm gone, there will be another, or maybe more than one, just as tall and full. Maybe you and Bill will be living in this house then. Or maybe Lily."

Lily says, "Yes, me, me!"

"Grandma, Billy and I ..."

Grandma catches Brenda's eye. "I think I understand why you took up with James. You've never liked being alone. But your husband is coming back to town now."

"Daddy's coming home! Daddy's coming home!" Lily begins to pull on Brenda's hand. "Mommy, can I go outside? I won't go far."

"We're not staying long, Lily."

Grandma says, "I could use some help pulling weeds out of the flower garden."

"I think it's going to storm, Grandma."

"Not for a while. This is the perfect time, while the earth is dry."

"Oh, well, then yes, Sweet Pea, I guess you can go out. In fact, I'll go with you and get started on those weeds." Lily skips out of the house and Brenda turns to follow.

Grandma stops her. "Don't you have any desire to see him?"

Brenda doesn't say a word at first, tears stinging her eyes. Finally she answers her grandma with her back still turned. "I don't know what I feel right now."

"I remember when I caught you two kissing behind the barn. What was that, ten years ago? I never saw two kids so much in love."

"It was a long time ago."

"Not so long ago."

Brenda remembers that day even though she wishes she couldn't. Even now, in this moment, the haunting images return. Billy's face moving towards her. The tenderness in his eyes. The urgency in the way his one hand cupped the back of her head to move her towards him. His lips ... soft. His tongue ... urgent, too. She shakes her head to clear the memory. She will feel nothing. She may see the images, but she will feel nothing. "I've got to get outside. I don't want Lily to be alone out there."

Grandma brushes dust off of the strawberries one by one. "There's nothing that's going to hurt her out there. Brenda, Billy is a good boy."

"And James isn't?"

"You love James?"

"I don't know what I feel."

"It's not that James is a bad boy, but he's just not husband material."

"People change, Grandma."

"I wouldn't bet on it. I like James. But you are better off with Billy."

"Well, it's too late. He will never take me back."

"You don't know that."

"I do know that."

"I know he loves you very much."

Brenda turns towards Grandma. "I received a letter from him yesterday."

Grandma turns from her task. "What did it say?"

"It was ... threatening."

"He's still angry. Do you blame him, Brenda?"

"He left me! He never even asked me how I felt about him enlisting. Yeah, he's good. But sometimes he's a selfish asshole."

"That was selfish of him. But he went and now he's coming back. Wounded to boot. He'll need you now more than ever."

"What about my needs?"

"Women have always had to place their needs second."

"Not anymore. That was the old days."

"Some things never change, Brenda."

"I did what I had to do." Brenda turns and walks out of the house, quickly wiping away her tears. She crosses the driveway and steps cautiously into the shed. Cobwebs, gray and heavy with dust, brush her face and arms. Uttering a sound of disgust crossed with fear, she flails her arms about, clearing the space, peering into the corners with suspicion. Every inch of the structure contains things. Shelves are covered with jars of nails, screws, bolts, and washers. Broken pots, burlap bags, and tools lie on the floor lining the walls. Out of the corner of her eye, she watches for movement. In the deepest part of her hearing, she strains for sounds. Quickly, she pulls on cotton gloves and turns to leave, but in the last moment she notices the grinding stone sitting in a corner. In her mind, she hears the sound of it turning, engaged and sharpening some metal tool.

Suddenly, she is ten again, Peter five, and they are alone together on the farm.

It was an October day with large puffy cumulus clouds floating like boats, and the hint of a cold bite waiting for the sun to drop. The leaves on trees and those already fallen were red, orange, and yellow, and would occasionally scuttle across the ground when the sweep of a wind blew through.

Grandpa Becker was sick and had been in the hospital for a couple of weeks. On this day, a Sunday, all the adults had gone up to visit him, leaving the two children behind for one hour. Grandpa had been moving hay with a pitchfork in the mow, when he fell down the chute to the lower level. One leg was stretched out before him, the other crooked precariously behind him. When he landed, his hip snapped and so did his will.

Brenda was playing on the stairs that day, leading to the second story of the house. She was engaged in an imaginary game of airplane, handing out leaves and twigs to passengers for their lunch. Peter stood in the shed, arranging and rearranging every pot, tool, and jar.

Brenda was bending over a stair offering a maple leaf as a plate to a passenger, when the voices of two men laughing and talking drifted out from the barn. The barn, painted red, sat forty feet behind the house. The large sliding doors on the bottom were closed, and the smaller one above open, where the hay could be seen stacked in bales held together with twine. Along with the laughter and the talk, other sounds could be heard: the grinding stone turning against metal, polishing a tool, in her mind, a scythe, a saw, or a large, long knife. This was punctuated by the sound of clinking glass.

Brenda stopped her game and looked towards the barn, her heart beginning to beat fast. She turned to see Peter stepping out of the shed, and each time his foot hit the ground, a voice of a man counted, one, two, three, four. Brenda remembers how she and Peter met eyes, their mouths hanging open, any gesture that they made, slow and heavy.

Peter said, "Did you hear that?"

Brenda answered, "Yes."

Their heads turned towards the barn as one, when a man's voice commanded, "Get the hell down from those stairs." The laughter erupted once again, the glass clinked, and the stone kept turning.

Brenda and Peter didn't have to exchange another word. She climbed down from the stairs and together they moved towards the back door of the house. They entered and climbed the four stairs, the voices of the men pushing them in. Bolting the door behind them, breathless with fear, they stared into each other's eyes.

One half hour later the adults returned. Their father told them their imaginations were running wild, as their mother held them close and stroked their hair. Uncle Sam turned and walked out to search the barn. Grandma Becker listened to their story and turned away with tears in her eyes. She knew something that no one else knew, but she didn't tell. No evidence of any men being there was found.

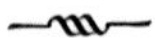

Brenda steps out quickly from the shed, searching for Lily in the adjoining field. The child squats, poking the earth with a twig, watching something with the absolute captivation only a child possesses. Brenda steps into the flower garden, moving across the clumps of dry dirt that lie in between bushes, bunches and stems of brightly colored flowers. The hot, early afternoon sun has drawn the fragrance into the blossoms, to burst into the air with a symphony of scent. Small golden honeybees and plump velvety yellow jackets buzz from flower to flower.

Brenda begins to pull up weeds from their roots, feeling a tug of guilt with each extraction. Even if the weeds prevent life, she didn't like killing them. But she keeps pulling, anything to keep from thinking about Billy and that kiss. She looks up to see Grandma step out of the back door wearing a sunhat made of straw and gaze up into the space of gray-blue sky, which only hours before the oak filled with foliage. When she turns back, her head hangs down as she strolls towards the garden.

Lily runs towards her carrying something in her outstretched open hand. "Nana, look! I've found a beautiful rock!" She holds up the black and white stone, the sun glinting off of the crystal flecks.

Grandma takes it from her hand and examines it briefly. "Oh, my. You've found a lucky rock."

"I have?" Lily asks with wide eyes.

"Oh, yes. Whoever carries this rock will always be very lucky."

"Well, then, I'm going to give it to my daddy."

"That's a wonderful idea, Lily Rose."

Lily places the rock in the pocket of her purple shorts and runs back into the field.

Brenda watches as Grandma bends and begins to pull out weeds, humming some old song that Sinatra used to sing. Suddenly a wind rises out of the still air. Brenda feels something soft brush her back. She stands up, looks around and sees nothing, except her grandma's skirt lifting up like a sail.

Grandma straightens up from the waist. "What's wrong?"

"I swear I felt something brush my back."

"Probably an angel."

"You still believe in angels, Grandma?"

"Well, yes. I've seen them."

Brenda looks around. "I don't see anything."

"Sometimes they choose to appear and sometimes they remain invisible."

"How can you believe in angels after all that has happened to this family and all that's happening out in the world? Aren't they supposed to protect us?"

"Maybe things would be worse if they weren't here."

"They sure didn't protect my mom, did they? Or Grandpa. Look what has happened to this farm. It's a ... haunted place now. I'm afraid to even come here."

"Don't be ridiculous. There's nothing that's going to harm you here."

"What about those voices that Peter and I heard when Grandpa was in the hospital?"

Grandma bends to pull a weed. "Oh, that."

Brenda touches her grandma's arm. "Who were they, Grandma?"

Grandma stands and looks directly at Brenda. "It was your grandpa's friends, passed already, waiting for him to arrive. At times they could be obnoxious drunks."

A shiver creeps over Brenda from head to toe. "You're telling me that those voices were ghosts?"

"There is a lot more to life than what we see with our eyes, sweet girl. If you remember anything I said, remember that. People die, Brenda. Sometimes in tragic ways. I don't think God wants us to understand everything." Grandma clears her throat. "I need to tell you about something that happened today."

"What?"

"A painting fell off of the wall."

"Didn't you tell me before ... that that's a sign of death?" Her voice rises. "Are you telling me that someone else is going to die?"

"We need to be careful now. Watch after one another."

Brenda grows louder. "I can't take any more death. I can't!"

Grandma grabs her arms to restrain her, to quiet her. "Try not to alarm that child."

"The letter. Billy said that James and I should get our things in order."

"Do you honestly believe that Billy is capable of hurting you?"

"I don't know. I don't know what he did over there in that desert. Or what he has become. You told me that he was getting therapy. He might not be the same person he was before."

"Calm down."

Lily runs over from the adjacent field. "Mommy, Mommy, what's wrong?"

Brenda quickly wipes away her tears and clutches her child.

Grandma answers, "Mommy is okay, Lily. You just keep playing. It's all right. Brenda, let her go."

"It's okay, Sweet Pea. Mommy is okay."

Lily turns and walks back into the field, occasionally glancing back towards the two women.

Grandma places her left hand on the top of Brenda's arm and touches her face gently with her right. "Now you listen to me. I've needed to say this to you for a long time. You are not a little girl anymore. It's time for you to step up and be a woman. Things have been tough for you. Use it for strength. Don't let it weaken you. That child needs you. Billy needs you. After I pass, you will be the woman in this family. Your brother, your father, everyone will need you. Step up. You are stronger than you know."

Brenda stares deep into her grandma's eyes.

Grandma bends to the ground once more. "Now let's get pulling weeds before those clouds burst."

Brenda bends beside her and her head starts to spin, but somewhere deep inside a resolve begins to form. She has no place left for pain. She is full to the brim, tired of the dark. Very, very tired of the dark. For the first time in a long time she feels a fight rising. A fight for what she wants. A fight for who she is. These thoughts are interrupted by the sound of a car pulling into the drive.

Grandma asks, "Now who could that be? I don't recognize that car."

Brenda does. The blue sports car belongs to Kate, Billy's sister. Brenda stands side by side with her grandma, as they watch the car come to a stop beneath the trees. The shadow of two heads can be seen. The passenger side door opens and Brenda watches as Billy slowly climbs out. She can see his head and torso from the waist up. He steps unevenly around the open door to the front of the car.

Grandma mutters two words. "Oh, my."

Brenda mutters none. She takes in this man's tallness, his sky blue T-shirt stretching tight across his chest and tucked into a pair of jeans. He walks with a carved wooden cane in his right hand. His face looks grim. Brenda feels like she cannot breathe.

"Daddy!" Lily screams and runs across the field, through the garden and into Billy's arms. He clutches her to his chest.

Brenda watches as he whispers something in her ear. He places her back down and Lily runs over to the open car door and climbs in. Billy hesitates for one moment, looking towards Brenda and her grandma standing in the garden. Even though he has shades on, she knows he stares directly at her. She screams, "Lily!"

Billy moves around to step back into the car.

Brenda runs towards them as fast as she can. The door closes and the car begins to move away. Her heart beats so loudly that she cannot hear the birds or the bees, the wind in the trees or the thunder beginning to rumble in the distance.

8 Savage

Friday 3:05 p.m.

Peter pulls into the parking lot of the local hamburger stand, scanning the loitering youth for one in particular. This one, new to town, will stand out with hair colored black and white. Peter doesn't see him among the crowd of girls in short shorts and guys in tees, so he pulls up beside a picnic table where two boys are blowing smoke rings.

He says, "Hey."

"Hey," one boy answers back.

"Have you seen that kid with the black and white hair today?"

"Todd? He left a few minutes ago."

"Do you know where he went?"

"Not really. But he headed that way," the boy replied, pointing north.

"What is he driving?"

"He doesn't drive."

Peter pulls out of the lot and heads north. Already his heart beats faster. He's had a hard-on for two days since he decided what he was going to do. He feels exhilarated and scared as hell.

Peter keeps an eye out for Todd as he scans the storefronts of this small, boring town. Though he loves flowers, the boxes of foliage that grace every other storefront bug him. Everything looks so inviting, yet he knows that behind every door stands a judge. They all go to church on Sunday where the minister preaches love for all, but back at home love for very few is practiced. If you drive an American car, dress in the latest fashion from Kmart, pursue heterosexual love in the spring, and shoot animals down in the fall, you are an integrated member of this town. Peter was not and never would be. If he could stop his midnight prowling, he might be able to save up enough money to blow this place. But he can't stop the prowling.

All of a sudden he catches a sight of black and white hair stepping into the tiny baseball card shop on the north end of town. Baseball? It didn't figure. He pulls over to park at a meter and wait until the kid steps back out. His hands are starting to sweat. As he draws his wet open palms over his jean-covered thighs, he sees a blue sports car coming towards him from the other way. It's his brother-in-law Billy with his sister Kate. A big smile pops up on Peter's face. Then he sees a little head bobbing in the back. It's Lily Rose! Kate and Billy wave to him as he turns to watch them pass.

As he turns back, he sees the kid step out of the card shop. Their eyes meet. The kid stops in his tracks and a little grin breaks. Peter quickly adjusts the hardness in his pants as the kid approaches. Peter leans over and opens the passenger door, looking at the red and black colors of the kid's grunge rock tee.

The kid pops his head in the open door. "What are you doing here?"

Peter's voice cracks as he says, "Get in."

The kid hops in, closes the door and turns to Peter. "Where are we going?"

"For a ride?"

"Out of town I hope."

"Definitely out of town." Peter starts the car and pulls onto the road, his wet palms sliding around on the wheel.

The kid says between lips that look like plump pillows, "I thought you were still in the closet."

"We're heading out of town, aren't we?"

From the corner of his eye, Peter watches the kid shimmy around in the seat.

The kid mutters, "Damn, these pants are tight."

Peter hears the sound of a zipper. He can hear his heartbeat banging in his ears. He glances over and screams, "Don't do that here! Jesus Christ!"

The kid re-zippers. "You really are paranoid."

"Not here."

Silence fills the car. Peter wipes away the beads of sweat popping onto the surface of his upper lip. He realizes he forgot to shave his sparse whiskers.

The kid reaches over and turns on the radio. The gruff yet tender voice of Kurt Cobain sings out in "All Apologies."

The kid speaks. "So, what's your name, anyway?"

"Peter."

Laughing, the kid says, "I never could understand why parents would name their kid that."

"Todd isn't that great."

"How do you know my name?"

"A kid back at the hamburger stand."

"You still hanging out at the bars in Three Rivers?"

"Yeah. How come you haven't been there?"

"I'm making a movie."

"A movie?"

"Well, I'm in a movie."

"What kind of movie?"

"Oh, I don't know. *Boy Toy Number Sixty Five* or some shit like that."

This stirs Peter further. Peter has been going to the two bars in Three Rivers for a year now, ever since he turned twenty. The bars are the only place in a fifty-mile radius where boys who like boys can hang. Three Rivers is a college town, but even then, actions can't be flaunted. Small-town locals sometimes stop by, acting gay, just to attract some prey. More than one patron has had the shit kicked out of him a block or two away. Mostly Peter drinks himself silly. He is too shy to initiate engagement and too frightened of the seduction tactics of most of the men. He usually drives home, more than one centerline leading him, and beats off in bed, fantasizing about Johnny Depp or Kevin Bacon or someone else he couldn't have. But this boy next to him had caught his eye. He was thin and tattooed, insolent and weary, and everyone knew about the snake in his pants. The kid had confronted him a time or two here in town, but Peter was just too damn scared.

The kid asks, "Where are we going?"

"To a favorite place of mine. If that's okay?"

"I'm sure anyplace will do." He pulls out a pack of Marlboro reds.

"You can't smoke in my car."

"Why not?"

"My dad will have a fit."

"It's his car?"

"No."

"Then fuck him."

Peter watches from the corner of his eye as the kid pulls a cigarette from his pack, places it between those lips, and lights it with a Bic. He can feel the nervous sweat rolling down under his arms.

The kid says through the smoke curling out from his lips and nose, "I bet you've lived here in this town your whole life, haven't you?"

"Yeah."

"What a bore. I can't believe my parents dragged me here. They think this town is going to tame me."

"If you don't drive, how do you get around?"

"Who told you I don't drive?"

"The kid back at the stand."

"I'm gonna have to cut his tongue out."

Peter turns to look at him squarely.

"Just kidding. I drive. They took my car away. The last tattoo nailed it. Stepped out of the bathroom one night and my mother saw it. But, I get around. The guy that's making the movie? He helps me out a lot."

"You're a senior, right?"

"Yeah. I might not finish school. It's boring."

"How do you get in the bars?"

"How do you think? By the way, the guy that's making the movie? He thinks you're real pretty."

"How ... where ... has he seen me?"

"At the bars. He's always looking for new talent."

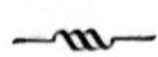

When he was a child, people said Peter was as pretty as a girl. This infuriated his father, who would turn and walk away. His father wanted him to be handsome. His father wanted him to play with toy trucks, action heroes, bats and balls. Peter wanted to dress up in Brenda's play clothes, paint his nails, and change diapers on her baby dolls. He knew he was different from other boys, and sometimes it made him feel like he didn't belong anywhere. His mother knew he was drawn to these things, and in the quiet hours when his father was away, she let him be who he is. In those hours, he was content.

One day, when he was five, he and Brenda were playing house. All of Brenda's baby dolls were sitting in chairs at a little table made of wood. Red, blue, and yellow flowers were painted on the corners of the table. He and Brenda were wearing old dresses from Grandma Martha's attic, sitting at the table, sipping on tea from tiny porcelain cups. He was wearing a brown hat with the beige-colored veil pulled down over his eyes, and Brenda was wearing a black hat with a small pheasant feather. They'd gotten into their mom's red lipstick, little did she know, and their cheeks were pink with blush.

The rain fell so hard that day it sounded like men marching. They didn't hear their father's car pull into the drive. He wasn't supposed to be home now. He walked into the house through the back door and screamed, "Hello! Anybody home?" Even from the back family room they could hear the ferocity in which he wiped his feet on the rug. Their mother came running back and stared at Peter and Brenda, wide eyed. She'd known about the tea party, but not the dresses, lipstick or the hats. As Peter was pulling the dress off over his head, the hat tumbling off and across the floor, his father stepped into the doorway. At first he smiled, when he saw Brenda and the dolls sitting around the little table. But then he saw Peter. Peter still remembers how loud his father's steps sounded, as he walked across the room and grabbed him by the arm. It hurt. It felt like his fingers were going to pop through his skin. He pulled him out of the room, down the hall, and shoved him into his bedroom. Peter remembers landing hard upon his bed. His father didn't scream the words, but said them slowly and distinctly between clenched teeth. "If I ever see you like that again, I'll kill you."

—m—

The kid reaches over and places his left hand at the crease of Peter's groin and thigh. "You know you're pretty."

Peter is stirred even more, this time down to the tip of his toes. He knows the kid, Todd, can feel him. "Whatever."

"Everyone in town must know what you are."

"Yeah, what's that?"

"A queer."

"I've been hoping that that's not as important as the person that I am."

Todd laughs. "That's hysterical, man! So, are we almost there or what?"

"We're almost there." Peter feels breathless. He looks out upon the fields of growing corn and blue-green winter wheat, and averts his eyes when they pass the barren one with rocks. He starts to imagine his mother's body lying there ... alone ... and he snaps the thought off. That is something he has gotten very good at. He cannot think of that.

Todd says, "Someone told me that your mom was murdered. That she was found in that field right there." He points to the rocky field.

"Look! If this is going to happen, we have to keep our focus here. Got that? Or it's not going to happen."

The kid puts his hands up into the air. "All right! You got it. But let's get to where we're going, because I want to see that sweet little ass of yours."

Peter turns left down a dirt road that leads to a clump of dense maple, white-barked birch and drooping willow. The clump is one mile off the road and sits around a small, tall-grassed glen near a creek. The heads of yellow, purple, and white wildflowers bob above among the grass. The heat of the summer has reduced the flow of the creek, but enough remains to run and gurgle over the rocks and reflect the beams of light filtering down through the trees. Peter stops the car, glancing over at the kid as they step out. He watches the kid move towards him dressed in his tight black jeans, ragged little tee, and scuffed Doc Martens on his huge feet. The kid has big hands, too. He hooks his left around Peter's head, drawing his face towards him, and his right he places securely on his ass. Peter falls into the pillow of his lips, and the kid starts aggressively probing his mouth with his tongue. It feels like he wants to eat him alive. Peter reaches down between the two of them to touch Todd. The kid pushes Peter's hand away and quickly unzips his own pants and pulls them open.

"Let's get this party going!" Todd says.

Peter says, "I have a blanket in the trunk."

"Get it. Get it fast."

Peter moves quickly over to the car, pops open the trunk and grabs the blanket. Tossing the native pattern of turquoise, red, and white into the wind, he guides the sail to the ground in a perfect square. The kid walks up, unzips Peter's pants, and begins to teach the twenty year old virgin.

"What about a condom?" Todd asks.

Peter gets down on his hands and knees. "No. Just do it."

"Look ... I've ...

"I know you've got it."

"Got what?"

"HIV!"

"How do you know?"

"I heard. Just do it! I want it. Do it. Do it!"

Peter can hear the kid, Todd, drop to his knees behind him.

When it's over, Todd squeezes words out through his gasping breath, "I hope you're happy. You are bleeding. What are you, some kind of savage? I didn't hurt you. You are the one who asked for it harder. You hurt yourself. You remember that."

As Peter lies on his side fighting to quiet the pulses of pain, he hears his car start up, and the tires pop across the gravel of the dirt road as it moves away. Unable to move, he tightens into a ball and whines like a dog that has been beaten. Already, he grows hard again.

9
Green Glass

Friday 4:00 p.m.

Lily loves parades. She doesn't know why, but every time she sees one she feels like crying. Not sad crying, but happy crying. Her heart beats real fast and she can't help but jump up and down and clap her hands. Right now she feels like she's in one. Sitting in the back seat of Aunt Katie's blue car, she can see everything outside the windows. People on the sidewalks are waving and passing cars are honking. Everyone seems real happy to see her daddy. Aunt Katie has a big smile on her face, but Daddy doesn't. He reaches back to squeeze her toes sometimes and his face looks sad.

"Daddy, can't I sit with you?" Lily asks.

He looks back at her, but Aunt Katie answers.

"She supposed to be in that car seat."

Daddy says, "One time isn't going to hurt." He reaches out his hand. "Come here, Peanut."

Lily unfastens the belt on her chair and crawls between the seats and into his lap. He wraps his arms around her tight and kisses the top of her head. She can see out the windows even better from here. She places her own hands over her daddy's. His hands are very big, and his fingers long. Lily feels very safe here. He still has his married ring on his left hand. Her mama doesn't wear hers anymore.

Aunt Katie asks, "Where you want to go now, big brother?"

"I don't care."

"You said earlier you wanted a piece of pie."

"Sure. That's okay."

'Where do you want to go? The Big Boy, the café?"

"I don't care."

"Let's go to the café then. The Kohlers have been asking about you."

Lily says, "I want some ice cream!"

Her daddy kisses her on the cheek this time and says, "I think we can manage that."

Lily looks down at his leg stretched out in a blue and white thing they call a brace. She reaches down and softly strokes where she can reach just above the knee.

"Does it hurt, Daddy?"

"Not much anymore."

"Do you have to wear that thing on it forever?"

"No, Peanut."

"Is it broken?"

"The doctors had to break it and put it back together again."

"Why?"

"During an explosion, pieces of metal flew into the bone of my leg. They had to take them out."

"Can I see it?"

"The pieces of metal?"

"No, your leg."

"I'll show it to you sometime."

"You promise?"

"I promise."

Lily's eyes follow as Aunt Katie and Daddy's heads turn to the right. Uncle James stands in the big open door of the garage where he works. A lady in a dress stands next to him. She has a big chest and wild looking hair.

Aunt Katie says, "Speaking of the devil."

Uncle James looks up and watches as they pass. His mouth falls open. He holds a cigarette in his right hand.

Her daddy asks, "When did he start smoking again?"

"I saw him in the bar the other night and he was smoking like a fiend. He probably started when he heard you were coming back to town."

Lily notices that Uncle James didn't wave. She says, "He took Growlie."

Daddy says, "What?"

"He took Growlie."

"What do you mean he took Growlie?"

"He buried him in the dirt. Jake found him."

Daddy's arms get tighter around her. She feels like she can't breathe and she coughs. Real fast his arms grow looser and he reaches up and pets her hair.

Lily watches as Aunt Katie looks over at her daddy. Her eyes look wet. She turns the car into the parking lot of the café and parks. Just then, Lily remembers her lucky rock.

"Daddy, I have something to show you." She reaches into the pocket of her purple shorts and pulls out the rock.

Her daddy picks it up from her open palm with two fingers. "That's a beauty. Where did you find it?"

"At Nana's. In her field. Nana said it was a lucky rock."

"Nana knows a lucky rock when she sees it. You need to take care of that."

"It's for you, Daddy. Nana said whoever carries the rock with them will always be lucky."

Daddy turns his head to the right and a sound comes up from deep inside of him. Another one follows as Daddy presses his thumb and finger into his eyes. He breathes funny for a minute, and then grows quiet. When he moves his thumb and finger, Lily can see his eyes are wet. It is then she knows that he was trying not to cry. She wraps her arms around his neck. "Oh, Daddy. I'm so glad that you're home."

He says softly, "Let's go get you some ice cream."

They climb out of the car. It takes a while for her daddy because he can't bend his right leg. He grabs his cane and they head for the front door of the Willis Café. She grabs her daddy's left hand and watches Aunt Katie lead the way. Aunt Katie wears high heels and a short skirt. Her nails are painted red and her hair is long and yellow like her own. When they get to the door, a man steps up and opens it, then moves to the side for them to enter.

He says, "Good afternoon, Kate."

Aunt Katie says, "Good afternoon, John. You remember my brother, Billy?"

"I think we've met a time or two." He sticks out his hand to Daddy, and Daddy has to let go of her hand to switch his cane. He sticks his right hand out to shake.

"Welcome home. You must be damn glad to be out of that desert." He uses a bad word.

"Yeah," her daddy says.

They walk into the café and Aunt Katie turns to her. "Where you want to sit, Lily?"

Lily points to the table near the front, next to a window. "That one! That's our favorite table, right, Daddy?"

A funny look comes over Daddy's face. He says, "That's right, Peanut."

Lily runs over to the table and sits. She loves this café. It looks like a log cabin with pretty flowered curtains and pictures of beautiful places on the walls. There are mountains and lakes and buildings that she has never seen. There is even an occasional animal head, which used to make her sad. But her daddy told her that the animals were hunted for meat. They fed hungry people so it was okay that they were killed. Before Daddy left for the desert, when her mommy and daddy lived together, they used to come here every Friday night for the fish fry. She hopes, oh she hopes, that they can all do that again someday.

The man and lady who own the restaurant walk over to the table. They are old like Nana. The man sticks out his hand to Daddy. They shake hands.

"Welcome home, Bill."

"Thank you, Mr. Kohler."

The lady says, "You look real good."

"Thank you, Ma'am."

"Anything you want, Bill. It's on us today," the man says. "You know, we never had a better worker than you."

"Thank you. That's very nice of you."

The lady turns to look at her and says, "Miss Lily Rose, you're growing like a weed. Going to be tall like your daddy."

Daddy, sitting next to her, puts his arm around her waist. Aunt Katie, sitting across from her, smiles.

All of a sudden, a huge noise comes from the kitchen. It sounds like a million dishes have crashed onto the floor. Her daddy throws his arms over his head, just like she saw in a movie one night that she wasn't supposed to see. Uncle Peter was babysitting for her, and he brought over the movie. It was a war movie. But not the same war as her daddy was in. There were a ton of loud noises and men falling to the ground and throwing their arms over their heads like Daddy did. She grabs his arm and screams, "Daddy!" He uncovers his head and looks around. She can see his hands shaking.

The lady says, "I don't believe it! That kid has done it again." She turns to her husband. "I told you not to hire him."

The man says, "Someone has to give him a chance."

"I know, but it's costing us a bundle. I'm terribly sorry, Billy."

"I'll go check on the damage." The man says.

"We'll send over a waitress right away. I'm ... I'm really sorry, Billy.

The man and the lady walk away. Her daddy's face looks red like a strawberry, and Aunt Katie reaches across the table to grab one of his shaking hands. She says, "Are you okay?"

He shakes his head yes, but he doesn't look okay. He says, "I ... I have to go to the bathroom."

"I'll go with you, Daddy."

"No. No, Peanut. You stay here with Aunt Katie. I'll be back in a minute." He stands up, grabs his cane, and walks in the funny way he walks now, over to the bathroom and disappears behind the door.

All of a sudden she feels so sad. Tears start falling out of her eyes. She feels so bad for her daddy and she's so afraid he's going to go away again.

Aunt Katie says, "Come here, Lily." She pats her lap.

Lily stands up and moves towards Aunt Katie, but then she's running over to the man's bathroom. She pounds on the door with both fists screaming, "Daddy!" She's got to get inside. She's got to. She's got to see if her daddy is okay. Aunt Katie scoops her up from behind and carries her back to the table. Everyone is looking at her, but she doesn't care. Aunt Katie sits down, holding her on her lap. She smells good as she always does, like cookies when they're baking.

Aunt Katie rocks her and whispers in her ear, "It's okay, Lily."

"He's ... he's scared."

"He's okay. It's just going to take some time."

"He's going to go away again."

"He's not going to go away again." She places her cheek against Lily's head. "Look, here he comes now."

Lily looks up to see her daddy walking back to the table.

When he reaches them, he says, "I have to get out of here. I have to get out of here now."

Aunt Katie says, "Okay."

Right then a waitress walks up. "I can't believe my eyes! It's Billy Bagwell. How are you?"

Daddy looks up at the waitress and says, "Hey, Donna, how you doing?"

"I heard you were coming back to town. You look real good...."

Daddy struggles to stand and reaches for his cane. "We ... were just on our way out."

The waitress says, "Oh ... Well, I hope to see you again soon. I ..."

Aunt Katie stands and they begin to walk towards the door. She says to the waitress, "He's not divorced yet."

The three of them walk out of the door and her daddy turns to Aunt Katie. He says, "You didn't have to be rude."

"You call that rude?"

Daddy closes his eyes for a minute then he opens them again. "I'm going to walk Lily home."

"What? It's got to be two to three miles from here."

"We can walk that far, can't we, Peanut?"

Lily begins to jump up and down. This is what she's been waiting for: time alone with Daddy. "That isn't far at all!"

Aunt Kate says, "But, you were just so upset."

"Walking helps."

"Your leg. You shouldn't be walking that long on your leg."

"I'm not going to baby it."

"I thought you said you were going to keep Lily. Why are you taking her back?"

"I can't keep Lily. I have to do it right, or I won't get her at all. I just wanted to show Bren and James who was in control."

"You'll run into them."

"I'm not afraid to see them. Come by the house in about an hour."

Lily and her daddy begin to walk down the dirt road. He holds her hand and they walk slowly because he has to use the cane. Clouds cover the sky. Thunder can be heard from far away.

"Is it going to rain, Daddy?"

"Hopefully not before we get you home."

"I'm so glad you're home."

"Well, I'm ... I'm glad to be home with you." He bends over and puts his hand softly on her cheek.

They begin walking down the road again. It is really quiet. There are no birds singing and Lily can't feel any wind. She looks up at her daddy to see him staring straight ahead. She can't tell what he is looking at. She says, "Daddy?" but he doesn't answer. Letting go of his hand, she starts to skip up ahead. When she turns back to look at him, he continues to walk slowly, staring. She spots something shiny and bends down to pick up a broken piece of green glass. She holds the jagged object up to her eye and looks through it to see the world. Things look different. The field in the middle looks like it goes on forever. The trees on the edges look a hundred feet tall. A house not far from her looks like a dot. A rock on the ground looks huge.

Her daddy walks past her. She looks up and watches as he stares straight ahead. If she didn't know better, she'd think he was a robot. Her mama told her he might not be the same since he was in a war. He is the same, but he isn't. Maybe he sees the world now like she saw it through the green glass. It's the same world, but it looks different. Did he see her the same way as he did before? Maybe he didn't see her as his little girl anymore. She starts feeling real scared again. Running up behind him, she grabs his hand with both of hers. "Daddy!"

All of a sudden he stumbles on a rock and falls forward, landing on his hands, his legs stretched out behind him. His cane rolls across the road.

"Daddy!" She falls to her knees beside him. For a moment he doesn't move. Then he pushes his upper body up from the ground and drags his bad leg around like it's real heavy. Sitting on his butt, he wipes the gravel off of his hands and presses his thumb and finger into his eyes. She can hear the sound. It sounds like he is choking. Lily throws herself into his lap, wrapping her small arms around him. "Daddy! Daddy. You're my daddy. My daddy."

The choking stops as he wraps his arms tightly around her. She feels so safe. They rock back and forth and back and forth like a chair, and Lily feels the wind begin to blow.

10
Rain Drop

Friday 6:01 p.m.

James watches as Doris Rentschler sashays her way out of the garage. He swears her tits are bigger. Her husband has the money to get them done. He owns half of Willis. James flicks his cigarette into a metal barrel and heads for the phone, wondering how the hell Billy got his hands on Lily. He picks up the phone and stabs at numbers, his teeth begin to grind. Brenda's voice clicks on the answering machine. James knocks the receiver hard against the edge of a shelf and stabs out another set of numbers. This time he hears Martha Becker's voice say, "Hello?"

"Martha? This is James. Is Brenda there?" There is a moment or two of silence. "Martha?"

"James, I know that you love her. I've known for a long time. But she's not your girl."

"Martha, with all due respect, stay the hell out of this."

"Now is not a good time to be starting trouble."

"Is she there or what?"

"Consider everyone involved before you make a move."

"Where is she?"

"She's out in the garden. I'll call her."

In the background he hears her call out Brenda's name. A minute or two passes as he fights the urge to light up another cigarette.

Finally he hears Brenda's voice. "Hello?"

"How the hell did he get that girl?"

"He ... he came by and picked her up."

"Did you know he was coming?"

"No!"

"You just stood there and let him take her?"

"It was a surprise. It happened really fast."

"How the hell are you going to get her back?"

"He'll bring her back."

"Are you sure?" A moment or two of silence passes. "Are you?"

"He's not going to hurt Lily."

"I'm not talking about hurting her. I'm talking about him keeping her and not giving her back."

"Can we deal with this at home?"

"When will you be there?"

"I'm leaving now."

James throws the receiver into a corner and begins to scrub his hands with a coarse brush. He could wear gloves to do his work, but he would feel like a fag. He rinses them, dries them on a towel, and checks himself out in the mirror above the sink. Sweeping his dark hair back out of his eyes, he leans in close to look at a grease smudge under his left eye. The girls have always liked his eyes. He's been told he looks like an Indian, but his mother has always denied there being native blood. In fact, who his dad is (or was) she has never said. He has had an interest in native ceremony and the long black hair of the women. But he feels like a white man.

James lowers the garage door to the ground, lights up another cigarette and jumps into his truck. He can't believe he started smoking again. He and Billy quit five years ago when Lily was born. It seemed like Billy was always leading the way. Fuck Billy. James was leading his own way now.

His tires squeal as he sharply turns into the lot of a party store. He runs in, grabs a six-pack of Bud, throws the man a five, and jumps back into the truck. He pops a can and takes a long deep draw. Wiping his mouth with the back of his hand, he heads for home. Sort of home. It's not his house and he feels like a stranger there, but it will have to do until he and Brenda buy one of their own. He watches the lightning crackle down out of the clouds in the distance. A few seconds later, the thunder rolls. This storm was going to be a good one. They needed the rain. The land was dry and hard, leaves on the plants drooping. The only brilliant fertile green was in the yards of the fortresses where the cost of water presents no object. The yards of these homes look like mini-nurseries, flush with color, lush with trees, bushes, and shrubs. Damn, is there anything those rich people don't have?

James finishes his beer down to the last drop. He throws the can into a black plastic trash bag behind the seat. The smell of old food drifts up. Must be the remains of the chicken and cheese burrito he bought at the convenience store the other day. He arrives at the house and pulls into the drive behind Brenda's wagon. Grabbing the beer, he jumps out and walks into the house through the back door. He lets the door slam hard behind him.

Brenda stands in the kitchen just starting to sauté green pepper and onion. A pot of boiling water sits on another burner with a crinkly plastic bag of spaghetti nearby. She has a little pink apron with white lace tied around her waist. Her ass, that ass, in her blue denim shorts sticks out in the back. He'd love to touch her, but he doesn't dare.

"I guess she's not back yet."

"No," she answers without turning.

"That's just great."

Brenda turns to face him. "Why does it matter to you, anyway? She's not your daughter."

"She has been for the last six months."

"She has not been your daughter. She's been a child you are helping to take care of."

"She's ... she's like a daughter to me."

"Oh, really. So that's why you stole her bear?"

"Jesus Christ. It was an old piece of crap. She's ... she's not a baby anymore."

"I know that you had to grow up quickly, James. But she doesn't. Her daddy gave her that bear."

"That's right. He gave it to her."

"You know what your problem is, James? You want to take everything that's his."

James steps over and grabs Brenda by the upper left arm.

"Excuse me? I took you? I remember you giving yourself to me."

Brenda says through a clenched jaw, "Let go of my arm."

He releases her arm and gives her shoulder a little shove. "You bent over at this sink."

Brenda turns back to her sautéing. James watches her bite her lip to keep from crying. The silence that follows balloons to fill the room. "Where's the mutt?"

"I don't know."

"You think he took him, too?"

"Maybe."

"I didn't see him in the car."

"What car?"

"Kate's car. That's how I knew he had the kid."

Brenda turns back to him, quickly wiping a tear away. "They were riding through town?"

"You'd think he was a fucking celebrity. People were honking and waving. It was ridiculous." James pops open another Bud and puts the remaining four in the refrigerator.

Brenda says, "I'll take one of those."

James pops the cap of another as Brenda reaches up into the cabinet for a glass. He can see the nipple of her right breast beneath her little striped shirt. He reaches down and quickly rearranges himself, just before she turns back towards him. She grabs the beer from his hand and pours.

He says, "You really think he's going to bring her back?"

"I don't know. God, I'm so confused." She gulps down a quarter of her beer.

"Confused? Confused about what?" Alarm makes his skin prickle.

"I ... I think I'd better show you something." Brenda places the glass of beer and the can down, and turns to pull out the letter from behind the canister. The delicate paper wavers in the air like wings as she hands the letter to James.

"What's this?"

"It's from Billy. It came yesterday."

James reads. *Dear Brenda. I'll be home on June seventeenth to straighten this mess out. You and James should get your things in order. I don't know why you two did this to me, but you're going to pay. There's no way out, Bren. No way out. Justice will be served. Billy.* James starts to ball the letter in his right hand.

Brenda screams, "No!" She pulls it from his hand. "We ... we might need it." She turns and urgently presses the paper against the counter top with both hands.

James doesn't like the way she does it, gently, like it's much more fragile than it really is. He says, "I'm going out to look for that mutt."

"That's all you have to say?"

"You knew this was coming, Brenda."

"Yes, but ... but not so soon."

"And you're confused," James mimics in a snotty voice. "What exactly does that mean? You still don't know which one of us you want to be with?"

Brenda turns back to the stove and stirs the vegetables with a wooden spoon.

"Well?"

"I don't know," she says in a tiny voice.

James steps out onto the sun deck, slams the sliding door behind him, and lights a cigarette. His heart thumps inside his chest.

Could Billy hurt them? Would he sacrifice everything he had for revenge? But then what did he have? An estranged wife, an occupied house, and some kind of injury that kept him healing in a hospital for months. The guy had nothing. Except a daughter. Imagine that. A guy who at one time had it all. This town's golden boy. Now, next to nothing. And he, James, was the cause of it. Or at least half of the cause. Maybe Billy did want to put a bullet between his eyes. Maybe he would. But could he kill Brenda?

James draws hard on his cigarette and watches the storm rolling in like a tank. The clouds are ominous, strangely colored, promising something severe. The time between lightning and thunder is five seconds now. The wind gathers force, pushing James' hair straight back from his face. Already the air feels cooler. The trees and flowers begin to dance first one way and then another in a wind that has no pattern. The sound soothes like white noise.

When his mother moved him and his three brothers to this town he was ten years old. She struggled to raise them on a low-paying factory job, working afternoons and then closing the bars with tattooed bikers, disgruntled married men, and other desperate single girls. He was embarrassed to go to school because his clothes were ragged, sometimes passing through three pairs of hands before his own. His black hair and brown skin made him feel like he stuck out against a vast majority of pale Caucasian skin. Girls would point at him from behind their books, giggle, and whisper in each other's ears. He didn't know at the time that they thought that he was cute, exotic, maybe even dangerous in their fantasies gone wild. The other boys kept their distance, sniffing at him from afar, circling and speculating as to whether he was friend or foe. In gym class he was often the last chosen, not because he wasn't fast and strong, but because his shyness made him look either not too bright or arrogant. He hid in the corner of the other classes, hiding behind his hair. One day Billy walked up to him after algebra and said, "We're playing a game of football after school. Why don't you come by?" That day Billy threw him a pass and he caught the ball in one outstretched hand, and clung to that ball running across the goal like a fire down a line. Everything depended on that play. His life got easier that afternoon as one of the most popular boys in school, and he and Billy became best friends.

They hunted rabbits, built forts, and tested their courage in every way they could. They raced through the fields on dirt bikes, flying over hills, threading their way through woods, and blasting down the straightaways like rockets. They jumped from bluffs into reservoirs of water and swung between trees like Tarzan.

Eventually their toys became snowmobiles and cars, James revealing a knack for fixing all things mechanical. Like some had an ear to crack a safe, James perfected the engine's purr.

James was fourteen when sixteen-year-old Sue Smith let him touch her. He was sixteen when twenty-eight-year-old Doris Rentschler grabbed his ass and dropped his drawers. The story was different for Billy. When they were fourteen, Billy confessed that Brenda Becker was the only girl he wanted. At fifteen James heard that they had finally kissed. As James banged his way through a string of females, Billy stayed faithful to just one. The one secret of James' that no one ever knew except Doris, who saw through him like a glass, was that James wanted Brenda, too. Brenda wasn't afraid to get dirty and she was as smart as or smarter than any boy. She didn't giggle and act silly, or play games to mess up heads. And at fifteen, her breasts were round and full, the nipples always taut, and her ass was, well, her ass was always perfect: a sweet ripe pear. What did Billy think, anyway, when the three would go skinny dipping together, and in the cold of the winter when they rolled into a ball? What did he think? James hadn't planned to steal Billy's girl. Not once. But it happened. And he couldn't imagine his life without her now.

James feels a big raindrop plop upon his forehead. Others follow upon his arms and head. One hits the end of his cigarette and he hears it sizzle. The wind-driven rain begins attacking him from all sides. He runs down the steps of the sundeck into the yard, and holding his arms up into the air, he moves around in a circle slowly and prays the only thing he can pray: *Please don't take Brenda away from me. I've had so little. Please.*

He didn't know if she loved him, but he knew that he loved her. At least as much as he could love anyone. Maybe she only turned to him out of desperation when she felt all alone. But she turned to him. When Billy left her alone, she turned to him.

James bounds up the stairs to the sundeck and re-enters the house through the sliding door. Brenda, standing at the stove, turns to watch as he peels away his wet shirt, unlaces and pulls off his scuffed brown boots. He watches as her eyes take in his brown and muscled chest. For an instant her eyes drop lower. Walking towards her, he takes the wooden spoon out of her hand, lays it on the counter and says softly, "I'm sorry, Brenda." He wraps his arms around her, but she begins to push him away and says, "Not now, James." He begins to kiss her softly on her neck and nuzzle her, running his hands gently but urgently up and down the length of her back and ass. She utters, "No," while struggling, but this time with much less resistance. He draws both hands forward to massage her breasts. She moans in pleasure as her head rolls back. Suddenly her limp body stiffens as she sucks in a breath. He looks up and sees her staring at something across the room. He turns slowly to see Billy standing in the doorway of the hall, leaning against the doorjamb. Lily stands by his side clutching his left leg. The dog, Jake, stands there, too.

11
Empty Eyes

Friday 7:14 p.m.

Bagwell will not take his eyes off the back of his former best friend. If he does, his eyes might slide over to Brenda, standing there so recently groped. He watched as she began to engage, open up, and surrender to the seduction of James. He will not look at her. He cannot look at her. If he could, he would will her into stone.

Every missile assault that had exploded above, beside, and below him meant to compel him forward now. Every skirmish he had exchanged with the enemy, every command barked into his face by an officer, every word of the Dear John letter carved into his mind now screamed inside his heart.

Without looking down at Lily clinging to his left leg, he says, "Peanut, go to your room."

She looks up at him with pleading eyes, "No ..."

"Go to your room."

Lily turns reluctantly and walks back down the hall and into her room. Jake the dog remains at the feet of his master.

By this time James has turned and stares wide eyed. Bagwell meets that stare until his eyes are drawn down to a crimson tattoo, six inches long and two inches wide across the left breast muscle over the heart: Brenda.

Bagwell rushes at James and pins him against the counter and the cabinet, cruelly twisting his right arm up high behind his back, and his own right forearm locked against his old friend's windpipe. His jaw clenches so tight his teeth squeak as he spits and speaks into James' defiant face. "Not now, because my daughter is in this house. But one day soon. I'm going to pick you off. I'm going to squash you. Some day when you least expect it, I will kill you." He twists James' arm up one-quarter inch further and pushes down harder on the windpipe until a gagging sound escapes, then he releases him.

A cross between a smirk and a sneer appears on James' face. "Not if I kill you first."

The moment breaks with the sound of a car horn bleating twice. Bagwell sniffs with disdain, turns to limp across the room to grab his cane left behind in the doorway. As he turns back to head towards the door, he catches one fleeting glimpse of Brenda from the corner of his eye, standing up against another counter, the back of one hand pressed against her mouth. Her eyes glisten wet in the light. Bagwell opens the door and steps out into the pouring rain, his war-torn body aching.

Bagwell feels like he might open the car door and roll out onto the road. His mother drives so slowly. True, the rain falls in sheets, visibility cut by half or even more, but he needs to talk with Sam now.

His mother speaks up, "You going to tell me what happened in there, Son?"

"Nothing. Nothing happened."

"Then why are you so riled up?"

Thunder cracks like a giant piece of wood being split by a hatchet. Both Bagwell and his mom jump.

She says, "I ... I think we better turn around and go home."

"No."

"I've never seen it rain this hard. The man upstairs is trying to tell us something."

"What's he trying to tell us, Mom?"

"That we are living immorally."

"How are you living immorally?"

"Maybe not me. But others. Like that girl," her voice cracks, "and that boy, who I used to like so much. They are living immorally in that house. Your house."

Bagwell sniffs with disdain once more. "One thing you learn in a war, Mom, there is no man upstairs."

"William John!" Bagwell turns to watch his mother turn her head up to the sky. "Forgive him, Father, he knows not what he says."

"For Christ's sake, Mom!"

She pulls the car over to the side of the road and parks. "Son, what have they done to you?"

"Like you haven't seen it before."

"Your father kept everything inside."

"Don't tell me you didn't see a change in him. I saw it and I was Lily's age."

"Then why did you follow in his footsteps?"

"It's in the blood." Bagwell turns to his mother, "I need to talk to Sam. Please."

"You've changed. Something's happened."

"The question is what's happened to you?"

Lightning flashes, momentarily illuminating his mother's face. But, in the darkness she says, "I've been born again."

"Great. Just great. Why couldn't Kate come pick me up?"

"She had a date. Billy ... Billy, look at me."

Bagwell reels in his right arm and as thunder rolls hard overhead he punches the dashboard, leaving a fair-sized dent. "Move this car!"

Crying softly, his mom puts the car in drive and slowly pulls back onto the road.

"That's his house right there."

"I don't remember it looking like that."

"He's been sick."

As fast as the rain started, the rain stops. The tiniest sliver of light from the rising moon breaks through the mass of clouds. Just before his mom turns the car right onto the dirt driveway, the moon itself appears in the opening.

She points up, "Son, look!"

Bagwell looks up, but doesn't say a word.

"It's a message for you, Son. The storm is over. Everything is going to be fine."

"Negative, Mom. The storm is not over. You can just drop me off. Sam will bring me home."

"I'd like to say 'hi' to him."

"Not this time."

"Are you sure he'll bring you home?"

"I'm sure." Bagwell turns to her briefly, but doesn't meet her eyes. "I ... I'm sorry I dented your dashboard. I'll fix it for you tomorrow."

"But when will you be home?"

"Later. I'll be home later."

Bagwell climbs out of the car and his mother drives away. Her face from the side, streaked with running rain, looks ancient. Sam steps out of his shop, a converted garage that sits to the right and in back of a slightly dilapidated white wooden house. In front on a tall pole is a single black and white flag drooping from the rain. Three letters are legible: MIA. Bagwell limps towards the shop as Sam moves towards him, stroking his long goatee with his right hand, holding a piece of sandpaper in the other. As the two men meet, Sam wraps Bagwell into a big hug. Bagwell allows the close hold but grows uncomfortable when his eyes begin to sting.

Sam draws back and looks at him squarely. "If you ain't a sight for sore eyes!"

Bagwell smiles.

"You look like shit, Bill."

"The girls have all been telling me I look great."

"Well, what do they know? Hell of a storm, huh? Did you see the moon break out, man? It will be full by tomorrow."

"Yeah, I saw it."

Sam pulls on Bagwell's arm. "Come on, let's go in the shop."

The two men walk into the converted garage. The pungent scent of damp wood permeates the air in the room. A long wooden work table splits the area in half. Carpentry tools line the walls, hanging on hooks, sitting on shelves, nestled on the cement floor up against the walls. There are clamps and glue, and nails and screws, and three different kinds of saws. A chisel and a lathe lie perpendicular on a shelf, and a confetti of wood pieces lie all around the table. Pieces of unfinished furniture sit in the right corner of the back. On the left sits a beautiful oak cabinet, doors open, vacant of glass. On the work table is an oak rocker, child-sized. Sawdust covers everything in the room with a thin coat, but the organization is impeccable.

Sam grabs the cane from Bagwell's right hand. "Let me see that thing." Sam studies the workmanship closely, tests the balance as it lies across the palm of his right hand. The thumb and the first two fingers of his hand are intact, the ring finger is missing, and the little one just a stub. "Not bad."

"I picked it up in Germany."

"Like I said, it's not bad. But you need something righteous. I'll carve you something real pretty. Maybe some dancing maidens or galloping horses."

"Surprise me."

"Oh, don't say that." Sam walks over to the work table where an ashtray made of turquoise glass, of a mermaid reclining on her side, sits on the right corner. He picks up half a joint, and lights it with a flip of a switch on a small torch. Inhaling deeply, he turns to look at Bagwell, then hands him what's left of the neatly rolled herb.

Bagwell waves his right hand and says, "Nah. They already got me on a half dozen meds."

Sam looks intently into Bagwell's eyes. Bagwell averts and turns.

"How about some dry clothes, Bill?"

"A shirt would be good. It's a real project getting my pants off this leg."

Sam walks over to a wooden coat rack, grabs a blue cotton work shirt, and tosses it to Bagwell. Bagwell strips off his wet shirt and pulls on the dry one, buttoning it from the top down with shaking hands.

Sam says, "You still wearing your dog tags?"

"No. They're ... they're the tags of a friend. A reminder that

I've got to call his mother or go see her. He ... didn't make it. I promised him."

"I doubt that you need a reminder to do that."

"Yeah ... well ... he wouldn't be dead if it wasn't for me," he mumbles.

"What did you say?"

"Nothing." Bagwell walks over to the middle of the work table to get a closer look at the little rocker. The top part of the back is decorated with delicately carved flowers. "Sam, this is really nice. Could you teach me how to do it?"

"Are you serious?"

"Yeah, I am. Who is this chair for?"

"Your girl." Sam flicks the roach of his joint out into the wet grass outside the shop.

"My girl?"

"Lily Rose. I asked her what she wanted for her birthday, and she told me she wanted a rocker. She said that every time she was sad or afraid, her daddy would rock her."

Bagwell turns and steps away from the table.

Sam continues, "Your daddy told me once, when we were over in that jungle, that you liked to be rocked as a boy, too."

"Oh, yeah? He told you that?" Bagwell remembers sitting in his father's lap, nestling into his clean-smelling green T-shirt. God, he felt safe. His father would gently stroke his hair and sing the words of a rock tune real quiet-like in his ear, keeping time by tapping the fingers of his free hand on the arm of the chair. Then he was gone, back to the jungle.

"What else did my daddy tell you?"

Sam brushes stray hairs back from his face and smoothes them into his long ponytail held back in a band. "He told me that if I made it, and he didn't, he wanted me to watch over you, and never ever let you take part in a war."

Bagwell turns to him. "Well, I did anyway, didn't I."

"And look at you. You see, the thing about war is, whether you come back or not, you're still a fucking casualty."

Bagwell draws his cane up and rams it down into the floor. The force of the gesture leaves the walking stick quivering. "I am not a casualty. This did not happen to me by chance."

"I'm talking about your soul, man. You got that empty look in your eyes. That somehow, someway, you sold the better part of yourself to the devil."

"Fuck you." Bagwell limps towards the open door of the shop determined to leave, only to see the rain screaming towards the earth on a slant, denting the skin with a force. The moon is long gone. As he turns back to Sam, the room begins to move; the walls spin slowly, and the floor grows distant. He falls against the nearest wall for support. Sam runs to his side and helps to lower him into one of two easy chairs sitting in the front of the shop. "I've got it," Bagwell says. But he doesn't.

Sam runs over to a small refrigerator and pulls out a bottle of water. He pours a glass full, walks back to Bagwell and hands it to him. He falls into the chair beside him. "What the fuck is going on, man?"

"I don't know. My body aches, I get dizzy, and I'm pissing blood."

"What did they tell you it was?"

"Oh, it's anesthesia coming out of my body, it's this, it's that, they don't know."

"You guys are probably coming back sick, too."

"Are you still sick, Sam?"

"They just diagnosed me with cancer again. Gave me six months."

"No way...."

Sam stands back up and moves over to his worktable. He picks up a piece of sandpaper, fine, and begins to smooth one bow of the rocker. "I'm planning on proving them wrong. Your daddy was the bravest man I ever saw. I have never witnessed a stronger will to live. I saw guys over there die of a wound that was barely a graze. Your daddy held his guts in his body with one hand, screaming orders, as we carted him around trying to get him lifted out. Nobody could believe he lived as long as he did. And he was talking. Talked about how pretty your mom was and how much spunk you had." He stops for a moment and sands, and then blows the dust away. "He almost made it." Sam walks over to Bagwell and leans over him, one hand on each arm of the chair, and looks him in the eyes. "You got to want to live real badly. You got to forget all the injustices. You got to forgive old debts and undoings. You got to look the devil in the eye and tell him that you want your soul back. You will have your soul back. Then the emptiness in your eyes will be filled again. You got that, Bill?"

"I can't."

"You can't what?"

"Forgive."

"You've got to try."

Bagwell looks at Sam squarely and barks, "Back off!"

Sam lifts his hands up as if at gunpoint and backs away. "You just aren't ready yet."

Using his cane, Bagwell struggles to stand up out of the cushions of the easy chair. He limps over to the open door again and watches the rainfall against the fading light. He poses as if to flee.

Sam resumes his sanding of Lily Rose's rocker. "You really want to run out into that rain?"

"I can't run. Remember?"

"You're telling me that that little wound is going to keep you from running? Your daddy kept his guts from spilling out with one hand."

"But he died anyway, didn't he?" The flag clinging to his father's coffin flashes across his mind. He remembers watching the Marines in their dress blues neatly fold it before handing it to his mom. The same flag Bagwell flew from his flagpole. What did she do with it? Would he really burn it when he finds it? The thought sickens him.

"I'll never forgive them."

"Who? The Marine Corps?"

"Them, too."

"I want to hear about it."

"You will." Bagwell glances down at his right forearm where his own tattoo of Brenda's name lies in a crimson heart. "I can't ever forgive ... her."

"She'll be back, Bill. I know my niece loves you."

Bagwell limps back towards Sam working on the table. "I'll never take her back."

"That's another part of that pact with the devil. The heart grows hard."

"I don't feel anything for her."

"If you say so."

"I feel something for him though."

"It's a bad thing being betrayed by a brother. A really bad thing."

Bagwell moves in close. "I want you to help me."

Sam stops sanding. "You know I'd do anything for you."

"I want you to help me kill him."

"Not her? Just him?"

"I can't kill Lily Rose's mother. I wanted to, but I can't."

"So, you're going to kill James. That ain't no way to fill those vacant eyes, brother." Sam reaches over and bounces two fingers on the edge of the rocker, causing it to rock. "You can't very well rock your little darling locked up behind bars."

"We can make it look like an accident."

12
This Boy

Friday 8:07 p.m.

Martha rinses the suds off the tumbler and carefully places it into the rack to dry. She glances out the window and a dot moving in the pouring rain catches her eye. The dot, growing larger, does not move in a straight line, but zigzags left and right, unsteady. She does not know if the dot is animal or human or even a ghost, but it heads towards the old farmhouse.

She feels wary of the fields, once so fertile and full of growing crops, now barren of planted food. Yes, there are the wildflowers and the long spiky grass, but the rocks foretell the future of this Mother Earth, untended, undernourished, turning back to sand. It is a testimony to the damage done by a race of people determined to make her theirs, every inch of her, to squeeze her and use her up until she must begin again. And so the people, too.

All those buried beneath the earth or scattered over her in ashes are the remnants of God's most progressive species, perhaps an experiment gone awry. The cries of those who have suffered echo broadly, and you can hear them if you try. Martha hears the cries of Jeanine, carried off into the night, left in one of these fields to pass away alone. She wonders if this dot now growing into form is her ghost coming home at last.

Martha watches the dot move forward into form, still small, but now distinctly human, though alive or dead she cannot say. The shoulders are stooped and the feet slide along the earth as if too heavy to lift; they are lead attached to willow. Martha feels like running out into the rain to catch this troubled soul before he or she falls. But she feels unsure that the figure is real. Would it fall through her arms without substance? Roll away into the rain and disappear? She closes her eyes and opens them again. Her breath catches as the figure sways wide to one side, then recovers. When she sees the angel perched up in an old oak watching the figure slowly pass, she knows that it is real. Angels do not watch over apparitions. The rain may prevent the angels from gliding, but their vigilance over living humans never ends. This angel, nestled into the branches and crouched with feathered wings folded in, looks more like a large snowy owl.

In some native cultures, the owl stands as a sign of death.

For one moment, the smallest moment, a sliver of the moon shines through the clouds and casts a single beam down upon the figure. As the figure drags itself along, a spot of darkness follows. A little shadow. An itty bitty shadow that the night swallows when the moon disappears. At this moment, the figure falls.

Martha runs down the four steps, out the back door, into the pouring rain without a hat, or coat, or umbrella, or anything else that would keep the grandmother covered. The thunder rumbles as Martha slips and slides across the driveway, her stiff old body struggling for balance. As she steps into the garden new challenges rear: puddles at the base of furrows suck at her feet, flowers and bushes from her garden, some with jagged branches, some adorned with thorns, grab at her clothing now wet, thoroughly wet. She can barely see through her glasses, a blur of running rain. Without them she cannot see at all.

From the lush garden into the barren field, she moves towards the figure, fallen and still. She looks up into the oak, but the angel has disappeared, proof floating down in the form of a feather. It lies on top of the body in the mud, no longer fluffy but drenched with rain. Martha plucks the feather with two fingers and pushes it deep into the pocket of her apron.

She falls to her knees and leans in soft. She sucks in a breath as the figure opens one visible eye and utters, "Grandma."

"Peter! My god!"

"Get me home, Grandma, please."

Peter lifts his upper body as Martha struggles to help him stand. She can feel currents of shivers course through his body from head to toes. Through a process of pulling, holding, and lifting, he stands. His tall, thin frame falls against her, but through her determination and his effort, feeble at first but growing stronger, they make their way towards the house. The lights in the windows beckon.

The memory of the picture falling fills Martha's heart with fear. Not this boy. Please. Not this boy.

"I ... I went through the field," he says.

"What field, Peter?"

"Where ... where they found her."

"Oh."

"I ... went through there." With the back of his free hand, he wipes salt water away with the rain.

"Let's get you home now."

"Why did someone kill my mom?"

"We're almost there now."

"Why did he take her away?"

The old woman and the young man step together around the rocks in the fields, stumbling over the smaller ones. They move through the lush vegetation of the garden, up and down over the furrows, the flowers stooping over, too, like the shoulders of Peter. As they step under the canopy of trees circling the house, they receive their first reprieve from the rain. The dark breaks through the halo of light that surrounds the house. In this light reflecting out, however dimly, Martha catches her first real glimpse of the boy, a young man really, though his face is bare of hair. She sees the red and swelling cheek, the puffy eye, the mud splattered on his pants in a design violently abstract. His T-shirt plasters to his body like a second skin.

"We better get you to a hospital."

"No! I'm okay."

"Just to check you out."

"No!"

The two figures working in a balance now enter the back door, climb slowly up the stairs and into the safe haven of the house. Martha draws Peter through the kitchen, down a short hall, and towards the high fluffy comfort of her bed.

"Grand ... Grandma ... I'm all muddy...."

"The bed covers can be washed."

Peter falls onto the bed on his side, curls his legs up and lies there shivering. Martha leans over and brushes the wet dark curls out of his eyes.

She says, "We've got to get you out of those clothes."

Peter, his teeth chattering, nods his head. He turns over onto his back wincing, and with the help of his elbows, pushes himself partially up. Martha unties the laces of his tennis shoes and struggles to pull the heavy wet canvas off of Peter's long feet. She succeeds and follows with the cotton socks, once white, now green and brown and black. Peter sits up slowly, pulls his tee over his head and falls back down upon the bed.

Martha says, "Unbuckle your belt, Peter, so Grandma can pull your pants off."

"No."

"What do you mean, no?"

"I'll ... do it."

"Just your pants. You can take off your underwear."

"I'm ... not wearing any underwear."

"Oh, you kids. You've got to get those pants off, so I can cover you and get you warm."

"You go. I'll ... do it. Just go."

"Okay, then. I'll make you a cup of tea."

"Could I have hot chocolate?"

"Of course you can."

Martha walks out of the room with a thousand thoughts racing through her head, including this one: what has Martin done to this boy now? This gentle boy. This good boy. This boy, misunderstood and abused, pointed at and talked about, as if being gay was something new. Dear God, is he the one to die? How can she give up any one member of her family? She must find a way. She must. Find a way to alter the destiny the fallen picture foretold.

She walks into the kitchen and lights the flame beneath the kettle, turns to grab a packet of Ovaltine from a brightly colored tin. She saw no blood or bruises on his body. But his movements were gingerly, like somewhere in his being there was pain. Turning, she heads back to the bedroom and enters.

Peter lies beneath a quilt he pulled up from the foot of the bed. One arm is flung over his eyes; the other is nestled down in the direction of his groin. His teeth continue to chatter.

Martha sits down on the edge of the bed. "Peter, what's happened? You must tell me. Are you sure we don't need to take you to a hospital?"

He lifts the arm off of his eyes. "No!"

"Are you injured?"

"No."

Martha tucks his arm under the quilt, then pulls it up to his chin. He glances into her eyes for one moment, and then closes his as if to sleep. She bends over to grab his jeans lying on the floor near the bed, and notices a dark red stain in the seat. She lets them fall back down to the floor, the belt buckle sharply striking the wood. Peter jumps. His eyes shoot open.

"There's blood on your pants, Peter."

"Just ... just a little blood."

"More than a little!"

"I ... I don't know. Don't worry about it."

"I am worrying about it."

"Well, don't!" as Peter rolls away from her, over onto his side, an uncontrollable moan escapes.

Martha places a hand gently on his side and leans towards him. "Did your father hurt you?"

"Not yet."

"Let me see."

"There's nothing to see."

"I've got to see." Martha, for an older woman, moves swiftly off of the bed and begins to pull the quilt up from the side.

Peter moves quicker. Turning, wincing as he does, his left arm shoots out to bring the quilt back down.

He screams, "I ... I had sex! Okay? I had sex!"

In that instant, the kettle begins to scream shrill and loud. Martha backs out of the room watching as Peter turns back onto his side, wincing again as he does.

It is one thing to know someone is gay, but something else to be reminded of what their acts together can be composed of. This gentle boy. This good boy. Injured from what she always thought should be an act of love. Bleeding. Blood. Tissue torn. Only the first time between a man and a woman. Was it the same between two men?

Martha tears the edge of the Ovaltine packet and dumps the contents into a cup. She picks up a spoon and stirs. Moving towards the icebox, she opens the door and grabs a can of real whipped cream. This boy has loved whipped cream on his hot chocolate since he's been small. She squirts out a mountain on top of the small lake of brown sweet liquid, and walks slowly back to where he lies. Placing the cup on the bed stand, she stands for a moment, still. She opens her mouth to speak, but before she can, he does.

"I'm sorry, Grandma. I'm sorry I told you that."

"Are you warm yet?"

From his position on his side he nods his head then says, "I'm in trouble."

"What do you mean?" Martha sits back down on the edge of the bed, placing her hand on his shoulder.

"He took my car."

"Your father?"

"No. The kid. The kid I did it with."

"He left you somewhere?"

"Dad is going to kill me." Peter begins to wipe the index finger of his left hand back and forth across his lips.

"Peter ..."

"Who knows what he'll do with my car."

"Why did he leave you?"

"I didn't know what to do."

"How far did you walk?"

"I didn't know where to go."

"You were right in coming here." She rubs his back softly.

"If Dad sees him in my car ..."

"It will be okay."

"How?"

"Maybe the kid will return your car."

"I don't think so."

"He'll leave it somewhere. Isn't that what they do?"

"Dad's going to kill me."

"Your father is not going to kill you," Martha says, but even she knows her words lack conviction. Not that she thinks her son Martin would ever kill his boy, but she doesn't doubt he might hurt him, at least with words, if with nothing else. He's hurt him many times before. The truth is, Martin has hurt many people.

"If he finds out what we did ..."

"Hush, now."

"He's going to kill me."

"Shhhh ..."

"I'm dead."

Thunder loudly cracks as lightning brightly flashes. Inside on this dark night looks like daylight for one moment. In the corner of the room Martha sees the angel backed up and flattened against the wall, not wanting to be seen, wings folded, eyes cast down, fingers intertwined. Dark once again, Martha stands up and moves tentatively towards the corner. She reaches out her hand, but feels nothing.

"Did you see it, Peter?"

She turns to look at the boy. His eyes are wide, his mouth open.

"Did you see it? Oh, tell me that you did."

"Why was it here? Why was it in this room?" he asks in a whisper.

"To watch over you."

"Or was it the angel of death come to take me away?"

"I don't think so because it left without you."

"Maybe it's coming back."

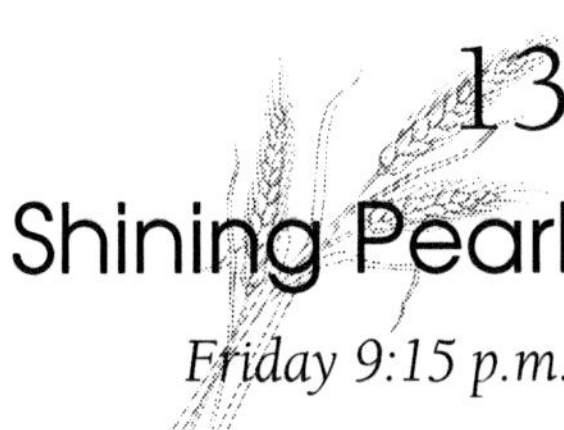

13
Shining Pearl

Friday 9:15 p.m.

Brenda lies in a tub of hot water up to her chin. The bubbles shining in the candlelight reflect the details of the room. Fragments of the white toilet, the blue flowered wallpaper, the brush, the cotton balls, the bath salts sitting in a jar. The razor. She considers slipping beneath the bubbles to a safe place, warm and wet, where she might feel buoyant, fed by another, able to let go for just a day. Or maybe forever. Brenda does submerge herself into the quiet and floats, lifting her hands and feet off the bottom of the tub. She experiences a lightness, a release of gravity, a clearing of her mind. All she has to do, she thinks, is to allow a trickle of water to enter her nose or her mouth, let it come, let herself go, let the trickle grow into a torrent, stop the air at last.

What has she done? No matter how she tries, she cannot rid her mind of the image of Billy limping across the kitchen floor. She longs to touch the wound.

Loud muffled thumps upon the door snag her attention. She thinks of James and decides to stay right here. She thinks of Lily Rose and moves up through the water, breaking the surface, through the collage reflecting on the bubbles, emerging into the air gasping. The thumps sound clear now, small and hard, arrhythmic, produced by two little fists.

"Mommy!"

"Lily, stop it!"

"I want to come in!"

"Why aren't you in bed?"

"I can't sleep."

"Go back to bed, Lily. Mommy will be there in a few minutes."

"You've been in there for thirty-three minutes now. I counted."

"Lily, please give Mommy a few more minutes alone. Please."

"How many?"

Brenda lifts her can of beer and feels it is still three quarters full. "A few more, Lily. I'll be there soon." Brenda guzzles most of the can and places it back down beside an empty.

Next she hears James' voice. "Brenda? What the hell are you doing in there? Why have you locked the door?"

Brenda sits up in the tub, bubbles and water sliding off her body. "Jesus Christ! Can't I have a few minutes alone?"

"You took the last of the beer. I'm going out for another six."

"Read a story to Lily first. Please!"

"Okay. But then I'm going out for beer."

"Make it a twelve."

Brenda leans over to turn the hot water on. She lies back feeling the fresh hot water mingle through the lukewarm. She watches as her nipples grow hard and round as berries. Reaching up with her right hand she touches them gently. This simple gesture ignites the longing. She wants something inside of her. She wants to be filled up now. The emptiness is killing her. Like she's all alone in the world with no arms and falling. But she will not end her life now. She cannot leave her child without a mother. Brenda knows all about that and the emptiness it brings. She will not kill herself because maybe there is a way to fill the hole. She longs for pleasure. The pleasure will fill the hole.

She slowly runs her right hand down her belly towards her groin and touches the spot, the shining pearl. In moments, she feels like she will burst. Kill herself? Slip beneath the water? In her mind, safety lies there. But through her desire she conjures her power. The boys long to be inside her. They want to fill her up. That's certainly why James is here. He pulls down her jeans and takes her, however and wherever he wants. He doesn't ask. Her whole body belongs to him.

Billy wanted to fill her up too, although gingerly. He had to light candles, put on Miles Davis' "Kind of Blue," nuzzle her neck, lick her toes, take her hard but never, ever hurt her. Billy would bring her flowers, touch her softly through her clothes, slowly but surely get inside, stay inside, telling her that inside her is the only place he ever wants to be. Inside her is his home.

Truthfully, both approaches leave her hungry, still empty. Why? How will she ever be fulfilled? God, please tell me how. Maybe this time, by her own hand. Brenda feels the inside of her contract, tight as a band. She could. She could stand up, step out of the tub, unlock the door and step through. Close the door to Lily's room, and lay down flat on top of the quilt she bought at JCPenney, brightly colored flowers splashed against the fur of an exotic cat. James will find her. Her scent will lead him in. He will tell her how he wants her to lie, where to put her arms and legs, always, always in the way that leaves her most vulnerable. She won't be able to get away. She'll be forced to feel the pleasure. He will explode inside and she, too, will feel her muscles flutter. Truthfully, the fulfillment is fleeting. He has filled her body and, for moments, her mind has swung free. But the emptiness remains.

In the middle of all this, her heart screams out for Billy. No. No.

It's his fault. It's his fucking fault for leaving her.

What has she done?

Grandma told her she's much stronger than she knows. Step up! Step up! How do you untangle the web that you did weave?

Brenda guzzles the last of the beer, letting every single bit of liquid trickle in. She drops the empty can to the floor and remembers.

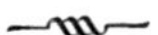

Billy and James had been out dirt-biking all day. Every inch of their leather riding gear and exposed skin was covered with a thin, pale dust. There were even a couple of leaves, and a small twig or two entwined in the long wavy curls of Billy's light brown hair, sun bleached to gold. They were laughing like hyenas as they undid the bungee cords holding their bikes upright in the back of James' pickup. Brenda had stepped out of the door of the apartment that she and Billy shared. They were all eighteen at the time, enjoying the early summer after their high school graduation.

Billy turned to see her standing there. He grabbed her hand, pulling her to him and kissed her once on the mouth. He said, "Hey, honey."

This was the day she knew. Young and naive as she was, she began to gather the signs. When Billy kissed her, James turned his back. When Billy lifted her long dark hair off her shoulder, James looked the other way. James could have been being polite, letting them share a moment to themselves, but James was never polite.

It was his idea. "Why don't we go to the pond for a dip? Bob Kohler gave me a little jug of raspberry wine. We can cool off."

Billy pulled a cigarette out of a pack with his teeth and lit it with the silver lighter Brenda gave him for Valentine's Day. Four words were engraved on the side: My heart is yours. "What do you think, Bren?"

"Sounds fun," she answered.

James said, "Let's do it."

Brenda ran back into the apartment for her bathing suit and Billy's trunks, two towels and a hairbrush. Little did she know, they would use only the towels.

There they were in James' pickup flying over the dirt roads, leaving a cloud of dust and dirt behind. Brenda sat between the two men with Billy's left hand hooked around her right thigh. The music pounded, the men smoked, and Brenda held the wine. Already she felt giddy. As James fishtailed around a corner, they almost collided with Doris Rentschler's Thunderbird. James brought the truck to a sliding stop with gravel flying, and backed up to where Doris sat in her car with a little smile.

At that time, Doris was thirty years old, already married, but there weren't any kids. Brenda and Billy knew that James was fooling around with her, and neither of them approved.

James leaned out of his window, and Brenda watched as he quickly reached down to make an adjustment. This made her feel uncomfortable ... mostly. She was taught not to touch herself. His gesture caused a stir.

He said, "Hey, sugar, what you doing?"

Doris answered, "Going over to see my mom."

Brenda remembers Doris's long painted nails, her bright-red lipstick, and eyelashes black and thick. Though she wasn't big breasted then, she wasn't afraid to show what she had. Doris had been very popular with the boys.

She added, "Donny boy went out of town."

James said, "Oh, yeah?"

"Yeah."

Doris raised her right hand and motioned with her index finger for James to move closer. James leaned out of his window so she could whisper something in his ear behind cupped hands. Brenda remembers the sound of their laughter. Devious. That was the word that came to mind. Devious. Doris pulled away with her own spray of gravel, as James did the same. He uttered a sound, something like, "Ooh-eey!"

Billy sniffed with disdain shaking his head. "You keep that up and you're going to end up with your nuts in a vise."

James grabbed the jug of wine out of Brenda's hands. "He don't care what she does."

Billy said, "Bullshit."

"It's not my fault these men don't take care of their women." James tipped up the bottle for a long swig.

"Don Rentschler could make your life miserable. It you want a license for that business you're talking about, I'd leave his wife alone."

"Living safe is your job, Billy."

The girls flocked to James like he was sprinkled with sugar. His dark skin, hair, and eyes made him exotic.

Ten minutes later James pulled his pickup into a glen, where the water of the creek gathered into a pool. Willow trees hung over one side, shading the water into a deep dark green. The other side, graced with the sun shining down through the water, exposed even the smallest of rocks resting on the bottom. The temperature was high that day, and the sky through the trees was blue. A wind, as gentle as a kiss, occasionally stirred.

James took one more swig of wine and then passed the jug to Billy. As Billy lifted his chin up to the lip of the tipped-up jug,

Brenda turned towards James, catching him staring down at her breasts. It was hard to admit to herself, but catching his eyes there made her breath grow shallow. He looked up to meet her eyes, and rather than being embarrassed as she thought he should be, he smiled. Then he jumped out of the truck, stripped off his clothes in a flash, and dived into the pool. Brenda and Billy looked at each other. They'd skinny dipped with James before, but only in the darkest night. In the bright daylight everything could be seen.

Billy turned to her. "Do I live safe?"

"Are you kidding? You're the bravest guy I know. Just because you don't sleep with married women. He's just trying to be a big shot today. Come on, let's do it." She grabbed the jug of wine and took another swig, and then she and Billy stepped out of the truck.

James was treading water with a big smile on his face, his dark hair slicked back and his muscled brown chest shining. "Get your asses in here!"

Brenda and Billy were swept up into the moment, too. Billy, laughing, stripped his clothes away quickly and dived into the pool. Brenda turned her back to the two men, and half-embarrassed but half-breathless with the thrill, pulled her shirt off over her head. Then she reached behind her back to unhook her bra, slide the straps down her arms, and pulled it away to feel her breasts dangle free. She remembers that her nipples were already hard. The jeans she wore were her favorites. They had a button fly, which she undid, then pulled her jeans down over her butt and kicked her legs free. She hesitated with her panties, but the thrill of the moment won out in the end. She pulled them down and then kicked them into the pile. Turning to see both men watching her, she crossed her arms over her breasts and ran into the water.

She swam over to Billy, and he took her into his arms. He was already tan from working construction. Brenda wrapped her legs around his waist and studied his face. She ran her fingertips over the cutting edge of his cheekbones, the bridge of his nose, and the velvet of his lips broken with small flecks of skin dried from a day in the summer sun. The truth was, Billy was almost pretty. His long black lashes were wet over his blue eyes. She could barely believe that he was hers. In three months they would be married. Glancing over towards James, she noticed he was swimming slowly the other way. Giddy with alcohol, her courage rose.

"Put it in, Billy," she said softly in his ear.

"Not with him here."

"He won't know."

"Yes, he will."

"You don't want it in?" she said, giving little kisses on his neck.

"There's nothing I want more."

"Then put it in." With her breasts pressing hard against his chest, Billy did as she asked. Dropping her head onto his shoulder, he held her to him, occasionally pressing her hips harder into his, but in a subtle motion barely making a wave.

James finally spoke up, "What are you two doing over there? You're going to make me jealous."

"I told you." Billy said to her.

Billy pulled himself out of her and let her float free. She remembers not wanting to let go. The three swam gently and separately, alternating between the sun and the shade until James crawled up onto the grassy shore. He rolled over on his back, and resting up on his elbows, turned his face into the sun. He closed his eyes. Brenda saw his genitals for the first time. She didn't want to look. No, that is a lie. She wanted to look, but didn't think it was right to do. But there he was. Once she had a peek she couldn't help but look again. She pretended to swim unbeknownst, and when Billy was turned away, she would glance again.

As she turned her head from her last peek, she saw her pile of clothes. James had crawled up next to them. Oh, no, she thought. My underwear. Did she hide it? Can he see it? She was afraid he'd think she was baiting him. It had been fun to be a little daring, but she would never hurt Billy.

Billy stepped out of the water and headed for the pickup. Brenda stepped out, too, crossing her arms over her breasts. She remembers thinking, "I've got to grab my clothes." As she walked onto shore, James dropped his chin out of the sun and opened his eyes. He watched her walk tentatively up to her clothes. She bent over, dropping her right arm to grab first her crumpled panties. She never forgot how he looked at her. For one second he looked into her eyes. Then he dropped them to her breasts and spent two seconds there. At last he dropped his eyes lower, without one bit of wavering. He lifted his eyes back to hers with a little smile. Though her heart beat fast, she swore he would never see her like that again. She was Billy's girl, soon to be Billy's wife.

At that moment Billy walked up with her towel in his hands. She never knew for sure if he had seen the way his best friend looked at her. Maybe he had, because his face looked grim. He said, "Here, baby," folding the large towel around her like a cloak.

—ꟽ—

What has she done?

Step up! Step up! You are stronger than you know.

But there is the longing for fulfillment. The cry of the shining pearl. Don't cry. Don't cry. It is not a safe place.

Just the dwelling of her power.

There is nothing that James wants more. Billy ... Billy ... would probably never touch her again. Since James touched her, she is tainted.

Serves you right, Billy, for leaving me. How can she ever trust that he wouldn't leave again? Following something that he believes in more than he loves his daughter and his wife. You're not a knight, Billy, even though I know you think you are. Serves you right. Fairy tales don't come true.

Brenda steps out of the tub and grabs a towel. She wraps it around her snugly and steps out of the room. James, sitting on the edge of Lily's bed with her new favorite toy in his hands, turns the kitty slowly as if searching for a clue. Lily sleeps in the center of the bed, not anywhere close to him. Brenda thinks of Growlie, and her stomach drops. But her need for fulfillment erases the thought. Maybe this time.

She asks, "You didn't go for beer?"

He shakes his head and looks at her, and she swears she sees sadness in his eyes.

Brenda turns to walk back out of the room, and heads for the quilt of exotic cat splashed with flowers. She drops the towel and crawls onto the bed, turns and waits. Seconds later James follows. Dropping his pants, he crawls up in-between her legs, and it feels good, so good, right there, right there, oh yes, right there it feels so good. But, no, oh no, it is Billy's face she sees. Suddenly she is crying. Billy limps across the kitchen floor. He does not look at her. He will not look at her.

James stops and asks, "Why are you crying?"

"I ... I ..."

"You don't like it?"

"I ... can't ..."

"Can't what?"

"I can't ... can't ..." She covers her eyes with the back of one hand.

"Brenda ..." James scoots his body up over hers so he can look into her eyes. "Brenda ..." His voice cracks. "Don't leave me."

14
Bony Cage

Friday 10:13 p.m.

Martin pulls out of the driveway of Harvey's Bar and heads home. He drives slowly and carefully, fully aware that he did drink one or two drinks too many. The rain has stopped for now; the first line of thunderstorms moved on east, with the second in the far distance of the west barreling in slowly like a herd of buffalo, the rumbling like their feet upon the earth, the gathering winds like the expulsion of their breath. But for now, an hour or two, the moon shines and the smell of wet earth and pavement, tar and plants, rises and floats; they are a strange perfume. Martin lowers the window on the driver's side and takes the scents in, breathing deeply. His eyes ache from the glare of the moon illuminating objects, the trees, an occasional house, casting shadows that are long, so long, like maybe the sky has fallen, resting on his shoulders, like maybe he will no longer walk in the world, but crawl.

Now that he has left the bar, he hungers for the laughter of his friends. Inside the car it is quiet, so quiet. He reaches over and switches the radio on. Willie sings out in his nasal twang about all the girls he's loved before. Not good. Not good. Jeanine's face flashes before his eyes. She is smiling; the string of pearls around her neck, the waves of her hair blowing back, the sweet smell, her smell, drifting up, better than the smells of the summer rain. Better. Martin reaches up and punches a different station out with one finger. The Beatles sing out "she loves you, yeah yeah yeah yeah." No. Martin turns the radio off.

He heads for home where his other life awaits him.

A car pulls out from a side road in front of him a couple of hundred feet ahead. The color and make look like Petey's car. When the car takes off like a little raped ape, Martin feels compelled to speed up and check it out. He has never seen his son drive recklessly. It is hard to imagine that he ever would. Martin's Lincoln is cumbersome, but the engine huge. In seconds he catches up behind the car, reads the license plate and knows for certain the car belongs to Petey. Music blasts out of the open windows with a rapid beat and someone singing like their nuts are being crushed. A hint of smoke moves out the driver's window and sweeps back towards Martin in the stream of the wind. The smoke blows back not from a cigarette. The smoke blows back not from a cigar. It's the wacky tobacky that his brother smokes. Martin's anger rises so fast that he doesn't even remember deciding to pull up beside the car. Suddenly he's there, looking over right, as the driver turns his head left and their eyes meet.

For a moment, Martin feels completely disoriented. The driver behind the wheel is not Petey, but some raggedy punk with black and white hair sticking up like porcupine quills.

The kid yells at him, "What the fuck you looking at, old man?" He throws his head back and whoops then stomps on the gas of Petey's Celica and pulls rapidly ahead.

When Martin turns his eyes back front, he sees a large truck rushing towards him. He swerves his car to the right as the truck roars past him, horn blasting, the force of the stirred wind sucking him momentarily in, then releasing him at last. Not good. Not good. Though Martin's heart is pounding, and his focus blurred with alcohol, he steps on the gas. In seconds he sits once again behind the boy. Who is he? He wonders why Petey has allowed him to drive his car. When he gets his hands on his son, he's going to ... Goddamn it! Petey knows how he feels about him lending out his car. What the fuck is wrong with his kid? Son of a bitch....

Suddenly the kid turns the car right down a dirt road, the car fishtailing and the tires kicking out gravel at the same time. Martin turns behind him, the weight of his car pulling it sideways as gravel peppers the windshield. By the time he has stopped the car and straightened out, the kid moves into the distance. Martin can't let it go. He can't. He punches the gas once more, kicking out his own vertical rain of gravel.

What if, he thinks, Petey didn't loan this punk his car. The punk could have stolen the Celica. What if the punk injured or murdered his boy and left his body in a field? Another body. In a field. That couldn't happen to the same man twice. Or could it? Martin may not be crazy about his boy, but he's his kid, after all. Martin suddenly remembers the painting falling off the wall. He remembers his mother telling him what the sign means. It can't be. It can't be. She's crazy as a loon.

Still, the Celica flies ahead, bouncing over the washboard surface, occasionally taking flight over the crest of a hill, landing with a thump. The Lincoln never leaves the ground, never fishtails, just continues to hug the road with its weight.

The Celica slides left around a corner, the echo of the thrashing beat of music reaching Martin's ears. The punk gathers distance once more as Martin's heavy car drags left behind him.

He could go home, crawl into the sack, and be free of worry. The glare of the stadium lights and the sound of his dream team grunting and groaning their way into victory call to him. But instead he jams the gas pedal of the Lincoln down.

Bethel Church Road lays out especially hilly and lined on either side by oaks, walnuts, and maples. Martin watches the red taillights of the Celica appear and disappear as the punk races over the roller coaster of small hills.

The body of his boy could be stuffed into the trunk. His tall lanky frame folded like an accordion ready to pop out the moment the lid is lifted.

Martin has never seen this punk before. He is either new to town or a transient passing through. Did he pass through ten years before, steal the life of his wife, and come back for more? Did the devil assign this dark angel to destroy him systematically? Martin shakes his head, disgusted with himself. For Christ's sake, the punk couldn't be more than sixteen. He didn't kill Jeanine as a boy. Focus. Focus.

At this moment, Martin remembers the hill. The big hill up ahead. The hill this punk may well not know about. A hill so steep, the Celica going at this speed could take flight for a quarter mile. Only one problem. Martin, in his present state of blurred vision and foggy thought, cannot remember exactly where the hill stands. He watches the taillights disappear and reappear, disappear and reappear.

At this point, Martin rumbles along one-quarter mile behind him, and moving closer. He travels at fifty-five miles per hour. Occasionally the bass reverberation of the music reaches his ears. One-eighth of a mile ahead of him, the red lights disappear, followed by the distant sound of the car hitting the ground very hard. Martin slams on his brakes, slides to a stop, and with his heart banging to get outside its bony cage, finds himself teetering on the crest of the big hill. He watches as the Celica slides sideways across the road, slamming the passenger side door into a large black walnut tree. The rapid beat of the music continues and the shrill song of the singer rings out – or is it the cries of the kid inside? The driver door opens and the punk tumbles out, sitting there dazed.

Martin noses over the crest of the hill and rolls down, coming to a stop on the opposite side of the road. He steps out of his car as the punk struggles to stand, wavering, two lines of blood, one moving down the side of his face, the other his arm, begin to drop into tiny pools on the ground. In those two pools, Martin sees the moon reflected.

"Where the fuck you think you're going, punk?" Martin growls between clenched teeth as he rushes over and grabs the boy. For a bony boy, injured, he fights like a little wild cat, until Martin, three times his size, pulls both of his arms back into a hold. "What are you doing with my son's car?"

The punk turns to look at him from the corner of his eyes. "I don't know what you're talking about."

Martin pulls the kid's arms tighter and he bows over with pain. "What have you done with my son?"

"Like I said, I don't know what you're talking about."

"Have you hurt him?"

The kid has the audacity to laugh a little to himself.

Martin leans into the kid and growls again, this time into his ear, "You think this is funny? Where is my boy? Where is he?"

"I don't know where your fucking kid is."

"Did you do something to him?"

"Nothing he didn't ask for."

"What does that mean? What have you done?"

"Old man, your son is a real pretty little queer." Suddenly, the punk stomps down on Martin's right foot with such force that Martin is left winded and his hands lose grip. The kid takes off into the field holding his right upper arm with his left hand. He wavers to the left and the right terribly unsteady. Martin hobbles off behind him.

Martin imagines what they look like from above: the young, thin boy running across the field of young soybeans, lopsided and headlong, holding one arm, a trickle of red landing on the green of plant and brown of earth; the middle-aged man, thick in the trunk, drunk on rage and VO, hobbling on one foot whose bones might easily be crushed; the moon shines down, illuminating the field like a stage, where maybe a final scene might be played.

The race offers no contest as the kid leaps over the rows of beans like a rabbit. He turns once to look at Martin and gives him the finger. Martin's last sight of the wounded boy is him entering a wood where Martin can only hope he stumbles and falls head first into a mossy swamp.

Martin falls to his knees and vomits. The soupy mixture of small pieces of turkey jerky and corn curls propels out with force, spraying the beans and the earth and any small living things passing through. The vomit seems to have no end, as Martin coughs, chokes, and heaves, feeling the acidic mixture lodging high up in his nose, leaving the air passage full as his stomach empties.

Get up. Get up off your knees. You are not here to pray. He

gave that up years ago. Get back to the car. You've got to find your son.

But Martin does not get up, even though he feels his knees sinking into the rain-soaked ground. His foot throbs, his heart pounds, his lungs strain for a sip of air. When he tries to stand up from kneeling, he falls back onto his ass and lower back; his eyes shoot up into the sky. Something flutters. What the fuck is that? Winged. Larger than a bird. He begins to look around frantically. He starts to feel afraid. Is he going mad? Get up. Get up. When he sees two lights approaching from the right, he grows disoriented again. For a moment he forgets where he is. The lights stop moving. He hears the sound of two doors slamming, then his name.

"Martin? Peter? Martin?"

Martin hears two voices conversing. Though teetering, he finally stands. "Hey!" He yells. "I'm here!" As he slowly makes his way back over towards the cars, remembering in detail now what led up to this moment, he sees two figures moving towards him. One moves quickly, the other with a limp, three legged with a cane. He feels relieved when he sees the face of his brother, and surprised to see that of his son-in-law, Billy.

"What the hell are you two doing out here?"

Sam answers, "I was giving Billy a lift home. What the hell are you doing out here? What the fuck happened?"

Billy asks, "Where's Peter?"

Martin answers, "I don't know." He slaps Billy on the back. "It's good to see you, Bill."

"Thank you, Sir."

Sam asks, "What do you mean you don't know where Peter is?"

"I was driving home, and this punk was driving Petey's car. I chased him. We ended up like this."

Billy asks, "Where's the kid?"

"Took off into the field. I chased him, but he got away."

Sam looks down at Martin's foot. "Are you limping, for Christ's sake, or what?"

"He stomped down on my foot. He was a skinny runt, but he had huge boots on."

Billy asks, "Which way did he go?"

"He's gone. Into the wood. Bill, see if he left the keys in the Celica."

Sam hovers near Martin. "Did you get a chance to talk to the kid?"

"He ... he seemed to know Petey."

"You're drunker than a fucking skunk. You were driving like that?"

"Spare me the fucking lecture."

Billy limps over and ducks into the Celica. Martin watches as he takes a look around the inside of the car.

"Anything in there, Bill?"

Billy ducks back out with keys in hand. "The keys are here. Nothing much in the car except some trash and a few pieces of clothes. Why don't we take a look in the trunk?"

The three men gather around the trunk, Billy tossing the keys to Martin. Martin turns the key in the lock and lifts the lid slowly. He looks inside. "What the fuck?"

Sam and Billy gather in closer to get a look.

Billy says, "What is that?"

Sam says, "Holy shit."

The night, not so dark, illuminated by the moon, is suddenly cut into by red stripes of light that revolve as a patrol car silently approaches. The three men looming over the trunk turn as one and watch. Martin reaches up and closes the lid behind him, hoping that the officer inside the car sits far enough away not to have seen the motion.

The officer steps out of his car and walks over to the three men. Martin recognizes him as the son of his old friend, Harvey Rankin. Before the kid can say a word to them, Martin speaks up, "How are you doing? Aren't you Harvey Rankin's kid?"

"Ah, yes, Sir, I am. What happened here?"

Martin steps towards the kid and extends his right hand. "Maybe you don't remember me. I'm Martin Becker, the county supervisor." The kid shakes his hand with a grip like a vise. This might not be as easy as he hoped.

The kid says, "I remember you, Mr. Becker. Would you like to tell me now what happened here? Is everyone okay?" He turns and takes in Sam and Billy from head to toe.

At that moment Sam crumples to the ground. Billy falls to the ground beside him on one knee, his bum leg stretched out to the side. Martin looks down upon Sam alarmed until he sees his brother wink one eye up at him.

The young officer, something Rankin, says, "Should I call an ambulance?"

"No! No! This happens all the time." Martin draws quickly on his ability to bullshit. "You see, my brother here, he's ... he's a Vietnam veteran and he has some physical problems. Blacks out periodically. He was driving my son's car home and he blacked out on this hill. As you can see, he plowed into that tree. But, he's fine. I was following him just in case this happened. Fortunately, Bill came along and he went over to Fred Tucker's place over yonder and called for a wrecker. How's he doing, Bill?"

"He's coming to."

Martin says, "Maybe, young Rankin, you could help us get him back on his feet. Then you can help Bill here, too."

Martin and the kid pull Sam up onto his feet, then the kid offers Billy a hand.

The kid says, "Hey, aren't you Billy Bagwell?"

"Yeah," Billy answers.

"I heard you were over in the Gulf."

"Just got back."

The kid looks down on Billy's leg in the brace. "Didn't Mr. Becker say that you drove up? How did you drive with that brace on your leg?"

"Oh, that," Billy says. He throws his left arm around the kid's shoulders and starts drawing him back towards his squad car. "I take it off to drive and put it on when I stand."

Martin laughs to himself as he hears Billy say to the kid, "Everything's covered here. I got a tip for you that you might want to move on. I heard the local boys are out racing on Austin Road tonight. The sheriff's been dying to catch them red-handed."

Martin turns to Sam. "Now, what in the hell are we going to do about the shit in the trunk?"

15
Torn

Friday 10:38 p.m.

Peter, lying on his side, wakes with a start and glues his open eyes to the opposite wall. The angel is gone now. Only a damp circle on the oak floor remains where the storm rain slipped off her folded feathers. He remembers her hands clasped over her heart in prayer and her face as soft and delicately carved as one of his grandma's porcelain figurines. Her eyes were soft, empty, and willing to take on everything the world willed to give. Maybe it was his mother. Come back at last to stand vigil over his dirty deeds? Perhaps she was the angel of death come to pluck his life away. Was Peter ready?

No.

He turns over onto his back wincing less now and throws one leg over the edge of the bed. The other follows. He must find Todd. He wants more of the pain and the pleasure. He will prove to the world that he is gay and there is nothing, absolutely nothing, he or they can do about it. They can beat him to within an inch of death or threaten him with descent into hell.

The truth is, he damn well better find Todd and his car before his father does.

Peter scans the floor for his dirty clothes. A dumb move. By now, Grandma has them fresh and folded, lying over by the door on the seat of a chair. He can smell their clean fragrance from where he sits with knees bent, weight forward with the impetus to stand. Knowing Grandma, even the bloodstain is ground free and washed away. He does stand, and walks over to the chair, pulls his ghost white tee over his head, grabs the jeans and sits down on his sore little ass. One leg at a time, he pulls the jeans on and zips them up; he's already partially hard. Yes, yes, he wants more.

The hands on the clock point to almost eleven, and Peter crosses into the hall on feather feet. He doesn't want to wake her. When his eyes spy the cabinet in the kitchen where the cookies are kept, he can't resist. He steals into a tin where moist nutty date bars snuggle between sheets of wax paper. Carefully he takes out two. In a corner under a red and white checked cloth, Dickie the canary dream talks in tiny, almost silent chirps. In the distance, Grandma exhales little winds in her sleep like she wills to extinguish candles. He is safe to leave.

Outside, the night sky spreads clear and vast, the stars barely perceptible beyond the moon's glow. The light wind blows cool from the storm, and Peter feels like he is swimming under water as he walks. Where will he go? Midnight. Cinderella's return. Peter's call to the wild. But this time with his cherry popped. Maybe those leering grins and crude gestures, like a brush against a nipple or a crotch, will look and feel inviting now. He feels like he's been torn from a protective skin. Tender and primitive.

Peter heads out across the fields, taking a short cut to town. A few hundred yards in he realizes that Todd would not be so foolish as to drive the Celica where he could be discovered. The kid would use his car to transport him to a place he wants to go. Maybe to the home of the pornographer. Better yet, to the bars. Or maybe he lit out across the land, destination unknown, to view turquoise seas full of dolphins, purple mountains capped in white, yellow rolling sands dotted with prickly plants, and green hills where grazing cattle eat the grass and brush line low. This land is their land, too. Gay or not. Fuck them. Fuck those with closed minds snagging quotes out of worn and leafy books, judging who is right and who is wrong. Inferior or superior. Dangling black people from limbs of trees. Chasing young girls ripe with child into back alleys to be butchered. Crucifying thin effeminate boys on fence posts where circling crows peck out their eyes. This land is your land. This land is my land.

Splashing through a puddle, Peter begins to laugh. He bets Todd headed to a place down the road in a neighboring town where the minds are open. At least within the four walls of the bars in Three Rivers where the boys gather.

Peter heads to the main road pointing there. He will not go through the field where his mother was found. Nor will he walk close to any house where rifles hanging on hooks in back rooms wait to shoot the foreign, the unknown, the dangerous, passing in the night.

He will hit the main road and stick out his thumb. Hunker down in the seat of a stranger's car and act ... normal. Peter furtively scans the fields for another soul, or the angel, or anyone else that he must hide his true self from. Then he remembers that he has been initiated and he doesn't have to hide anymore. He laughs and laughs and laughs until for one moment the laughter breaks into a sob. But for just one moment. Soon he will belong. He won't be alone anymore. He picks up his pace.

The night feels so fresh after the rain. The retreated storm looks like a wall against the eastern horizon. In the west, in the distance, another storm is brewing far, far away. He can sense it. But for now, he sucks in a huge breath of the fresh air. This boy ain't a boy anymore. He's a man.

When Peter was sixteen, his dad hatched a plan. Being a county official, he knew everyone in town. This included Doris Rentschler, wife of the local land mogul. According to his father, Doris was "hot to trot." Although the label "chicken hawk" was generally applied to men, Peter understood Mrs. Rentschler to fit the bill. She had a taste for teenage boys. Many suspected this, though few knew with certainty, and Peter was informed of this tasty tidbit by his brother-in-law's best friend, James, now his sister's lover and the current scorn of the town. Daddy decided a few years after Peter's first wet dream, and observing his lack of interest in girls, to set him up. With the promise of initiating him in a good way, his father made arrangements to drop him off at a local motel, where Doris waited for him behind a door. They pulled up in his dad's Lincoln and his dad said, "Get out, son."

Peter remembers shaking so hard that no matter how he

clenched his jaw, or squeezed his hands beneath his thighs, his wavering voice gave him away, "Dad ..."

"Get out. Before everyone in town's wondering why the hell I'm parked here."

Peter opened the door. It squeaked. He climbed out of the car. His quaking legs barely held him upright. By the time he reached the door, painted blue, number 22 in white metal, his dad was a mile down the road. He turned and stepped out with his right foot to flee when the door opened and a hand grasped his shirt from behind.

A woman's voice said, "Not so fast."

He'd never been in a motel room. Hotels, yes, on the rare occasion when his father took the family on a trip. Everything in the small room looked made of pressed wood and polyester. The bedspread was burgundy and green geometrics with plastic-backed matching drapes. The shag carpet was baby-poop brown, dotted with stains of various shapes, sizes, and colors. A swag lamp hung from the ceiling where a couple of flies on the shade had clung and fried. A small table stood by the side of the bed where a bottle of Wild Turkey sat next to the *Bible*. A cigarette with red lipstick on the filter burned in a clear glass ashtray, the smoke curling up in a signal for help, or so Peter prayed. No such luck.

He turned to look at Doris, who was now sitting on the edge of the bed. She was wearing a black lace slip, one strap falling off the shoulder. Leaning back on her elbows, she drew one leg up and let the smooth shiny limb fall slightly to the side. Peter glimpsed her private place and darted his eyes to her face. She was pretty, very pretty. Her wavy brown hair fell down her back, though a thick strand covered the right side of her face. The one dark eye that could be seen sparkled and the half of her mouth smiled like she was dying to tell him a secret. She reached down with her right hand and touched herself, drawing his eyes.

"I want you to look here, sweet boy. I am so ready for you. Don't you want some? I bet a tall, big-handed, long-footed boy like you has a really lovely schwantz."

The truth was, he didn't want it. The pinkness looked like a flower or the inside of a shell. In its own way the place wasn't bad to look at, but he did not feel compelled to smell, or taste, or touch it.

"Come here." She sat up and reached out her hand to grab his, and pulled him towards her. When she stood up to face him, he was engulfed in flowery scents. They smelled good, but they didn't stir him either. She began to unbutton his shirt, pulled the two sides apart and lick and bite at him. He felt like he was going to throw up. Then she undid his belt, zipped down his pants, and reached into his white jockey shorts.

"Oh, yeah," she said. She slid his jeans down over his hips and went to work, and work she did, but still nothing happened. He still felt like he wanted to throw up. As he turned to sprint to the john, he tripped on his pants and fell to his knees, and hurled into that baby poop brown rug to leave yet another stain. He was surprised to feel her by his side, rubbing him gently on the back, leaning in to speak softly in his ear.

"You're not just afraid. You don't like girls, do you? It's okay. Your secret is safe with me. I'll tell your father you performed like a stud."

He turned to look at her. "No!"

Doris drew back. "No? What do you want me to tell him?"

Wiping his mouth with the back of his hand, he said, "You don't have to tell him anything. He doesn't need to know."

"Petey ..."

"My name is Peter!"

"Peter, I have to tell him something. He'll ask."

Peter stood up and began to pull his jeans up. "I'm sorry. I'm sorry I threw up. Just tell him ... that it's our little secret. What happened here. I don't want you to lie. And you can't tell him the truth. Please."

"Okay, Peter. Sure."

And he left, hovering outside until his father came at last.

—ɯ—

Peter hits the main road and prays, hoping God is all forgiving, that he will find one ride for the forty miles to the bars. He's never hitchhiked before, but he has to find Todd. And his car. Maybe he can save himself yet from the wrath of his father and in the meantime become an integral part of his new family.

He'd be lying to say he isn't worried that someone he knows might drive by and see him. As for strangers, what person in their right mind would stop to pick up a hitchhiker in the middle of the night? He hopes the angel feels protective and somewhere somehow still looking over him. If she is the angel of death, so be it. The story, already written, will unfold in destiny.

The road stretches out fairly empty with an occasional car or truck flying by fast. When headlights appear, he steps out, one foot off the shoulder and thrusts a thumb into the air. One semi zooms by, laying on his horn, sending Peter to dash into the ditch, his heart thumping like a pounding fist inside. After the shaking stops, he steps back up, hearing a loud bass reverberation heading his way. The car approaches and slows, then pulls over to the shoulder. Peter, with sweat rolling down his sides, steps up to the passenger window. He recognizes the music: Motley Crue. He does not recognize the two passengers, but they look like poster boys for another community on the fringe: white trash meth junkies. Their red eyes dart around like loose balls caught in a square. Their lips pull back tight against protruding teeth. Peter can smell sweat, cigarettes, and a recently passed fart. The passenger holds a small brown glass pipe in his right hand.

"Where you going, man?" The passenger asks and then the two druggies look at each other and laugh maniacally.

Peter realizes that if he refuses, they will be offended. If he says yes, he'll never arrive where he wants to go. "Where ... where are you guys going?"

"Isn't this the highway to hell?" Their laughter rattles Peter to the bones. The passenger holds up the pipe to Peter. "Want a hit?"

Peter shakes his head no. The driver stomps on the gas and leaves him coughing in a spray of gravel and dust and coats his ghost white tee in brown. How bad does he want more of the pain and the pleasure? Bad enough that he remains on the shoulder hoping for another pair of headlights. He shakes off the gravel and the dust and looks up into the sky. Just then a star falls, arcing from right to left. He can make a wish. What does he wish? He wishes for every hungry mouth to be fed, and to find Todd and his car. The next pair of headlights approaches slowly. Peter steps out, thrusts his thumb into the air and watches the car, a late model Ford painted blue, slow down, drive past him, then pull carefully onto the shoulder. The driver leans over to roll the window down. He's a small man with a halo of wispy hair, wearing wire-rimmed glasses and a white shirt buttoned up to his neck.

The man asks, "What are you doing out on this road at night, son?"

Peter bows over to talk with him through the window. "I ... ah ... well ... someone took my car...."

"Someone took your car? Get in, son. Get in. I can't believe the unchristian-like behavior of people. Get in. I'll help you any way I can."

Peter opens the door, climbs in, and the driver pulls away from the shoulder.

"Did you call the police?"

"Well ... actually ... I know the guy who took it. He's in Three Rivers. I'm going there to find him."

"He's in Three Rivers, is he? Well, good. That's just where I'm heading. I live there. I'm just getting back from a week-long Bible camp."

The car pulls away from the shoulder of the road as Peter's stomach sinks. He remembers the so-called sacred book in that motel room and the death count of the Inquisition. Peter takes in a deep breath and lets it back out as he furtively steals a look around the car. The crucifix hanging from the rearview mirror extends six inches long and so realistic that even in the dark Peter can see the red paint drops masking for blood. The wooden cross swings back and forth in a rhythm that threatens to hypnotize him. He pulls his eyes away. Papers lie strewn across the dashboard, and he notices one book, black. When a car approaches from behind, illuminating the car's interior, the gold letters on the spine of the book can be seen: *End of Years.* Peter drops his eyes to the space between the seats, where a crumpled paper and cup from Subway sit askew. Just peeking out from beneath a corner of the paper, a part of one other object can be seen: the silver snub nose of a revolver.

"He died for your sins, you know," the man says.

"Excuse me?"

"Your sins. He died for them."

"What sins would that be?"

The man turns to Peter, tips his head down and looks at him over the rim of his glasses. "All of them. You are a Christian, aren't you, son?"

"Isn't everyone in these parts?"

"Not quite, but we're working on it. We're the chosen ones, you know. It's unfolding just the way we were told."

"What's that, Sir?"

"Armageddon. It's all being set up over there in the Middle East."

Peter turns to the man to study him more closely. He's familiar with the word Armageddon. The word means the end of the world. He's never heard anyone talk about it as if it's impending. This man seems to want the world to end. The man has a sticker stuck to his white shirt. It says John. A wedding band on his left hand glitters in the headlights of passing cars. Peter recognizes his aftershave: Old Spice. Why the fuck does this man have a gun beside him? More importantly, is it loaded?

"We've done a bad job. The Lord gave us a chance and we blew it. This country is rampant with sin." John pounds his right fist against the steering wheel. "People lying and cheating, using the Lord's name in vain. Spending all their money on possessions rather than helping those in need. Children killing children." He leans in towards Peter. "Did you know that children killing children is one of the final signs? Nudity and indecent acts. And worst of all, homosexuals. This is a sick society. Sick. As a Christian, you know it's true."

By this time, Peter fears the man can hear the pounding in his chest. He can't believe it! After he prayed and everything. Made a wish on a star. There can't be a God. There can't be. If God does exist, how could he end up in a car with this guy? And angels. What bullshit! That wasn't an angel. Just some optical illusion created by the lightning. No angels. No God. No one looking over him. No one forgiving him for his sins. He was doomed. But with this revelation came freedom. Fuck it. He was free. No one to answer to.

Peter turns to the man. "Yeah, those fags, they are really a problem."

"There's a bar in Three Rivers where they hang out. It's despicable."

"No way!"

"Oh, yes."

"Do you think they fuck each other right there in the bar?" Peter watches as the man, John, clenches the steering wheel with both hands. He turns to Peter slowly.

"Wh... what did you say?"

"You heard me. Do you think they get down on their knees and suck right there?"

The man's jaw drops and his eyes widen. He drops his right hand in-between the seats and scurries through the Subway wrappers for the gun. He lifts the revolver up in a shaking hand and points the firearm at Peter.

"You ... you're one of them, aren't you?"

Peter leans in towards John and says, "Boo."

16
Mortal Coil

Friday 11:11 p.m.

Bagwell sits with Sam and Martin at a back table in Harvey's Bar. The three are hunched over, talking in hushed voices. The barmaid brings over three drinks on a small plastic tray lined with cork. She places a tall ginger ale in front of Sam, a cup of coffee in front of Martin, and Bagwell grabs his shot of Jack off the tray and immediately tosses it back. Fuck the meds. He needs something to loosen the coil before it springs to life like a cobra.

Martin says, "We're damn lucky that punk officer didn't look in the trunk. You're sure it's marijuana?"

Sam looks exasperated. "Of course I'm sure. I haven't tasted it yet, but it looks and smells like California sinsemilla."

"And you're not going to taste it either."

"Too late, bro. I already snagged a big sticky bud."

"Well, put it back!"

Sam's eyebrows shoot up and his eyes widen. "Why?"

"When the fuck are you going to grow up?"

"Hey! You drink your poison, I'll smoke my weed."

Martin shakes his head with disgust.

Bagwell speaks up. "Can we get to the point here?"

"That's right," Sam says. "We need to find Peter."

"First we get rid of the stuff," Martin says.

"The stuff is safe locked up in that trunk."

Bagwell clears his throat. "Not necessarily. Towing the car to Martin's house was a good first step, but I think we better move it again and hide it. That kid or whoever owns that porno might know where you live."

"So, you don't think it's my son's?"

"No, Martin. I don't."

Sam scratches his goatee. "We could put it in my old barn."

Martin adds, "We hide the car and burn the shit."

Sam says, "It would be a shame to burn that weed. I know people who could use that for pain management. It's not like you can track the weed."

"Give me a fucking break! The 'weed' and the tapes go!"

Bagwell calls to the barmaid, "Another shot over here, please!"

Martin closes his eyes and shakes his head. "I ... can't believe it. I ... I mean ... I knew he was probably ... a ..."

Sam speaks up, "For Christ's sake, say it. Your son is a homosexual. That doesn't mean he's got anything to do with that porn or weed in the trunk. The kid could have stolen the car and was using it to transport the stuff."

Bagwell adds, "That's right. Peter's gay, but I really don't believe he's a ... into kids. I don't believe it."

Sam asks Martin, "Did you call Mother?"

"No. I don't want to upset her. She was already upset earlier about that tree."

"Peter might be there. He's pretty close to his grandma. Or maybe he's at Brenda's." Sam turns to Bagwell. "Why don't you call over there?"

"Me? Negative." The barmaid places the shot glass of Jack in front of him. "Thank you." He tosses the dark amber liquor back.

Martin turns to Bagwell. "Don't you want to fight for your wife?"

"You're telling me, Martin, that you could forgive your wife cheating on you?"

"It's for the baby. She needs to have her mother and her father raising her. Just like my kids did."

Bagwell grabs his cane and stands up slowly. "I will never forgive your daughter. Ever. So, don't even talk to me about it."

Martin lifts his left palm in the air like a stop sign. "Fine. I'll call her."

"No, I'll call her. For Peter, I will call her." Bagwell heads over to the pay phone over by the johns. The coil is starting to loosen and he feels like he can breathe again. As he reaches the phone, a guy he knew from school, Jason, steps out of the men's john.

"Bagwell?" The guy reaches out his right hand towards him. "Fuck! It's good to see you."

Bagwell shakes his hand. "Thanks. Good to see you, too."

"I heard you were getting back. Hey, the wife and I are having a pig roast tomorrow at the house. In the afternoon. Why don't you come by? We're going to toss the ball around a little. I've got a great strip of lawn for it."

"Ah ... I won't be playing ball ... for a while."

Jason glances at Bagwell's cane. "Oh, shit. I didn't know you were injured over there."

"Yeah." A beat or two of silence passes. "Well, I've got to make a call."

"Come by tomorrow."

"I'll try." Bagwell grabs the receiver of the phone and listens to the dial tone hum for a count of five. He doesn't want to hear her voice. He doesn't want to remember how she looked today standing out in the garden. What was it about that girl? The minute he saw her he wanted to grab her and hold her. Then he remembered she was sleeping with James. All those months over in the desert that felt like hell, he thought only of her. The other guys were jerking off to magazine photos of nude girls sitting spread eagle or buying a weathered and worn out piece on leave. He only wanted his girl. Smart, pretty, and fun. His girl. Not his girl anymore. Shit! Drop the quarter! Dial the phone! Be a man. Pretend you just don't care. He drops the quarter. What if *he* answers the phone? That would be easier. The phone rings four times. Finally she answers in a sleepy voice tinged with fear. Calls in the wee hours were always hard for Brenda.

"Hello?"

"Bren? It's Billy."

There is silence for a couple of beats. To his surprise she starts to cry. "Bill ... I'm so sorry ..."

He'd be lying to say her crying doesn't affect him. But he

pretends it doesn't. "Cut the crap. Is Peter there by chance?"

"P... Peter?" She sounds confused. "No. Why?" Alarm sets in. "Has something happened?"

"We're looking for him. Your dad and uncle and I."

"Why? What's happened?"

"Some kid had his car. We don't know where he is. He's probably fine. If he shows up there or calls, tell him to get his butt home."

"Of course. You're ... you're not telling me everything."

"It's probably fine. Try not to worry." In his mind's eye, he sees her in a little flimsy nightie, maybe pink and short, sitting up in bed beside James. "In the meantime you can suck James' off."

"God ... I can't believe you just said that. I can't suck his ... He left."

"Yeah, right." He replaces the receiver with a bang and feels pissed that his eyes are stinging. He presses his left thumb and index finger into them, takes in a deep breath and reels in his right fist to explode into the wall. His action is interrupted.

"I know you've got better things to do with your money than pay for a wall repair." Sam drapes his arm over Bagwell's shoulder and says, "The whole thing is going to take some time to work out. However it works out. Peter's not there, is he?"

"No."

"Martin's over there talking to one of his cronies abut towing Pete's car. I'm going to call my mother. I'll meet you back at the table."

Bagwell nods his head. As he walks back, he wonders if James has really left Brenda. If he has, that means he's somewhere out there in the night. He could hunt him down like a rabid dog. Brush up on the old skills. Sniping with infrared. There is nothing worse than a man who betrays his friend. In the corps you learn this. You learn about fraternity, loyalty, and the power of the oath. You will lay down your life for a brother if necessary. He never dreamed, ever, that James would someday let him down. He never dreamed it. If someone had looked into the future and told him this would be, he would have called him or her a liar. They cut their arms and mixed their blood, kicked ass together out on the football field, jumped out of planes, off of bridges, found their way home twice when they were lost. For Christ's sake! Some years back, James even saved his life. Was Brenda the payback? Bagwell knew James had private pain, things that happened to him that he never talked about. Was it this private pain that made James turn?

The son of a bitch seduced his wife. Bagwell couldn't believe that she seduced him. But maybe he didn't know her as well as he thought. Bagwell half falls into a chair at the table. He feels unsteady again. He'd better stop the alcohol. Okay, so he is mortal, not Superman like he dreamed. He can still take care of the matter at hand.

Martin and Sam arrive back to the table at the same time.

Martin says, "Okay. Bob is going to tow the Celica over to the barn. Did you find Petey?"

Sam pulls his ponytail over his shoulder and shakes his head. "He was at Mother's. Came walking through the fields in the rain. She said he was hurt."

"Hurt?"

"She said he was ... okay." Sam looks Bagwell in the eyes, but Bagwell is unsure what he's trying to communicate. Something he doesn't want Martin to know. "She put him to bed. Then she went to bed. A half hour ago she noticed he was gone."

Martin says, "Let's go."

"Where to?"

"I don't know. But we have got to find my boy and find out what the hell is going on."

Bagwell stands up and the three men leave the bar.

—~—

Something about this night reminds Bagwell of that desert. Maybe because the billions of stars, sprinkled against the black, sparkle like a city in the sky. Maybe because of the warmth in this early morning hour, as if the moon held the fire of the sun. Maybe because of the silence of nature pressing against the only sounds that can be heard: the occasional whoosh of a vehicle traveling on the main road or a dog barking at a random hopping hare.

Bagwell thinks about James, not the back-stabbing homeboy, but his buddy overseas. Glover. There wasn't a day that man from Atlanta wasn't smiling. In the mess hall, men fought to sit beside him on the bench. In scrimmage, they fought to fight on his side because no matter what, he always kept his cool. He was a man of few words with a big old heart. Now he was six feet under or burnt to ashes deep inside an urn. Gone.

Martin speaks up from behind the wheel of his Lincoln, which Bagwell has to admit rides smooth as silk. "Well, he's not in town. Where the hell is he?"

Bagwell sits in the passenger side where he can stretch out his leg, which is pounding with pain. He's been up on it for too long and his painkillers wore off hours ago. "Maybe he's at a friend's house."

"Petey doesn't have a lot of friends."

"You said he's been out 'til the wee hours of the morning. He's got to be hanging out with someone."

"I don't know who. I lost track of Petey a long time ago. He could be hanging out with potheads and ... and ... child pornographers."

Sam speaks up from the back seat. "No way. I've offered him pot a dozen times. He doesn't smoke it."

Martin says, "For Christ's sake! Don't offer my kid illegal drugs!"

"He's not a kid, Marty. He's intelligent and socially aware. Not to mention he's a good person. A really good person. I'd be damn proud if he was my boy."

Suddenly a doe bounds out of the ditch on the left side of the road onto the pavement, turns, and freezes in the headlight's glare. Martin swerves to the left behind her, sweeping onto the shoulder, and around as she leaps into the ditch on the right.

Sam exclaims, "Holy crap!

Bagwell says nothing, but the shaking begins.

Martin doesn't miss a beat, unfazed by the near collision. "So, maybe he's hanging out with pedophiles."

"No way," Sam says and hesitates before his next few words. "Look, I might know where he is."

"Oh, now you tell us!" Martin says.

"I just thought of it! He told me he hangs out in a couple of bars in Three Rivers."

"Three Rivers? How would he get there without a car?"

"Where there's a will, there's a way." Sam leans up towards Bagwell. "Maybe we should drop you off at your mom's. It's been a long day for you."

"No. I'm going. Pete's like a brother to me." Besides, Billy couldn't possibly sleep. The coil was beginning to tighten up again. "Could we make a quick stop at the 7-Eleven for a pack of smokes?"

"Smokes? Martin asks. "I thought you gave that up."

Bagwell shrugs his shoulders. "Now and then."

Martin pulls the Lincoln into the parking lot of the convenience store. Bagwell glances at the pickup they pull up next to and gives a longer look at the late-model Jaguar parked on the other side two spaces down. He's always admired the graceful lines of the British car, but knows that mechanically they demand too much. James told him that years ago. Not James, his brother in arms, but James the back-stabbing prick. Sitting behind the wheel is a white man with slicked-back black hair, smoking a big fat cigar. Bagwell turns back to the matter at hand. "I'll be right back. Need anything?"

Sam says, "Grab me a Snickers. The munchies are setting in."

"You got it." Bagwell opens the door, grabs his cane, and steps out onto his right leg, his hurt leg, and it cries shrilly. He can't help but wince. Making his slow way into the store, he walks over to the counter, grabs a Snickers on a shelf and asks the skinny, pimply kid working at the register for a pack of Marlboro Lights. He glances over his shoulder to see a kid step up behind him with spiked up black and white hair. Though the kid looks fairly fresh, he sports an egg-sized bump on his left temple and a fresh ten-inch scratch down his right arm. Bagwell pays for his items and turns to see the kid nervously darting looks outside the door. Bagwell figures he's paranoid with speed and heads back outside the store. As he approaches the Lincoln, he sees Martin turned around in heated debate with his brother. Hand gestures are flying and muffled profanity can be heard through the closed glass. Bagwell opens the door to climb back in, reluctant to enter the scene, and watches as the kid scurries out of the store and into the sitting Jaguar like a fugitive. Bagwell hopes that the man behind the wheel is the kid's father. But, he doesn't think so.

"I don't give a rat's ass, Marty. I'm done with all that crap."

"You're going to die without it!"

"I might die faster with it! I'm not putting any more of that shit in my body!"

"Then die, you little son of a bitch." Martin turns, facing forward again. By the time he does, the Jaguar has backed out and taken off down the road.

Bagwell tosses the candy bar back to Sam and begins hitting one end of the cigarette pack into his open palm. "If ... I'm going to ride forty miles in a car with you two, you're going to have to cool it. I'm serious here. My sanity is hanging by a thread. I'm this close" (he illustrates a quarter inch between two fingers) "to going ballistic. So, please, let's just focus on the matter at hand. Finding Peter. Figuring out what's going on with the goods in his car. Okay?"

Sam leans up and pats Bagwell on the left shoulder. "I know where you're at, bro. And you're right. We need to focus."

Martin says, "Three Rivers, here we come."

Bagwell pulls a cigarette out of the pack with his teeth and lights it with the silver lighter that Brenda gave to him one year for Valentine's Day. He hits the switch on the door to roll the window down and readies to toss the lighter out, then hesitates. He reads the words engraved on the side: My heart is yours. He pockets the lighter and swears he's keeping it because it works. As he takes in his second draw, he's back in the desert with Glover beside him. He remembers the nervous look Glover threw him when he lit the cigarette outside their cave of sand. But Glover didn't say a word. The rockets came flying one, two, three. He lit the forbidden cigarette and some crazy Iraqi with the eyes of an eagle spied the smoke. He was sure of it. Yes, Glover broke the three-second rule on the radio. The Iraqis no doubt triangulated them as well. They didn't have a chance. But the attack began with Bagwell lighting that fucking smoke. If he hadn't, Glover would still be alive and he would still have two good legs. His impetuous nature bit him in the ass at last. His mother told him that it would. Someday. Bagwell never ever wanted to take someone with him. But, he did. He killed his best friend. No, not the back-stabbing half-breed that he taught how to fly. The man from Atlanta that no one could get enough of. Bagwell remembers that he's got to contact Glover's mom. What will he say? *I'm sorry, but I killed your boy. I killed your boy and I am deeply ashamed.*

"Did you kill anyone over there, Bill?" Martin asks.

Sam leans up quickly. "Goddamn it, Martin, you've got some shitty timing. Don't be asking him that."

"It's okay, Sam," Billy says. "It's okay. I shot a few people. Yes, Sir, I sure did. On top of that, I took out the best man in our company."

Sam warns, "Don't go there, Bill."

"I read that letter from her and I had to smoke. I lit up. I lit a fucking cigarette. They saw it just like the lieutenant told us that they would. We got hit with rockets, Glover and I. The impact is impossible to describe." He turns to the back seat. "You know what I'm talking about, Sam. I was sure I was dead at one point. Knocked out, I dreamed I was back here on a summer day. Lily Rose and I were dancing around in the grass. When I came to, I was half buried in the sand. My buddy was blowing air bubbles out of a hole in his chest. Jesus. I couldn't figure out where they were. Not the Iraqis. Our guys. They knew exactly where we were. They had to have seen the explosions. I pumped Glover full of morphine and started carrying him. He was holding on by a thread. After some time, I don't know how fucking long, it could have been ten minutes, it could have been an hour, our guys showed up. Goddamn it, I was pissed. If they'd come sooner, he might have lived." Bagwell inhales hard. "The whole thing was fucked up over there. The masks were faulty. The radios didn't work. Good thing the Iraqis were outnumbered and ill-equipped worse than us. I mean they had nothing. If they had been a mighty force, we would have been doomed. As it was, we mowed over them. I'll never forget the stench of death rising off those corpses burnt like toast. And for what? Jesus. What did we do?"

Sam leans forward. "You did what you had to do, Bill. Just like I did what I had to do."

Bagwell smothers his cigarette out in the ashtray. "It's not okay. It will never be okay."

Martin speaks up. "You've got a wife and child to think about."

"Cool it on the wife stuff, Marty," Sam adds.

"James Tillman isn't going to stay with one woman and you know it."

"Oh, and I'm going to slip back in like nothing happened?" Bagwell asks.

"Like I said before, you need to think about what's best for the child...."

Bagwell's voice gets low. "You know what I think is best for the child? To grab her and get the hell out of here. I don't know where. But, somewhere less complicated, less ... tainted. I feel like ... like an alien in this land now. When you've been away and you come back.... My mother is watching her TV evangelist on a forty-two inch screen. She says she actually feels like she's in his church watching him life-sized. My sister spends three hours a day in front of the mirror. And she still doesn't seem to feel good about herself. And I can't believe it, but half this town is fat. You just don't see that over there. Everyone drives around here like they're oblivious. Like there are no starving people on the planet. Like there are no people struggling just to be alive. And you, Martin, with all due respect. After all these years you still haven't accepted your son for who he is. We're not all cut out by a machine. There were guys over there from every corner of this country. Underneath the different colors of skin and beyond the basic preferences, we were all ... just guys and a few girls, of course. Some of the guys were gay. They fought righteously beside us, just like all the rest. The war was never over in the Pacific, Europe, the Gulf, or Vietnam. This land is the true battlefield. Right here in the good old USA."

17 Unearthly

Friday 11:32 p.m.

Foolishly, James thought that once Billy was gone, he would always be gone. James would simply take his place. Brown-haired, blue-eyed man, yellow haired in the summer, would vanish. In his place, black-haired, brown-eyed man, almost black skinned in the summer, squeezes in as his replacement. The daughter, always loyal to man number one, an obstacle. But, with enough discipline and direction, shaped into a sweet, obedient stepdaughter. This was the plan once Brenda spread her legs at the kitchen sink and let him slide into a stable home. He gave up every married lady with a negligent husband and young maiden lusting for what they'd heard whispered in their curious, but tender ears. He gave up all the other females just for her.

Not that he wanted Billy to die. No way. He secretly hoped that Billy would find another girl, black-haired, buxom, and brown, beneath the veils worn in that scorching desert. Billy would learn a trick or two he never learned before. Instead of Brenda sending a letter to Billy, he would send one to her. *Her name is Jasmine, Hannah, or Maria, and I can never leave her.*

Where can James turn to now? He can't go home to Mom, busily brushing the dust off of boyfriend number eleven. Another ne'er-do-well she picked up on the fringe of the factory, throwing dice at midnight, crawling into bed with her at dawn. If she checks his record, he is probably wanted in six states for passing bad checks, stealing the Social Security income from gray-haired matrons, or wagging his weenie in a bush by a local school.

James' experience with her string of boyfriends was brutal. A few had stolen into places he struggled to protect, breaking into satisfied grins when they reached down and found out that even as a boy, he was endowed. The whole thing confused James. The touches felt good, but even as a boy he knew it wasn't right. When he told his mother about the covert rendezvous, she laughed and asked him if there was a limit to his appeals for attention.

Once upon a time James had a little bear. Brown and fuzzy with yellow buttons for eyes and red stitches hand-sewn into a half-moon smile. James called him Teddy, and he went everywhere with him. "Uncle" Mike cut Teddy into quarters and warned him that his fate would be the same if he told. Touching him was good. Telling Mama was bad, very bad.

Sitting outside under the stars beside the natural pool where he, Billy, and Brenda had such good times, James tips up the bottle of 150-proof rum and guzzles.

He wants to kill the two men that are left who touched him. If he knew where they were he swears he would. At this moment, a life behind bars looks as attractive as any other. Maybe he could share a cell with his brother Jack, who wasn't up for parole until 1995. Jack was the only one who fought to protect him.

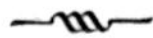

When James was ten, his brothers Jordan, Jeff, and Jack were fifteen, seventeen, and nineteen. Jordan was quiet and artistic. He could draw anything and make it look real. He would sit outside for hours and reproduce the countryside with the long, light strokes of a pencil. Even when Jordan was a freshman in high school, the art teacher latched onto him as a future star. Jeff was always restless and wild. He taught James about cars and possessed the fastest ride in the county, a cherry red Pontiac GTO with oversized tires on the jacked-up rear end and hood scoops that helped the car to fly. That year Jeff was arrested twice for breaking and entering and spent more time in juvenile hall than he did in school. Jack was tall and muscular, working out with weights long before it was considered to be cool. He worked construction and could drive a nail into just about anything with one blow. Jack didn't speak much, but when he did people listened. Jack played the father role, even when their mom had a boyfriend around. The boyfriends were generally useless, and no matter how hard Jack tried to steer his mom towards a better breed of man, she just kept bringing home mongrels.

Sisko was no exception. A slobbering drunk, who got mean as hell and cruel with his words. In fact, Sisko drove Jack out of the house into a small apartment a mile away, free of the four walls, but close enough to keep tabs. Jack didn't want to leave his brothers, but he loved his freedom and feared he might kill Sisko one day. And one day, he almost did.

That summer day was hot and stormy, too. Sisko decided to grill up a few racks of ribs, cigarette dangling from the corner of his mouth, gray ash dropping onto red meat laced with pale fat. He'd ordered a keg of beer and rolled it into the backyard of their tiny home and sucked on the tube like it was a lifeline. He wanted all the boys there, and even Jack showed up, not because he wanted to share the time with Sisko, but because he wanted to be there to intercept potential violence. His plan backfired.

By this point, Sisko had snuck into James' bed six times. Jordan slept beside him in a neighboring bed like a dead man, and Jeff was locked away for his thievery. James would smell the alcohol fumes before he felt Sisko run his hand over his ass. He would tighten into a ball and count. Usually by the count of forty or fifty, Sisko's hands had completed their tour, and he had grunted and groaned his dry humping into climax. James felt so confused when he grew excited. Did it mean he was a fag? He strove to put that fear to rest every time he pleasured a woman from the age of fourteen to the present.

The day of the rib-fest, fifteen years ago, Sisko got drunk and careless and before the eyes of his brother Jack, walked up behind James and patted his ass with one cupped hand. James remembers turning to see Jack stride over, grab Sisko by one shoulder, and throw him up against the house. Jack stepped up into his face and said, "Did I just see what I think I seen?"

Their mother flew up behind Jack crying out, "What are you doing, Jack?"

Jack turned and said, "Get back, Mother! James, get over here!"

James walked over. He remembers his face feeling hot and his stomach turning and turning like he might hurl. Oh, good, they'll finally know. Oh, no, what will they think of me?

Jack boomed out, "Has this weasel-like little son of a bitch been touching you?" His big brother turned to him and James nodded. Jack started banging Sisko up against the house. "You fucking piece of shit!"

If Sisko hadn't been three-quarters drunk, he might have been smart enough not to utter the next few words, "He likes it."

Jack threw Sisko on the ground, and kneeling over him, beat his face into a pink, red, and yellow pulp. One eye popped out and dangled on his cheek, and his nose was splintered beneath an empty tent of flesh.

Jeff and Jordan struggled to pull the fury that was their brother off of the now-unconscious Sisko. Clearly the drunk was an inch or two from death. Jack received twenty years in the state penitentiary for felonious assault.

Jordan was killed in a hunting accident two years later, sitting with his back against a tree sketching Mother Nature, when a stray bullet struck him. Jeff ran off and joined the pit crew of a stock car circuit. Their mother, ever desperate for love, became more discriminating in her choices, but never enough to hook what others may describe as a "good" man. Four years later, at the age of fourteen, James began his parade of conquests, each helping to put his greatest fear to rest. All that was finished now, done, because of his love of one. Brenda.

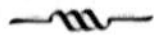

James tips the bottle of rum up again and lets it trickle down into a flow that becomes a river. When he places the bottle down and looks around, the world he sees looks fuzzy. Sitting there, on the edge of the pool where he, Brenda, and Billy once skinny-dipped in the brightness of the day where every nook and cranny was revealed, he feels helpless. At the same time, he knows that he must decide whether to fight or surrender. How bad does he want her? Will he face off with his former best friend or pull up stakes and move on?

He remembers sitting on the couch with Brenda three months or so ago watching the sun go down. Her back was up against his chest as he counted her heartbeats to make sure the organ was running right, and matched his breaths with hers to pretend that they were one. Lily Rose was sprawled on the floor humming to herself, whisking her Barbie around in a white plastic sports car. That evening, later, Brenda talked about the night her mother was taken away, half convinced that whoever or whatever had done it was unearthly. Why didn't she or Peter hear anything, like a scream, a door, a struggle? Why weren't she and Peter taken, too, but instead left in their beds to dream? In the morning they woke up, stretched and yawned, wandered into the kitchen where their mother always was. Nothing. She was nowhere in sight. Brenda clutched James' hands in hers resting on her middle and asked why? Why, Billy, why?

Billy?

It was so dark that night, she said. How could he ... it ... even see to carry her mama away, enter her against her will, and steal her breath? Leave her to lie alone in the cold night? It, whoever or whatever, must be a thing mysterious and unknown. Isn't it true, Billy, isn't it?

Billy.

James realizes now, gazing out into this fuzzy world, unearthly in its own right, that the man who possesses Brenda's heart was always Billy. He just stood in. Now Billy was back, not lured away by a brown-skinned girl in veils. He didn't send a letter to Brenda telling her he wasn't coming back. Although the world looks fuzzy in his present state, his mind runs crystal clear. Billy's out to get him. Should he put a target on his head? Or does he have what a man needs to give it one last fight? What does he have besides his golden dong to lure her away?

He could kill Billy first, couldn't he?

James remembers that day when the three of them, naked to the world, jumped into this pond. James was pissed. Billy made him look like a pussy out on their dirt bikes. The guy had no fucking fear. He would take off across the fields, over hills, soar into the air, glide back down, sliding, fishtailing, practically laying the bike on its side, all with a smile. Chasing after Billy, he found it difficult to keep up. They finally stopped for a rest, pulling out their canteens, brushing the dirt and dust off of their faces. To make things worse, Billy brought up Doris.

James finishes off the pint of rum and lets it slip out of his hand onto the ground, where he watches as the bottle rolls to the edge of the pond. Maybe he could stick a message into the bottle and hope that somebody answers his prayer. Somebody besides God, who never answers his prayers. He feels like the odd man out. Nobody nowhere cares.

"Why do you keep seeing that woman?" Billy asked.

"She's as flexible as Gumby," he answered with a grin.

"There's a ton of single girls out there."

"I've been with more than a few."

"Don't you worry about diseases?" Billy pulled off his helmet to let his hair dry.

"I'm eighteen years old! In my sexual prime."

"You keep acting like you do, no girl is going to want you."

"Oh, yeah?"

"Yeah. Don't you want to get married, have kids?"

"Maybe. If I decide to do that, I'll have to go look in some other town."

"Why?"

"Because you've got the number one girl in this one."

Billy turned and looked James straight in the eyes. "She's pretty special."

"That she is." Billy didn't blink or turn his eyes away. "Why are you looking at me like that? I wouldn't touch her. That doesn't mean I don't appreciate her."

"Look, I know that things weren't easy when you were growing up."

"What's that supposed to mean?"

"It had to be tough. Your mom and all her boyfriends."

"What are you getting at?"

"I'm just saying...."

"Saying what? You haven't got a clue, golden boy. Everything you touch ..."

"James, listen ..."

"No, you listen. I'll live my life the way I want to. You live your life the way you want to. Got it?" James climbed back onto his bike and took off with a spray of dirt.

Maybe they know. Maybe the whole town knows how he was molested in the night. Same as it ever was. Whispered voices behind shielding hands. Everyone secretly shaking their heads and saying it's all so sad. Half-breed boy used like a blow-up doll.

Boy turns to promiscuity to chase his fears away. Abused boy turned horny man seduces every girl in sight. No more sympathy now. One step too many over the line, boy.

Meanwhile, the women wait, lying back with their legs spread.

Even Billy's friendship turns into a sham. Golden boy befriends the mutt because he cannot help but shelter the underdog. He'd do the same for a stray cat.

By the end of the afternoon dirt-bike ride, even though he and Billy were laughing together once again, the kernel of resentment at his friend's reprimand ate away at him. James cast his caution to the side and solicited the one girl he wanted above all others: his best friend's fiancé. He dared to glance at her breasts as they rode in the pickup. He bared his jewels before her eyes. He sent something out, that he guesses is desire set out upon a wave, maybe a song, or a rhythm, an emotion into substance that stirs the woman. And he saw that stirring for a moment in Brenda's eyes. But, only for a moment, swiped away by fear and put to rest when Billy draped her body in the towel.

Billy must have sensed or glimpsed his betrayal, but he never said a word.

James did not do it again.

But the seed was sown and sprouted while Billy fought in the heat rising off the blistering sand, and Brenda's loneliness led her into unfaithful alliance. Like the others, she laid waiting for him, but her heart was under lock and key.

They all know – every one of them – how his innocence was stolen in the night. They used to feel sorry for him, but now they just don't care. Nobody. Nowhere. Cares.

James falls back onto the long cool grass and peers into this fuzzy world and realizes he likes it. He wishes he had some pot to dull the edges even more. Now the clarity of his mind begins to fade, and all the fears, the doubts, and concerns lift, and he begins to float in a cloud of nothing, nothing, dark.

He awakens enveloped like a pea in a pod. The billion stars are gone, and above and around him all looks black. When he lifts his right hand to brush his hair out of his eyes, his elbow brushes something soft. He sucks in a breath and lifts both hands to feel around him. Feathers! He's enveloped in feathers! He begins to shake. Sitting up with a start, he sees darkness lift up into the air, revealing the jewel box of stars that faintly lights the night. He scrambles across the grass on his hands and knees towards his truck, emitting grunts of fear. When he reaches his truck he stands with his back against the cool metal and looks up into the sky. What the fuck? A giant bird? A ... a ... white against the black ... He's dreaming. He must be dreaming. Or is he dead?

18
Prayer

Saturday 12:01 a.m.

Sam sits back and settles into the cushy rear seat of the Lincoln. All stands quiet now, Billy working on cigarette number three and Martin gazing ahead, red eyed and exhausted from the evening's events. If either of them turned to glance back at Sam, they'd see his teeth clenched, and the subtle shift of his hips as he struggles to find a seating position that will make the pain in his gut go away. Fuck. Beads of sweat break out above his upper lip, and if he were to lift his hair, he'd find the short down damp and clinging to his neck. He drops his head into his hands and prays, his lips moving in silence:

I'm not good at this. I never have been. I'm only half convinced that you exist at all. I may have believed before I lived in that jungle for two years. War challenges faith in ways nothing else comes close to. But on the chance that you do exist, I've got a couple of things I'd like to say and a couple things I'd like to ask you for.

I did things over in Nam that I know you'll never forgive me for. I could tell you I was just following orders, which is the truth, but I could have gotten out of it if I really tried. I could have shot myself in the foot or the hand like Hendricks and Castaneda did. I could have shot into the ground or the sky and hoped that the lieutenant didn't notice. Probably I did shoot a kid or two, or an old man or woman who weren't hiding explosives under their shirt. Probably some part of me really did enjoy slitting the throat of that gook, I mean that Vietnamese that killed someone in my platoon. There were times when my fatigues were splattered with blood and brains, and I emitted the cries of a madman, incensed, out of control and acting like an animal. Did we take trophies? You bet we did. Body parts, objects from their pockets, gold from their teeth. Small things we had room to carry. I was half stoned most of the time. I was comfortably numb like Pink Floyd sang about. Didn't feel the insect bites, the jungle rot, the extended days of two hours' sleep. There wasn't a moment when one eye wasn't open. I didn't want to taste my di.. in my mouth. Didn't want to feel my body fly apart in a million pieces. Didn't want to hold my guts in with one hand. Why did you have to take Chris Bagwell? Couldn't you see how badly he wanted to live? How hard does a man have to fight for his life before you believe him?

There was a guy in our platoon who was a Native American. Navaho or Hopi or something. We called him Red Feather. His father was a medicine man who was passing his knowledge onto his son. One night, God, everything was quiet. We were in the jungle, stationary, gathered around telling stories in low voices. We'd lost a few men the day before, feeling bitter and revengeful, wondering how one man dies of a grazing wound and another survives looking like he was torn apart in a combine. Red told us that death has a presence and it comes in two forms. One is Benevolent Death. It arrives without ceremony, closing your eyes with an illness or collecting you swiftly after an accident or an act of nature, gently carrying you up to meet your maker. Then there's Stalking Death. Red said when he stepped off the plane onto the land of this place far away known as Nam, he could sense Stalking Death rolling, skittering from and into all eight directions. The place was permeated with it. Stalking Death hunts you down. It captures you in its sight and follows you tirelessly, snatching you away because it wants you. You could have a broken toe and you're done. You can scream, cry, or pray, attempt to fight it off like a bear, but forget it. The will of the individual sits crushed in the hand of this relentless force. I guess that's what happened with Chris. He never had a chance.

Are these two forces a part of you, God? Or is one force yours and the other a renegade without a father, or perhaps risen from the place of fire and smoke down below? Which one moves among this family now? I can't tell. I just can't tell.

My mother told me tonight that a painting fell off the wall in the old farmhouse. She told me that this falling marks a sign of impending death. Is it my time? Will Benevolent Death close my eyes with a kiss? Or is Stalking Death crouched behind me ready to spring? I can't say

I'm ready to go at this moment, but I'll volunteer if it means saving another soul. The doctors gave me six months to live. How much do you give me?

I look at these kids, and I'm not a crying man, but my eyes fill up with tears. The boy in the front seat, Chris's boy. I've never seen such a fearless character. Neither pain nor the fear of death could deter him. I witnessed this when he was growing up. Always the first one to jump, the last to give up, a leader in every situation. And he's a good boy, hardworking, accountable in word and deed. I look at him now and see someone beaten down, the spirit stolen from his eyes, his heart broken. In the past, a bum leg wouldn't have gotten in his way. He'd be out there already dancing a jig.

It's her. My niece. It's him. My brother. He sent her running out into that cornfield long ago, huddling for cover, her little arms crossed across her eyes. I know damn well she was simply looking for a safe place where Marty wasn't dictating their every word and move. Then you took her mom away. Well, now, maybe you didn't. Maybe that was the dirty work of Stalking Death. Jesus ... I mean God, whatever, whoever you are ... she was a good woman, Jeanine. My God, she loved those kids. Can't blame Brenda and Peter for being afraid of the dark, the unknown, with the mystery surrounding that affair. I can't blame them. I think Brenda was afraid Billy was never coming back. Like her mom. I honestly think that's what she thought. She should have realized that nothing would stop Billy. He's like a cat with nine lives. But she did break his heart. I'm pissed at her for that. Personally, I think she still loves him.

I've always liked James Tillman. He can't keep his...in his pants. I do apologize for that. The guy likes to be with the ladies. That doesn't make him a bad guy. I'd rather the kids of today be exposed to tits and ... I apologize ... I ... um ... sensuality and sexuality I mean, than the violence and devastation of war. Now, my niece, Brenda, is a good-looking girl, and I'm not saying it's right but ... she was really pissed that Billy left her, and like I said before, she's used to people not coming back. Loss ... she's had her share. Maybe James intended to steal her, but I don't think so. You *can't be friends like he and Billy were for all those years and just turn on him. I don't think so.*

Another very important thing I need to talk to you about is my nephew Peter. What the hell ... I mean heck ... is going on here? We need your help on this one. That boy ... has had it tough, too. His father, my brother, Marty, has a set view of the world that will not budge. Anything outside that view is extraterrestrial. I don't know how you view homosexuality, but for me, it's just the way it is. I don't know if it's biological or environmental, or whatever, but it is. Sure, I'd like to see the kid married and settled down with kids, but look at me.... Anyway, we have a real problem on our hands with this pound of weed and dirty, stinking tapes. Please, I just don't want Peter involved in all that. Please ... let us find him safe. Let us clean up this mess without the police being involved. I guess that's too much to ask because whoever is involved with this porn is going to have to fall.

God, I'm not sure that I believe in signs like that painting falling off the wall. Even though I must admit that when it's happened before, someone did pass away. Please. Please. If you do exist, please, don't take away one of these kids. Not the baby, Lily Rose, not the others. I know my mother grows old, but she's the ... the ... heart of this family. We still need her. It's a hard time. Maybe I have to pray to that renegade without a father, too. Or is Stalking Death an uncontrollable force, outside your jurisdiction and outside so far, nobody can touch it? I'll go. Even though I have fear because I did what I did over in that jungle, I might not cross over to a place I want to be. I'll take my punishment if that means giving these others a chance at a longer life.

Billy asks, "What the hell you doing back there, Sam, talking to yourself?"

"Oh, something like that." Sam strokes his goatee.

"You were praying, weren't you?"

Martin speaks up, "Well, good, put a word in for Petey."

Billy adds, "Yeah, and put a prayer in for James, too. Tell 'the Lord' to get a seat ready for him."

Martin turns to Billy, "So revenge is the answer, huh?"

Billy leans up to stab another cigarette out in the ashtray. "I know it's not the same, but what if you knew who killed Jeanine, and he was running around out in the world free?"

"Bill, you said it. It's not the same. Murder deserves death. Betrayal? Beat the shit out of him, but don't kill him. You'll ruin your life."

"My life is already ruined."

Sam closes his eyes and resumes his prayer, *Lord, God, Jesus, whoever you are, please cool the fire in that boy's belly.*

Part II
Benediction

19
Leftovers

Saturday 12:10 a.m.

Martha sits in the oak rocker and rocks back and forth, and back and forth, and back and forth. The moon shines so brightly outside the night almost looks like day. She stares out the north window past the open space where her blessed tree once stood, down the road that leads to a neighboring town. Down, down, down the road of memory where sadness and joy sit silently side by side. She hesitates to go there, but she has no choice. Worry and concern propel her to study the events of the past in search of a pattern, so maybe, just maybe, she can capture a glimpse of the unfolding future.

—∿—

July 1970. Brenda had been lost for one hour now. Somewhere in the fields of corn, she was running away or hiding. Five years old, like a midget among giant stalks, she trekked across the damp earth wearing her new patent leather shoes. Her dress shredded on the bristly edges and sharp corners as she passed. Her skin scraped away, punctured, insects alighting, biting, leaving small red swollen mounds. This vision traveled through Martha's head as she covered her designated area, the calls of the searchers ricocheting in the early night, the controlled beams of flashlights occasionally visible.

Where was that child? Martha had yet to discover why she ran into the fields at all. She came upon Jeanine, using one hand to wipe away the tears rolling slowly from her eyes.

"Oh, Martha, where is she?"

Martha slipped her arm around the younger woman's waist. "She can't be far."

"She might have fallen into a hole ... or ... maybe an animal got her. She could be ..."

"Jeanine, she's probably fine. Just hiding. Don't worry your mind with what might be." Martha turned to look her in the eyes. "What happened? Why did she jump out of the car?"

"I'm ... I'm not sure. Well ... maybe it was her father. He was upset with me."

"Why?"

"Oh ... just ... he's always upset with me."

Martha stopped walking and firmly gripped Jeanine's arm. "You've got to stand up to him. Don't let him get away with that crap. He'll run over you like a bulldozer. That boy has always been a handful. Strong willed just like my mother."

"It's so hard ..."

Suddenly, from a short distance away, Sam's voice was heard. "I found her! She's over here!"

Martha and Jeanine broke out into a run, weaving their way through the corn, until they emerged out of the stalks into a field of wheat. There, Samuel, the grandfather, stood holding the semi-conscious child in his arms. When Martin arrived, five beats before the women, he grabbed the child from his father.

Samuel said, "She's fine. She's coming to. Got a nasty bump on her head."

Martha watched the child's eyelids flutter and the rise of apprehension as she focused on her father's face. The child turned her head to see her mother, reached out her small arms and said, "Mama."

—∞—

Martha pushes on the arms of the rocker into a stand and walks over to peer out of the north window. Martin. What a trouble that boy has been, trying to mold everything that comes up in his path. She shakes her head with frustration as another memory creeps up. Sammie. Her boy who's suffered so.

—∞—

November 1971. Thanksgiving day and there was one empty chair at the long oak table covered with an off-white linen cloth. The leftovers sat cold in their array of color. The orange of the squash, the green of the beans, the yellow of the Jell-O pineapple salad. The turkey stood half eaten with the remnants of dressing spilling out upon the plate. The men were groaning, ready to push back their chairs, stand, and retire in front of the TV, where they'll watch a game of football. The women, resting their chins on the bridge of their hands, chattered and stalled. The prospect of cleaning up the mess was always overwhelming. The children were anxious to run outside, hungering to play in ways their holiday clothes won't allow. For these last few moments the group was intact except for one.

Jeanine asked, "Where did Sammie go?"

Martha answered, "I don't know, but he's been gone for quite a while."

Martin said, "He probably snuck off somewhere to shoot up."

"Kids, you can go out and play now," Jeanine quickly added, softly rubbing her belly where Peter was inside growing.

Brenda and her cousins jumped up and ran out, their small feet tapping upon the hardwood floor.

Sandy, Sammie's longtime girlfriend, stood and threw her napkin down upon her plate. "He's clean! He's fucking clean, Martin."

"Well, then, where the hell is he?"

Samuel pulled a toothpick out of his mouth and said, "I think he's in the bathroom."

Sandy walked out of the room and Martha followed. The younger woman knocked on the door. "Sammie, are you in there?"

A muffled reply could barely be heard. The two women looked at each other and silently agreed to move inside. Sammie was crumpled on the floor, lying on his side, his arms crossed hard against his guts. The women fell down upon their knees beside him. Sandy gently lifted his head and cradled the damp, heavy bulb in her lap.

"Honey, what's wrong? Are you sick again?"

"Yeah," he answered weakly.

Martha asked, "Again? What do you mean again?"

"He's sick, Martha. Ever since he came back from over there."

Martha placed her right hand upon the cheek of her second born. He was hot to the touch and trembling.

—~—

Martha draws her eyes away from the ribbon of road and begins to search her violets for a sign of budding life. There they are. The unfolded tendrils containing the small clusters of life waiting for the sun to pull them out from underneath the leaves. Soon her violets will be covered with lavender, purple, and white flowers. The discovery makes her smile.

—~—

October 1975. They arrived back from the hospital to find the kids inside the locked house with a chair jammed under the knob of the back door. They called through an open window and the kids came running, their eyes wide and their little chests heaving.

"We heard voices in the barn!" Peter exclaimed as he threw his arms around his mom.

"What's this all about?" asked Martha.

"I was playing on the stairs and Peter was in the shed. We heard men laughing and we could hear them sharpening something on the stone wheel," Brenda said.

Peter jumped up and down. "Yeah! And I heard glass bottles!"

Sammie turned towards the door and said over his shoulder, "I'll go check the barn."

Martin turned to Jeanine exasperated. "See what happens, Jeanine, when you let those kids watch spooky movies?"

Jeanine, bolder now than years before, said, "How do you know, Martin? Maybe there was someone in the barn."

Martha's chest began to constrict as she sat down in a chair with a plop, one hand clutching up for her throat. She knew immediately what this meant. The hours, minutes, seconds of her husband's life were numbered. They've come for him. They've come to take him home. She wasn't ready. *I'm not ready,* she said silently in prayer to God.

"Ma, are you okay?" Martin asked.

She looked up at her son and wondered if she should say a word, knowing that he would discount her. She looked at all the faces turned to her, large and small, and knew that only one, gone now to the barn, would believe her. Sammie saw the angel when he was young, and what he saw in Nam she doesn't know, but he came back with a newfound respect for the mysterious.

Finally, she answered, "Yes, yes, I'm fine. But I think I'd like to lie down for a while."

Martin said, "So you don't believe there was anyone in the barn either."

Martha stood up and began to move slowly towards the hall leading to her bed. "Martin, you always have lacked imagination."

Underneath the plump and verdant upper leaves of the violets are those few that are wrinkled, fading, turning pale. With the timing and efficiency of a cherry picker, she plucks them away one by one from each and every plant.

Where there is life there is also death.

Baunmiller Funeral Home. Martha overheard chatter passed in low voices.

"He fell down the chute?"

"That's what I heard. Right into a stall of pigs."

"The Beckers have never raised pigs."

"The hell they haven't. And you know pigs. They eat anything."

"For Christ's sake. That's all bullshit. Does that man over in the box look half eaten to you? He fell down the chute, broke a hip and ... you know those old farmers. After a fall, they never recover."

"I heard he was drunk."

"I never saw Samuel Becker drunk. Not once. Though he did like his beer."

"Well, anyway, he was a hell of a man."

"That he was."

—∾—

Martha turns away from the violets and out of the corner of her right eye marks the spot where the fallen painting had hung. She wonders what would happen if she just hung the painting back up onto the wall as Martin had suggested. Would it change anything?

—∾—

September 1980. The phone rang at 9:03 a.m. Martha picked up the receiver to hear silence on the other end.

She said, "Hello? Hello?" Just as she decided to place the receiver back down, she heard the voice of Martin.

"Ma?"

"Martin! For crying out loud. Speak up!"

"You ... need to get over to the house."

Martha heard something in his voice she had never heard before. "What is it? What's happened?"

"It's ... it's Jeanine. She's dead."

"Wh... what?"

"She's been found dead. Ma, please, just get over to the house. The kids are alone."

"Where are you?"

"I'm still in Gaylord. I'm catching a plane back in an hour. Just go. Please."

When she walked into the back door of Martin and Jeanine's house, she found Brenda in the kitchen wearing her mother's red and white checked apron, fixing French toast on a griddle. Peter sat at the kitchen table finely filling in the lines of a costume he designed for some big musical dancing in his head. Brenda stopped her motion in midair, a piece of egg-covered toast suspended on a spatula. Peter jumped up from his chair at the table and ran over to wrap his long thin arms around Martha's waist.

Brenda asked, "Where's Mom, Grandma?"

Peter looked up at Martha with his big blue eyes, "We can't find her anywhere."

Martha debated all the way over to the house what she should tell the kids. Maybe Martin should be the one to tell them that their mother died. Knowing Martin, however, who had always shied away from addressing the uncomfortable, he might very well leave it up to her. Ultimately, she didn't have to make the decision. Brenda, being the intuitive teen that she was, looked intently into her grandmother's eyes. The spatula and bread dropped to the floor with a plop and Brenda ran out of the house heading for a field of corn emitting a long shrill scream. Peter continued to stare up at Martha, his strong sinewy arms squeezing her like he would never let her go.

Martha leans over the back of the sofa to pull the painting up, but it won't budge. The frame and canvas, heavy as lead, wedged in fast, or perhaps became encumbered now with a life of its own. She attempts to slide the painting back and forth, and pulls hard to lift it. The fallen soldier stands imbedded.

Baunmiller Funeral Home. Martha overheard chatter passed in low voices.

"Who found her body?"

"Willy Lutz was flying over the fields looking for a calf."

"He saw her from the air?"

"Lying among the rocks. He could tell she wasn't just sleeping."

"I heard she was raped."

"Well ... she was penetrated with something."

"What do you mean?"

"Look, this isn't the place to talk about this."

"I heard she was strangled."

"Broken neck. Let's be quiet now."

"Just one last thing. I heard there was some kind of evidence."

"There wasn't a clue left anywhere."

—~—

Martha now feeling fatigued, lifts up off of the sofa and heads back to the rocker. She drops onto the crocheted seating pad with a deep sigh.

—~—

June 1981. Brenda was sweet sixteen today and the family had gathered in the yard of the old farm underneath the trees. The oak stood especially tall and full that year, allowing just the tiniest slivers of the summer sun to shine through. The slivers reflected upon the ground like a fist full of diamonds had been cast. Martha made Brenda's favorite cake, chocolate with strawberry filling, decorated with yellow flowers, green leaves, and sixteen white candles standing in columns. Blasting through the air was the music of Brenda's favorite band, The Police. Martha had to admit, the beat of the music was contagious, and even she found herself moving to the rhythm. Brenda wore a new pink cotton blouse with the top three buttons undone, revealing a bit of her already ample bosom. Her jeans were so tight, she must have poured herself in and her feet were bare, toes painted carefully to match her ensemble. Billy stayed close to Brenda, anticipating her every need. Every time they passed within an inch of each other they touched. There was the grazing of fingertips, the warm whispered breath in the ear, and the subtle collision of young, firm hips.

James sat off to the side, brushing his hair off of his forehead, drawing on a cigarette, and tapping his foot to the time. Martha walked over to join him, sitting down next to him in a chair.

"How are you doing today, James?"

"I'm doing fine, Martha."

"You seem kind of quiet."

"It's Bren's day, not mine."

Why didn't he look her in the eyes? "Does your mom have birthday parties for you boys?"

"Not really. She works a lot. Besides, my brothers are all gone now. I'm the only one left at home. She ... she just forgets." He shook his head and shrugged his shoulders. "It doesn't matter."

Martha placed her hand upon his knee. "I hope you know, James, that we all consider you a part of our family."

James cast his eyes down and she watched him swallow as he put his cigarette out in an ashtray sitting on the ground. He looked up at her for one moment. "Thank you." Then he darted his eyes away.

Later, watching from afar, she couldn't help but notice how James subtly bristled every time Billy and Brenda touched. Only someone watching very close could tell that James was jealous. But was he jealous of Brenda or was he jealous of Billy?

—ᴥ—

Martha begins to rock again, back and forth, and back and forth, twisting one corner of her thin and faded apron into a ball. How did all these years pass so fast? Wasn't there any way in the world to slow time down?

—ᴥ—

July 1982. Martha and Brenda were driving down the main road outside Willis, heading towards Martin's house. They just left the Methodist Church, where Martha had convinced Brenda to join her at an ice cream social. Brenda went kicking and screaming, not happy to spend an evening away from Billy, surrounded by mothers and matrons swapping recipes and remedies, and reliving choice moments of their favorite soaps.

Martha turned to Brenda in the car and said, "I ... I want to talk to you about something."

"Oh, no."

"Oh, no. Why, oh, no?"

"What is it, Grandma?"

Martha said, "I know you are seventeen, but I want to make sure your mother or father talked to you about ... sex."

"Grandma! Mom talked to me about that years ago."

"So, you are protecting yourself?"

"You don't even have to worry about that. Billy won't do it." Brenda rolled her window down halfway. Martha watched the air blow back her long dark hair in waves.

"Oh."

Brenda rolled the window down further and leaned out, letting the air pour over her face. "I know they say guys get blue balls, but what do girls get? Sometimes I feel like I might explode."

Martha turned left onto Ellis Road. "Billy is a real decent young man."

Brenda pulled back her hair with one hand so the air could circulate around her neck. "He wants to wait until we're engaged."

Martha reached down to rub her right knee where her arthritis tells her the weather is about to change. "In my day, we used to wait until we were married."

Brenda turned to her grandmother. "Did you really?"

Martha turned left onto Austin Road, a long, flat, straight road. "Most of us did. You kids these days. You want to grow up so fast. Billy just wants it to be real special."

"My friends have all had sex."

Suddenly, up ahead on this paved road, two sets of headlights appeared side by side. Through the window, Martha could hear the very distant rev of engines. As the headlights quickly moved closer, the sound of the engines grew. Her foot fell off of the accelerator as she asked, "What is going on here?"

Brenda dropped her hair and sat up, her eyes wide and alive with excitement. "Pull off! Pull off of the road, Grandma!"

The pair of headlights rapidly approached as Martha clumsily found the accelerator and pulled the car onto the side of the road. Five seconds later two cars flew by side by side in a running color blur.

Brenda turned smiling, her face more animated than Martha had ever seen before. "He's crazy!" Brenda exclaimed excitedly.

"Who?"

"James. That was James in the red GTO. He has the fastest car around."

"He's going to kill himself. Or somebody else."
"James wouldn't wait to have sex."

—⁂—

Martha pushes herself up into a stand again and shuffles slowly out of the room towards the kitchen, where she stops at the sink to gaze out onto the fields. Fast cars. Fast sex. The fast passing of years. She shakes her head and leans into the counter. There appears to be no way to convince the young to slow things down.

—⁂—

August 1986. The temperature was eighty-eight and the humidity was high. The family was gathered in a neighboring city to watch Billy ride his dirt bike in a state competition. Everyone watched and withheld breath as he flew over hills, around corners practically laying the bike down, and shooting down the straight sections like a bullet. His motions, as well as the other riders, were sometimes obscured by large and looming clouds of dust sitting stagnantly in the moist air.

Brenda stood at the fence, never taking her eyes off her husband, holding their newborn daughter close to her body like an extension of her own. Occasionally, she brushed her lips in Lily's downy, golden curls, or across her cheek, plump and pink as a sun-ripened peach. She rocked the baby when her eyes fluttered open, and when her tiny mouth opened for a cry, she sang softly in the shell of her ear. Lily Rose was a good baby and Brenda a better than average mama.

Occasionally, James stepped up beside Brenda holding an unlit cigarette down by his side. He and Billy gave up smoking when Lily Rose was born. He looked at the little baby and said simply, "Wow," like he'd never seen one before.

Sammie sat in a folding chair, weak from chemo, his once long hair short and thin. His eyes, too, never left Billy, the young man, the son of his dead best friend. The young man that Martha knew was like a son to Sammie, never having had his own, his seed dried by chemicals that once reduced the jungle vegetation of Nam into a long-forgotten dream. Her son was weak in body, but his eyes still sparkled.

Martha watched Martin and Peter standing side by side, the father trailing the path of his son's eyes, nervously anticipating that they may fall upon another boy. Once, when a buxom blonde balancing on high-heeled boots walked by, Martin jabbed his son in the ribs with his elbow and remarked, "Ain't she something?" Peter grinned and nodded, but Martha could see that his heart wasn't in it. Finally, Peter stepped away from his father, and took a seat next to Sammie. Martha watched as the tall, gawky, but handsome teen from time to time stole a glance at another boy standing at the fence down the way, occasionally glancing over his shoulder to meet Peter's eyes. You can't fight nature.

With two laps to go, Billy was in first place, with a boy in black leather hot on his tail. From where they stood, the crowd strained to see every move, as the two bikes headed into the final lap. The bikes were impossibly close, moving in and out of the stagnant clouds of dust. They fishtailed, they left the earth for seconds, they sped along side by side. Until, in one moment, Billy's bike careened off the trail, sliding riderless on its side, Billy tumbling head over heels a half dozen times or more.

Molly, Billy's mom, standing beside Martha, broke into a run, as did Martin and James, as the boy in black crossed the finish line holding up his arms in triumph. Before they reached Billy, he stood, threw his helmet to the ground and ran towards the boy who beat him. In moments they were rolling in the dirt, punching, kicking, screaming as anyone who could fit in gathered 'round. James and another of Billy's friends pulled Billy up as supporters of the boy in black did the same.

Billy screamed, "He kicked my fucking bike!"

The other boy screamed, "You're fucking crazy!"

A judge stepped forward to say that what Billy said was true.

Molly turned to Martha and said, "That's my boy. He always fights for what's right. Just like his daddy."

—~—

Fighting for what is right. Billy's daddy dying in Vietnam. Martha's own son coming back ravaged with disorders. Billy now back from the Persian Gulf with injuries of his own. War seems to be at the bottom of every kind of strife. When will they learn? When will they learn? Martha turns from the window with disgust.

—∞—

December 1989. Christmas was cold and snowy that year, with three-foot drifts and twelve-inch ice stalactites hanging from roofs. Sitting around the long oak table covered with the linen cloth, they raised their glasses in toast to the year full of blessings. Sammie's cancer had been in remission for three years now, his hair long and full, people beginning to come from far and wide to buy his woodwork. Billy was now the foreman of a construction crew, busy building houses for city folk moving into the country for a break from the congestion and the smog. Brenda worked side by side with the town veterinarian, thinking about going back to school once Lily Rose began hers. Martin was re-elected county supervisor and now played cards with friends every Friday night, something he hadn't done since Jeanine died. He didn't talk anymore about how he wanted to hunt her murderer down and kill him with his bare hands. Peter graduated from high school and seemed to be coming out of his shell. Lily Rose was three and passed through the terrible twos with barely a stir. James was there, too, his mom out carousing with her newest beau. His mechanics shop was now the place most people brought their broken and ailing cars.

Billy spoke up, "This time is as good as any for me to tell you some news." He hesitated then went on, "I've joined the United States Marine Corps. I leave in fourteen days."

Brenda stood up from the table and moved quickly out of the room, her soft sobs barely audible. Lily Rose looked after her, her small brow furrowed in worry.

—∞—

Martha grabs the blue watering can off the top of the

refrigerator, fills it with water, and shuffles out of the kitchen back into the living room, where she proceeds to lovingly water her violets. Her jaw tightens.

—~—

February 1991. Little Lily Rose entered the back door of the old farmhouse quietly and climbed the four stairs into the kitchen. She was covered with snow from head to toe. Her cheeks were red as cherries, and the small chunks of snow in her golden hair clung and sparkled under the ceiling light.

Martha stooped down to help the child unwrap the purple woolen scarf from her neck, pulled off her wet purple and white striped mittens, and lifted her out of her white rubber boots. At four years old, Lily demanded her daily outfits to be color coordinated.

"You're very quiet, Miss Lily. Does the cat have your tongue?"

Lily shook her head.

"Did you have fun out there in the snow?"

Lily nodded.

"Would you like a cup of hot chocolate?"

Finally, the child spoke, "With marshmallows?"

"I have the little pink and yellow ones you like."

Lily's blue eyes widened, "Oh, goodie."

Martha turned to put the gas on to heat up water. "Did something happen out there?"

Lily silently nodded.

"Do you want to tell Grandma?"

Lily beckoned with one finger for her grandma to stoop back down. The child said softly, "I saw an angel."

"You did?"

"I was lying in the snow on my back making a snow angel. When I looked up, she was standing over me. She was a lady with big white wings."

"Did she say anything to you?"

Lily nodded. "She said my daddy would be coming home." The

child broke into a huge smile then suddenly sobered. "Nobody is going to believe me."

Martha gathered up the child into her arms. "I believe you."

"Nobody believes in angels anymore, Nana."

"I do. I believe in angels."

—∾—

The room where every family celebration and mourning takes place still echoes, and darkens, as one large and puffy cloud crosses over the moon. A sudden spasm in Martha's right forearm causes her hand to release the watering can, which drops to the ground with a plop, falls over, and the liquid quickly streams free. Rather than running for a towel to stanch the flow, she simply watches the water traverse a course around the legs of the violet stand and darken the edges of the carpet. She knows now whose destiny has come to call, and raising her voice to heaven offers her own life up instead.

Bless the family and let them live, she prays. *I am old and tired.*

20
Swallowed

Saturday 12:45 a.m.

Brenda places the tea bag in the cup and hangs the tag over the side just like her mom used to do. She walks down the hall, her eyes tracing the horizontal lines of the throw rug, and stops in front of Lily's door. Pushing it open, she steps inside her sweet daughter's room where the moon shines in like a spotlight and falls upon the rocking chair in the corner. Jake the dog lies beside it. He lifts his head momentarily to look at her, releases one soft little whine, and lays his head back down. Brenda knows beyond a doubt that Billy has recently sat in that chair. Earlier, when he was in the house, he probably rocked Lily in his lap, just like he always did. She walks across the room, watching as her small daughter stirs in her sleep and mumbles. As she drops quietly into the chair onto the purple crocheted padding, the smell of him wafts up. The scent contains a delicate mixture of the deodorant he wears, the aftershave and the shampoo, earthy smells, as familiar as coffee brewing in the morning. The smell stirs her.

What the hell has she done?

The stirring stops as guilt, remorse, shame, and all the other dark forces that arise to shut out the light accost her. She experiences this as a pain in her belly, which she covers with her crossed arms to cradle.

Then she remembers her grandmother's words: you are stronger than you know. And Brenda remembers that she has already taken one step to fix it. She cut off her lust for James.

—ᴧᴧ—

Brenda had never heard desperation in his voice before. When he uttered those words, "Don't leave me," there was a pause in her crying. She looked into James' eyes and saw a frightened little boy.

She felt for him. God, she did. But still she scooted herself up off her back into a sitting position and said, "I can't do it, James. I can't do it anymore."

In the few seconds it took to say those words, she watched as the frightened little boy was turned off. What replaced that vulnerability was cold, defiant, and what she feared the most, cruel.

James bent down to grab his black jeans, stood, and pulled them up, tucking all that he was endowed with neatly inside.

"You are really something," he said.

"I'm sorry."

He turned to her. "It was all a game to you, wasn't it?"

"No ..."

"Parading around in that little robe with your ass and tits hanging out."

"No ... James, please be quiet. I don't want to wake up Lily."

He dropped the volume of his voice. "You don't give a shit about me."

Brenda pulled the sheet over her naked body. "I ... I do care about you. Just ... just not like that."

"Brenda, you don't care about anybody but yourself. You never have."

James stooped again and plucked up his black and blue pullover, stuck his head through the collar and his hands and arms through the sleeves.

"I ... I really thought I did. Love you. Like that. I really did."

"But, you like to fuck me, don't you? They all like to fuck me."

Brenda, holding the sheet over her breasts, leaned forward. "I do care about you, James. You're ... you're a friend...."

"Oh, great. You think you're so damn special." He leaned in towards her now. They were one foot apart. "You're just another fucking twit. Game playing, head fucking twit. Billy knows that now, too. So don't think for a minute that he's going to take you back. I'll bet you anything he won't. You'll be all alone, Brenda. And that's what you fucking deserve." And then he left.

—m—

Brenda jumps up from the rocker, remembering the hot water she put on for the tea. She tiptoes out of the room, down the hall, and into the kitchen. As she pours the hot water into a cup, she begins to cry. Not a sob, not a wail, but a gushing of water from her eyes. Maybe she is selfish. Maybe she is a twit. Maybe Billy never will take her back again.

Step up. That's what Grandma said. Step up.

A voice inside her head says, *do you really want him?* For some reason, she had not considered this. She pulls the tea bag out of the cup and adds her honey and a little milk. *Do you really want him?* Billy could also be very selfish. He raced dirt bikes at the risk of injury or death. He jumped out of airplanes, tumbled off of trestles on a cord, enlisted knowing he might very well fight, maybe die in a war. The truth is, Billy has done everything he wanted to do mindless of perhaps leaving a wife and child behind. Suddenly she's hot. She feels like she cannot breathe. She places the cup of tea down and heads for the sliding door. Tired. So tired, but propelled forward now, out into the night, darker now, as a large cumulus cloud passes over the moon. With no flashlight in hand, she descends the steps, walks out into the yard and remembers.

They are looking for Peter.

Her little brother, not so little at six feet tall. Her little brother disappearing into the night to find his family. Kicked out, beaten down by their father, for behaving in what daddy sees as unnatural ways. Peter could shine if he were given half a chance. Their father could send him to a design school where Peter could do what he does best. Instead, he disappears into the night, undercover, slipping away to those bars where those boys can be boys, or girls, or whatever else they want to be. She should have told Billy that Peter might be there. Why didn't she think of it? Because she was thinking about herself.

As she walks over to her small garden, the moon breaks through and she realizes how truly dark the night was only seconds before. She can't believe it. She felt no fear. The truth is, she forgot about her fear of the dark. Brenda looks up and sees the blanket of a new front approaching, ready to swallow the moon into the night.

Like Peter, who has been swallowed. Why are they worried about where he is? Something has happened. Their father has finally succeeded in pushing Peter so far away that he has disappeared.

She bends down to feel the shape of the young green beans, long, but not yet firm. The tomatoes, round and tiny, flesh threatening to burst through the tender skin. She caresses the textured flesh of the baby cantaloupe, carefully avoiding the spiky leaves of the zucchini. In this way, she sees in the dark. She has found a way to navigate her way in the dark. Reach out and touch, unafraid to feel, with open hands.

Suddenly, she feels a brushing across her back, just as she did earlier in the day, when her grandma told her it was probably an angel. She hesitates for one moment, then she starts to laugh. But she doesn't turn to look around. Her ears strain for footsteps in the grass, or the flutter of wings, or an exhaled breath, something. Still she doesn't turn. Next she feels anger rising. How could she possibly believe in angels? No way do angels exist in this world where loving mothers are carried off into the night, and men and boys are wounded and brutally killed in senseless wars, and people crucified for daring to be different. No way. And even if angels do exist, they wouldn't come to visit her. In the eyes of the church, she's a fallen woman. A selfish, heartless twit. If God does indeed exist, she is forsaken.

Brenda counts to three, stands up and turns. She sees nothing. Turning towards the house, by the light inside, she watches as Jake trots down the deck stairs and heads towards her. He plops down on his haunches, leaning into her, looking up. When his ears perk up and he begins to look around, a small sense of panic rises. The dog moves off slowly, muzzle in the grass, a whine or two escaping.

Is there something or someone really here?

Brenda strains in the dark to see around her. Should she lift her hands and feel her way? In the old days, even yesterday, she would run into the house and lock the door. But today presents a new day of nothing to lose. There exists no one left to protect her. Daddy, Billy, James. They are all gone. She remains left alone to protect her child and herself. And she will.

Brenda speaks, "Is there someone here? Damn it, is there someone here?"

She steps forward into the darkness, reaching out with her hands, and walks the entire perimeter of the house. Jake does the same, ears alert, tail wagging, until suddenly he takes off into a field to the right side of the house.

"Jake! Come back here! Jake!"

Brenda runs after him, not so much to catch him, but to see what he will find. The long edge of a new storm front has obscured the light of the moon and every star. She can see forms in the darkness, but they are void of features. Running with her arms outstretched, she realizes that for the first time since she ran into the corn looking for the safe house, she is running towards something, not away. Her feet sink slightly into the tilled earth, and occasionally she slips and slides, following the bobbing back of the dog as he navigates his way.

Around an occasional tree they go, skirting around or hopping over rocks. Rocks. The field. The one where her mother was found, her torso curved into the letter q. No. Maybe Peter lies here now. Maybe this spot stands as the unofficial family burial site. Bodies found lying on the hard unforgiving ground, the spirits hanging in the trees like cobwebs.

Lily. Lily. She left her Sweet Pea alone at home.

"Jake! Stop!"

The dog stops at an old pear tree and barks up into the gnarled branches where at one time sweet white fruit used to grow. His tail wags as he alternates between sitting on his haunches and pressing his chest to the earth and his hind end up to the sky. Brenda, breathless, standing beside him strains to see up into the branches, her heart pounding. She sees nothing, but the darker forked wood against the dark night sky.

Brenda kneels beside the dog, and taking his handsome head between her hands looks him in the eyes. "Stop now. Stop! You come home. Come!" She stands and turns and suddenly loses her bearings. Which way is home? Panic does begin to rise, but unlike the old days when she would let it take her over, she begins to breathe deeply, calmly, telling herself she can find her way.

Across the cemetery of her ancestors, or so it seems. She does not see Peter lying on the ground. She feels no ghosts. And she certainly doesn't see an angel. The damn dog, however, stops again, alternating little sniffs and cries, and he begins to dig, moist clumps of earth shooting up. Then he steps back and barks.

Brenda moves over to the freshly dug hole and for the first time tonight sees white. A cluster of pebbles? Maybe teeth. Or marbles left from another time. She slowly moves her hand into the shallow hole and with her fingers plucks up a few and brings them up before her eyes.

Pearls.

Lily.

Slamming the emotion down, she bends to empty the hole, place the pearls into the pocket of her shorts, and stick her fingers into the hollow one last time, to find one final object. The gold clasp that secured the circle of pearls around a neck. Slam the emotion down. She must get back to her daughter. She stands and turns, heading into the direction she knows points home.

By this time, her eyes have gotten accustomed to the dark. She moves smoothly around the trees and rocks, no longer needing to reach out with her hands. Breaking into a trot, Jake beside her, she begins to feel a fearlessness that she has experienced only in her dreams. She sees the lights in the house ahead and even from here, hears the distant ring of a telephone. Her trot turns into a sprint as she enters the yard, the pearls and the clasp jiggling in her pocket with a life of their own. Up the stairs, into the house, she grabs the ringing phone off the counter.

"Hello?" She can barely speak with her breathlessness.

Uncle Sam says, “Are you okay?”

Brenda turns to see Lily Rose clutching her stuffed kitty standing in the doorway rubbing half-closed, sleepy eyes. She walks over and scoops her up into her left arm. “Hey, Uncle Sam. I was out jogging.”

“At this time of night?”

“Jake took off into the fields. I went after him.” Brenda kisses Lily Rose on the cheek and squeezes her tighter. “Did you find my brother?”

“I was hoping he turned up there.”

“No. He hasn’t.”

“Well, we’re almost to Three Rivers. Had to stop so Billy could take a leak.”

“You’re going to the bars?”

“Yeah. It’s going to be interesting to see how your dad handles that.”

“For sure.”

Lily Rose says, “Mommy, I had a bad dream.”

“You can tell me about it in a minute, Sweet Pea.”

Sam asks, “Is the baby up?”

“Yes, she is. Uncle Sam, why are you looking for him? He’s my brother. I have a right to know.”

“It’s one a.m. We don’t know where he is.”

“It’s not unusual for him to be out into the wee hours.”

“Some kid had his car.”

“That’s what Billy said.”

“And we found a couple of interesting things in the trunk.”

“What kind of things?”

“Trouble, Brenda. We’ve got to find your brother so we know what the hell is going on.”

“What was in the trunk, Uncle Sam?”

“Try not to worry.”

“Tell me!”

“Some ... porno and some marijuana.”

“Really?”

"We'll call you as soon as we find him."

"You know where the bars are?"

"In Old Town. Bars? You said that before. Is there more than one?"

"Yeah. There's The Stud. But he sometimes goes to a hole in the wall named Eddie's or something like that. It's a block or two away."

"Get some sleep."

"Yeah, right. This family is so unlucky."

"Now don't go thinking that."

"Did Grandma tell you about the painting falling off the wall?"

"What painting?"

"It's a sign."

"A sign? That sounds like her."

"A sign of death."

There is a pause. "Not every picture that falls off a wall is a sign."

"You don't believe it?"

"Everything is going to be fine."

"Uncle Sam, how is Billy, really?"

"He's not good, kiddo, he's not good. But, he'll make it. If Peter shows up, keep him there."

"Of course."

Brenda scoops Lily back up and heads for her bed, kicks off her shoes, and lies down with the child beside her. They cuddle together as Jake jumps up on the foot with muddy paws. "Jake!" But the dog places his head down between his front paws, and Brenda, too tired to fight, relents.

"I'm sorry I left you alone, Sweet Pea."

"Where's Uncle James?"

"He left. He won't be living with us anymore."

"Oh, goodie." Lily snuggles deeper underneath her mommy's arm. "Does that mean that Daddy is going to live here again?"

"No. No, it doesn't. I don't know what's going to happen between your Daddy and me yet."

"Oh. Mommy, I had a terrible dream."

Brenda brushes the hair from her daughter's eyes. "Tell me about your dream."

Lily becomes animated. "There were these two cars and they crashed. One was driving this way and one was driving this way." Lily illustrates a head-on collision with her little hands. "It made a really loud noise. And the cars went all over, just like in the movies."

"The movies? Where have you seen movies like that?"

Lily looks sheepish. "With Uncle Peter."

"I should have figured that. The car accidents weren't real in the movies or in your dream."

"So, nothing really happened to the people?"

"No. Nothing really happened to the people." She cuddles her child tighter, kisses her on the forehead, and waits for her to fall asleep. Worrying. Worrying. Where is Peter? What will happen to everybody now? Billy, James, her sick Uncle Sam, Peter.

In minutes, Lily Rose falls asleep and Brenda slides her over and covers her with the quilt. She walks back into the kitchen and takes a sip of her long-cold tea. Dropping her hand to open a cabinet door, her arm brushes the cluster of treasures in her pocket. She reaches in delicately, as if the pearls may disintegrate even with the gentlest of touch. One by one she recovers them from their temporary tomb, most single, but occasionally a chain of two or three held together with a string as thin as a gossamer thread. They have been hidden in the earth for years. One final object lies in the bottom crease, the clasp, the gold still yellow, the metal still sturdy, which held the string of pearls in a circle around her mother's neck.

21
Ground Down

Saturday 12:59 a.m.

Martin watches Billy lean over and punch a new station on the radio. Some rock and roll bullshit with screaming guitars and a reverberating bass tone that irritates him down deep into his bowels. What is it with these young people? The next bathroom stop might be for him.

From the corner of his eye he's been watching Billy grow from quiet and composed to a squirming agitation that sets his teeth on edge, on top of his churning bowel. The guy's been chain smoking and adjusting his tall frame in the seat, readjusting, muttering under his breath, and rolling wads of foil into bullets between the thumb and finger of his left hand. For one instant he imagines the tortured young man jumping out of the car like Brenda once did, and rolling across the land, knocking down his adversarial imaginings one by one. They shouldn't have brought him along.

Martin's brother, a lifelong thorn in his side anyway, sits in the back seat muttering, too, the subtle vocal sounds somehow reaching his right ear through the musical cacophony threatening to make him drop a load.

"Jesus, Billy, turn that shit off," he finally says.

Billy starts as if he has forgotten the two men are with him. "Oh, sorry, Martin." The wounded Marine reaches over and with one fluid poke fills the air with some other rock bullshit. Even Sam has ceased with his desperate whispered pleas to God.

Dog spelled backwards. The great cosmic joke. Martin doesn't need a "holy book" to tell him what constitutes right and wrong. Some things are natural and some aren't. Obviously, you do not kill, unless of course someone is trying to kill you, or has killed someone before and needs to be stopped. If he knew who killed Jeanine, who carried her off and tortured her, he would kill that person with his bare hands. He would delight in doing so. Secondly, you do not get friendly with your neighbor's wife, no matter how good looking she might be, and regardless of her dangling cleavage or rounded behind as she bends over. A little nooky on the side isn't worth the untangling. Thirdly, you don't lie if at all possible. It's just too damn hard to keep the chain of deceit straight. And finally, you do not have sex with kids, animals, or someone of your own gender. It's just not right.

Martin wonders where the punk is who took off across the fields, throwing him the finger like he's some big bad man. He has to admit, he has imagined breaking that finger off and shoving it up the kid's ...

Sam pipes up from the back seat, "Did you see that sign?"

"What sign?"

"The one that said Three Rivers the next four exits."

"Jesus Christ, Sammie. I'm not some hick. I've been to this fucking city a few times over the years."

"I was just checking, Marty."

Martin looks up in the rearview mirror and watches as the headlights of passing cars illuminate his brother's face. He sees the pain there. Pain he's seen on this weathered face before.

Martin briefly softens, "Thanks for the reminder, Sammie."

"You know where Old Town is? The bars are in Old Town."

"Bars? I thought you said bar before."

"When I talked to Brenda she mentioned another one."

"How does Brenda know about 'the bars'?"

"Marty, that generation doesn't have the same aversion to homosexuality that you do."

"Oh, balls."

Billy turns to him. "You're a redneck, Martin. Plain and simple."

"I'm a ... what? I am not a redneck. And turn on some fucking country music, will you? I've had it with that rock crap."

Billy and Sam break into laughter that feels like a saw grinding upon Martin's last nerve.

"If you two keep up with that, you're going to be on the outside looking in."

Sam answers, "Shit, Marty, lighten up."

Lighten up. Sure. Not once have they entertained the idea out loud that Petey might be dead. No doubt, they're thinking it just like he is. The boy wasn't folded like an accordion in that trunk, but that doesn't mean he's not lying in a shallow grave or pitched head first into water. Or maybe he is in "the bars" exchanging phone numbers with some muscle-bound guy who talks like someone is stepping on his dick. Jesus, he'd almost prefer to find him in the ground or in the water. Almost.

It's that ... sweet edge that the boy has. Like instead of one daughter, he has two.

Martin glances outside the car windows to look at something besides the uncurling ribbon of the road. The next storm front slowly, but surely, rolls in, extinguishing the light of every star. Most of the houses lining either side of the street are also dark, the families inside tucked securely in their beds, where he should be, lying beneath a downy quilt, his real life reeling inside his booze-soaked head.

—∾—

One Sunday afternoon when Petey was maybe eight or nine, he came running out of the house with a drawing in his hand. Martin was sitting in a chaise lounge in the shade, nursing a VO and water, and reading the sports page of the Sunday *Gazette*. Petey proudly held out his drawing for Martin to see, and there it was, colorful penciled sketches of men and women wearing things that Martin had never seen before.

Jeanine walked out of the house with a plate of snacks and placed them next to Martin on a small wooden table.

"Aren't those costumes amazing?" she asked.

"Is that what they are?"

Meanwhile, little Petey was squirming and jumping up and down, throwing out his hands in tiny bird-like moves. His face was lit up, and his smile, even Martin had to admit, was what people might describe as "cherubic." A word Martin would never use, but it did come to mind. Cherubic. Jesus.

"What are you drawing those for?"

"I like to," Petey said.

"Why don't you draw cowboys or soldiers or dogs or something like that?"

"I like to draw these."

"Martin," Jeanine said, "These drawings are really good."

"Oh, yeah?"

"His teacher said so."

"Well, what do you know?" Martin handed the drawing to Jeanine, as Petey began to crawl up into his lap.

"Hey, what are you doing there?"

"I want to hug you, Daddy."

Martin gave him a tentative squeeze as he picked his newspaper back up with one hand. The boy clung to him, resting his little head on his chest, his legs falling easily into the ravine between his own. Martin felt divided. One part of him wanted to stroke his boy's bony back, and the other wanted to cast him to the side. He loved his boy, but a boy needs discipline. He needs to learn when young that the world rules brutally, and somehow, someway, he must manage to carry himself strong and tall. The world is no place for wimps. Life will grind you down into dust and blow you away in a single puff.

"Now, come on, Son. Your dad wants to read the newspaper."

Reluctantly, the boy crawled back off of him and ran into the house.

Jeanine said, "It's not wrong to show that boy a little tenderness."

"I'll leave that up to you, dear. You're so darn good at it."

—∞—

Here they are riding down the streets where the only lights are those of the street lamps casting long triangular shadows. All those lucky people safe inside their houses dreaming.

"Turn left here, Marty," Sam said. "It's a shortcut. I use it when

I need to pick up carpentry supplies at a little shop up here."

Martin turns left.

Memory isn't done with him yet. He doesn't want to go there. No. He doesn't want to go.

"Right here, Marty."

Martin turns right.

Martin fights to imagine himself inside his bed, under the quilt, where all remains safe and fine. But images of another kind continue to bubble up. Martin turns his attention to the radio and some new country singer whose voice he recognizes but whose name escapes him. He's singing about his broken heart. Yeah, yeah, yeah. That's all they ever sing about. And still the images bubble up to haunt him. He tries to push them back, he tries, but in the end they win.

Martin's dad bought him the small black and white calf when he was eight. The calf was all pink nose and pink tongue, which were in constant interplay. It was Martin's job to feed the motherless, helpless animal with a bottle and make sure there was enough clean yellow straw lining its pen. Martin named the little creature Obie, even though his father told him he should not name the calf. He watched it grow from little calf to steer, and the animal and the boy grew attached, though his father warned him not to. Martin scratched his ears and pet his sides, and Obie followed him out into the fields and came to him when he called. He brought him special treats and even bathed him after a rain when Obie splashed through puddles and rolled from side to side in the mud. Martin won a blue ribbon for Obie at the Willis fair, and hung it proudly on the wood of his best friend's pen.

The day came when Obie was taken away and brought back in pieces, and even now Martin can't stand to think of it. He had cried and begged his father to let him keep Obie as a pet. But times were hard for the family and they needed the meat that Obie provided. His father sat him down and explained to him that this was the way of the world. He told Martin from the beginning that this was the way it would be. This was the cycle of life, Son, the cycle of life.

Martin swears that Obie knew where he was going. When they loaded the animal onto the truck he watched the boy with one eye. That eye was pleading, Martin swore.

The boy began to scream and shout until his father made his mother take him away into the house. Martin felt then as if he had let his friend down, and to this day he feels the same, though he would admit that fact to no one.

Several months later, his father took him over to the Johnsons' place. Ralph Johnson butchered for all the local farmers, and Samuel Becker expected his son to watch. The first time Martin watched as a pig was hit over the head with a mallet and its throat slit from ear to ear with one swipe of a blade. The blood began to pour out and the boy ran from the room and threw up his breakfast of oatmeal and orange juice into the green grass. Again it was the eyes. The eyes that went wild with fear when the animal sensed impending death. And the pig fought for its life. He or she squirmed and squealed, fighting to escape, twisting and turning this way and that to avoid the hands that would hold it down. Martin felt the fear. He felt it. He couldn't stand that feeling and, even now, he would do anything rather than feel that fear again. It was primordial, watching the animal fight for its life, unleashing some memory maybe thousands of years old, of when Martin, then another man from another land, fought for his own life, now somewhere in his genes. Cellular memory. Tangible fear. Survival of the fittest.

After that came the witnessing of other butchery, all bloody, all violent, always the eyes wild with fear. But he learned to harden his heart. He learned to avoid looking in the eyes. He learned to poke fun at the situations rather than allow himself to feel. Never again did he have another pet. Never again did he reach out to scratch the ears of an animal or pet the velvet of their sides. But neither did he become a farmer.

—ɯ—

"You can start looking for a parking place, bro," Sam says, breaking Martin's fall into the past.

"Where is the joint?" Martin asks.

Billy speaks up. "You said the name of the place is The Stud, right?" He points to a small building built of red brick one block down. "It's right there."

From here, Martin can see a few men milling around outside the bar. His stomach drops. Jesus Christ. He's going to have to walk into a scene full of queers. Already his skin begins to crawl, his heart pounds, and beads of perspiration begin to fall. He prepares to parallel park, years of experience sliding his boat of a Lincoln into a tight squeeze. He completes the mission, shuts the engine off, and the three men turn and look at each other.

Martin says, "So, who's going in?"

"I'm going in," Billy answers.

"I'll go in, too, if you don't want to go, Marty," Sam adds.

"No, I'm going."

"Well, keep a cool tool."

"I'll keep cool."

Martin and Billy climb out of the Lincoln and head over to The Stud. Martin notices that Billy walks now with a more pronounced limp. In fact, with every step, Martin can see a wince on Billy's face, even though his jaw clenches against it.

"Are you okay, Bill?"

"Don't worry about me, Martin. Let's just keep focused on the task at hand," Billy says.

"Let's just hope he's here."

The handful of men standing outside the bar are smoking cigarettes, talking and laughing, and touching each other periodically. Martin watches as one tall guy wearing leather pants grabs the hand of another. And two lean against the red brick wall, standing inseparable with their arms around each other's waists. As the two men approach, all eyes turn to Billy, and Martin watches the men blatantly take in Billy's handsome form from head to toe. Billy doesn't flinch, simply nodding to them as he climbs the four stairs into the establishment with a jaw of iron, not a wince visible. The men have the audacity to turn and watch Billy from the rear, then break into frenzied whispers. They don't give Martin as much as a glance, and although this ignorance is desired, some part of him feels a twinge of hurt. He can barely believe it himself. But, he, too, was once tall and handsome, and the ignorance reminds him of his receding hairline and growing gut. He passes up the stairs and into the bar barely noticed.

By this time, it's after one o'clock, and the inside of the bar reflects the early hour. The music blasts, making Martin's ears vibrate, and the neon signs look dreamy through the cigarette smoke. In the center of the room, a glittering disco ball shimmers as it slowly revolves on a wire. Under the ball, a few men are bumping and grinding, periodically emitting shrill little laughs. Standing around long-legged metal tables are mostly men, but much to Martin's surprise, an occasional woman. Maybe a woman. A couple certainly are. As with the outside, all eyes turn to Billy, and Martin feels invisible again.

They walk up to the old wooden bar, where the bartender stands, resting his ass against a cooler. He wears a pair of jeans and two black leather armbands around bulging muscles. His hair is pulled back into a ponytail and Martin swears he's wearing lipstick. Billy has to shout above the din. Martin assumes he's going to ask about Peter, but instead he orders a Jack and coke. Billy leans in towards Martin and shouts, "You want something to drink?"

Martin shakes his head. He turns from the bar and takes in every person in the room, one by one, hoping, sort of, that Petey is one of them.

Billy turns with his drink in hand and joins Martin in his glance around the room.

An effeminate blonde boy sitting on a stool next to where Billy stands nudges Billy's arm and beckons for him to lean down so he can speak into his ear. Martin has no idea what Billy retorts, but the boy instantly recoils, turns, and goes back to his business of drinking.

Billy leans in towards Martin and shouts, "I don't see him."

Martin shouts back, nodding towards the bartender, "Ask him if he's seen him."

Billy sucks up a third of his drink through a straw then leans in towards the bartender. Martin can't stand the way the bartender acts all flirty with his son-in-law. The juxtaposition of his feminine face with those bulging muscles makes Martin nauseous. He feels like he's in a nightmare and he wants to wake up. Now there's a switch. Usually he can't wait to go to sleep.

Billy leans in towards Martin again and shouts, "He says he hasn't seen him. I don't believe him. I think he thinks we're cops."

"Great," Martin shouts back. But he has to acknowledge the relief that runs through him. Billy doesn't believe that Petey lies dead somewhere. He believes he might have been here.

Martin turns back to the room and gets the shock of his life. The face looking back at him also startles. Standing before him is the loan officer from Willis Bank, John Henderson, still decked out in his conservative suit. John breaks into a little smile, and then shouts at Martin.

"Martin! I didn't know you came here."

Martin shouts back, "Don't be ridiculous!"

"Then why are you here?"

"We're looking for someone."

"Your son, by chance?"

"Well, yes. Have you seen him?"

"The tall boy with the dark curls and lovely ass?"

Martin grabs him roughly by his suit lapels, bringing his face within an inch of his own. "If you touch my son, I'll kill you."

"Not a chance. I like the bottom, too."

"What the fuck is that supposed to mean?"

Billy interrupts, shouting into Martin's ear, "Let him go, Martin. We don't need any trouble."

Martin releases John's lapels. John, fairly inebriated, sways over towards Billy. "I could suck you off for that."

Billy says, "Save it."

Martin says, “Does everyone at the bank know you hang out here?”

“I’ll just tell them you were here, too.”

Billy says, “Have you seen Peter Becker here tonight or not?”

“I’ve seen him.”

Martin adds, “How long ago?”

“Oh, a half hour or so. He was with Eddie.”

Billy asks, “Who the fuck is Eddie?”

“He owns the bar down the way.” He leans in real close to Martin. “He wants to turn your son into his love slave.”

Martin steps forward to accost John again, but Billy stops him with one muscled arm.

Billy says, “Cool it.” He nods to John, then says to Martin, “Let’s go.” He turns to place his empty glass on the bar and leads the way back through the tangled throng. All eyes turn again to watch the golden boy step out into the night. The invisible man follows.

22
Drive

Saturday 1:42 a.m.

Not only is he a member of the family now, but he's being escorted around by a local celebrity. Eddie, the man who owns the bar, walks up to him in The Stud and asks if he can buy him a drink. Two drinks later they're sitting in the back room of Eddie's bar. The walls of the room are paneled in some dark wood and on top of the cement floor lies an Oriental rug, brightly colored in deep reds, blues, and greens. Peter leans forward and brushes his fingers across the velvet of the carpet. A long, heavy-looking wood desk sucks up one half of the room with the two cushy chairs, one of which he's sitting in, and a lamp, balancing out the other.

Peter slumps down into his chair while Eddie ceaselessly paces, asking him questions about his likes and dislikes, his family dynamic, and his plans for the future. Peter doesn't know why, but the guy has really taken an interest in him. Eddie, an older guy, dresses in jeans and a Polo shirt. He wears his dark hair slicked back and occasionally puffs on a fat cigar. Peter doesn't know if the man has a nervous tick or what, but he brushes his hand over his crotch every few minutes or so. Does Eddie want to fuck him? He wants something.

"Did you drive here from Willis?" he asks.

"Ah, no. I hitched a ride. Actually, I'm looking for someone."

"Who's that?"

"A kid named Todd. Do you know him?"

Eddie stops his pacing, crosses his left arm over his chest and puffs on his cigar with his right. "Why are you looking for him?"

"He took my car. I've got to get it back before my father finds out."

"It's your father's car?"

"No. But, it might as well be."

Eddie takes a step closer to him, bends over and touches the ridge above Peter's left eye. Peter flinches, not only because of the pain, but because he never anticipated the touch, gentle-like for such a beefy man.

"Where'd you get the shiner?"

"From the Christian."

"The Christian?"

—m—

So there he was, sitting in some nondescript Ford with a revolver pointed at him. He didn't feel scared, mostly because the revolver was completely unsteady, strangely animated through John's shaking hand.

"So, what are you going to do?" he asked. "Shoot me because I'm gay?"

The whole situation seemed ludicrous. John's head moving back and forth between the windshield, looking out on the road to drive, and him sitting to his right. John reminded him of one of those toys, whose head bobs and bounces loosely on a stationary body.

"I might. I might. Jesus would certainly understand."

"You sure about that?"

As John began to pull off onto the shoulder of the road, Peter grabbed the revolver from his hand. John gave up the wheel and began to strike out at Peter wildly with both fists. Holding the revolver in his right, Peter used his left to ward off the blows. He caught a good one in his left eye before he realized he could use the revolver himself. As the car rolled to a stop, a car coming up from the rear blasted its horn, further agitating the Christian. Peter held the gun steady, pointing the cold heavy metal straight at him.

"Stop it!" Peter screamed. "Fucking stop it!"

John held both his hands up in the air, his eyes as wide and round as the moon. "Don't shoot me, please. Please, don't shoot me," John pleaded.

"I'm not going to fucking shoot you." Peter rolled the window down and threw the gun into the night. He turned back to John. "I need to get to Three Rivers real bad. Just drive me there, please. I'm not going to touch you. You're not nuts about queers, and I'm not nuts about Christians. We're even. So get over it and drive the car."

"Drive," Peter said again. And John did.

—∾—

Finally, Eddie sits down in a chair opposite Peter with his legs wide, and continues to puff away on what is now a brown stub. An old joke runs through Peter's head. Hey, you remind me of a movie star. Oh, yeah? Who? Lassie, taking a shit.

Eddie says, "You know, it's not just Christians who think that homosexuality is aberrant. Other religions adhere to the same principle."

"Yeah, I know." What does this guy want? By this time, slumping down into this comfortable chair, Peter feels like he could nod off. The day has been long, so long. But one throbbing need persists.

"So you don't know where your car is?"

"No. Todd took off in it."

"Where were you?"

Writhing on the ground in pain, Peter thinks. But, he says, "I guess he thought it would be funny."

"You were ... just hanging out with Todd?"

Todd just fucked me real hard, he thinks. But he says, "We were just hanging out by the creek."

"Sometimes Todd is a little too mischievous for his own good."

Peter sits up straight in the chair. "So you do know him. Where is he? Where is the car?"

"Todd's around. We don't know where your car is."

"What do you mean *we* don't know where my car is?"

"Todd left it in Willis." Eddie places the butt in an ashtray and stands back up. "I want to talk to you about something else."

Here it comes, Peter thinks.

"I make movies and I'm looking for new talent."

"Oh, so you're him."

"Him, who?"

"The guy who makes the movies. Todd told me about you."

Eddie grabs a box of Marlboro reds from his desk and holds it out to Peter. "Care for a cancer stick?"

Peter hesitates, but then reaches forward and pulls out a cigarette. He's tried smoking only a few times. But right now his heart pounds and he's getting hard.

"You're not ashamed of your homosexuality, are you?"

"N... no," Peter answers. That's not completely true.

"All you have to do is follow directions." Eddie leans over Peter and lights his cigarette with a square silver lighter, an American eagle embossed on the side.

Peter takes a puff and immediately coughs.

Eddie laughs. "Nobody needs to know except me and you."

"Oh, and everybody else involved with the movie."

"We're like a family. Everybody involved is very discreet."

Peter takes another puff. This time he doesn't cough.

"Look, Peter. You have fun, you make some money. It's a win-win situation for everyone."

This could be a way out, Peter thinks.

"Can you follow direction, Peter?"

"Does that mean I'm a slave?"

Eddie laughs again. "Not a slave. You're an adult. You can say 'yes' or 'no' to everything."

"How ... how much money?"

"Enough for you to live on your own. Maybe it's time to say goodbye to Daddy."

Say goodbye to Daddy. Peter's been dreaming about that for years. To be out from under the roof where all he ever feels is shame. Not just shame, but also guilt for never being the person that his father wants him to be. Shame. Guilt. Self-loathing. God, he's tired of the self-loathing. He's never dreamed about being in porn, but maybe he can meet some people involved with the big shows. Broadway. Maybe he will get the chance to design his costumes after all.

"I can follow direction," he says.

"Let's see."

—∞—

That was his father ten years ago, trying to bond with him after the murder of his mother.

"I'm going to teach you how to trim the trees and prepare the lawn for winter. Don't worry. I'm going to tell you exactly how to do it."

And he did. He and his father worked side by side and for moments Peter felt like they actually were related. Peter, however, made one fatal mistake. While he was trimming the branches of a crabapple tree, and his father was bending over, picking up the pieces and placing them into a barrel, Peter asked, "Do you miss Mom?'

His father stopped what he was doing, stood up slowly and said, "Now what do you think, Son?"

"I guess we all miss her."

"That's right. We all miss her. Now let's leave it alone." His father bent back over to retrieve a fallen branch, the smell of the severed wood pungent.

Peter felt compelled to ask one more question. "Don't you want to know who murdered her? I want to know who did that to her."

Slowly his father bent back up. "Of course I want to know who ... killed her. What do you want me to do, join the police force and lead the way?"

"No, I ..."

"And look at what you're doing." His father stepped over towards him, grabbed the trimming shears out of his hand, and butted him to the side with his left hip. "I told you exactly how to do it. You don't have to be afraid to cut it all the way back to here. Can't you do anything right? You're useless, Petey. Sometimes you're absolutely useless. Go draw your pictures or something." With a wave of his hand his father dismissed him.

—ɱ—

"Get on your hands and knees and crawl over here," Eddie commands.

Peter leans forward and falls out of the chair onto his knees and begins to crawl across the velvety carpet. When he reaches Eddie, he looks up to see the older man looking down with a little smile, almost a sneer on his craggy but handsome face. The ghost of acne and a deep scar near his left eye makes him look like a gangster.

"Unzip my pants."

Peter lifts up his torso, balancing on his knees, and reaches up with his left hand to grab the waist line of Eddie's pants, undoes the button there, and with his right pulls the zipper down. Peter feels more excited than he ever has before. He pulls the pants open and can see the bulge of Eddie's genitals through his white Fruit of the Loom underwear.

"So far so good," the gangster says. "Now let's see what else you can do."

Five minutes go by, then ten, and he does everything Eddie tells him to do; even though he gags at times, he does not stop, he cannot stop, his will held hostage in the gangster's hands.

At this point, through Eddie's grunts and groans, Peter hears muffled voices just outside the door. The gangster pulls away from Peter's mouth, as the door bursts open. Peter looks up to see his father and his brother-in-law, Billy, standing in the doorway. Peter quickly wipes his mouth as Eddie turns.

Eddie says, "What the fuck?"

Before Eddie can even get his genitals back into his pants, his father bounds across the short distance, grabs Eddie by the shirt collar and throws him back down upon the desk. A container of pens and pencils, papers, dust collectors of different kinds all go flying into the four directions.

Peter falls back onto his ass and watches as Billy throws his cane to the side and crosses over the short distance to pull his father off of Eddie.

"Martin!" Billy shouts. "Stop it!" and pushes his father to the side.

His father looks at Peter and commands, "Get out of this room."

Peter says, "No."

His father takes a step closer. "I said, get out of this room."

Peter stands up. "No."

Billy looks at his father and says, "Close the door."

As Peter's father reaches the door, Todd steps into the doorway, takes one look at the scene and turns to flee. But his father reaches out, grabs the black- and white-haired kid by the tee, and pulls him into the room, kicking the door closed behind him.

"You fucking little punk. I ought to ..."

"Martin!" Billy screams. He looks from Eddie to Todd and says, "I've seen you two before."

His father screams, "It's him! The punk who had Petey's car."

Todd turns to flee again when Billy reaches out, grabs him, and tosses him into one of the cushy chairs. "Stay put, you little fucker."

Eddie pushes up off of the desk, stands and turns. "What the fuck do you two think you're doing?"

Peter's father moves towards him. "I'll kill you. I'll kill you."

Billy holds up his hand. "Stop! Pete, sit down in the chair." He turns to Eddie. "I think we have something of yours."

His father says, "What the fuck?"

"I saw them, Martin. At the 7-Eleven."

"Why didn't I see them?"

"You were in deep debate with your brother, that's why."

"Petey," his father says. "Tell me you're not involved with these guys."

Billy turns to step towards Peter and sways to the side, an expression of pain contracting his face. Peter jumps up and moves over quickly to pick up Billy's cane. He hands it to Billy. Billy takes the cane out of Peter's hand with a nod of thanks.

Billy asks, “Do you know what was in the trunk of your car? Be honest, Pete.”

Peter answers, “The trunk of my car? What do you mean?”

“That’s what I figured.” He turns to Eddie who has seated himself behind his desk. “We have something of yours.”

His father says, “And you’re not getting it back.”

Finally Eddie speaks up. “I don’t know what you’re talking about.”

Billy says, “You know what we’re fucking talking about. You’re stupid if you think we can’t trace those tapes back to you.”

Eddie grins. “There is nothing on those tapes to identify them as mine.”

Peter’s father says, “No fingerprints? No, nothing?”

Eddie looks at Peter, who feels divided. This man could be the ticket out of his father’s house. But, what are Billy and his father talking about?

Eddie says, “Let’s not forget, they were in your son’s car.”

Billy says, “We don’t have to tell the cops where we found them.”

“Oh,” Eddie says, “You just plucked them out of the air?”

“You leave Peter alone, and we bury the merchandise. That’s the deal,” his father says.

Peter says, “Hey! Who said I want to be left alone?”

Billy turns to him. “You don’t want to be involved with these guys. Believe me.”

“I’m almost twenty one. I can do whatever I want.”

His father turns to him. “Son, I know we don’t see eye to eye, but listen to us.”

Eddie says, “It’s a deal.”

“Wait!” Peter says.

“Kid,” Eddie says to him. “You’ll never follow direction.”

“I did. I did just what you said.”

Billy walks over and puts his arm around his shoulders. “Let’s go, Pete.”

Peter turns to Eddie, who refuses to look him in the eye. He turns to Todd, who sits all comfy in the cushy chair just smiling.

As Peter walks reluctantly out of the room with Billy and his father, he hears Eddie say, "Todd, you're in big trouble, boy."

23
Mushroom Cloud

Saturday 2:51 a.m.

Bagwell steps out of the Lincoln on his left leg and uses his cane to stand. Even the slightest pressure on his right leg now creates a searing pain. But he must walk into the house. He refuses to crawl or accept help from Sam or Martin, who are both more than willing to assist. He could jump up the driveway on one leg like a kid, but even the jarring motion would cause pain that he is now too exhausted to bear.

In the driveway sits a car that he does not recognize. As he approaches from the rear, stepping oh so gingerly, he hears moans and groans. He walks by, glancing into the front seat where he sees his sister, shirtless, entangled in a tight embrace. The man running one hand up and down her back and cupping a breast in the other notices Bagwell and stops. He's the same man who held the door open for them earlier at the café. A man twice as old as Kate and possibly married. Her choice in men has never been that good.

Bagwell says, "You can't find a more comfortable place to do that?"

Kate disentangles and rushes to cover her breasts.

The man says, "We were just saying goodbye."

Bagwell limps on, not just feeling cut in half but severed into quarters. He steps through the back door of the house and the booming voice of a television evangelist dripping with honey and spiked with conviction accosts him. Bagwell stops in the kitchen, opens the refrigerator door, and grabs a carton of milk. He pours himself a tall glass full, replaces the carton and limps on. His mother lies on her back on the sofa fast asleep, her mouth hanging open, one arm dangling over the edge. Bagwell stops long enough to set his glass of milk down and throw an afghan over her lower body. The night is warm, but he knows his mother likes to be covered when she sleeps. Grabbing his glass, he turns the TV off, and moves on towards his own room where a waiting bed sounds like heaven. He stops in the bathroom to wash two, no three, pain pills down with the milk, throws water on his face, and stares into the mirror. Bagwell does not recognize himself anymore. The face looks too tired, too drawn, and too dry from the Arabian Desert, which even after four months continues to leave its mark.

Suddenly, his sister's face appears beside his own, the family resemblance unmistakable, but her face young, firm, fresh, untainted.

"Well, that was embarrassing," she says.

"I didn't see anything, if that's what you're worried about. Isn't that guy married?"

"He's separated."

"The pickings are that slim in this town?"

"Yes, they are."

"Then leave town, Sister. Leave town."

"Where would I go?" Kate turns to walk away, then turns back. "Where have you been?"

"You wouldn't believe me if I told you."

"With Brenda?"

"No, not with her."

"Did you see her?"

"I don't want to talk about her, Kate."

"Are you okay?"

"Sure," he says, fighting to keep composure. "I'm great."

"You're not great." Kate sits down on the edge of the tub. "Is that leg hurting you?"

"Yeah. Want to grab an axe and cut it off?"

"That's not funny."

"I wasn't trying to be funny." He squeezes toothpaste onto a brush and begins to brush his teeth.

"Joe Bailey wants you back working with him, you know."

Bagwell spits into the bowl. "How the hell am I supposed to

climb up on a roof with this leg?" He rinses.

"You can supervise."

"There's too many things I won't be able to do."

"Then what are you going to do?"

"I don't know."

Kate stands back up and talks to Bagwell in the mirror. "I've never seen you let anything get you down. Why are you letting this get to ya?"

Billy slowly shakes his head from side to side and stares at her.

"You're not there anymore," Kate says.

Bagwell turns from the mirror and speaks directly to his sister, "Oh, I'm still there. You better believe I'm still there." He places the toothpaste and the brush back into the cabinet, and then turns to head out of the room. "I've got to lie down before I fall down. I'll see you in the morning."

"Sweet dreams, Billy."

"Yeah."

He slowly makes his way into his bedroom, rests the cane against the nightstand, and falls onto his back on top of the bed. The explosions begin as soon as he closes his eyes. He shoots them back open. Goddamn it. Not tonight. Closing his eyes again, he mutters a prayer, and then remembers that he no longer believes in God. No God would allow fighter jets to turn people and property alike into charcoal. Children, too. He saw them, the people in their cars trying to escape before the destruction came. No God would allow hospitals to be leveled when a rocket went off target, or let much-needed oil burn off into the night, creating a dense and filthy rain of black. Or give questionable drugs to allegiant Marines and soldiers. Or send them off into hell with faulty masks, broken radios, and a list of commands that change every day. Waiting and waiting.

He closes his eyes again.

The explosions pound down upon him like fists, knocking him first this way, then that. He rolls out of the bed onto the carpet, pulling a comforter off behind him. Spreading the blue comforter onto the floor, he rolls on top of it, reaches up and pulls two pillows off the bed, then places one under this head and covers his face with the other, which he holds in place with one hand.

Please, stop, please.

Pain pills. Kick in. Three should knock him out. A collage of images begins to wash over him. The smiling face of Lily Rose. The beautiful long dark wavy hair of his former wife. James' brown strong hand in a clasp with his own. Martha bending over in her garden, cutting flowers. His mom holding up a square glass container of lasagna. Kate patiently painting her long perfect nails. Peter on his knees wiping his face with the bottom of his shirt. Martin frowning behind the wheel of his Lincoln. Sam lying in a hospital bed, connected to tubes. His dad ... his dad ... standing proudly in his dress blues. Brenda in a nightie, curled in a ball. Glover staring up at the stars just before ... just before ... he died. All Bagwell's ever known or wanted moving up into the sky in a mushroom cloud.

—m—

He's walking alone across a barren field with an AK-47 in his hands. His steps are careful and calculated, for underneath this crusty lid of earth lies hidden land mines. The air, cold and crisp, lovingly receives his warm expired breath. The sun, veiled behind a thick gray fog, dimly sparkles off the small crystals clinging to the low-lying shrub. No other human can be seen, but somewhere they are there, his enemies hunting him as he hunts them.

He inhales sharply when over by a good-sized rock he spies the skeleton of Jeanine Becker. The bones are half fallen into dust, but in one clawed hand is a crumpled four-by-six photo of the children she adored. An apparition kneels down beside her. The fog dances through this suggestion of a form that turns to wave to Bagwell as he passes. Martin, when he had a head of hair and twenty-five pounds less of whiskey and turkey jerky on his frame.

Anger flares when much to his dismay he spies, from the corner of his eye, the shifting light of a television perched up upon a flat-topped rock. He reaches the screen in time to see the goose-stepped marching of Nazi soldiers urged on by cheering masses. The locust invasion of boats landing on the shores of Normandy during the Second World War. As the men depart, they fall, drowning in the shallow water before their body of blood can run out. The blue choppy water, where bodies bob, turns into the dense green jungle of Vietnam. American soldiers dangle from branches with severed genitals in their mouths, as old Vietnamese men, women, and children are ushered into ground holes like corralled cattle awaiting slaughter. Boys of every color running through lush green fields with plastic guns in their hands, their faces camouflaged with the charcoal from the blackened bodies of the Iraqis who did not escape intact from the Arabian Desert. The screen shifts to a line of religious leaders chanting in time, "Thou shalt not kill. Thou shalt not kill. Thou shalt not kill." Behind them stands a line of political leaders holding up play cards that read: "The few. The proud."

From the corner of his eye, Bagwell catches movement appearing and disappearing in the fog. He feels drawn behind the figure like a magnet, stepping gently but swiftly through this barren land of hidden explosions. Suddenly, his assault rifle transforms into a musket and the fringe on his jacket and his pants dances in taps upon his body. He catches up upon the figure who hesitates and turns long enough for Bagwell to recognize him. James. Dressed in a loincloth with glistening long black hair, a tomahawk held firmly in his right hand. Bagwell raises his musket and fires as James ducks and disappears deeper into the shroud of fog.

Suddenly, Lily Rose runs towards him with outstretched hands begging for a lift. She disappears. From his right comes Lily Rose running towards him once again. She disappears. Then from his left. Then from behind. He's sweating. God, he's sweating even in this cold. The last thing in the world he wants to see is his daughter raining down upon him. He begins to hyperventilate, peering into the fog, like searching into the sandstorm of the desert for his Peanut.

Instead he spies James sans loincloth, his tight-muscled buttocks pumping away in a woman bent forward over a rock. Brenda. He can tell by her long, dark, wavy hair cascading gently over her face. James grabs her hair with one hand sweeping it into a tail, and talks dirty, oh, he talks dirty, as she moans and groans and comes.

Billy now bends down before his M40A1 sniper rifle with Glover by his side. His partner whispers the parameters as Billy sets the crosshairs and hovers his finger over the trigger. One shot, one kill. One shot, one kill. One shot, two kills. He fires.

Once again he's running behind James Tillman through the mine field around rocks, leaping over dry creek beds, rustling through patches of damp, dead grass. There's no time to raise the musket, load, and fire, so he tosses it to the side. He looks up just in time to see James turn. His enemy aims and throws his tomahawk, and Bagwell watches the weapon turn blade over handle, blade over handle to miss him by inches before the weapon strikes into the carcass of a tree. The tree, old and bloodless, crumples where the blade embeds. The tomahawk falls heavily to the ground.

Again they are running. Their paths are more erratic now, setting off explosions that rock the earth, and sway the desolate landscape. After what seems like hours, James turns and smiles, confident with his lead. Bagwell watches as the right moccasin steps down and James transforms in seconds from solid to a rain of colorful confetti, not red and bloody, but like an explosion of color, every shade in the spectrum, spraying out and raining down, evaporating before it hits the earth. In the end, nothing remains except a trail of bloody footprints that continue past where James just was, leading into the distance. Bagwell follows.

In the sky, circling in and out of the gray soup, are the vultures marking some shallow grave. He moves towards the spot, heart pounding, sweat breaking, breath erratic and thin. Who can it be? Closer and closer he moves up a hill over a crest and peers down below into a crevice. There lies a pile of charred body parts, a thin ribbon of smoke rising, the stench so ripe and sour that he has to cover his nose and wipe his eyes of tears. He stands over the fetid mess searching for clues, and he finds them. Half falling out of one curled hand is the lighter Brenda gave him with "My heart is yours" still visibly engraved on the side. A few long strands of dark, wavy hair are attached to what once was a skull, now matted to the tan earth. Enmeshed into the charcoal of a smaller frame are the remnants of a bear that Lily Rose once called Growlie. Bagwell shakes his head slowly from side to side until the increased speed of the motion threatens him with whiplash. He tips his head back and opens his mouth into a long deep wail.

—∞—

"Billy, Billy," he hears as he is softly shaken. He opens his eyes to see his mother kneeling on the floor beside him, worry and concern contracting her face. "It was just a dream," she says as she gently strokes his brow.

Bagwell rolls away from her over onto his side. "I'm okay," he tells her.

Placing her hand on his side she asks, "What are you doing sleeping on the floor?"

"This is how it was over there," he answers, as the last fleeting images of his nightmare silently disperse.

"What do you mean?"

"We slept on hard surfaces."

"Well, you don't have to now."

He wants to tell her to leave him alone, but he can't hurt her.

"You were having a nightmare."

"Yes, Mother, that's right."

She pulls on his side to turn him. "Look at me."

"No. Leave me alone." There, he said it.

"I will not. Reverend Johnson says ..."

"Don't tell me about what some reverend says."

"You've hardened your heart."

"I didn't harden my heart. It was hardened for me."

"Aren't you supposed to take that brace off your leg at night?"

"I was too tired." Billy feels like he's going to fall back into the nightmare at any moment.

"Let's get you into bed."

"Will you leave me alone then?"

"Yes, if that's what you want."

He lifts his torso, which feels like a thousand pounds, throws his arms over the edge of the bed and begins to pull. His mother pulls, too, and soon he is lying on his back. He fades out for a moment, then recovers to see her undoing the buckles on his brace. A loud moan escapes as she lifts the inflamed leg free.

"I'm sorry," she says.

Next she's undoing the belt and zipper on his jeans and pulling them straight off by the cuffs. He wants to protest, but his attempt is feeble, muttering half-formed words. Soon the quilt covers the lower half of him.

"There," she says. "Doesn't that feel better?"

Billy feels her sit down on the edge of the bed beside him. Fluttering his eyes open, he sees her facing him and leaning towards him slightly. Her light brown hair is mussed from her own earlier sleep, and her face looks sweet and soft. The rolls of her belly up against him, that she fights so hard to hide, feel nurturing. She places her hand on his chest. "I don't know what happened to you over there. I don't want to know what you heard or saw. But you made it back alive, and you need to be grateful to Jesus for that. I know you came back to a mess. It breaks my heart that Brenda took up with James. Breaks my heart. And that child, my only grandchild, being pushed and pulled between people." Bagwell lets his heavy eyelids drop. The explosions, however, begin again in his head. Now he doesn't know which is worse. His mother talking about subjects he longs to forget, or the assault of bombardments beating him down. He flutters his eyes open as she says, "I can smell alcohol on your breath. You've got to find a better way." He allows himself to drop off and this time he finds himself adrift in a small boat on a huge body of water filled with the passing fins of sharks.

—~—

He awakens, lying on his belly in bed, with a stream of drool half dried on his mouth and pooled on his pillow. From the corner of his eye, he catches a flash of white, drawing him over on his back wincing as his wounded leg rolls. What he sees he doesn't believe, so he blinks his eyes repeatedly to clear them. But still she stands there at the foot of his bed. An angel. There's no way. No fucking way. He must be dreaming. Her skin and hair are dark. Angels of the Black Madonna. Her gown shines white like the color of pearls. The wings are tucked behind her like huge hands praying. When she speaks, every hair on his body stands.

"You are still the man you have always been."

Though his eyes grow misty he does not cry. The sharks in the water swim away. Something solid settles over him and all that he dwells upon as a weight lifts. Before his eyes, the angel disappears, one moment solid, the next an empty space. Bagwell lets his eyes drop, crosses his hands upon his chest, and falls at last into a deep calm sleep.

24
Bow Out

Saturday 7:17 a.m.

James rolls over and one ray of light peeking around the edge of a curtain hits him in the eyes. Morning has come and he groans with a head that feels like a watermelon, throbbing with each and every beat of his heart. Where is he? He doesn't recognize the interior of this room. Blue and white pom-poms and team flags hang on the wall next to a poster for the movie *Dirty Dancing*. He turns his head to the right with another groan to see a tall white chest of drawers with bras, panties, and socks spilling out. Uh-oh. Slowly he rolls to his left to see a bare back and a head of straw-colored hair. Who the hell is that? He lifts the covers slightly to catch a glimpse of the ass, sweet and round, and decides he must have been invited here. He reaches out to run his right hand over the baby-smooth butt cheek to test whether the invitation remains open. A moan of appreciation says yes. He runs his fingertips around the edge of the cheek heading inside. His morning hard-on begins to throb as hard as his head.

Just as he prepares to slide over, she turns. She is a pretty girl, a very pretty girl, petite, with large round breasts. The nipples protrude, inviting. He reaches up to pinch one as she wraps a hand around him. For one so young, she certainly knows what to do.

"Oh, James," she says as she leans in to kiss him. Morning mouth or not, the tongues mingle, and she pulls him on top of her. She likes it hard, so he gives it to her, as she throws her head from side to side making all kinds of noise. He wonders if there is anyone else in the house. Could he get caught with his pants down? He pulls away in a bit of a panic.

"Hey!" she says, reaching out for him. Then with a little smile she adds, "You can do anything you want with me."

He thinks, *okay.* "Roll over on your stomach."

When it's over, he falls over on his back as she rolls over on her side to look at him. Holding her head in her right hand, she runs her left over his chest, playfully.

She says, "I've always wanted to be with you."

"How old are you?"

"Old enough to know better, but too young to resist. Isn't that what they say?"

"Ha ha. No, really, how old are you?"

"Eighteen. Want to check my ID? You didn't care last night," she says.

"Where did I meet you?"

"You don't even remember?"

"Ah, not really."

She rolls over on her back. "You don't remember anything?"

"Uh, not a whole lot."

"I ... I thought something special happened."

"Special? I'm in no place for 'special'. I'm involved with someone."

"I know. You called me by her name a couple times. If she's so special, why weren't you with her last night?"

"Is this your room?"

"Yes."

"Where's your parents?"

"Away for the weekend." She turns towards him again. "All weekend."

James sits up and throws his legs over the edge of the bed.

She pulls on his arm. "Don't go yet."

"I have to open my shop." He stands up and glances around the room, looking for his clothes. He finds them lying in a pile at the foot of the bed, grabs his pants and pulls them on.

"Am I going to see you again?" She asks in a tiny, almost whiny voice.

"I doubt it."

"I'm eighteen! I swear. There's my purse over on that chair. Check my ID if you don't believe me."

James pulls his shirt over his head. "I've got to go."

"Are you going to the Jedeles' pig roast today?"

"I don't know."

"Take me!"

"Take you? Why would I do that?"

"Because," she says, running one finger over her plump little lips. "I'll do anything you want."

James pulls on his boots, then walks over to grab the girl's purse. He pulls out her wallet and glances at her ID. She is eighteen and her name is Debbie. He puts her purse back down, walks towards the door to leave and says over his shoulder, "Call me at my shop around noon."

Debbie squeals with delight once more.

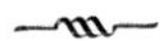

James does not fly over the washboard roads as he loves to do. The throbbing in his head slows him down, as does the nausea gathered in the pool of his stomach. The hell with opening the shop at eight. This morning it will have to be 8:30. He needs three Tylenol and a plate full of bacon and buttermilk pancakes. But first he has to drive past Brenda's. Is Billy there? Brenda's wagon sits in the driveway. No action can be seen, but that doesn't mean a thing. Billy can't drive with that bum leg, so he could well be there between the sheets that James so recently slept upon himself. James doesn't like the feeling threatening to well his eyes with tears. Never to touch Brenda again, or kiss her, or hold her. God! He doesn't like how he feels. So he shoves that one down and lets another rise. Anger. Now *that* he can deal with. He'll kill Billy. Then the man she ... loves... will be gone. James might not get her back, but at least Billy won't have her. Somehow, someway, he has to get rid of Billy.

James pulls into the driveway of the Willis Café, no doubt reeking of last night's booze and sex. The hell with that, too. Maybe he is losing it. After all, no man in his right mind would think he saw an angel. For Christ's sake, he was enveloped in the wings. It can't be. Must have been an alcohol-induced hallucination. But the memory of the wings soft as water haunts him.

He walks into the café and heads for the counter, nodding to a handful of people who he knows. Joe Schmidt turns to him as he sits down next to him on a stool at the counter.

"Got some time to look at my truck this morning? Sounds like a belt is loose."

"Sure. Bring it by."

The middle-aged waitress, Linda, approaches James with a pot of coffee and a big smile. "Morning, James. Cup of coffee?"

"Yeah. You got any Tylenol back there?"

She pours him a cup of coffee. "I've got some kind of pain relief in my purse."

"Bring it on."

"You hang one on last night, James?"

"Just a little."

She leans in towards him over the counter. "Must have got lucky, too. You still got lipstick on your face." Linda reaches out with one finger and rubs a spot on his right cheek.

"Oh, shit." He could have at least looked into a mirror.

"So, what can I bring you besides the pain relief?"

"Pancakes and bacon. A couple of eggs, too. Scrambled."

"You got it."

James sweeps his hair off his forehead and takes a quick look around the café. Nestled back in a corner at a small table sitting all alone is Martin Becker. Maybe Martin will ignore him. The man looks like hell, with dark circles big as tires creating shadows around his eyes.

Linda returns with three white capsules in her right palm. "If I remember, you take three."

"You have a memory like an elephant, woman."

"Yeah, well ... Your food will be right up."

James washes the capsules down with coffee and grabs the front-page section of the *Willis Gazette* lying on the empty stool on his other side. A few minutes later, Linda places a plate of food down before James and warms up his coffee. He folds the paper in half and reaches over to place it back on the stool, but the seat is now occupied.

"Warm up my coffee a little, too, will you, Linda?" Martin says.

James dives into his food, not even turning the least bit to acknowledge Brenda's dad. But he feels Martin lean in towards him.

Martin says in a low, but strong voice. "He's back now. It's time for you to bow out."

Without turning, James says, "With all due respect, Mr. Becker, I'm in love with your daughter."

"That's too fucking bad. She loves him."

"How do you know who she loves? She doesn't even know herself."

"If you know what's good for you, you will bow out."

"Are you threatening me, Mr. Becker?"

"I'm promising you. If you like your business in our little town, you'll back off. Got that, boy?"

James turns, fork in his right hand suspended in the air, and the two men lock eyes.

James walks into the back room of his shop and throws his keys onto a table with a clang. He strips off his clothes and steps into the shower thankful, very thankful, he set up this back room. He could live here if he had to, with a sink near the shower, a cot in the corner, and a metal locker with clean clothes inside. Might as well stay here until he figures out what to do. He won't move back in with Mom, unwilling, no – unable – to witness her desperation. Maybe he'll rent an apartment or a small house, though the thought of sleeping at night in a bed alone does not sound appealing. Sure, he can find some girl to share it, but not the one girl he wants. Maybe Brenda will reconsider, thinking of the sex that he knows she enjoys, or remember some facial expression or gesture of his she just simply can't live without. Yeah, right.

He lathers up and rinses off, making sure his armpits and his genitals are squeaky clean. Damn it! That girl better have been protected. That's one thing he always stays sober enough to do. Until last night. That's all he needs. Some young girl popping out with a baby. He should stick with the older women like Doris who are in it, too, purely for the fun.

Fun.

Is it really fun anymore?

James steps out of the shower and dries himself off with a brightly colored beach towel. He dreamed of heading out to the West Coast one year for a vacation. Hasn't gotten there yet.

After throwing on work clothes, he lights a cigarette and walks over to open the door of his garage. Fuck if Brenda isn't waiting outside the doors in her wagon. He can see the back overstuffed with clothes, his guitar, and who knows what else. The girl sure hasn't wasted any time. She climbs out of the car and walks hesitantly up to him. She looks great in blue jeans, sandals, and a little purple sleeveless shirt. Her eyes though are red, puffy, and glazed with fatigue. At least she's not laughing and happy.

Turning to flick his butt into the sink, he says, "You afraid my things might burn a hole in your house?"

She shrugs with her hands stuck into her back pockets. "I've got to get on with my life."

"What does that look like exactly?"

She shrugs again, shaking her head.

"Is he back?" God, that was hard to ask.

"No, he's not back."

Maybe he still has a chance. "Can I see you sometimes?"

She reaches out and grabs his hand. "I'm sorry, James. I'm really sorry."

He tosses her hand. "Well, if I can't have you, he can't have you either."

Brenda takes a step towards him. "Please. Just leave him alone. He's still healing from that desert. He's already suffering."

She does still love him. Fuck. Oh, the anger rises. He hates to admit it, but God, he wants to hit her. In his mind's eye he backhands her hard across her right cheek and pushes her up against the car. His teeth are locked and his right forearm presses on her throat.

Instead he pushes it down, packs it down, doesn't feel a thing, and asks her for her keys. He plucks them out of her open palm, walks over and opens the rear door of the wagon. The air stands still and humid, and not one song of a bird can be heard. It's going to rain. He'll let the sky cry for him.

Brenda walks over to the back of the car to help. He reaches up and places his right hand on her upper chest and pushes her away.

"I'll do it. Where's the kid?"

She places her hand on her chest where his just was. Maybe he pushed her too hard. Tough.

"At Grandma's."

James unloads his possessions into the back room of the garage, his new home, as Brenda leans against the car looking uncomfortable. The kid must be at Grandma's to give Brenda a day free. Free for what? Making love to Billy?

"Why's the kid at Grandma's?"

"My brother is going through a tough time. I want to spend some time with him."

Yeah, right. Lies, all lies.

"You going over to Jedeles' today?" he asks.

"I don't know."

As he returns from the back room with the last load, Joe pulls into the parking lot with his truck. Shit. His timing couldn't be worse. Right behind him, Mike, James' friend, pulls up in his gold metal fleck Camaro. Jesus. It's a fucking three-ring circus.

As both of the men step out of their vehicles, Brenda holds out her hand for her keys.

"I've got to go, James."

He steps up close to her and drops the keys in her palm. "I'm not giving up. I ... love you."

Speaking in a voice real low, with tears in her eyes, she says, "You said I've never loved anyone but myself. Well, you, James, have never loved anyone or anything. Maybe it's time for both of us to grow up."

He swears that if those two men weren't standing there, he'd hit her for sure. The fucking twit bitch. Instead he clenches his jaw and watches her walk away, her pretty little ass sashaying, for the first time leaving him untouched, not stirred, simply cold.

James tells Mike to go grab a coffee as he lifts the hood of Joe's truck and pokes around. His head spins, not with the hangover, but with a fury he's felt only one time before. After a football game one year when Billy and he were leaving a party, they were surrounded with six bullies from the opposing team. They didn't want him as much as they wanted Billy. The cowards attacked from the rear, two grabbing James and pinning him down while the other four set out to break a few of Billy's bones. Being the golden boy ain't always what it's cracked up to be. James watched as they kicked Billy in the kidneys and the ribs and punched him in the face, bent back his arms into impossible positions, and pulled his long brown hair, unbleached from the winter sun. Finally, after kicking and flailing, James set himself free and he honestly doesn't know what happened after that. Billy described him as a fury, a hurricane that swept around him, as he was down on his hands and knees reeling from the blows. Invincible Billy said and he must have been, for all six boys scuttled away like the whiny bitches that they were. That's what Billy said. James threw Billy into the back seat of his GTO and took him to the hospital emergency room, where he was released six hours later with stitches and bruises and a cast on his arm. Billy thanked him for saving his life and James simply shrugged. He did it because he had to do it. The bullies pulled an unfair fight. Or something like that. Why the hell was he so furious now?

He repairs Joe's belt and sends him on his way. Mike returns with two steaming coffees, way too hot for this humid day. But the caffeine helps to shrink his swollen head.

"You look like shit," Mike says.

"So would you if you drank as much as I did."

"You going over to the pig roast today?"

"Jesus Christ! All I'm hearing about is this fucking pig roast."

"They throw a great party. Having a band and everything. You should bring your guitar."

"I doubt it." As James sips his coffee, he glances up to see Doris drive by in her new green Jaguar. She waves as he nods.

"How's the Pontiac running?" Mike asks.

"I haven't had it out in a while."

"I know. Time to get that baby out again. We're meeting later out on Austin."

"Who's 'we'?"

"The usual with a stranger or two from Dexter."

"I don't know."

"The pot stands to be hefty."

"We'll see."

"Let's see how's she's looking." Mike walks over to the other side of the garage and with one hand pulls the thin, shiny, black plastic cover off the GTO. He stands back and whistles, bringing a smile to James' face.

Mike turns to go, tossing one last line over his left shoulder, "Is she still the fastest?"

Bow out? Fuck Martin Becker. No way is he bowing out.

25
Open Hands

Saturday 10:11 a.m.

Brenda stops by the bakery for two muffins and two coffees, strong and creamy, then heads over to her dad's. She doesn't like still, muggy mornings when nothing seems to stir but the insects. The smell of manure – cow, sheep, and pig – wafts slowly through the thick wet air from the local farms. The branches of the trees droop and the flowers struggle to lift their heads. The pig roast could be rained out, but knowing the Jedeles, they will be prepared with tents. Nothing stops this yearly party. Part of her wants to go. She can pretend she's a carefree teen again, drink and dance, flirt with the cute boys, lead them on. All the things she missed because at fifteen she was already Billy's girl.

Every day for six months she has had sex in the morning. Passionate, hard sex missing a few key ingredients, like quiet conversation, gazing into each other's eyes, limbs entangled so intimately you don't know where one body ends and the other begins. She's read about those things in *Cosmopolitan* magazine. James knows the mechanics. He knows where the parts are, the buttons that make things go, the timing on how they stop and start. But he knows nothing about romance. He plays her body like an instrument, but forgets that somewhere beneath the flesh and bone beats a heart that can draw two together closer than the pleasure. Climax occurs, but then he turns to light a cigarette, begins to distance himself away, leaving a girl to feel lonely, even deceived, by a hope that maybe this time he will let his guard down. Maybe someday for some girl, he finally will. That girl will be lucky. The girl that gets the wild man to open his heart at last.

At one time she thought she was that girl.

Brenda pulls into the driveway of her father's house. Yes, his, even though not a piece of furniture has been moved, or a dust collector shifted since her mother died. A cleaning lady comes in, but the house stands as a museum to her mom. Brenda both loves and hates to go there. She's always fifteen years old again, expecting to see her mom walk around a corner, call to her from another room, be standing in the kitchen wearing one of her aprons. She thinks that if only she had awakened that night, heard the intruder or her mother's panicked call, or the closing of the door.... Whatever the case, Brenda wishes and wishes she had been able to stop it. But, she wasn't. Who killed her, and are they still walking around? Someone she knows? A stranger from afar? This was one more reason for the dark to become scary, very scary, terrifying at times. If only she had learned to reach out into the dark with her open hands before. But monsters can also attack from the rear. Can't they? She shakes her head to let it go. Let it go. Those days are done. Aren't they?

Neither her father's car nor Peter's are in the driveway. Are either of them home?

Uncle Sam called at 2:00 a.m. to tell her that they had found Peter. Everything was okay. Go back to sleep now. Don't worry.

She had fallen into a slumber as still as death, where even dreams do not form, waking up to find Lily Rose in the kitchen standing on a chair looking for her Cheerios. Twelve trips to her car later, all physical traces of James were packed into the back, except for stained sheets, a rumpled towel and an ashtray full of butts.

Brenda steps out of the car, greeted by her mother's cat, Muffin, now fourteen years old, a few pounds overweight and half blind. She bends over to pick her up, cuddle her, and give her a kiss on the side of her face near the whiskers. The cat purrs like a little motor and jumps out of her arms when a horsefly zooms by.

Quietly, evenly reverently, Brenda enters the house through the side door. There it is, her mother's kitchen, with a black and white tiled floor, white cabinets, red countertops and green and yellow flowered curtains. Held onto the refrigerator face with magnets are pictures of Peter and her as they grew up. Riding bikes, riding ponies, playing games on the lawn. Sitting in the bathtub, eating hot dogs on the porch, dressed up on Easter in their Sunday best. Occasionally, they are smiling. The pictures stop when Peter reaches ten and she fifteen, as if time had somehow stopped, too, except for one picture of each of them snapped at graduation. Oh, and over in the uppermost corner on the right side is a snapshot of Lily Rose when she was two, with a smile as big and radiant as the noonday sun.

In the living room, on the back of the couch, lies an afghan her mother crocheted when Brenda was ten. Up until two years ago, Brenda could still smell her mother settled into the tightly woven fibers. She picks up one corner of the textile now hoping that maybe just maybe one lonesome trace is left. But there isn't. When she walks past her father's recliner, his fresh scents rise. A mixture of oily skin, Old Spice aftershave, and a hint of cigar. Beside the chair on a table sits a cocktail glass with diluted VO and water, her father's drink of choice.

Where is he? Golfing? She's glad he isn't here.

Slowly, she walks upstairs heading to Peter's room. As she lifts one foot, she swears she hears her mother call her name. She stops, her heart pounding, and looks over her shoulder. This isn't the first time. It probably won't be the last. As usual, she sees nothing.

Moving on towards Peter's room, she glances towards her own, but the door remains shut. Good. She doesn't want to see inside, doesn't want to remember her life beneath her father's roof. Wants to wipe that slate clean, except for memories of her mother smiling when she was alone without her father.

Pete lies in his bed on his back staring up at the ceiling where, four years ago, he painted a universe. When she walks into the doorway he starts.

"Jesus, Brenda! How about making a little noise?"

"You aren't showered yet? You told me a half hour ago you were jumping into the shower."

"I did. Then I crawled back into bed."

"I brought us muffins and coffees." She holds up two white bags.

"Great!" Peter slides up into a sitting position. "Have a seat. We'll have a picnic."

Peter dives into the muffin like he's starving, intermittently sipping on his coffee. Brenda nibbles on hers, not really hungry. In fact, she's eaten very little over the past two days.

"So," she says. "Are you going to tell me what happened or not?"

Peter looks up at her and then back down. He looks up again and says matter-of-factly, "I'm not a virgin anymore."

"Well," she says. "Who's the lucky guy?"

"You don't know him." Peter finishes his muffin and wets his finger to pull up crumbs off his napkin.

"Someone that you like?" She hands him her muffin. "I'm not hungry."

"Are you sure?"

She nods.

He says, "Liking the guy wasn't really the point."

"What was the point?'

"Having sex with someone that I wanted to have sex with. He's new in town. I ran into him in the bars a few times."

"And?"

"We ... did it. Then he took off with my car."

"He took your car? Where were you?"

"Out at that nice little bend on the creek."

"How did you get to Three Rivers?"

"I hitchhiked."

"Peter!"

"But you're missing a whole other part of the story. The storm broke out and I didn't know where to go. I was too far from your house, and I sure couldn't come back here without my car. So, I walked to Grandma's."

"You're kidding?"

"I barely made it there. Grandma took care of me and I fell asleep. When I woke up I freaked out. I remembered Todd taking my car, and I knew I had to find him. So, I left."

"In the meantime, Dad ran into the kid driving your car."

"I guess Todd smashed it up."

"He did? Uncle Sam didn't tell me that. He did say that they found some things in your trunk. Did you know about that?"

"No, not at all. I still don't even know what they are. They wouldn't tell me last night. Billy and Dad didn't say a word all the way back."

"Well, I know." Peter looks up at her expectantly. "Some grass and porno."

He doesn't seem surprised. "Really," he says.

"Where did Dad and Uncle Sam find you?"

"And Billy. Billy was a big part of it."

Brenda stands up and walks over to the window to look out. "Okay. So where did they find you?

"At Eddie's bar."

Brenda turns to watch a little sly smile break out on her brother's face. "So, what's so special about Eddie's bar?"

Peter jumps out of bed and throws on a pair of jeans and a pullover shirt sitting on the back of a chair. "It's not the bar. It's Eddie."

"Eddie's special?"

"He makes movies." Peter steps over in front of a mirror on the wall and attempts to style his head of unruly hair.

Brenda turns and walks back over towards the bed, her arms crossed over her chest.

"What kind of movies?"

"You know."

"Porno. Jesus, Peter."

"He might know people who work on the big shows."

"Porno people don't know people who work on the 'big shows'."

Peter turns to look at her, tossing the brush onto the top of a chest of drawers. "How do you know how it works?"

"Peter, you're not seriously thinking about doing that ..."

"Who cares if it's porno? The guy did some training on me last night. I liked it."

"What?"

Stepping towards her, he says, "It's just sex. Don't tell me you don't like it. Messing around with James Tillman. How many holes has he poked you in?"

Brenda feels the heat of a blush moving up from her neck to cover her face.

"See! I'm right, aren't I?"

She turns away, waiting for the blood to recede. Once she feels the heat fade, she turns back to see Peter sitting on the bed pulling on socks. "Oh, I see, it's a big game to you now."

"Not really. But, I need to get out of this house, Brenda."

"Find someone who needs a roommate."

"I need to get out of this town."

"Yeah. I guess you do. But, not that way."

"I'll take any way I can."

"How about finding somebody to love? How about that?"

"Love? I don't know anything about that."

"You wouldn't like to find someone to share your life with?"

"I'm twenty years old! Well, almost twenty-one. There's more to life than finding 'someone to love,' isn't there?"

"How come you knew that before I did?" Brenda watches Peter pull on sneakers. "James is gone."

"What do you mean he's gone?"

"He's gone. Moved out."

"Are you happy about that?"

"Pretty much."

Peter stands up from the bed. "I think you should know, Bren, that Billy looks like shit."

"He does? He didn't look bad when I saw him."

"He looked bad last night. You should talk to him."

"I will. At some point. When I'm ready."

"He's a good guy."

"And I'm a good girl. Pete, you need to remember something. He's the one that wanted to go over there. He left Lily and me behind."

"You said it was a big fat game to me. What do you call what you've been doing? Sleeping with James. Billy's best friend. Now Billy's back and you dump James. You know, Sis, that sounds fucked up."

Brenda's eyes begin to well. "Of all people, Peter, I thought you understood." She turns, and quickly heads for the door, but turns back again in the doorway. "Screw you. Screw all of you."

"Hey, I thought we were going shopping."

She rushes down the stairs past all of the reminders of her mother, and out the side door into the muggy day. Just as Brenda reaches her car she hears Peter's voice behind her.

"I forgot to tell you something!" This last bit sounds important.

Brenda stops and turns to see him hanging out of the back door. "What?" she says.

"Grandma and I. We saw an angel."

Brenda shakes her head with disgust. "You people are all delusional!"

"We saw it, Bren."

"Yeah? Well, I have something to tell you, too. Jake found Mama's pearls."

"What?"

"He found her pearls. Buried in that field where she was found."

Brenda climbs into her wagon as Peter calls out for more.

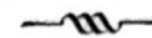

She exists alone in the world, just like James said. There isn't one person who understands her. Putting the car in reverse, she steps on the gas, and squeals out of the driveway. She puts the car in drive, and with a spray of gravel begins to fly forward, passing trees and low-lying brush in a blur. A determination glues her foot to the gas pedal, diminishing every other thought. She will not bolt from the car and disappear into the fields that surround her. She will not crawl on her knees to Billy and beg him to take her back. She will not forget how she can traverse her way through the dark with outstretched arms and open hands. She will not be afraid anymore.

They can call her a selfish twit and accuse her of playing games. When her husband left her and their child behind without asking her how she felt about it, she gained the right to actions of her own. Should she have slept with his best friend? No. Should she have moved James into their house? No. But she learned about herself, who she was as a woman and a sexual being. She learned that she can make decisions for herself. She learned how to protect herself from being beaten down. Her grandma told her to step up, she was stronger than she knew. And she feels stronger, and nobody can take this newfound strength away.

The air streaming in through the open windows of her car carries her long hair back in a stream. The manure scents flow past her. The car rocks and rolls over the gravel and the holes on the road. She doesn't see the fair-sized rock that has somehow found its way onto the middle. Her left front tire hits it, and the car jolts, fishtails, and begins to slide. Brenda struggles to hold the steering wheel steady as she moves her foot from the gas to the brake and pumps on the pedal. When the car slides to a stop, twelve inches this side of a tree, she begins to laugh.

Brenda backs up the car, carefully shifts the gear into drive and proceeds, on her way over to Grandma's to pick up Lily Rose.

Expecting to see her daughter romping around in the garden or the fields, she feels surprised when she isn't. She jumps out of the car, buoyant with her newfound determination, and climbs the four back stairs into the house at the farm, or what used to be a farm. Finding no one in the kitchen, she calls, "Grandma!"

He said they saw an angel. They're all losing it, she swears.

From the living room, she hears the rustle of paper and heads that way. She walks into the room, where the family ghosts would be if there were ghosts, to find her grandma rocking in her favorite chair, one foot crunching into a bag of Cheese Puffs. Grandma stares into space.

"Grandma?" Brenda grabs the old woman's arm and gently shakes it. Her grandma turns to look at her. "Are you okay?"

Grandma nods her head.

"Where's Lily?"

"She's with Billy."

"You should have let me know before you let her go with him again."

"He's her father. He needs to see her right now."

"How do you know he isn't going to run off with her?"

"Billy wouldn't do that."

"So you talked to him?"

"We talked for a while."

"About what?"

"When are you going to talk to him?"

"He knows where I am if he wants to talk with me." Brenda slides down onto the couch up against the wall where the painting of the winter scene once hung.

"I thought you were spending some time with Peter."

"That plan got changed. Why haven't you hung the painting back up?"

"It's wedged between the sofa and the wall."

"Maybe it wasn't a sign, Grandma."

"Oh, it was a sign all right."

"You still think someone's going to die?"

"We saw an angel. Your brother and I. Did he tell you?"

Brenda shakes her head with disgust. "Yeah, an angel."

Her grandmother looks at her directly. "The angels loved you so when you were a child."

Brenda jumps up from the couch. "You're all crazy!"

"I'm working on striking a deal with God, but it's not looking good."

"So who is it going to be, Grandma?" Brenda says with a little laugh.

"It's very important that we keep everyone as calm as we can. Do you understand?"

"What do you mean, calm?"

"We have to keep tempers from flaring."

"And how are we supposed to do that?"

"By softly reaching out to them."

"To Dad? To Peter? To Billy? To James? None of them know how to be reached out to softly."

"Well, they better learn fast."

"As long as it's not my daughter, I don't care."

"That's the coldest thing I've ever heard you say."

Tears spring into Brenda's eyes. "You're right. That was awful. I didn't really mean it."

Her grandmother turns to her. "Don't make becoming stronger cold, Brenda. That would be missing the point."

26
Judgment

Saturday 11:00 a.m.

So here he sits, flying over the country roads again. At least this time sober but certainly deprived of sleep. No matter how hard he tries, he cannot remove the picture from his mind of Petey down on his knees before that ... pathetic excuse for a human being. Martin doesn't know for certain what his son was doing, but he did see him wiping away at his face with his shirttail. If he and Billy hadn't gotten there when they did, God knows how they would have found them. Martin regrets striking a deal now. He'd like nothing more than to see the ugly fuck behind bars, but keeping him from his son rates second.

He's on his way to his brother's barn to destroy what's sitting in the trunk of the Celica. He's going to dig a hole so deep, the tapes will not resurface for a thousand years. No, he'll burn them first and then bury them. Watch the perversion, the filth, rise up out of the fire and return to the earth in ashes. Some will blow away. Those held down by weight, he'll bury. Not a trace will be left.

He'll burn the marijuana, too. Sam needs to realize that pain management or not, cannabis sativa lists as a controlled substance.

Martin stops at his brother's before heading over to the barn. He pulls the Lincoln into the long dirt driveway and moves up close to the house. The double doors of the shop are shuttered up and Martin can see Sam standing before the long wooden table working on a small rocker.

Sam turns to look at him as he steps into the shop. Unbelievably, at ten in the morning, his brother is already smoking a jay, a joint, whatever the hell you call it.

"Why can't you start the day with coffee like everybody else?"

"Pain management, bro, like I told you."

"You're in that much pain?"

Sam suddenly arches his back forward and groans. "Yeah, I've got pain."

"Why don't you get some pain pills from your doctor?"

"They don't work, that's why. Plus they're full of side effects. Let's not get started on that shit again."

Sam turns back to the little rocker he's working on, and with the tiniest of brushes, begins to paint in the flowers engraved on the top panel of the back.

"Who's that for?"

"Who else? Lily Rose."

"Oh, yeah, she's got a birthday coming up."

"Yep. She's a Libra, just like me."

"I'm heading over to the barn to take care of the shit in the trunk. Can I have the key to the barn?"

"It's open."

"It's open? What if someone wandered in there and ..."

"Jesus, Martin. Are you ever going to get that stick out of your ass?"

"You never worry about ..."

"Marty, go to the barn. I don't feel like dealing with you today."

"That's just too ..."

Sam turns to look at him squarely, "Out!"

Martin shakes his head, turns, and climbs back into the Lincoln. He can't remember a time when his brother ever talked to him like that before. He feels a little ganged up on – Billy getting on him last night about his son, and Sam standing up to him this morning. Maybe he's losing it. What, he doesn't know. But whatever kept other men at bay. Maybe his confidence. God, he hopes he's not losing that.

A mile down the road the barn sits back about fifty feet. The red paint peels like the dead skin after a sunburn, and the advertisement painted on one end for Quaker Oats appears barely legible. Old straw protrudes from the half-open door of the haymow, and the overgrown grass at the base of the structure makes it look completely unused except, of course, for the double set of tire tracks from the tow truck and the Celica fresh from yesterday leading right up to the door. An idiot could see them. But the chance of the porno king stumbling upon the scene would probably be slim to none.

Martin slowly climbs out of the Lincoln, his old football injuries beginning to catch up on his exhausted, hungover body. He walks up to the large double doors, catching a whiff of something dead. Out of the corner of one eye he spots the ragged remains of a decaying rodent, gums pulled back stiffly into a wicked grin. Flies buzz and light, feasting away on the last few measly shreds of flesh.

He takes hold of the handle on the right side of the door and pulls sideways, exposing the inside of the barn as two doves inside lift off with a flutter of wings and startle him. They fly out into the summer day. The inside of the barn looms dark except for slivers and slices of light filtering their way through the decaying wooden panels. In the fractures of light he can see dust and gnats dancing, rising, falling, floating. The space looks large, the small smashed car sitting in the center. The haymow sits up ten feet on either end, reminding Martin of the section of the church where a choir stands. That's what the empty, hollow space reminds Martin of, a church. He hasn't been inside of one for years, six years that is, since Brenda and Billy were married.

Martin walks over to the trunk of the car, sticks the key into the lock and opens it. At first he thinks his eyes are deceiving him in the dim light. Although the cardboard box containing the tapes sits there, the black plastic bag full of marijuana is gone. He reaches into the trunk, moving his hands around in the half-light, hoping the bag was shifted into a corner from the towing.

"Fucking Sammie!" he says out loud, turning from the trunk with disgust. How the hell did he get into the trunk without a key?

As he turns back to the trunk he hears a soft, deep voice say, "What have you done?"

Startled, he turns away from the trunk again, then revolves in a circle peering into the dismal light like a man half blind.

"Who's there?" he asks.

No answer.

Shaking his head, he turns back to the trunk and reaches in with both hands for the box of tapes.

The voice comes at him once again. "You have been unkind."

Okay, he thinks. That's it. He lets go of the box, steps away from the trunk, and begins to walk into what feels like the immensity of the cavern. He looks carefully into every corner, his heart pounding at the same time as his anger flares. Someone is fucking with him, and when he gets his hands around his or her neck ...

"You have hurt enough people."

Goddamn it! Someone dares to judge him for his actions? He's never been anything but a straightforward, standup guy.

"Where are you?" he yells.

He begins to climb the ladder up to the haymow on the right side. Peering into the twilight of the cavern, he sees nothing but old straw scattered in clusters or tied into neat tight bales.

"In your heart."

Now the hair on his head and arms begins to stand, though his anger does not fade. He can't tell if the voice is male or female, so distant, so soft, but also insistent. It can't be real! He's losing his mind. Maybe he's actually going insane. He's heard of people hearing voices. Is he one of them?

"Let them live their lives."

That's it. That's it. He climbs back down the ladder, the old body moving faster now. There must be someone in this barn. Quickly he moves across the expanse to the ladder on the other side and begins to climb again. When he reaches the top, he peers around and suddenly a movement in the straw startles him. The shock throws his body back. He loses the grip on his right hand and his left foot slides off the ladder. For a moment he precariously dangles, but regains his balance when his right hand resumes a grip. A good-sized field mouse scurries out of the straw and heads hurriedly for a corner. He knows damn well that mice can't talk. Seeing nothing else in the mow, he climbs back down the stairs, wanting to hear the voice again, so he can vent his fury, half not wanting to hear it, because he'll know he's gone insane. But an insane person doesn't know he is insane.

Martin thinks, *the hell with it*. He trudges over to the trunk of the car and reaches in to grab the box again.

"Only God can judge."

That does it! That does it!

He turns from the trunk and screams, "Who the fuck are you? Leave me alone! Leave me the fuck alone!"

Grabbing the box, he lifts and carries it straight out the thin opening of the door, out into the humid day. He walks around the barn to the back and half drops the box to the ground where a few of the tapes tumble out. There are no pictures on the tapes, just titles, except for one. Two young teenage boys stand half dressed, no shirts, only jeans, barefoot, staring sullenly into the camera; the tape is labeled "Boy Toy 13." With disgust, he throws this tape back into the box, where all the others read, "Boy Toy" with a number. There must be two dozen. Filthy, fucking monster.

Martin walks back around the barn to the trunk of the Lincoln, opens it, and takes out a shovel, a few pieces of newspaper, and a BBQ lighter. He walks back around the barn and begins to dig a hole.

Only God can judge. Bullshit. Anyone can see that these films are filth, the perverse toys of sick men. *I can judge,* Martin thinks. *I will judge.* The dirt flies as Martin's thoughts go wild. Let them live their lives. He will not. Any chance he gets, he will tell anyone who wants to listen that sex with children is not right. You have hurt enough people. Damn right, they have. The voice must have been directing the statements to them. It had nothing to do with him. That's right. I have been unkind? When the fuck have I been unkind? You. Not him. Them. It has nothing to do with him.

Martin dumps the contents of the box into the hole, tears the newspaper into strips and covers the tapes like a blanket.

He stoops down and with good riddance, lights a corner of the paper, but it doesn't take. The paper must be damp with humidity. He walks over into the field behind the barn, and breaks off a few pieces of brittle grass, walks back and drops them on top of the paper. He stoops again with the lighter and this time a spark breaks into a small fire. Martin stands and walks back to the front of the barn and hesitates before entering, half frightened, but half curious if he will hear the voice again. He walks into the dusky cavern over to the trunk of the car and feels around to see if he left anything behind. Nope. All clear.

"Not them, you."

Goddamn it! He doesn't believe it. Not them, you? I didn't film those filthy tapes. What does this voice possibly mean? In my heart. In MY heart. That's it. That's it. Martin slams the trunk door of the Celica down, turns, and screams, "Fuck you!" He stomps defiantly across the ground and prepares to slide back through the opening in the door.

"Let your family live their lives."

He hesitates, then pounds on the door with his fury. Since when hasn't he let his family live their lives? He must be going crazy.

He walks back around the barn one final time to watch the fire, black toxic smoke rising, the smell acrid and offensive. Mesmerized, he stares into the flames.

Then the guilt begins to roll over him. The misgivings begin with Jeanine and the way he beat her down. Telling her she didn't look good when she did. Telling her she didn't do something right when obviously that was a lie. He had to keep her in the house and all to himself somehow. She was so beautiful, so good, so sweet smelling, every man must have wanted her. So what if he was the quarterback and the king of the prom. No matter how good you had it, someone had it better, waiting to push you into second. And they pushed hard. God, they pushed hard.

He knows for a fact that Michael Finkbeiner had his eye on Jeanine. He didn't even engage in contact sports, but he played a real mean electric guitar. Michael F. had his own band at sixteen, and all the girls stood at the foot of the stage drooling. His band, The Desperadoes, even played at the homecoming dance. He had dark hair he wore slicked back with some kind of grease, and wore jeans cuffed at the bottom and a leather jacket. The guy looked like he came from another world in Willis. Martin caught Jeanine watching him one night at a party from a corner of the stage. She had that look on her face that they call dreamy. On her left hand was his class ring, not Michael's, his, but she was letting the vision of another man transport her to another place and time. Martin remembers walking up to her and pulling her from the front of the stage by one hand, his grip like a vise, her pretty face contorted with pain. But even that didn't do it. When he wandered back into the party after catching a quick smoke with the other guys, he found Jeanine talking with Michael F. under a tree. He didn't ask any questions, just grabbed the tall, thin guy by the neck and threw him down. Tall, thin, dark haired. Tall, thin, dark haired, like Petey.

Martin stands up from his stoop and begins to kick at the ground, and flail his arms around wildly. Goddamn it! Maybe Petey isn't even his kid. He's wondered at times. Oh, he has wondered.

"You have been unkind," he repeats under his breath. "Like others have been so fucking kind to me!"

That's it. That's it. Petey's not his boy. He's Michael F.'s kid. Michael F., who left for New York one day after graduation never to return. But Jeanine received a letter. He remembers now. A letter asking her to come, pursue her own dream of designing women's clothes. She didn't go, swearing Michael was just a friend. He never touched her, she swore. "Not one time Martin, not even one time."

Sure.

Martin walks in circles around the fire, the smoke trailing straight up in the windless air. He sees visions of Indians from Westerns past, dancing around the fires before a war party goes out. Whooping and hollering and making other strange vocal sounds, primitive and dangerous. He feels like he's spent his entire life doing just that. Preparing for battle. With known, but mostly unknown adversaries.

He's tired now. God, he's tired.

He sits, half falling to the ground.

Let them live their lives.

He looks around to see if the porno king has found him.

You've hurt enough people.

He feels like he's hardly gotten started.

Never has he told his daughter what to do. Not once did he ever lift a hand to hit her. Still, that precious girl bolted from the car and took off into the field. For Christ's sake! He didn't say anything. He was only talking to his wife. The worst part was later when they finally found her. She was lying lifeless in his father's farmer hands. Martin reached for her and there she was lying safely in his own. But when her eyes fluttered open, he swears he saw fear, as she reached her tiny outstretched hands to her mother.

She didn't even want to lie in his hands. He was supposed to be her provider and protector, but his precious jewel couldn't wait to get away from him.

Maybe he did do a rotten job. He never showed her how much he really cared. He couldn't. She might be carried away with terror in her eyes like Obie. The same terror most likely present when Jeanine was carried away. He'll never know. When he identified her in the morgue her eyes were closed, too tightly it seemed, her mouth slightly open in a crooked way, the sweet smell that always drifted off of her was gone.

In your heart.

There's nothing there.

Nothing can live in something that cold.

Martin stands up and begins to kick the ground again, but this time whatever soft surface dirt he can loosen up, to kick into the fire. What's left of the filthy porno has been reduced to small odd shaped balls of brown and black. He covers them with dirt, then wanders out into the field to find a few medium rocks, but settles on just one, large, that he pushes and rolls over to cover what was the fire pit. The headstone for the porno. The cap for the grave. If only this grave served for all porno made with children being manipulated by men. The death of innocence. The ruination of the planet. The evil of the world buried deep in a grave, covered with a rock, never again to rise.

Only then does Martin spy one lone tape lying under a clump of brittle grass. He can't believe it. After all of that, he missed this one. Bending over, his hungover and fatigued body creaking like a loose stair, he plucks up the tape and studies the cover. "Boy Toy Four." He tucks the tape into the waistband of his trousers.

Martin looks up into the horizon to see a subtle line of darkness in the approaching march of clouds. Another storm. Definitely a storm. He can see the traces of yellow and brown that mark a bad one.

Quickly, or as quickly as his abused body will let him, he walks around the wooden structure and peers one last time into the church that is a barn. Before any chance of hearing the voice again, he pulls the old, heavy door shut with a slam. He walks over to his Lincoln, places the shovel and lighter in the trunk, opens the driver's door and sinks into the leather with a sigh. Pulling the tape from his waistband, he places it carefully under the seat. He puts the car in reverse and moves swiftly out over the matted grass, then into the drive down the long road home, where he cannot wait to fall into the comfort of his bed. His real life awaits him.

27
Silent Song

Saturday 1:29 p.m.

Bagwell watches as Lily Rose prances through the long green grass, then leaps just before she reaches the ball, landing with a gleeful squeal. Running back towards him holding the purple plastic ball dotted with white stars, she throws it towards him underhand using both hands and arms. He dashes towards the ball awkwardly using his cane, but manages to catch it with his open hand and guide the roll down into the crook of his elbow.

"Peanut, we better stop now before we wear out your daddy's leg."

He reaches down with his left hand to take Lily's right and tosses the ball over near a wooden picnic table sitting alongside the creek. Sitting down on the table, he pulls his daughter up onto his lap and balances his cane against the edge.

"I want to talk to you about a few things."

"Okay, Daddy. Oh, look!" She points over to the grass at the foot of a tree. "A squirrel! Isn't he cute, Daddy?"

"Yes, he's cute. Now listen up."

"I like coming to the park, Daddy."

"I know you do."

"Can we walk over and see the crayfish before we leave?"

"Yes, we can." He squeezes his arms tighter around his girl, and rests his chin on top of her head. This may be the last time he plays with his daughter or holds her closely against his body to protect her from every foul and unfair happening in the world. Who will protect her from now on? Martin? Maybe. Definitely Sam while he's still alive. Peter? Bagwell's not sure Peter can protect himself, clearly attracted now to the seedier side of life. Brenda? He doesn't know a damn thing about her anymore. He can only hope that threads of what originally drew him to her ten years before remain recoverable, or perhaps intact, just buried now, pushed to the side, complicated through an impulsive nature. He must believe she will come to her senses.

Nothing can steer him from his conviction. The few. The proud. A man's got to do what a man's got to do.

The hell with making it look like an accident.

Though the vision of watching James' brain exit his skull in a pinkish red mist excites him, staring him in the eyes as he kills him excites him more. He will not attack and run. He will kill and surrender.

The apparition that came to him in the early hours told him he is still the man he has always been. Somehow then he will be victorious.

First, he must say goodbye to his daughter. "Now listen up, Peanut."

"Daddy, can I have ice cream after we leave the park?"

"You had ice cream yesterday. I don't think it's a good idea to have ice cream every day."

"Why not?"

"It's more important that you eat fruits and vegetables, and cereal and meat and things."

"Can I have ice cream tomorrow?"

"We'll see. Lily, I want to talk to you about some things."

"Okay."

Where exactly does he begin? He has so much he wants to say. "Really smart people say that there is nothing to fear but fear itself. Do you know what that means?"

Lily shakes her little head resting up against his chest.

"That means that you only get scared because you want to get scared. It means that no matter what happens, you can be brave enough to face it." He's a good one to talk. He's afraid to get too close to Brenda. Afraid he might grab her and pull her into him or maybe punch her in the face instead.

"I don't want to be scared about monsters, Daddy. But, I am."

"There's no such thing as monsters, Peanut." Just people who do monstrous things.

Lily turns to look at him. "So, I shouldn't be afraid of anything?"

"You can be afraid, but you face it anyway. You have to act like you're not afraid. When I jumped out of a plane with a parachute, I felt afraid, but I did it anyway. I was afraid to go overseas to the Persian Gulf because I might be injured or killed. But, I went anyway."

"But, you were injured, Daddy."

"It was one of the consequences, but I went over there anyway." And I pissed my pants when the rockets landed. Some responses are out of our control. Do I tell her about that?

"I'm afraid of Uncle James."

Bagwell's arms tighten around Lily's little waist. Some responses are out of our control.

"He took Growlie. He buried him in the ground. Growlie didn't even have his jumper on to keep him warm."

"I can promise you, Peanut," he kisses Lily on the cheek, "that 'Uncle' James will not be doing things like that anymore."

"Oh, goodie."

"The second thing I want to tell you is that there are things in your life that you are really going to want to do. They are your dreams."

"I had a bad dream last night, Daddy."

"I don't mean your dreams when you sleep. I mean your dreams when you are awake."

Lily becomes animated. "Two cars hit like this!" She claps her hands together.

"Lily, scoot around sideways so I can look at you."

Lily scoots around and hangs her legs over Bagwell's left thigh and looks up into his face with her sweetest smile.

"When you want something really bad, Lily, you have to go after it. The things we want really badly mark the path of our life." He wanted a wife, a loving wife and children. He wanted Brenda. Should he tell Lily that sometimes the things we want don't work out?

"I really want ice cream, Daddy."

Bagwell laughs. "There's going to be other things that you want. You have to be fearless and go after them. Regardless of the consequences."

"What's consequences?"

"That's the end result of what you do."

"Daddy, can we go see the crayfish now?"

"In just a couple of minutes. Just listen a little bit longer."

"Okay, Daddy."

"Sometimes we have to do things that have very bad consequences. But we do it anyway because we feel very strongly about it."

"Do you feel very strongly about something, Daddy?"

"Yes, yes I do."

"And there's going to be very bad consequences?"

"I want you to know and always remember that I love you more than any other person now and forever."

"But what if you and Mommy have another baby?"

God, he hates it when his guts twist into a knot. Let it go. Let it go. Keep focused on the mission at hand. "Lil ..." His words choke in his throat.

Lily pulls the dog tags out of his T-shirt. "Can I wear your doggie tags for a while, Daddy?"

Great. Not only are his words choked off, but tears are threatening to spring. "They're ... they're not mine, Peanut. They're ... they're my best friend's, James."

"Uncle James?"

"N ... no. They belonged to my friend overseas. His name was James, too. James Glover. He ... died over there."

"Oh." Lily lets go of the tags as if they burn her. She looks up searchingly in his eyes. "Are ... are you going away again, Daddy?"

Bagwell cups her head with his right hand and holds her closer into his chest and begins to rock. Why the fuck can't he let it go? Why is the betrayal by his old friend an unpardonable sin? All he can think about is pounding James into a bloody pulp. He cannot let the betrayal go. James betrayed him with the woman that he truly loved. Loves. Loved. She betrayed him, too, but he will not harm the mother of his child. James must have seduced her. He must have.

"You are, aren't you?" She asks in a voice as tiny and high as a tinkling bell. Lily breaks his hold with a will much bigger than her size and begins to run.

"Lily!" he calls after her. His heart begins to pound as he watches her head towards the busy road that parallels the park about forty feet away. Oh, my God. Oh, my God. Leaving his cane behind, he begins to trot awkwardly, but as Lily moves closer towards the road, his trot evens out, adrenalin silencing the voice of his screaming leg. Bagwell watches from the corner of his eye all the heads of people in the park turning to watch the golden haired girl running towards the road, and he following some distance behind. The scene becomes dream-like, time seeming to slow down, the distance between him and his Peanut growing larger. He dares to take his eyes off the small back of Lily to glance left and right down the uncoiling road. Though the streams of traffic are not seamless, the distance between passing cars appears short as his child begins to ascend the bank separating the park from the road.

Bagwell is not alone now, as a woman from his left and a man from his right join in the chase realizing his uneven gait, stronger than it should be on his still-fragile leg, but his run obviously compromised. They bypass Bagwell and begin to gain on Lily, who never glances over her shoulder once or responds to his calls.

Up the bank she runs, the incline slowing her down slightly, as the man, younger than he and no doubt stronger, moves up behind his child, reaching out to grab the back of her shirt.

The pain in Bagwell's leg screams him into slowing, his next few steps a hop on his left. He watches Lily crest the bank without breaking speed or hesitating as if she cannot see that what lies directly ahead is a sporadic stream of cars. The man directly behind her reaches out one last time to stop her, but she runs out onto the road, and with horror Bagwell hears the honking horns, the squeal of tires, the shouting voices expelled out of the open windows of the cars.

He has to and he does begin to run again, mindless of the pain, the former slow motion gearing up into fast time as people in the park gather up around the road. Bagwell pushes his way through them, his breath held, and there she stands screaming and crying. The young man who almost succeeded in stopping her stoops down beside her, and the people have stepped outside their cars, already creating a traffic backup. Lily spots him maneuvering his way through the crowd and runs towards him with her arms outstretched. He bends to scoop her up and she throws her arms so tightly around his neck he almost chokes, his tears of relief streaming from his eyes.

"Daddy! Daddy!'

Bagwell doesn't say a word, just turns and winces, and with Lily in his arms half slides down the embankment and at the base he allows himself to plop down on his ass and hold Lily tightly to him. The people from the park move past him, worry etched onto their faces. The young man stops to say, "I tried to stop her...."

"Thank you," Bagwell says. "I know you did." To his daughter he says, "It's okay. It's okay now."

A woman whom Bagwell recognizes, but can't remember her name asks, "Is there something I can do to help you?"

"Yes, Ma'am, you could walk over to that picnic bench over there by the creek and grab my cane."

"Aren't you Molly's son?"

"Yes, Ma'am, I am."

"You just got back from the war over there, didn't you?"

"Yes, Ma'am."

"He was injured," Lily says.

"I see that," the woman says.

An older man stops as he passes, "You should take better care of your child. She was almost killed. You young people. You let your kids run wild."

Bagwell says, "If I were you, Sir, I would step away before I break off one of your arms and shove it up where the sun don't shine."

"You could barely run. You telling me you could fight me?"

"Oh, yes, Sir. I could hurt you."

The woman jumps to Bagwell's defense, "You just back off. Most of the people in this town know this boy. If you knew him, you wouldn't ever say that."

The man moves on grumbling to himself as a young girl of maybe ten runs up holding Bagwell's cane. "Here you are," she says.

Bagwell says, "Thank you." Grabbing Lily tightly in his left arm, Bagwell uses his cane to help him stand even though at least three people, including the woman, volunteer to help him. "Tell these people thank you for helping us, Peanut."

Lily turns her red and wet face from his shoulder and mumbles, "Thank you." She turns her face back into his shoulder.

As Bagwell turns to walk away, he sees Kate running towards them. "Look, Peanut, it's your Aunt Katie, our chauffeur."

"What happened?" Kate asks. "Why is the road backed up?"

"My daughter here decided to take a little run."

"What?"

"Let's just go now. We've caused enough of a spectacle." Bagwell could kick himself. He could just kick himself. What the hell was he thinking? He should have realized that Lily was bright enough to read between his lines. For Christ's sake, he was five when his father left him again to go back into that jungle. He remembers how he felt not knowing if or when he'd ever see him again. Lily knew he was saying goodbye. He should have left well enough alone. But he had things he wanted to tell her, things she might remember years from now. His father didn't tell him much of anything. In fact, he barely connected with him at all. Bagwell realizes now that he couldn't. He'd already seen and felt too much. But there was one scene that he does remember, where everything his father thought important was summed up in a few simple lines.

—~—

Bagwell was curled up in his father's lap, his father tapping the arm of the rocker to some song only he could hear. Bagwell loved the green color of his T-shirt and was fascinated with the metal tags he had hanging around his neck. Though his father held him tightly he said little, and every time he looked up at his father's face, he was staring off. Sometimes his father would blink his eyes and shake his head lightly as if to ward off something he didn't want to see.

"Daddy, how long will you be gone this time?"

"I don't know, Son."

"Are the Americans any closer to winning?"

His father laughed a little laugh. "It isn't about winning anymore."

"What's it about then, Daddy?"

"Revenge, Son. They kill some of ours and we kill some of them."

"But if we kill more, won't we win?"

"Win what? That's the question. Son, I don't ever want you fighting in a war. No matter what happens to me, I want you to remember that."

"But, I want to."

"No, Billy, you do not want to." His father lit a cigarette and took a deep long drag. What he said next was the single longest statement he remembers his father saying and the closest to exposing his personal convictions.

"Mankind is so damn self-righteous. Everybody thinks they're right. They have the right religion, the right political beliefs, the right way of doing things. Son, there's been wars since the beginning of time. And each war is supposed to be the war that ends all wars." His father inhaled deeply again on his cigarette. Bagwell remembers the tip of the cigarette glowing. "Revenge is like that. One man gets back at another for some wrongdoing, then that man gets back at him or someone close to him. It's the snake eating its own tail." Bagwell watched as his father stared off for a few seconds, then returned. "That does not mean that some people do not deserve punishment for the things that they do." There he was tapping his fingers to that silent song containing a beat and a drive that only he would know. He ended with this, "It's never going to end. The wars, the revenge, the self-righteousness. Every man is a slave to it. Driven to prove somehow, someway that what he does and what he thinks is right. In the end it will destroy us all." He took one last drag of his cigarette, then squashed it out, muttering things under his breath he didn't want his son to hear.

—∞—

That does not mean that some people do not deserve punishment for the things that they do.

Lily lies asleep now in Bagwell's arms. He rubs the back of his fingers across the velvet of her cheek. Yes, the world is cruel, but here lies one of the angels among us. But even her sweet innocence and beauty cannot deter him, driven forward by his own song. He says to Kate, "We need to get Lily back to Martha's. I've got a score to settle."

"Billy ...," she says.

"I can't let it go, Kate, and you know it."

28
For Keeps

Saturday 2:16 p.m.

Lily watches a fly land on the golden petals of a marigold. She blinks and the fly is gone. Everything comes and everything goes. She can't pretend that things stay around anymore, because they don't. Except for Nana, but she's old, and old people die, so she won't be around either. Her mama stays around, but she sits alone a lot staring out the window. She's there, but she's not there. Uncle James is gone now and that's good. But Growlie is gone and that's bad. Her daddy keeps coming and going, and coming and going. Lily feels afraid because not one thing stays. She wishes just one thing would. Mama and Daddy. Two things. Then she would never be afraid like her daddy said. He said she shouldn't be afraid of anything. Right now, right this minute, she feels afraid of everything. Every single thing. There's bees that can sting her and horse flies that bite. Wild dogs waiting behind rocks and bad men that steal you away in their cars. There's monsters. She's seen them on TV. Daddy said there's no such thing as monsters, but he's wrong. Her grandpa said there's no such thing as angels, but there are. She saw one. Is she going to see a monster, too? Who will be there to protect her? Everything comes and everything goes.

Her Mama calls her from the back door of Nana's house. She doesn't want to go in. Inside is the yelling.

—m—

When Aunt Katie and Daddy dropped her off, Mama came to the back door. Her face was all red and she started yelling at Daddy. She slammed the door and Daddy went into the house after her. It was awful. Lily followed him up the four back stairs into the kitchen and they yelled really mean things at each other.

Mama yelled, "If you want to see Lily, you need to call me and make an appointment. You can't just take her anytime you want."

"Why the hell not? She's my daughter."

"It doesn't work that way."

"You are not going to tell me when I can see my daughter and when I can't."

"I'm the mother. I can tell you."

"And what a mother you have been. Taking up with another man right in front of her."

"At least I didn't leave her."

"I wasn't gone that long. Why couldn't you wait? All this. Why?"

"What did you do over there?"

"You know why I went over there."

"Was it for anything? We needed you."

Mama began to cry, but she made a sound in her throat and her tears stopped.

Daddy didn't say another word.

He bent over and picked up Lily and held her real tight. She started coughing. He put her back down and brushed his hand back over her forehead to ruffle her bangs.

"Bye, Peanut. You remember what I told you in the park."

He walked out of the house and climbed back into the car with Aunt Katie.

—m—

Lily Rose pretends she doesn't hear her mama calling. She continues walking through the flower garden looking for new buds and bees, and the sun hides behind clouds now and only the flies seem to want to play. In the distance, thunder rolls. God bowling in heaven. That's what Nana told her. God or not, the sound makes her feel funny in her tummy. Maybe she should go back into the house. It's safe there, isn't it? But she feels mad at her mama for yelling at Daddy.

Daddy's gone.

Again.

What she wants more than any single thing, even more than ice cream, is to find one thing that will last forever. One thing that is hers and hers alone that will never leave her. She thought Growlie was that one thing, but she was wrong. What could it be?

Suddenly her mama yanks her by her left arm. Yanks. A new word she heard on TV. Her Uncle Peter told her what it means.

"Lily Rose! Didn't you hear me calling you?"

"I heard you."

"Why didn't you come?"

"I'm looking for something."

"I want you to come when I call you."

"You're hurting my arm, Mama."

Her mama lets her arm go, falls to her knees, and throws her arms around her tightly.

"I'm sorry, Sweet Pea. I'm so sorry."

Mama begins to cry. Lily's tummy begins to hurt. Things don't just come and go. They also fall apart.

Her world is falling apart.

Where will she go to feel safe?

"I never wanted it to be like this," Mama says.

Lily does not feel sorry for her. She feels nothing, but a hurting in her tummy. Twisting and turning, she breaks free of her mama's arms.

"I'm looking for something, Mama."

Wiping tears away from her cheeks, her mama asks, "What are you looking for?"

"Something just for me."

"You're mad at me, aren't you?"

"Everything comes, everything goes."

Lily walks deeper into the garden and her mama stands.

"Lily, I want to go somewhere for a while. Will you be okay staying here with Nana?"

Lily turns to look at her. "Are you going to look for Daddy? How can you be so mean to him?"

"No, I am not going to look for him. As for being mean, well,

I told you ... there are a lot of complicated feelings. I am feeling all kinds of things. Someday you will understand better. When I come back, we'll go get some ice cream, okay?"

Her mama walks away and her tummy stops hurting. In the distance, the sound of God bowling grows louder.

She'll pretend.

She'll pretend that she's the mama, and Daddy is her husband and he never goes away. She begins to walk on her toes like the ladies she watches on TV wearing shoes that make them tall. She imagines that she is a princess wearing a long purple dress that trails behind her. Her hair is piled up on top her head and her white gloves cover her arms up to her elbows. Around her pile of hair sits a crown covered with sparkly rocks, and she wears bracelets and rings that match. The king and the queen have called for her, and she walks down a long red carpet where people stand on either side. Near by the king and queen, sitting in big chairs, stands her daddy dressed in a white suit with a purple shirt. He smiles as she approaches and there isn't a brace on his leg or a cane in his hand. Jake sits next to him wagging his tail.

They live in a castle that sits on a hill overlooking a big green lake. On the lake are boats slowly crossing the water, and big colorful balloons are floating in the sky. There are no monsters. There are no bees that sting, wild dogs that bite, or mean men waiting to steal things away in the night. There are no people yelling at each other, no people sick or dying in their beds, and God is not bowling. There is only rain when the flowers need a drink, snow when an angel needs to be made, and wind when the air feels too hot.

Princess Lily tells the maids to sweep the floor, wash the windows, and make the ice cream – strawberry, of course. When they do their work well, as they always do, Princess Lily throws a ball where everyone dances.

Lily Rose begins to dance around the garden on her toes. The skirt of her dress, which she holds out to the side with her hands, is very full. She swirls around the dance floor in her daddy's arms, passing everyone else in a blur. The floor falls away as they lift into the sky and begin to dance around upon the clouds. The day changes to night and the stars begin to shine and fall all around them like fireworks, but without the loud bangs. She looks around to see angels sitting around on the clouds, some playing the thing with the strings that sounds real pretty, and others singing in really sweet voices. Her daddy and her swirl and laugh and twirl and smile and they turn, and they turn.

Everything comes here, but nothing goes.

It's all hers in this world where Daddy and she live happily ever after.

Then Lily stumbles on a hard piece of dirt and falls. When she opens her eyes she is in Nana's garden sitting on the ground, a few drops of blood beading from a scrape on her knee. The blood is very red. She does not cry, though she feels sad that the magical world that she was living in is gone. For now.

On the ground walks an army of ants. That's what Daddy called them one day when they discovered them in the yard. An army. These ants are busy walking in a line carrying pieces of something much larger than they are. How can they be so strong? And they walk for a very long way. Her daddy is a Marine. He's not in the Army, but he told her they are kind of the same, only the Marines are stronger and less afraid. Braver. That's what he said. They were braver. Do Marines carry pieces of something much larger than they are? He told her he was in a desert so large that you couldn't see the end. He said it was very hot, much hotter than it ever gets here. Poor Daddy. Is he going back? He's going somewhere. She knows because he said goodbye. Her tummy begins to hurt again.

Behind the castle, which shines as yellow as a marigold or the sun, sits a zoo. But this zoo doesn't have cages. All the animals play together like friends. They wander over the hills that are very green, and they, too, have no end like the desert, only here the air feels cool. The elephants walk behind each other in a line, like the ants, their trunks and tails connected. In the trees, the happy monkeys swing from branch to branch laughing. The lions lie on their backs in the warm sun, purring like kittens. Here they don't hunt other animals for their food. No animal has to hunt. All the animals are fed exactly what they love to eat. In the green lake swim whales and dolphins and fish of every size. The dolphins jump out of the water playing, sometimes giggling, as they swim backwards on their tails. Also in this water swim sharks, but they have no teeth, and snakes, but they do not sting. Snakes sting, right?

In one valley among the hills are the horses, her favorite. There are white ones and black ones and also gray. But the one she likes best is yellow, the color of sand. Palanimo, or something like that. She'll name her horse Star because he has a white star on his forehead. When he sees her, he comes running, and she jumps up on his back and they race across the hills, her hands wrapped tightly in his mane. At one point, Star runs so fast that he lifts off the ground into flight. Wings pop out from his sides, and she and her favorite horse fly.

Hers.

All hers.

No one, not even Uncle James, can take these things away.

A loud crack of thunder makes the earth shake. Suddenly, Lily Rose is back in Nana's garden and the sky looks dark.

"Lily Rose! Lily!" her Nana calls.

But Lily does not want to answer. She doesn't want to be in the garden. She wants to be in the world with her castle.

Everything comes.

Nothing goes.

Her daddy is going to kill Uncle James. She doesn't know how she knows this, but she does. He's going to kill Uncle James because he stole Growlie. And because he slept with Mama in her bed.

Then Daddy will have to run away.

He's not going back to the desert. He'll have to run away or be locked up behind bars.

No.

Behind the castle sits the zoo. None of the animals live in cages. None of the animals hunt.

"Lily!"

She doesn't want to go into that house. It isn't safe in there. In that house, people yell.

Inside the castle it feels very warm. A huge fireplace in one wall sits full of wood and flames. Princess Lily and Daddy are lying in bed snugly under thick fluffy quilts. The quilts are purple flowered with little kitties and puppies on them playing with balls. Daddy holds her tightly in his arms, softly petting her hair and occasionally kissing her cheek. She feels safe. She feels so safe.

The loud sound of God bowling shakes the ground again. Lily finds herself back in the garden. Daddy told her that if she wanted something very bad, she had to go after it. How can she find the castle? Can she find it before Daddy has to go away?

Suddenly, Nana stands beside her.

"Didn't you hear me calling you?"

Lily doesn't look up at her Nana. "I heard you, Nana."

"Why didn't you come?"

"I'm very busy."

"What are you doing?"

"I'm playing a game."

"What kind of game?"

"Daddy and I live in a castle."

"Not your mama, too?"

"No."

"Lily, look at me."

Lily looks up at her Nana.

"What happened?"

"We live in a castle by a green lake. There's a zoo behind it and all of the animals live together without cages ..."

"No. I mean when you were with your Daddy. Did something happen?"

"I ... I ran away. I almost got hit by a car!"

Nana drops to her knees and grabs her shoulder. "Why did you run away?"

"Because ... because Daddy was saying goodbye."

Nana puts her hand on her cheek then stands back up and turns away looking worried.

"Doesn't anything stay forever, Nana?"

"Well, Lily Rose ..." Her voice fades off as she watches something intently.

Lily turns to see what Nana is looking at. It's Uncle James driving by slowly in his red car. The color is so pretty. Uncle James is looking towards them, but he doesn't lift a hand to wave.

Nana says very softly, "Oh, no."

Uncle James wants to kill her daddy. She doesn't know how she knows this, but she does. He wants to. He's already killed Growlie, and he wants to be back in Mama's bed.

Lily covers her tummy with both hands.

29
Red Hot

Saturday 3:44 p.m.

The GTO glides along the road, rumbling from the dual exhaust. James slows her to a stop at the red light. When it turns green, he slides the dual-gate shifter to the right to take her through the gears. Although he hasn't run her in at least seven or eight months, the Pontiac doesn't miss a beat. The guttural growl blends in with the thunder and the gas pedal begs for the run, with 450 horses vibrating beneath the scooped hood. Nobody has to tell him he looks good, riding along in this blood-red car that once belonged to his brother, Jeff.

—m—

Debbie let out a squeal when she crawled into the passenger side, stroking the black leather of the seat like it was a puppy. Her little skirt grew shorter as she squirmed this way and that, craning her neck to take in every nook and corner. When she turned to take in the back, she leaned in towards him, making sure he could sneak a peek down the little tee straining to hold her breasts in. He began to fantasize about doing things to her he hadn't done yet. That he remembered anyway. Damn it, if Brenda didn't come to mind. Her breasts, her ass, her... Not this child endowed with the body parts of a woman. But he didn't resist when they moved into the outskirts of town, and Debbie turned to him and shot her hand out to touch him, and she began to knead like dough. Who the hell taught this girl her licks?

"I didn't have much breakfast. Mind if I chew on a little sausage?"

"That's not a little sausage," he said.

As she unzipped his pants, she said with a giggle, "You're

right, it's not." As she began to pleasure him more, he reached down over her back and snuck his hand in under the waistband of her skirt, He pulled the GTO off the paved road down a dirt lane real slow so as not to raise the dust. Lifting her head gently by the hair, he said, "Come here." She drew the tee over her head in a flash and threw the thin cotton into the back seat as he began to nibble at her nipples. They weren't hers, they were Brenda's. The hole wasn't that of a half-grown woman, but the one he dreamed of filling with his seed. When Debbie began to squeal, his senses returned, and he pulled Debbie off, both of them breathless.

"Let me get a condom," he said, as he reached over to open the glove box.

"I'm on the pill," she said.

"I always use these," he said as he tore open the little package with his teeth.

"You didn't last night."

His stomach sank.

"I want to feel you inside of me without that thing on," she continued.

"Never mind," he said as he began to push her back over into the passenger seat.

"No!" she whined. She pulled her panties off and resting her head against the passenger door, said, "Don't tell me you can resist this."

He pulled her by the hand back on top of him and tossed the condom to the side.

Back to the task at hand. Locating Billy and beating him into a bloody pulp as red as his car, as red as the heart of a flame, as red as a sunset can be at the end of a hot August afternoon. He brought her along on the outside chance of making Brenda jealous. He'll go to the fucking pig roast that everyone keeps talking about because he can't find Billy anywhere else. He'll taunt him and tease him until his old friend blows. He'll show the whole town once and for all that Billy is not the golden boy. Not anymore. He's a gimp now returned from the war, no longer strong as a bull, no longer handsome as a movie star, no longer the husband of Brenda. Just another guy. James will beat him to within an inch of his death then let him live out the rest of his life in shame. If afterwards he has to run he will, heading west to use that striped beach towel, or if necessary, farther south, over the border, where he'll spend the rest of his life gloating, surrounded by bronze-skinned beauties cooling him with a fan. The time has come.

"Why are we riding around and around?" Debbie asks.

"I'm looking for someone."

"I thought we were going to the party."

"We are."

"Do I look all right?"

James turns to glance her way, taking in the wavy blonde strands of hair, the flush of orgasm in her cheeks, the sparkle in her eyes. *Everyone will know what we just done,* he thinks. Good. They wouldn't expect less from him.

"Sure. You look fine."

She drags a lipstick across her lower and upper lips, then presses them together as girls do. Every girl he's known except Brenda. Most of the time she didn't even wear lipstick. She didn't have to. She was a natural beauty by any standard. Fuck her. Fuck him for thinking about her.

"So is your girlfriend going to be there?"

"Probably."

"You know ... everyone says she's going back to Billy."

That's all it takes, even though James swore he would keep his cool until later. He pushes it down and manages to ask, "That's what they say, hah?"

"I'm available. I could be your girlfriend."

James laughs, shaking his head. "You're a kid."

"A kid? A kid doesn't do the things I just did."

"It's not all about that." Even he's not sure what that means. "Where did you learn all that, anyhow?"

"Well," she says under her breath, turning to look right out of the window. "Step fathers," she whispers. She turns to look at him and lowers her eyes and turns away again, her pretty little mouth twisted into something sad.

What do you know. A comrade of sorts.

He doesn't say anything.

As they approach the Jedele farm, the white plastic fabric panels of the tents droop in the humid day, and the smoke from the cooking meat rises and hangs in the air like fog. James carefully pulls the GTO into a field where twenty-five cars or more are already parked. He pulls up next to a black Camaro he's never seen. As he and Debbie step out of the car, a young man dressed in a white tee and blue jeans standing in front of the Camaro turns from taking a leak.

"Whoa!" the guy says. "Didn't expect anyone to pull in just then. Good thing your engine made enough noise to warn me."

"Next time you might want to step into the trees," James says.

"What's under the hood?"

Debbie steps up close to James.

"Standard V-8," James says.

"Hardly standard."

Debbie pipes up, "He's got the fastest car around."

"You've got your very own showgirl?" The guy asks James.

James takes in a deep breath and lets it back out slowly.

"I'd guess 450," the guy says. "The tubed wells look good. You going out to Astin Road tonight?"

"Austin. Not Astin. Maybe." He turns to Debbie. "Let's go, showgirl."

"Not very friendly, are you?" The guy says.

"Not very," James says as he and Debbie head towards the crowd.

"Sub-thirteen?" the guy asks.

"Sub-twelve," James throws over his shoulder. He turns to Debbie and says, "I brought you here to be seen and not heard."

"Well, you brought the wrong girl."

"That's what I'm afraid of."

—⁓—

One hour later, two beers and two shots down, James starts to relax. Though he's not giving alcohol to Debbie, she's getting it from somewhere, slinking around giggling and smiling and catching every man's eye.

James doesn't dance, but Debbie pulls a few volunteers in from the crowd, or dances alone, pushing her long gold hair up off the back of her neck, unnecessarily undulating to the beats of the pop rock cover tunes. Like a homing pigeon she keeps returning to his side, slipping her hand into his or interlacing their arms, both of which he shakes free. One time she dares to step up close, staring him in the eye as her right hand reaches between them to softly rub.

He steps back growling, "Not here."

She pivots away on one foot, turning back to glare, her lips drawn together in an angry pout. Off she goes, no doubt hunting for another pushover of a man who will feed her more booze.

At one point, his friend Carl steps up beside him, a huge plastic cup of beer with a thick frothy head in one hand and a filter-less cigarette in the other. "I hear she came with you," he says, nodding at Debbie, who was jumping up and down to a rapid beat, her breasts jiggling, her lovely little ass firm and unmoving.

James draws smoke from his own cigarette. "Yeah," he says, shaking his head, his eyes rolling.

"Taylor Jacobs' daughter, isn't it?"

"I don't know."

"How old is she?"

"She's legal. I saw her ID."

"Yeah, but was it real?"

James hesitates, his cigarette halfway to his mouth. Now why the fuck didn't he think about that?

"Just kidding," Carl says. "She graduated last June. But obviously trouble. Big trouble."

"Yeah."

Now maybe it is James' imagination, but he feels like all eyes are turned towards him when he's not looking, and he doesn't know how many conversations he's heard delayed as he's walking by. He's the center of attention. Now maybe the attention springs from his showing up with Debbie – the widows and the matrons, the mothers and the prudes blaming him for her loose behavior. A few of the women, those he's bedded, act torn between jealousy of the young girl and longing for a repeat of their own pleasure. They greet him warmly until their backs arch up whenever Debbie sashays near. The men, too, are torn between respect for his mechanical expertise and his blatant womanizing that sets their teeth on edge. Half of them want to throw him out of town and the others want to walk a year or two in his shoes.

"Billy's here," Carl says, looking at him out of the corner of his eye.

With those two words, James feels his entire body tighten and the blood, the blue blood not yet introduced to the air, pound inside his head.

"Is he alone?" James asks.

"Came with Katie."

Ah, yes, James thinks. Billy's sister, Katie. Does Billy know that maybe a year ago he and his darling sister made out for an hour and a half? She let him feel up her breasts, small and perky, but when he slid his hand down lower, she pushed the advance away.

"How about Brenda?"

"Haven't seen her."

James brushes his hair up off of his forehead and takes one last long drag, drops his cigarette to the ground, and grinds the red of the ember into ash.

"You guys going to get into it or what?" Carl asks.

"So everyone is standing around waiting for it to happen?"

"Oh, I don't know," Carl says. "I just thought it was inevitable."

So that's the deal. He and Billy facing off serves as a sideshow for the party. While the rock star wannabes pound away on their cover tunes, and the townsfolk pull away their greasy roasted pork with their teeth, they're silently counting the minutes until the skirmish breaks out. Are they taking bets? Finally, the face-off they've been dreaming of for six months, knowing Billy, the golden boy, will return and avenge the seduction and theft of his wife. Damn if they care that Brenda was a willing partner, reaching up to bare her ass, bending over to make sure he gets all the way in. Damn if they care that James has loved Brenda every day, every minute since he saw her one day in school when they were thirteen. Already, his stepfathers had stolen their pleasure and Doris Rentschler had earmarked him as her own. Damn, they didn't know anything except their own driving need for the sight and smell of blood.

The iron-like richness.

The sticky aftermath.

Their own secret needs satisfied.

James would give it to them. Triumphant.

James begins to walk around the crowd, nodding to those who will acknowledge him, turning away smiling from those who glare. He pours himself at least a jigger from a decanter of whiskey and tosses the smooth hot liquor back. He lets every injustice, and underhanded doing, every heartbreak and pain, surface to make him seethe.

He wonders how a small town can produce a crowd this large. Must be the news travels far beyond the borders. Pork on the spit, juicy inside, crispy outside, calls to the animal in all. Kegs of beer, pumped like oil, beads of sweat glisten and roll down the metal sides of the barrels. Pasta salad and potato salad, pickled pears, and radishes sliced just right into petals. Chips and dip and a bowl of baked beans, brownies and Jell-O topped with a tower of whipped cream. Paper plates stuffed into plastic cans with forks and knives tumbling free. Used cups dotting the scene with various levels of unused liquids, cigarette and cigar butts floating, standing, sinking.

The cross section of humanity. And the party was in full swing.

There's Bob Aikens from the John Deere dealership surrounded by at least six local farmers cleaned up for the day, smelling pretty in their checked shirts and stiff new jeans. Mabel Downey from the flower shop holds a double plate of heaping food, which her short fat frame doesn't need. Doris stands in the shade off to the side with her husband the land mogul. He's one who glares at James, but still Doris manages to squeeze James' hand as he passes. Bart Jones, sergeant of the police force, dressed in street clothes, stands with his arms crossed like he's still on duty, his gun strapped to his side. Is he here in case a fight breaks out? The teenage girls whisper, as they always have, behind raised hands, riled over the loose behavior of their peer, Debbie. Secretly, they all want to be just like her. Don't they? The kids, squealing and laughing, weave their way through the crowd in some annoying game. Shouldn't they be out in the fields playing catch, or football, hide-and-seek, or tag? There's those he graduated with, those whose cars he repairs, those whose names he doesn't know, but has seen around a hundred times.

There's Katie. But, no Billy.

He decides to mess with her.

He walks up to her with a little smile, letting her see his eyes take her in from head to toe. She's a pretty girl, but her nails are too long, her clothes too clean and pressed for him. James wants the trace of a scent drifting from under the arms and, if he's lucky, the distant waft of a musky cave. Katie smells like lotions, oils, hair spray, and cologne – like the cosmetic counter of a department store that he makes a point of walking around. He watches her take him in from head to toe and the subtle fear that appears in her eyes.

"Hi, Katie," he says, making sure he walks up close enough that she can feel his breath on her cheek when he speaks. Close like they were good friends. Until six months ago, before Brenda, they were. Sort of.

"Hey, James," she says, her eyes glancing over her shoulders. She's looking for her brother, he thinks.

"You're sure looking good today. What's that perfume you're wearing?"

"Leave him alone, James."

"Who?"

"Don't be an asshole. You know who."

"What if he doesn't want to leave me alone?"

"It takes two. If one of you ..."

Just then, of course, Debbie, sweaty and smelly, saunters up, glaring at Kate, and puts her little hand around his well pumped biceps and says, "James, please, please come dance with me." Her smell stirs him, but her tiny whiny voice holds him down.

"I told you, honey, I don't dance."

She cups her other hand over his left pectoral, flutters her lashes and says, "Just once."

James laughs as Kate looks on with disgust, and he glances over her shoulder to see the red-hot glare of his blood brother.

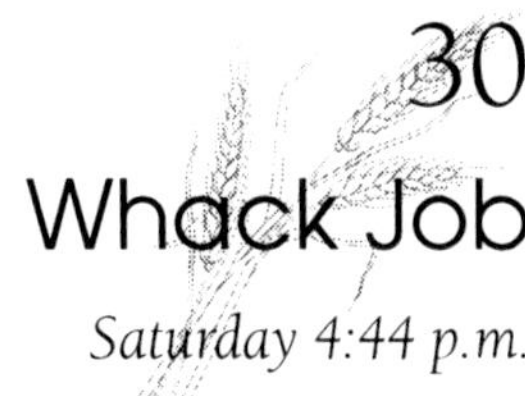

30 Whack Job

Saturday 4:44 p.m.

No way can Peter ever see the world with the same eyes as he has before. His eyes are now open. He always wondered what that meant, and now he clearly knows. In effect, he has become worldly. In a twenty-four-hour period, he dropped from the imaginary universe painted on his ceiling into a world of desire, danger, and opportunity. He was fucked by an infected wild boy, walked for miles across fields in the gushing rain, saw what appeared to be an angel, pointed a gun at a devout Christian, and sucked off a scar-faced gangster. No way can he remain in Willis hiding his lusty urges, pretending he's the average guy wishing his world would open up. He'll keep this new world pried open with his will. He'll place a wedge in the opening so he can pass through cleanly. He'll close the escape hatch behind him so as to never be the boy he was two-dozen hours before.

From now on he'll be known as Pedro.

Pedro follows directions impeccably.

Pedro begins rifling through his father's bedroom drawers looking for money.

Not his father. The man who used to be his father.

The cleaning lady has all of the man's once-white Fruit of the Loom underwear folded into neat, square piles. The socks are rolled into balls beside them. In the second drawer are his shirts, flawlessly pressed, collars perfect, all white and suitable shades of pastel. Beside them sit his selection of belts, coiled like snakes. In the third drawer, Pedro hits the jackpot, but not what he expected. He plops to the floor cross-legged and sorts through the disarrayed treasure of this chest. Obviously, Molly Maid was told to keep her hands off this one. Three porno tapes in dog-eared cardboard sleeves. On the covers are exceptionally large-breasted women, licking their lips, or pinching their nipples, or lying back leisurely with their plump thighs spread. Half-buried under the tapes lies a red file with newspaper clippings of the man who used to be his father, smiling for the cameras, trophy in hand, or caught in the action of throwing a long high pass. He stands handsome and well-muscled. Rolling in the bottom of the drawer are a few golfing tees, a couple of golf balls, and matchbooks and coasters of clubs where he has dined, drunk, and ridden across emerald greens. On the far right of the drawer, a thin pile of papers lies face down. Pedro picks the pile up and turns it. On top lies the clipping from the *Willis Gazette* announcing the murder of his mother. A photo accompanies the news, his mother smiling, dressed in a summer dress, holding Brenda in one arm and him in the other.

Before he has the chance to hold the word back, it squeezes through – "Mommy." The worldly man becomes a boy again for seconds. A pain in his gut flares with the threat of tears and the anger at a God he now distrusts. Suddenly, he is ten again and all alone. His chief ally gone forever, and he feels like he will never again be understood.

Until he remembers Todd and Eddie. New friends from his new world.

Aren't they?

He throws the papers back into the drawer, slams the heavy wood shut and stands.

Where the hell does his fa ... the man who used to be his father hide his money? Everyone hides a little cash somewhere. Don't they?

In the second set of drawers, Pedro finds neatly folded sweats, pajamas, and robes starting from the bottom up. In the top drawer, he hits the jackpot again. Ten twenties folded in half lie under a box of cufflinks and beside them, a small pearl-handled revolver, more pretty than deadly, but nonetheless able to wing a man or perhaps lay him down, depending on the shot. Surprisingly, the fag, the queer, the gay boy shoots pretty darn well. The man who owns this gun taught him how when he was ten.

Pedro tucks the revolver into the back waistband of his jeans, like he's seen in the movies, but he takes the gun back out. He's looking for excitement, not trouble. He places the gun back into the drawer and pockets the cash.

He walks over to the large window in the master's bedroom and gazes out at the dark clouds laced with yellow marching into town. All is still, all is humid, all is waiting for the storm. Pedro wonders if he will ever peer through this glass again, the same glass his mother cleaned of every smudge, smear, and insect poop, and lost herself inside. She wanted escape. He knows it. No doubt she never daydreamed her escape would be through death. He will not imagine again what she went through. He's been over that a thousand times before. He will not go there. He grabs the revolver from the top drawer and carries the cold metal in his warm hand.

Pedro walks back over to his bedroom and pulls the blue knapsack out of the closet. He looks around the room and wonders where to start. What does a man with open eyes take with him when he's about to leave his old life behind?

Clothes.

He opens drawers quickly, pulling out two sets of socks, jeans, shirts and underwear, and piles them into the bottom of the sack. In the bathroom, he falls to his knees before the cabinet, and rifles through cans, canisters, soap bars, double-edged razors, and old sponges, looking for one of his mom's old cosmetic bags. He finds one covered with pink and blue flowers, and fills the plastic inside with razors, deodorant, toothbrush and cologne, zit cream, Excedrin, toothpaste, and a few cotton swabs. Pulling the cord of his hair dryer out with a snap, he coils it, grabs his brush, and returns to his room.

He begins to write his farewell note in his head.

Dear ... old Dad. No way.

He's older now, more mature. Perhaps he'll call him Martin.

Dear Martin.

No.

Dear jerk, control freak, bastard.

Is that necessary?

After packing his toiletries on top of his clothes, he still has space for ... what? He pulls a sketchpad from underneath stacked paper on his desk, grabs a couple of pencils, an eraser, pink as a baby's butt, and one pen. All of these things he places carefully in his bag.

I've left because I can't be under this roof for one more day.

Remembering the look of the sky, Pedro walks back into the master's bedroom to peer out again through the large window his mommy loved. If he leaves now, he's sure to be rained upon in the not-too-distant future. Maybe if he walks his ass out on that road, he'll quickly catch a ride. Hopefully this time the person who picks him up will be a handsome young gay man, or someone connected to the big shows on Broadway.

Actually, he's planning on heading straight to Eddie's. Eddie didn't mean what he said. He just said what he knew his father and Billy wanted him to say. Didn't he?

As Pedro stands in the window watching the zigzag of lightning crackling through the clouds, he catches a late-model Jaguar driving slowly by from the corner of his eye. The car travels past before he can see who sits inside. Probably a friend of ... Martin's ... hoping to drag him out for a drink in the bar, or a round of golf. No, not golf with a storm threatening to break. Pedro turns from the window to finish his packing. On top of the pile in the knapsack he places his rain slicker.

If only you could have accepted me for who I am.

On top of his dresser and his desk are framed photos of family members. He grabs the small one of Lily Rose lying on her back in the grass, laughing. He will miss watching his little niece grow up. Tucking the photo in a pocket of his knapsack, he looks up at the wedding photo of Brenda and Billy. He has to take that one, too. But, it is the photo of his mother sitting on the porch on an autumn day that he grabs from his bedside table, holding the oak frame for a moment upon his chest. She stares out wistfully, unaware that a photo is being snapped. That photo, he tucks into a pocket in a special place. If only he could have protected her ... saved her ... from him. Martin snuffed out her spirit. The other guy just stole her remains. He slowly slides the revolver down into that special pocket beside her.

I hate you. Could he really write those words?

The ringing phone startles him. Should he answer it? Or slip out the back door as if he never heard the ringing, never shared the drama, never felt that sense of not belonging.

But his curiosity gets the better of him. Maybe Brenda still wants to go shopping.

"Hello?"

"Petey ... I'm glad you're there."

What do you know? It's him. No one else calls him by a baby name anymore.

"What you doing?" he asks.

"Just ... just hanging out," Pedro answers.

"I just stopped by my office for a minute. I thought maybe we could drop over by the pig roast."

"What?" Pedro can't believe his ears. His father ... the man who used to be his father ... hasn't tried to share time with him since he was a teen. Pedro figured his father would show up and try to ground him or something. Instead, he wants to spend time with him. Something tightens up inside him. Suddenly, he's struggling to breathe.

"I can swing by and pick you up in a few minutes."

"No! I mean ... Brenda's coming by. We're going shopping."

"I thought Brenda was going over to the party."

"Later. She said she was going later."

"Oh. Did you get some sleep, Son?"

"Yeah."

"Look ... what happened last night ... I hope that ..."

Pedro can't believe his ears. His father is actually bringing it up.

"We're ... worried about you."

Save it.

"Dad, I've got to go. Brenda is out front honking her horn."

"Why don't you come by the party with her later?"

"Yeah, I probably will."

"We'll have a beer together."

What the ...

"What do you say?"

"I don't like beer. I've never liked beer. If you knew me, you'd know that. Bye ..." He utters the second word under his breath, "Dad."

Pedro turns and heads back to where his knapsack sits on his bed. He lies down on his back beside the bulky canvas and stares up into his own private universe. In moments he's lost inside the blue-black of the background and the bright light of the stars streaming by. To the right, he spots the rings of Jupiter and, far off into the left, the distant speck of Pluto. He sails through the cluster of lights that constitute the Milky Way, and watches the tail of a comet recede into the mysterious endless dark.

What is he doing? Turning tail and running, so as not to feel the piercing blades of old pain? Or is he daring to look forward to a day when his father not only accepts him for who he is, but even calls him Peter. Or Pedro.

The blades are rusty.

Infection has set in.

How will he amputate these oozing wounds and retain enough of himself to move on?

Get up off the bed. Finish packing your meager belongings. Stick that thumb out and take another chance.

Forget me, Dad. And I'll forget you.

Instead he pictures his father as a piñata swinging from a tree. In his hand he holds a stick, long, hard, and thick enough to leave welts and multicolored bruises.

Pedro begins to flail.

One whack for all the times you told Mom the food she prepared was tasteless.

One whack for all the times you told her she had a funny smell.

One whack for all the times you talked to her like she was a child.

A slave wearing her little cotton aprons just for you.

A piece of ass you could access with a snap of your fingers. A slight brush on the soft flesh of her upper thigh. The not-so-subtle separation of her legs when you were ready.

Two whacks for appraising Brenda's budding sexuality from the corner of your eye.

One whack for telling her she'd never be good enough for Billy.

Two whacks for not protecting and supporting her when her husband was away.

One huge whack for making Pedro feel like a stranger in a strange land.

Two more for dragging him down the hall, throwing him onto his bed, and glaring at him with devil eyes.

For slapping his hand away when he dared to touch his weenie.

For holding him at arm's length when he needed a hug so badly that he was afraid he might burst.

His heart did.

Burst.

The bloody tattered remains are still splashed against each and every wall inside this house, but not a home.

I will never be able to forgive you.

I am no longer your son.

Goodbye.

Pedro shoots up from his position lying on the bed, throws his legs over the edge and stands. Maybe he should walk out of the house and leave it in flames behind him.

He would, except that he cannot burn what is left of his mother hanging on the walls, tucked gently into drawers, carefully displayed on every surface of this house. His sister calls this house a museum to their mom, and it is. Beneath the taunting, the abuse, he, Martin, must have loved her more than he was capable of showing. Where did he learn that? Why do so many men keep those they love most at arm's length?

Pedro swears that he will not do that.

Pedro walks into the bathroom and stands before the mirror, runs his fingers through the dark unruly curls of his hair. He leans forward and looks deeply into his own eyes. Can he do this? Can he walk out of this house confident that he can take care of himself?

Or will he find someone else to do that for him?

No. He will be okay. He will be okay.

Pedro walks for the last time back into his bedroom. He glances up at his private universe and realizes that it, too, will become a part of the museum. Every room will reflect the members of the family who once lived here, but no more. The man who used to be his father can pretend that they are all still here. The splinters off their spirits, which he so rudely pried away, will echo, ricochet, and haunt.

Pedro zips up the pockets of his knapsack, throws the heavy bundle over one shoulder, and walks out of the room, bounds down the stairs and, before he can think twice, steps out of the house into the stormy day.

Halfway down the driveway he remembers that he forgot to write and leave the farewell note behind. He hesitates for one moment, his right foot suspended in the air.

If he leaves now, will he ever see the angel again? Lily Rose? Brenda, Billy? Grandma Martha and Uncle Sam?

They love him. Why is he leaving them behind?

His right foot falls and propels him forward. He cannot live in this community except undercover. Already the people of the town know that at twenty he's never had a girl. No doubt behind a few of the manicured doors live other men who want men, and he has his suspicion of who they are. But he wants to hold the hand of a man in public. Kiss his lips when the notion strikes. Tattoo his arm and pierce his nipple and not have people point like he is a circus freak.

Here in Willis, conformity holds the town intact. The pioneering spirit of those who had been outcasts, too, settled this land, only to be forced undercover by the words from the pulpit, the actions of the elite, the soothing murmurs of their desperate rocking mothers.

Pedro has found a new family.

When he hits the main road, he pulls his rain slicker from his knapsack and rests the crinkling plastic guard on top. The thunder rumbles like an approaching train, and the jagged intermittent forks of lightning look scary.

Maybe the angel will travel with him. Isn't that what they say? Everyone has a guardian angel. Is his the one he saw?

He steps up onto the shoulder of the road and sticks his thumb out. Pedro figures that a vast majority of the town stragglers are half drunk and happy at the pig roast, carving away at the sacrificed lamb, spilling the blood over the tilled land where crops will grow. They wait breathlessly to see if Billy will avenge.

Pedro thrusts his thumb out with greater intent. A station wagon slows down, drives past him, and pulls over onto the shoulder.

Without even bending over and checking out who sits behind the wheel, he opens the door and climbs in, dragging his heavy knapsack onto his lap.

31
Blow Hard

Saturday 6:13 p.m.

The sight of seeing James standing so close to his sister, Kate, like maybe he might brush her ass with his hand or lick her ear with a flick of his tongue, catalyzes Bagwell's fury. His old friend's actions are lizard-like, his eyes half shaded with puffy lids, his head snapping back and forth from side to side, the trademark smile one beat away from cruel. Bagwell has seen this James before. One shot of bourbon too many. An old memory or personal offense tightening inside him like a wire about to break. James is going to blow. Bagwell plans to meet that blow halfway.

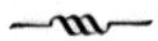

Two hours later, rain begins to pitter-patter on the plastic tent as the wind dances through and lifts the edges. Some of the people have left, not wanting to be squeezed beneath the plastic, forced into hard-backed chairs, humidity rising off the confined bodies mixing with the smoke of meat, the smoke of cigarettes and cigars carried forth by sneezes, coughs, and incessant chatter. When thunder strikes, squeals rise from the children, expletives from the adults, howls from damp-furred doggies like Jake who couldn't resist a romp through the falling rain. A fair share of the townsfolk have remained and the fun has not diminished, but has taken on an edge, as alcohol loosens the tongues, lifts the inhibitions, and fuels old wounds. Though it appears on the surface that one and all are tied up into their own dramas, the whereabouts of James and Bagwell are carefully monitored, their words telegraphed from table to table, the outcome of their final meeting speculated upon while quiet bets are exchanged beneath the tabletops.

Bagwell knows all this because he's seen it before. The names of the warring parties are Bagwell and James today, but someone always captures the eye of attention in a small town. The people think they know all the details of the dispute, but in actuality they only know the story each has created from the scraps of gossip passed from house to house like a relay.

Yesterday Bagwell was the golden boy, today he's the gimp come back from the desert with a Purple Heart. James remains the outsider, the brown trash who doesn't bother to curb his lusty urges. He's a hotheaded young man who acts without scruples, half-hated, half-pitied, people partially aware of his mother, her lovers, and how James the young boy became their toy.

Still, even in the rain, a few people arrive, the cover band delivering a rhythm for their steps, each looked over from head to toe, greeted by some, ignored by others, as all wait for the arrival of one. The woman. The county supervisor's daughter. The girl that couldn't wait for her husband to return, who had to satisfy her own urges as women in wartime often do. The women will tell you they have needs, too, for they are women after all, only a few decades free from the label of a man's property. They are dizzy with newfound freedom as the blonde girl demonstrates out on the square of grass kept clear for dance. At this moment she begins to wiggle up her wet T-shirt inch by inch, exposing firm and tender flesh.

Bagwell watches as James rushes out on the dance square and pulls her by the arm into the fold. She throws her arms around his neck and he unwraps them and holds them down by her sides. He's talking into her ear with a disapproving look on his face. Next he pushes her down into a chair. When he looks up, his eyes meet with Bagwell's once again.

Where the hell is Brenda? It's looking like James came here with the blonde. Bagwell knows her as the daughter of Taylor Jacobs, the local antiques dealer. He remembers her as a little girl, hardly that now, out there dancing with the smell of sex all over her.

James has been in her. He's two-timing Brenda? His estranged wife told him last night that James was gone. Could she have thrown him out or did he just leave? Is this performance playing out between James and the girl just for him? James wants a fight. He wants a fight real bad.

Bagwell limps over to the table where bottles of booze stand in disarray, some empty, a few half full, one or two overturned, lying there like dead soldiers. Or Marines. Occasionally a rocket explodes inside Bagwell's head, forcing his jaw into a clench, and the one hand holding onto the head of his cane to tighten like a vise.

Through the ringing in his ears he hears a voice, "Bill, how the fuck are you?"

He looks up to see Joe Bailey, his old boss on the construction crew, beaming at him with his right hand stretched out.

Bagwell steps towards him, his wounded leg screaming from the morning run in the park, his face no doubt still red from watching James manipulate another female. The girl could even be underage. When he gets his hands on him ...

But he says, "Hey, Joe. How are you?"

"Jesus, Bill, it's good to see you. When you coming back to work? We've got developments happening all over the county."

"So I've seen. At this rate, pretty soon country life's going to be a thing of the past." He's talking, but he's got one eye on James. Not going to lose sight of him. James isn't going to leave the party sitting in his shiny red car. He's leaving in an ambulance or the coroner's wagon. There's no doubt about that.

"I've brought a jug of home-brewed stuff. Let's have a drink together." Joe reaches down under the table and pulls out a jug, just like he said, and pours two small plastic cups half full.

"Whoa," Bagwell says. "I'm on meds."

"This ain't going to hurt you. Put a little hair on your chest."

The two men tap cups and toss back. Joe's goes down like water on his 250-pound frame. Bagwell watches the large man stroke stray droplets away from his mustache and his beard. Then he glances over where James stands, tipping a beer back, hovering over his date.

"So, when you coming back to work?"

"I don't know, Joe. I've got this leg problem." Damn it, if Kate isn't standing over next to James again. Bagwell lights a cigarette, fighting to keep his hands steady.

"What was it like over there?"

"Hot," Bagwell answers.

"Didn't take long to clean up the problem."

Bagwell laughs, shaking his head. "It's hardly cleaned up."

"What do you mean?"

Bagwell watches from the corner of his eye, as the bear of a man follows his gaze.

"I guess you haven't settled things with him yet."

"No, Sir."

"It's not worth ruining your life over."

Bagwell looks Joe straight in the eyes. "Betrayal by another brother is unpardonable."

"That's just military gobbledygook."

"No, Sir, it is not."

"It's just a woman."

"No, Sir, it is not." Bagwell turns and limps away, heading over closer to where his nemesis stands.

Joe calls after him, "Call me when you're ready to work!"

They do not understand. None of them.

When Bagwell swapped blood with James that day tucked inside their little reed hut, he thought that he, too, knew what friendship and allegiance were. He didn't have the slightest clue. The Marines taught him about true brotherhood, and how each and every one becomes an extension of your own body, something you protect, you covet, you carry through wind, water, and fire, if necessary. You never leave your brother behind, whether the heart is beating or the heart is still. Even his remains and spirit floating overhead are included, as you tug the corpse across the ground, heave his lifeless hulk across your shoulder, feel his dangling hands tap a rhythm upon the back of your legs as you walk.

James couldn't get close to this profound allegiance. He couldn't wait to sweet-talk his way in between Brenda's pearly thighs, just like he couldn't resist snatching and destroying Lily Rose's little bear.

All those years James must have been planning how to plunge a knife into his back. All the laughs, the adventures, the shared experience was pretend. It doesn't matter that he saved your life that one night after the game when he turned into a hurricane and knocked down those arrogant punks one by one. A fluke. A lapse in normal behavior never to be repeated. A generous moment that James now regrets. Right?

As Bagwell moves closer, he sees James still hovering over the girl who now has her head down on her arms upon the table, maybe passed out, maybe resting. His right arm encircles Kate's shoulders as she steps away from the gesture, speaking insistently towards his ear.

What the hell is she saying?

The scene becomes magnetic, drawing Bagwell as if on a cable, his concentration unbending, the screaming of his leg numbed through homemade hooch.

He's fifteen feet away when a gust of wind bursts through the party scene, lifting the edges of the tent and plastic table covers, scattering empty cups, plates, and utensils, billowing the ladies' skirts, and forcing gasps from people who had been caught by surprise. The rain begins to drive down harder.

One cable snaps as Bagwell dives into service, helping to scoop up the renegade plates wheeling across the grass, and retie the strings holding the flapping roofs intact. He looks up when his name is called, seeing a classmate from high school, a girl from his woodshop class, his favorite class. His eyes slide past her onto two figures to the left, Brenda and Dr. Sheppard, the vet she works for. The doc is a good-looking middle-aged guy whose wife died a couple of years back. The son of a bitch has his hand in the crook of her arm. Did they come here together?

His eyes, looking for James, race over the faces in the crowd. It's his fucking fault. If she is here with another man, it's because James ruined her, turned her sweet innocent nature into a wanton lust. Bagwell saw James' glances at her breasts and ass through the years. He didn't miss the little sly comments. He mistook seduction for appreciation, being young, stupid, and allegiant to a fault. He knows better now.

He knows.

"Billy, how are you?" The old classmate asks.

He simply nods as he passes, heading towards the girl who continues to rest her head on the table, but James is nowhere to be seen. As he turns back to glance over at Brenda, their eyes meet. A little smile breaks for one moment, then she reaches down to unhook Dr. Sheppard's hand from around her arm. So, she doesn't want to be with him? She didn't come with him? What does any of it matter?

God, what he would give to hold that girl in his arms again. Turn back time to when they were inseparable.

But time only moves forward.

As storms often do on these hot summer days, the fury that so recently reigned stops, leaving the world in a stillness that feels like a long-held breath. The crowd spills out from under the tent onto the green field, lively and merry, keeping one eye on the fun at hand and the other on the triangle of drama that he, James, and Brenda represent.

He can't hold that girl in his arms again ever.

She doesn't want him anymore.

Does she?

Doesn't matter, doesn't matter.

James has been inside of her. That particular knowledge makes him want to puke.

Where the fuck is he?

Way out past the port-a-john, Bagwell spies James from the back, half immersed into the edge of the woods taking a leak. James never did like those toilets on wheels, claiming claustrophobia and unsanitary conditions. He's holding himself with both hands as a cigarette dangles from the corner of his mouth.

James Glover never smoked.

James Glover supported him through thick and thin.

James Glover was the best man he ever knew, though Sammie Becker stands a close second. Bagwell never knew his father, holding his guts in as the helicopter sought a place to land.

James shakes off and zips up. He turns and when his eyes hit Bagwell he smiles that smile that by now looks like a sneer. He throws his cigarette into the wet grass. Bagwell swears he can hear the sizzle as the fire dies. All his senses come alive through the adrenalin pumping. James hooks his thumbs through his belt loops and leans causally. Bagwell knows James can spring out of that casual stance like a cougar.

"So, is this it?" James asks.

"This is it. I was going to blow out your brains from a distance with my sniper rifle or loosen up your axle, but I decided I didn't want to miss the sound of your bones cracking and the feel of them as they give way."

"I know what you mean."

"Why'd you do it, you asshole?"

"Ask her."

"You just had to have every woman in town."

"She seduced me."

"You son of a bitch. How dare you say that."

"I just stopped by to check on her and the kid. She came out in that little flowered robe, showing me her ass."

"You were my best friend."

"She bent over at the sink ..."

Bagwell throws his cane down to the ground, loosens the brace on his leg and pitches it. In a flash, he closes the ten feet between them. He dives on top of James, knocking him over on his back. The ground gives, squishy with saturation, as they begin to roll, Bagwell doing everything he can to get on top. They grapple for minutes that feel like hours, rolling first one way and then the other. Bagwell holds position on top for seconds staring with hatred into James' eyes, only to be forced over on to his back while his old friend grunts with effort. Back and forth they go, taking turns reigning until Bagwell summons a surge of strength that dominates James at last. He pins James' arms down to his sides between his legs, sits up, and begins to whale upon his face with both fists, violently forcing his head from side to side. At one point Bagwell feels his fist sink deeply as the cheekbones break. Bagwell knows that he's crying, and spitting out profanity and promises of all he plans to do. *Stop the fucking crying,* he thinks. Stop the crying. You hold a Purple Heart, though right now his own heart in his chest feels black. The blood in his aorta and the veins like oil.

Suddenly, with one very strong arch of his back, James bucks Bagwell over, and his old friend sits on top of him whaling away on his face. The blows hurt like he's getting hit with cannonballs and he feels the blood splatter when his nose cracks and falls to one side. His eyeballs feel like they may become embedded. Finally, he manages to free his right arm, which had been pinned against James' leg, and he lands a blow dead center on James' jaw, snapping his head back. The piece of shit flies off onto his back and lies there for a moment stunned. Bagwell sits up and moves forward, struggling to stand, drops of blood dripping to land on the bright green grass. James kicks up his right foot with the force of a horse into Bagwell's groin, missing his dick and his balls by less than an inch. Bagwell now lies on his back again as James scrambles onto his feet and steps over to pin his wounded leg to the ground. The searing pain brings everything to a stop, including his mind, his breath, his will.

"I never planned on it. It just happened," James says, tears streaming from his eyes.

With a gathering force fueled by every ounce of betrayal that Bagwell feels, he springs his torso up and grabs James' leg and pulls, knocking the fucking bastard down on his ass. He struggles to stand quickly and wavering over James on his throbbing leg, begins to kick James in the kidneys and other organs so neatly held in place by the shell of his ribs and the flesh stretching over everything as tight as a glove. He lands two strong blows into his rib cage, hearing bones crack and watches as James rolls over onto his side and throws up yellow liquid laced with red.

At this point, Bagwell looks up to see the people of the town standing in a half circle around them maybe fifteen feet back. Some of the faces are smiling, some looking distressed, and some in the middle of turning away.

Here's your fucking show. Here's the blood you have been craving.

Kate breaks out from the crowd and runs towards him and James and hysterically shouts, "Stop it! Stop it!"

Brian Jedele steps out and pulls her back into the crowd.

Where the hell is Brenda?

Before he knows what hit him, Bagwell thuds to the ground again onto his back with James on top encircling his neck with his hands, surprisingly soft not callused, as he begins to squeeze with all his might.

The motherfucker is strangling him.

Bagwell reaches up, fighting to loosen James' grip as every sight, every sound, every thought he's ever had spirals downward into black.

32 Reunion

Saturday 8:36 p.m.

Brenda opens the glove compartment of her station wagon and begins to tear through the collection of restaurant menus, paper napkins, maps, matchbooks, marbles, a plastic kewpie doll, and a small container of pepper spray.

Billy had bought her that last item just before he left for the Persian Gulf. He always took good care of her.

But where are those fucking pictures? She swears she last saw them in the car. Slamming the compartment door closed, she bends down to search under the passenger seat, half-in, half-out of the passenger door. More stray marbles, an empty juice container with the tiny straw still stuck in it, a flashlight, a tennis ball, a tuning fork. That last thing had to be James', rolled under when she was packing his things. She grabs the fork and sticks the cold metal into the pocket of her jeans. She'd give that to him later if she could muster up enough courage. Seeing him with Debbie Jacobs didn't make her jealous, but seeing the young girl pawing at him unashamedly did trigger a moment of regret, just one moment, knowing she may never again feel that much pleasure.

Where the fuck are those pictures? Recent shots of Lily Rose wrestling with Jake in the backyard. She wanted to show them to Billy. What the hell is she thinking? Not Billy. She didn't mean to think about him. She meant her neighbor Mary, who she just ran into at the party.

She does not want to think about Billy. Seeing him limp around with that cane ...

Brenda stands up and slams the passenger door of the car and opens the back door on the same side. Kneeling in on the seat with her left knee, she bends back over to rifle through the few things on the floor behind the driver's seat. She will not think about Billy. He was one of the few who jumped to help when the wind burst through the party, loosening the tent and scattering stray items everywhere. That was Billy for you.

The pictures!

She starts to cry. She feels so fucking frustrated. Must be that time of the month. So what if she forgot to take a couple of her pills? She couldn't have gotten pregnant that fast. The whole thing makes her feel torn. Part of her still craves the lustful pleasure that she and James shared, the other part feels revulsion.

Just find the fucking pictures! Tears stream down her face, dropping with little splashes on the vinyl of the seat.

When she hears a voice behind her, a shock runs through her and her face grows red. Did someone witness her acting like a wild woman? She turns from her position, head down, ass up in the air, to see Dr. Sheppard.

"Dr. Sheppard." Putting her ass down on the seat, she scrambles out of the car, wiping the tears away and swallowing hard.

"Are you okay?" he asks.

The concerned look on his face appears sincere, but what the hell was he thinking looking at her ass stuck up in the air? He was acting too friendly today, touching her arm and all that.

"I'm ... I'm fine. I was just looking for something in my car."

"Could I be of help?"

Brenda glances over towards the tent. The crowd looks considerably thinner. She turns back to look at the doctor. He's a tall, good-looking older man, though she's never thought about him like that. For crying out loud, he's her boss.

"I ... I was just looking for some pictures. Where did everybody go?" She motions towards the tent with a quick gesture of her head.

"I ... I'm not quite sure." He shrugs his shoulders.

"What's going on?" She asks with suspicion rising. Pushing the car door closed, she steps out to walk back towards the party. Dr. Sheppard grabs her arm and pulls her back.

"I don't know if you should go back over there now."

"Why?" She realizes that the thinning of the crowd must have something to do with Billy or James. Maybe Billy and James. She steps out again to run, but the doctor grasps her arm tighter.

"Brenda ... just let it be."

She pulls her arm away from him. "The hell I will."

Brenda steps out and begins to jog, then breaks out into a full-on sprint. No, she thinks. No, no, no. This is not what I wanted. I swear I never had this in mind. Why do they always have to do this? Men. What the fuck is wrong with them?

The scattering of people standing beneath the tent turn to look at her as she searches in every direction until she sees the crowd, huddled around a clearing near the johns. She begins to push her way through firmly, even rudely, until she breaks out onto the green and stops. James straddles Billy and his hands are wrapped around his former friend's neck, thumb touching thumb, the flesh red, veins blue and thick, her husband's mouth open, his eyes looking ready to pop out of his skull.

No one is stopping them?

What the fuck is wrong with these people?

There are drops of blood covering both of them, like maybe what had fallen from the sky wasn't rain at all. Billy's hands are pulling on James' wrists, his one strong leg, bent, as his heel digs into the earth for traction.

"Stop!" She screams at the top of her lungs.

Suddenly, Billy's head shoots up off the ground as he slams it into James'. James' head flies back and Billy bucks up, throwing him over onto his back.

"Stop!" She screams again.

Brenda turns around to look at the faces of the town's people, and what she sees horrifies her. They stand as if mesmerized, the grease of the meat they had recently devoured like savages still glistening around their mouths. Holding their beers and their whiskey, their cigarettes and cigars, their eyes are animated, only a few reflecting the fear, the revulsion she feels.

Their words tell it all.

"Kill him, Billy! Kill him! Kick him again, Billy! Kick him! That's it, Billy! Smash him!"

Billy straddles James now, punching with one fist and then the other into the sides of his head. Even from here, Brenda can see Billy's nose lying crooked, his lips torn and ragged, his eyes half closed shielding from the spray of blood flying up from the impact of such brute force. The red mist. Billy wrote her about the red mist that satisfies the successful sniper shot. Does a spray of blood also satisfy?

One of James' eyes lies buried beneath a puff of flesh as his body rocks erratically from side to side. Sounds of pain escape with each exhale.

"What's wrong with you people?" she screams. "I thought you were our friends!"

Finally, Brenda finds one other person in the crowd who looks as frantic and desperate as she feels, Billy's sister Kate, her arms held behind her back by the host of the party.

Until this moment, Brenda felt helpless, thinking somehow that it would take a man to separate them, to run over and pull them apart, fearless that they might get pulled into the fray. But, desperate, she moves towards the two men, once boys whom she had grown into a woman with.

"Stop it, Billy! Stop it!"

Suddenly, out of nowhere, a young blonde girl appears running around the edge of the crowd to the left. She reaches the two fighters seconds before Brenda does, and begins to pull at Billy with both hands.

"Don't hurt him! Don't hurt him!" the girl screams.

Billy turns and pushes her to the ground with his left hand, then resumes his pounding.

The girl scrambles to her feet and both she and Brenda begin to pull on Billy with all their strength. Brenda notices that the girl is crying, too, and now their words are not delivered in screams, but in soft pleads.

"Billy, Billy stop it. Don't kill him. Please. I'm sorry. I'm sorry," Brenda says.

"Don't kill him. Don't kill him. I love him." The girl says in unison.

Finally, Billy falls back upon his ass, half dazed. Drops of blood fall and soak into his sky-blue T-shirt from the deepest cut on his right upper lip and his nose. The left side of his face is badly swollen and his knuckles on both hands split open into tiny ravines. He falls back and stares into the sky as Brenda kneels and reaches out to cradle his head. He moves one hand up slowly and pushes her away.

Brenda turns to James, who lays still, both eyes now hidden behind swollen folds of flesh, his shiny black hair matted with blood. The girl kneels to cradle his head and she meets with no resistance. James doesn't move at all.

"He's dead. He's dead. You've killed him," the girl cries.

But Brenda can see the slightest movement as his chest rises and falls with a feeble breath. Brenda looks back to Billy as his sister, Kate, kneels down beside her brother, shooting her a look that feels like a barb.

Kate says, "You get away, Brenda. He doesn't want you here. And I don't either. This is all your fucking fault."

Billy lifts his hand and says, "No," very weakly.

"No?" Kate asks. "You want her here?"

He nods.

"Call an ambulance!" the girl screams, wiping away the blood from James' face with her hand.

Dr. Sheppard appears out of the dispersing crowd carrying his black bag in his right hand. He lifts his container of medicine and tools and says, "Since they've been acting like jackasses, maybe I can help."

—∾—

Brenda stares out upon the road and the intermittent headlights that one by one are swallowed into dark. The storm front now sits to the east, pelting rain on neighboring towns, neighboring counties, destined to move from state to state until what's left meets the shore and a fresh new body to drink from. The moon peeks out from behind the last string of cumulus clouds and star by star appears. In a patch of dark when no car passes, she glances up to see the belt and arrow of her favorite constellation, Orion. The warrior. The brave one who runs into battle on foreign shores, through desert sands, through jungles so thick machetes are used to clear a path. The battles never stop. Were they ever meant to? Is war one of God's population controls? Or an arena in which our morals are examined? So much blood spilt, the poor souls left behind or returning in war-torn bodies to face the world with new eyes, tired eyes, eyes willing to close on all they've seen that haunts them. Maybe God never intended war. Maybe war was invented by man, arrogant and territorial, greedy and grasping, to fill a hole meant to be filled with quiet moments, deep reflection, a search for connection between heaven and earth. Grandma Becker knows about such things.

Billy sits next to Brenda, his head resting back, nose packed with gauze and salve, his eyes closed, his left hand lying palm up on the seat between them.

She wants to reach out and lay her hand in his. He must be able to hear the pounding of her heart. If one were to look upon her chest, they could see the bones and flesh rise and fall with every beat. If she gently placed her hand in his, would he snatch his back? Like the touch burned him? Singed his flesh of hair? Left a red mark that would fill with water, later to be popped?

Or would he accept her hand and squeeze it?

Does she want to lay her hand in his because she wants him back? Or because after ten years he is a habit she cannot break?

Can she imagine herself wrapped inside his arms?

Would he leave her again after she allows her heart to swallow him whole once more?

None of that matters. Reunion or no reunion, she's not afraid to be alone now.

—∞—

The night Billy gave her the diamond, they were both eighteen and virgins. He had taken her to the Three Rivers Inn for dinner, an old stone mill renovated into a dining hall with white linen tablecloths and fresh carnations sitting on every table. On Saturday nights, a man strummed love songs in the background and both Billy and Brenda ate fresh fish. Billy pulled the small black box out of his pocket, opened it, and placed it in the center of the table. Gently, he pulled the gold-banded rock out of its satin bed and pushed the metal and mineral onto her finger. They stared into each other's eyes through a veil of tears. Did he have an erection at that moment? She had waited so long. Now that they were engaged, Billy was ready to do it.

They stopped at the bend in the creek where the willows canopied a soft bed of long, cool grass. All the way there, Brenda sat squeezed up against him in the cab of his truck, holding his right hand in hers as it draped across her shoulders. Their hands made love squeezing and stroking as Brenda hooked her left hand high up on his inner thigh. She could feel him and felt as if she would go insane, waiting now three years for this night to come.

She could not wait to feel him inside of her. She was softly panting like a dog. Could he hear her?

Billy spread a blanket out on top of the grass and they fell to their knees facing each other. He reached up with both hands to caress her face and run his hands through her long hair. Leaning forward, he brushed his lips against hers once, but when she eagerly opened her mouth for more, he pulled away. He drew his hands down to cup her breasts, and his breath became as shallow as her own. He pulled her shirt over her head and reached back to unfasten her bra. Her breasts fell free and he gasped, as if it was the first time he had seen them fall. An urgency grew in him, though he remained gentle. She fell back as he moved on top of her. Finally, he leaned over to kiss her, moving his tongue inside her mouth as she unbuttoned his shirt and pulled it down his arms. His chest was so firm, so finely muscled, as she reached up to touch him. She didn't want to wait. She made her way to his zipper next, but he pulled away, drawing her skirt down. She reached up again, this time wrapping her arms around his neck, pulling him over her.

"Fuck me, Billy, Please," as she opened herself to him.

"No. But I will make love to you."

She felt a little tear and for one moment pain, then he was inside her and the pleasure began. He grabbed her hips, and they did indeed make love. She cried. She couldn't help it. The pleasure begged for her tears. Never taking his eyes off of hers, he made his own sounds of pleasure, and soon they exploded together. He fell down upon her and they rolled into each other's arms, kissing and giggling and counting the minutes until he would be hard again.

—⁓—

Out of the corner of her eye she watches Billy's hand. Does he want her to reach out and touch him? Why else would he leave it there, palm up, just inches from her for so long?

"Where are we going?" he asks.

"To my house. Our house. I mean ... the house."

"Take me to my mom's."

"I want to clean you up a bit."

"No." He withdraws his hand back into his lap.

"Yes."

When they walk into the back door of the house, Jake dances on his hind legs and jumps up on Billy, who moans and groans and finally has to speak sharply to his most devoted friend. "Jake! Down!"

"Sit down at the table," Brenda says. "I want to wash out those wounds."

Billy pulls out a chair and sits down gingerly. He won't even look at her at all, not a sideways glance, nor a quick sweep. Nothing. Slowly, he stretches his wounded leg out, free of the brace, tossed aside in the fight. The grimace contracting his face clearly tells her how far away the limb is from healing.

Brenda fills a bowl with warm water and walks over to the table with a soft cloth, hydrogen peroxide, and a couple of powdered herbs. Billy quietly sits scratching Jake's ears and the back of his head. She bends before him and begins to wash the scrapes, cuts, and contusions free of mud, plant material, and blood.

Billy doesn't utter a sound, but sits still as a rock, his eyes softly focused on some distant point.

Look at me, she wills. Look at me.

She says, "You could use a few stitches in a couple of these cuts."

"That boss of yours must not have thought so. Just pack them with goldenseal. They'll be fine."

She takes the yellow powder and packs the wounds. When she brushes the golden curls back from his forehead, she does not fight the urge to throw in a gentle caress. Suddenly, his eyes meet hers.

"I didn't plan any of it. It just happened," she says.

His eyes drop.

"Why couldn't you have talked to me about going over there?"

His eyes lift again to meet hers. She remembers now how they looked, his eyes, so soft, so yielding, when they stared into each other's eyes for hours.

He turns his head away from her.

"Look at me. Look at me," she commands.

Slowly he turns his head back and meets her eyes once again.

"I'm sorry, Billy. I'm sorry." She bends in further and brushes his ravaged lips gently, so very gently with her own.

He reaches out with both hands and wraps his arms around her waist, pulling her to him, and buries his face, wounds, yellow powder, traces of blood and all, into her breasts. He rubs, kneads, and squeezes her ass through her jeans, and the excitement builds, though the roughness of his handling makes her feel a little scared.

Startling her, he stands and lifts her and begins to carry her down the hall, his steps urgent, but uneven. When they reach the bedroom, he throws her down on the bed on her back, and bends over to unbutton her shorts and pull them off. He tosses them into a corner. Next he unzips his pants, drops them, and pulls them off, kicking them across the floor. Brenda watches with alarm, her eyes on the wounded leg. The wound. A cavity pink and raw like a mouth opening. Not large, but deep. Pulsating with an eternal beat of its own. Still her breath remains erratic and shallow. He kicks off his underwear and moves over her quickly. She gasps loudly as he thrusts away harder than she ever experienced with him or James and certainly deeper. His tears fall down upon her face as his grunts and groans match her own. The ache of pleasure feels almost unbearable and when it ends, his eyes finally meeting hers again.

He says, "You always wanted me to fuck you. So there you are. I've fucked you." Pushing himself up off of her, he grabs his clothes and walks out of the room.

"Where are you going?" she calls after him.

"Where's the keys to my truck?"

"You can't drive with that leg."

"Fuck the leg."

Brenda falls back again onto the bed, aching. She reaches down to touch the wetness and draws her fingers back to see the color red. Is the warm sticky blood Billy's or her own?

She rolls onto her side and draws into a tight little ball.

"On the nail by the fridge," she says softly.

33
Heaven's Mouth

Saturday 9:44 p.m.

Martha knows without anyone telling her that the explosion has occurred. Maybe the clearing night sky gives her a clue, as the last stormy clouds sail unencumbered, unchained, free to make their way at last. Or maybe she knows because the churning deep inside her viscera has slowed to a slight murmur. The certainty rings inside her in the hollow that has no name, provides no proof that can be traced or followed. You either trust this inner voice or not. They are silent words spoken from heaven's mouth.

Now comes the release of the repercussions and the promise of one death, hopefully no more. Though Martha fought to ward off the warning message of the old wives' tale, and bargain with a higher power to snatch her life away rather than one of the young, she has failed. Hasn't she?

But promises can be broken, can't they? It's not that Martha sees herself stronger than the powers that be, able to move mountains or unbury hidden treasures, but there remains human will, given voice through prayer, that can crash through the gates of heaven and drift into an open ear.

Action results when human will refuses to surrender. Tenacity that will not slow down, will not go to bed, will not stop driving until defeat deadens the urge.

Her urge is not dead yet.

First, she picks up the telephone receiver and punches Brenda's number with her index finger. The phone rings, and rings. Second, she calls Martin, the one man who comes closest to the town crier. The phone rings, and rings until a recorded message clicks on. She tells Martin to call her. Third, she calls Sammie, her second born and the kindest man she knows.

"Hello?" he answers with a voice full of gravel.

"Sammie, is that you?"

"Yes. Though the flesh is disintegrating and the blood runs thin."

"What? Are you smoking that pot again?" In the background, a female giggles. "Do you have company?"

"Just doing a little pipe cleaning."

"Have you seen Billy or James?"

"Those boys have to settle what's between them. I talked to Billy and I prayed."

"But did you talk to James? Has anyone talked to James?"

"I haven't seen him."

"I thought maybe you went to the pig roast."

"I got waylaid. I mean laid. I mean waylaid."

"Well, I'm happy for you, Son."

"It could be destiny. The thing between Billy and James. Maybe you should let it go."

With Lily Rose in tow, she grabs her purse, pulls a sweater on, walks out her back door and greets the cool, clean night with a sigh. After opening the garage door, she climbs into her car, buckling the child into the rear, backs out, and moves down the road ready to meet any repercussions head on.

Martha forgets how much she hates to drive in the night, when the lights and shadows interplay and confuse an old woman's mind. But, she drives on, thinking at one point that a deer is about to bound across the road and, at another, that the approaching headlights are on her side of the road. She has forgotten where the stop signs are half hidden behind hanging branches, and the stripe running down the center of the road wavers. She takes a deep breath and lets the moon light her way. Her little granddaughter sits quietly, somehow understanding the mission at hand. They will stop at Martin's first.

His Lincoln sits in the center of his drive. Even in the night, she can see that the sides of the car are splattered with mud and the tires are caked. Where the hell has he been? She pulls her Chrysler in behind.

"You sit tight, Lily Rose. I'll be back in a minute or two. I have a feeling that you don't want to see Grandpa tonight."

Martha climbs out and firmly knocks upon the side door. She cannot see detail through the delicate lace of Jeanine's curtain, but she tries, and does see Martin's large looming figure approaching. He jerks the door open and stands there, ruffle-haired and weaving, a dark stubble shadowing the lower half of his face.

"What the hell are you doing here?" he growls.

"Are you going to let me in or not?"

"Hell, I don't care."

She opens the door and follows him through Jeanine's kitchen as he shuffles and sways into the living room and half falls into his recliner. Martha perches on the edge of the couch. He lifts a short glass containing his VO over ice and takes a deep, long drink.

"Can I get you a cocktail?" he asks.

"You know I don't drink."

"What are you doing here?"

"I'm looking for Billy and James. Have you seen them?"

"I saw Billy last night and the little prick this morning. I set him straight with a little warning."

"You didn't go over to the pig roast?"

"I'm tired of the people in this town."

"How's Peter?"

"W... what?"

"I said, how's Peter? Your son."

"He's gone."

"What do you mean gone?"

"Packed some things and left."

"What did you do to him?"

"Oh, just support him and provide for his every little need."

Martha hates to hear his slurring and the angry indignant tone beneath his words. "Everything but love, unconditional love," she reminds him.

"Don't start that shit again. Why didn't Brenda come in?"

"I'm not with Brenda."

"You mean to tell me that you are out driving?"

"I'm not a feeble old woman."

"Jesus Christ, Ma. What the hell are you doing?"

"I'm looking for those boys."

"Oh, I see what this is about. It's that fucking picture, isn't it?"

Martha stands, wavering slightly. Martin leans forward to stand up out of his chair.

"Never mind, Son. I can see you are going to be of little help."

"Why don't you stop worrying about those two and worry about our family, our blood. The hell with them! My son is gone! He needs help! He needs help." Martin sets his glass down and covers his eyes with both hands, trying to hold his tears in.

But, they begin to fall, and for Martha it is a wonder to behold. She walks over next to him, and drops her hand upon his shoulder and softly rubs. She says, "It's about time that armor around your heart cracked."

"Get out! Get out!"

And Martha does, heading now for Brenda's, keeping her eyes peeled for James' bright-red car and Billy's sister Kate's little blue Mustang. Not that it will be easy to spot the colors in the dark. But, she'll know.

"Where are we going now, Grandma?"

"I'm taking you home, Lily."

"I don't want to go."

"Don't be mad at your momma."

"I want to find Daddy."

"I'll find your daddy. Does your tummy still hurt?"

"Only a little."

"That's good."

Martha gazes off into the fields alive with moisture, the air thick with the smell of earth and greens. The tires of her old Chrysler splash through puddles in the ruts of the dirt roads, and through the open window she hears the calling of the night birds. They are out plunging and picking away at the small skittering animals dashing to and fro. Tonight the earth sings alive, and Martha sees the parading ghosts of the people who once populated this land. Pioneer women with their white-capped heads and aprons, walking side by side with the wagons. Their children running through the fields beside them, the open space fertile with tall grass and wild flowers of brilliant hues. The men on horseback and driving the wagons, eyes peeled for distant fires, ears open for unnatural sounds almost natural that signal subtle verbal exchanges between the savages.

The savages living in harmony with all the worlds of nature: plant, animal, mineral, and spirit. Spearing and killing only what they need. Using every inch of the blessed sacrifice for their survival. They are the caretakers of this land. Their teepees, their hogans, their longhouses. Their clothes on their backs beaded, painted, tanned, and fringed. Their blankets woven and the bowls, pots, and jugs formed by hand and fired. Every member accepted into the fold, each encouraged to share their gifts, no one relegated to the sidelines because their gender identity or their character appears perverse.

The pioneers and the savages meet head on. The blood seeps slowly into the earth as the spirits rise.

Ashes to ashes. Dust to dust.

The shadows of the trees bow across the road as Martha and the child pass through, the grandmother wondering how it could be possible for accident or violence to occur on this seemingly peaceful night.

Where will she find the fallout from the explosion?

The pair of headlights approaching seems to zigzag and move towards them very fast. Martha veers over to the right, allowing a distance for the vehicle to pass. When it does, Martha sees the blur of a pickup, the color hard to see, identification of the driver impossible. But the child knows.

"Daddy!"

Martha turns to see Lily's face flush with excitement.

"Are you sure?" she asks.

"He's driving! He's driving!"

Martha hits her horn again and again, but the truck is now a pair of red taillights receding into dots.

"Let's follow him, Nana!"

"By the time I turn around, he'll be way far away." Driving too fast and too erratically through this calm but portentous night.

"I'll find him later, Lily. Right now I'm taking you home."

Martha feels the little girl sulking behind her. She turns into the driveway of Billy and Brenda's home and expects to see Jake, but he doesn't appear. Brenda opens the front door and steps out upon the porch. She runs down the steps barefooted, wearing a short, flowered, flimsy robe.

Martha steps out of the car more tired this time, as Brenda pulls Lily out of the car seat in back.

"Grandma, I told you I'd come over later and pick Lily up," Brenda says.

"I had to get out of the house."

"You shouldn't be out driving at night. You know how your eyes play tricks with you."

"Leave the old lady alone, okay?"

"Are you coming in?"

"Mama, we saw Daddy drive by. Was he here? Is he coming back?" Lily cries.

Martha and Brenda meet eyes over the roof of the car. Martha sees something sheepish on Brenda's face. The corners of her mouth struggling between turning up or down.

"Go in the house, Sweet Pea. I'll be in, too, in a minute."

"Is he coming back, Mama?"

"Go in the house," Brenda says sharply.

Lily turns and runs up the stairs into the house, the fall of her feet pounding.

"Girls and their daddies," Brenda says. "Or most girls and their daddies. Why don't you come in for a while, Grandma?"

"What happened between those boys today? Did something happen at the party?"

"They ... fought. They almost killed each other."

"Billy's up and moving. Where's James?"

"I don't know. Billy beat him unconscious, and he came to. I know Dr. Sheppard tried to talk him into going to the hospital. But, I saw him drive off in his car with this girl. It's over, Grandma."

"What's over?"

"They fought. It's over."

"It's not over, Brenda. Go back into the house. You shouldn't be out here in that robe."

"No one died, Grandma."

"Where was Billy going when he left here?"

"To his mom's, I think."

"He was driving erratically."

"He ... he was a little upset at me when he left. At me. Not James."

"Go back into the house now."

"Where are you going, Grandma?"

"I'm ... I'm going home."

"Good. I'll talk to you tomorrow."

Martha climbs slowly back in behind the wheel. She has no intention of going home.

She pulls back out into the night where the shadows grow large when the moon shines bright. This night full of revenge and loss. Her grandson somewhere out on foot again escaping from his torment. Looking for a new life now. If death had wanted him, he would have died last night. Wouldn't he have? He will go out into the world now, a dangerous place for someone who challenges the norm. Bleeding from the act of uniting in cruel ways. Bleeding from the act of trying to pull love out of a father who has lost his heart. Bleeding from a society that has set out to destroy everything given it as tools for survival. Her eyes race across the fields searching for his hunched and dragging form, then remembering that wherever he walks at this moment, his head is held high, his back erect, he moves free at last.

Let him go for now.

Martha heads for Molly Bagwell's house to see if, indeed,

Billy arrived there. Has his venom been released? The thirst of his revenge quenched? How many blows did he deliver and receive until the last one finally satisfied the need? When James' eyes closed with unconsciousness? When his once best friend's chest barely moved with his breath? Or is he sitting in a corner somewhere plotting out his next step?

Earlier today, when memories moved through Martha in slow waves, she knew who was in the greatest danger. One of the few people in town whom the people love to hate. Don't ask her how she knows. She'll simply tell you that the answer came to her. One of those unlucky souls whose home life as a kid was torture. More profound than Martin's needling. More humiliating than Martin's threats. No support in any direction, so that the abandon and isolation seal the heart and the emotion into an iron box.

Somewhere in this night, he drives his cherry red car up and down the rolling hills. She sees him in her mind's eye. His eyes puffed into slits, a tooth or two missing, purple and red patches in abstract designs upon his face. His hands aching, a finger or two broken, the knuckles red and raw like steak. Disappointment clawing at his insides, so sure, for a moment or two, that in the end Billy, not he, would triumph.

But this boy can never be the golden boy.

Martha reaches Molly's and there sits the truck up close by the house in the driveway. Good. Now to find James.

Driving slowly down a paved road watching the ghosts of the distant past parade, Martha catches a form from the corner of her eye sail by. The angel. Too large for an eagle or a vulture, too low for a small airplane, too dark and still of a night for a parasail. But like a bird of prey, the angel searches. She can feel the intent. Gliding across the fields, peering into each direction, systematic with her task. Could the angel be looking for James Tillman, too? Protection? Absolution? Or retrieval?

Where is he?

One memory from earlier in the day revisits. Brenda and she driving down the road when the pair of headlights threatened to hit them head on. James in the cherry red car flashing by, the look of pure exhilaration upon Brenda's face. Martha has heard Martin speak about the nighttime races when the boys from neighboring towns meet and prove their manhood. Brenda told her James had the fastest car in town. Could the boys be meeting this full moon night, fueled by pig and liquor at the party, drooling for a title besides son, grandson, brother, father? They all want to be the fastest man around.

What road was it? Martha hit the long gray stretch by accident that night seven years ago. She'll find him. She'll pull James from his car and carry him home like a babe. She won't let anyone near him or touch him. Not the stepfathers, not the mother, not the angel, and certainly not the hands of fate. She can't move mountains, or unbury hidden treasure, but she will keep one young man alive.

Austin Road.

Yes! Austin Road.

Now, where is it?

She turns right down a dark dirt road remembering, yes, Austin should run parallel to her right. Keeping one eye on the gliding angel hoping to become invisible to her in the long shadows of the trees, she moves slowly, crackling over gravel, splashing softly through the standing water, listening to the night birds call. Suddenly, though, her foot pushes down upon the gas, the car begins to slow, dwindling and dwindling in speed into a full-on stop. The engine dies as she watches the angel coast into the distance of the west.

34
Fall Out

Saturday 11:49 p.m.

James pulls away from the eight drivers and their cars thinking about Martha Becker. He slides the shifter that pushes the GTO through the gears in seconds flat, not the twelve she's capable of, but fast enough to show the punks behind what they missed. Martha would be proud of him, turning away from challenge. His heart isn't in it anymore. Owning the fastest car in a few counties doesn't feed him like it once did. Martha Becker has always been kind to him, making him feel like she sees something redeeming beneath his crust of flaws. He wants to thank her before he leaves this town. Billy beat him fair and square, but that's not what's pushing him out. The words are to blame here. The words he can still hear now, through the aching bruises, the stinging cuts, the stabbing pain of his cracked or broken ribs every time he breathes.

Kill him, Billy. Pound him. Break him. The town took glory in watching Billy beat away. James knows he got a few good licks in there, too, but in the end, the golden boy will always be golden, walking with a cane or wheeling through in a chair. A core of decency exists inside Billy that he will never get close to. Larceny in the heart cannot be absolved overnight. Perhaps never.

James turns to look at the girl, her head resting back, mouth open, hands resting on her flat little belly. She turns her head to look at him.

"I think you better pull over, James. I'm going to throw up again."

He pulls the car over to the shoulder of the road. Before the car has come to a complete stop, Debbie opens the door, leans way over to gush out food, but mostly alcohol, onto the ground with a splash. How can that little body hold so much? She sits up, wiping her mouth off with the back of her hand. Turning to him, she smiles sheepishly.

"I'm sorry, James."

"Don't worry about it."

She slides towards him across the leather and dropping her body behind the shifter, places her head in his lap. There it lies, gold curls and all, as she closes her eyes. James stares down in wonder at this angelic face. He lifts his right hand off of the steering wheel and hesitates. Can he touch her gently? Can he stroke her cheek with his fingertips? He drops his hand and touches her soft hair, the smoothness of her cheek, pulls one curl up off of her eye.

She says, "I love you, James."

A girl this age doesn't know anything about love. But the words feel good. They feel really good.

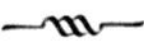

After the fight was finished, he opened his eyes, slits that they were, to see the girl leaning over him. He thought it was still raining, but the drips felt too warm. The girl was bawling. When he turned his head to the left, he saw Katie leaning over Billy, and Brenda sitting nearby looking sad. She must have felt him looking at her, because she turned to meet his eyes.

She mouthed two words, "I'm sorry."

He turned away and saw the veterinarian walk up to Billy with his little black bag.

Brenda said, "Take a look at James first."

The doctor fell to his knees and wiped away blood, looked inside his mouth, felt his head, ran his hands over his ribs and limbs. James grunted and groaned though he tried not to.

Dr. Sheppard said, "I think you better go to the hospital and get some X-rays, James."

Debbie stood up and said, "I'll call for an ambulance."

"No!" James said. "I'm fine."

"You're not fine," Dr. Sheppard added.

"I'm fine."

Dr. Sheppard stood up off of his knees and went over to stoop by Billy.

"Help me get up," James said to Debbie.

Debbie tried to pull him up as Brenda stepped over to help, and between the strength of the two girls, he was able to stand. He pulled his arm away from Brenda, refusing to look at her, and draped his arm around Debbie's shoulder. Together they walked away.

Of all people, they ran into the punk who was pissing near the cars when they first arrived. The dumb shit was emptying his bladder by the car again. Before Debbie and he could slip into the GTO unseen, he turned.

"I'm going to have to tell all those dudes out on Astin Road that you won't be there tonight because you got the shit beat out of you."

Debbie said, "Fuck you, asshole. James has the fastest car around, and he always will."

James just stared at the guy and didn't say a word. But before he pulled his door closed, he jerked it against the guy's legs, knocking him off kilter.

"Oh, big man," the punk said.

Debbie, a little spitfire, James had to admit, stepped up into the guy's face and said, "James has more gifts in his little finger than you'll ever have."

"Get in the car, Debbie," James said.

Debbie walked over and climbed into the car, as James uttered three words to the punk, "Austin. Austin Road." Pain in his left elbow or not, he slammed his door closed.

"Are you going out there?" Debbie asked.

"I've got to."

"Dr. Sheppard said you should go to a hospital."

"He's a fucking vet. What does he know?"

"Dogs and horses have the same body parts as we do."

"I'm okay, Debbie."

"You want me to give you a blow job so you'll feel better?" She reached over and put one hand on his crotch.

He lifted her hand off of him. "I'm fine. Just be still."

Then she started hiccoughing. She was still blasted.

So they rode through the fresh air of the June night with windows down, the GTO rumbling. As they approached the crossroad of Austin and Mason, Debbie painted on lipstick, and James pulled up driver window to driver window with his friend Mike in his gold fleck Camaro.

Mike said, "Jesus Christ, James. I guess you did take a pounding. I hear Billy doesn't look much better."

"He doesn't," Debbie threw in.

James glared over at Debbie, raising his swollen right hand and cutting it through the air. She turned her head away.

Mike asked in a low voice, "Who's that?"

"Debbie."

"Looks young."

"Old enough."

Another guy James knew from town, Brad, stepped up between the cars. "Whoa, James. Should you even be here? I saw the fight. Bagwell might have got the last blow in, but you were both really strong."

"Who were you rooting for?"

"You, man."

"How come I didn't hear anyone screaming out my name?"

"It was just the old timers screaming out for Billy. Christian mothers. Veterans. You know. So how much does one of those Ram Air packages run?"

"Less than you think. I can set you up. So, what's happening here?"

"The dude from Dexter in the black Chevy is running against good old Mike here next."

"That fucker is a weenie wagger. Can't even step into the bushes to take a leak."

Mike added, "He's a smart-ass fucker. I'm going to dust him."

Brad asked, "You want the winner?"

"I'm not sure what I'm doing yet."

The punk from the party parking lot walked up next, puffing on a cigarette, grinning like a little chimpanzee.

He said, "Seeing how the chick seems to run the show, I'm surprised she's not behind the wheel."

Debbie piped up again, "James doesn't need anyone running his show."

"See what I mean?" The punk said laughing.

James said, "Why don't you get that little weenie of yours out again? We just didn't see enough."

"Yeah," Debbie added, "and I'll get out the magnifying glass. James has one the size of a jungle snake." James turned and glared at her, shaking his head.

The local boys cracked up as the out-of-towner grew red. Still he added, "Well, he's not driving with his prick, is he?"

James answered, "I wrap it around the wheel to steer and smoke with one hand, and stroke her with the other."

"Ha ha," the guy said. "Let's get this race going."

Mike and the punk started up their cars with a roar and pulled out on Austin Road to travel up a quarter of a mile to ready for a race. The other seven drivers pulled up and spread out under the trees of the perpendicular road. Everyone stepped out of their cars and crowded at the edge of Austin to watch the cars fly by.

With a squeal of tires they were off in the distance heading this way. The two pairs of headlights looked like a four-eyed monster bounding out of hell. James, his body throbbing in places he never knew existed, and Debbie, a bit unsteady, stood side by side. She wrapped her left arm around his waist and he let her. They watched as Mike's car crossed the line two seconds ahead of the punk, and all the locals broke out into cheers. The two other drivers from Dexter cussed and swore, kicked up dirt, and flung their arms around.

James felt fucking bored. He thought about getting home and sinking into a hot bath. But he remembered that he was now living in the back room of his garage with only a shower and a cot as hard as clay. Maybe he'd stay at Debbie's. She said her parents were gone for the whole weekend long. Yeah. A hot bath. A soft fluffy bed. A sweet girlie body to hold onto like a pillow. Not Brenda. But a girl who clearly liked him. When everyone else was calling out for his beating, he heard her soft cries through his haze.

He turned to Debbie and said, "Let's go."

"You ... you're not racing?"

"I think those days are done."

He and Debbie climbed back into the GTO, the taunts of his friends and foes not nearly bad as he imagined. He guessed he must have looked as bad as he felt.

With the angel in his lap, James gazes down the road into the future. He feels free now. Released at last from a decade of struggling to be something that he's not. The golden boy. His life consists of a different pattern, more of an erratic rhythm, a walk down a path where he confronts his demons one by one. A mother who can't be a mother because she cannot define herself outside of her coupling with monsters. Their roving eyes and wandering hands in search of the innocence they were not born with. What they cannot have, they will break. James, the boy toy, subject to their dark desire. If he could see them now. If only he had been stronger then to push their hands away, squeeze their balls 'til they were blue, pound their faces into hamburger. If he could see them now. Point them out in a lineup, detail their dirty deeds under oath, seal their fate behind bars. They should be in jail, not his brother who fought so hard to protect him. Next week he'll go to see Jack on his way out of state.

The road lies before him like a silver river in his headlights, the center stripe begging him to follow. He will pack the striped beach towel into his bag and set out and see those craggy mountain peaks of the West with his own eyes. Maybe some will even be snow covered. He'll drive up as far as his truck will take him and climb to the top of the peaks and see for himself what it all looks like from above. From there he'll descend into the sprawling desert and study the fossils from the beginning of time. Witness the life of those who know better than any how to survive on so little. A drop of water a week for the little mouse. One tiny sprig of green for the long-legged hare. The belly of the snake on the fire of the sun without a burn. He will learn from them.

The girl awakens, her head still cradled in his lap. "James, are you okay?"

He pets her head softly. "I'm good. Real good. Can ... can I stay with you tonight?"

"Oh, yes," she says, squeezing his legs tightly.

He'll cross the Indian reservations and search for the face of his father. Eat their food, listen to their stories and their songs, and see if the seed of memory encased in his DNA awakens. He may suddenly lift his feet to beats he mysteriously knows, and utter sounds and cries that have been just waiting in his heart.

Maybe a raven-haired beauty will become his bride. Not fair-skinned like Brenda, but brown as a chestnut, with pretty but callused hands rough with the work of her survival. Children. Maybe. All the seed he's spilled and wasted through his own selfish pleasure, incubated now, in the womb of the mother. Can he protect them from the roving eyes and the wandering hands? Can he instruct them on how to become a golden boy, even if he himself never got close? Can he quiet, once and for all, the larceny in his heart that has tormented him forever?

More importantly, can he show them love?

He lightly brushes back the bangs on Debbie's forehead.

He has proof, he can be gentle here.

The final destination will be the sea, where the waves roll in to lick the sand, and the sea birds call sharp and shrill. He'll watch from the shore as huge ships pass on their way to exotic places, or on their return to this land with stowaways tucked tightly in the darkness of the belly. When he dives into the waves at last, he'll swim in the water saltier than our tears. A vast body of released emotion that in its own strong way will unleash his own. He will cry because he never has. The amount he's held inside, once released, will cause the level of the seas to rise. What remains left of him will dry in the sun as he lies upon the shore. The sea birds may carry him away in pieces. The remnants left will blow away in the onshore breezes. The prisms in the flecks of flesh will sparkle as they lift.

What is life, after all?

The moon shines down on James and Debbie in the GTO. Glancing out to the sides, he notices how the moon's rays illuminate them as if they were on a stage. To his left, from the corner of his eye, he sees the dark little shadow of the car moving, much smaller than it really is. The shadow running parallel like a small sidecar, heading west with them, alongside, but with them, yes, just an extension of them really.

At this moment, James looks up into the rearview mirror to see what lies behind. He sucks in a breath deeply, as his left hand on the wheel tightens. No. It can't be. It's not possible, he thinks. The face of the angel in the back seat looks so sweet, so kind, and she holds out one hand, the color of his own skin, to him in invitation. Her feathers glowing white in the moonlight tuck around her like a cloak.

Debbie sits up, her eyes wide. "James, what's wrong?"

James glances forward at the ribbon of the road, then back again to lock with the eyes of the angel. A shiver races up his spine as the hair on his arms stands. She has come for him.

Suddenly, Debbie screams, "James, look out!"

He darts his eyes forward to see a large pickup pulling out in front of them from a dirt road to the right. James jerks the wheel too sharply as he knows, but too late to retract. He feels the first few rolls of the car as it turns into the night, and the heavy bump of Debbie's body as her bones and flesh are flung against his own.

35
Benediction

Wednesday 7:03 p.m.

A small crowd of Willis townsfolk mingle inside the curtained viewing room. The plain silver casket balances on a wooden stand with James' senior picture, framed in oak, standing guard on top of the closed lid. His handsome face with high-ridged cheekbones and eyes dark as dates appear daring. I dare you to get too close. I dare you to get to know me. I dare you to pry open the safe that contains my heart. The corners of his mouth turn up slightly, his full lips ready to smile, the bigger part of him unwilling. You all amuse me, but life does not, that attempt at a smile seems to say. There sits no montage of photos to document his life. No favorite songs picked out carefully to express his spirit. No captured words that he uttered when he was still alive printed on the inside of a handout. Even the photo, offering a slim reminder of his being, was supplied by Martha Becker. James' mother couldn't find hers.

—᠁—

"How come I've never seen his mother before?"

"You must have seen her somewhere. I saw her out at the Brown Bear a few times. Drunk and loud with some man or other hanging on her. She works out at the bottling plant."

"Didn't he have some brothers?"

"One got shot a few years back. Don't you remember? Some freak hunting accident. One's in prison. Jack. I heard that they're letting him out for the funeral. He was a good kid, but had a hell of a temper. The other one, I don't know where he is."

"Well, she looks like a real piece of work. I never seen a woman wear a shirt so low cut to a funeral."

—᠁—

The funeral director, small, wiry and balding, carries another spray of flowers into the room with stiff arms, keeping the blossoms a distance from his nose like he might be allergic. In fact, after he places the arrangement of flowers to the right of the casket, he quietly sneezes again, and again into a white cotton hanky.

—ᨓ—

"Has Brenda been here yet?"

"I haven't seen her."

"How about Billy?"

"Do you think he'd come?

"I think he might. His sister Kate and his mom were here a little while ago."

"I'm glad the Tillmans decided not to show him."

"I heard that his face was smashed in."

"Really?"

"That's what I heard."

"That's terrible. He was so cute."

"He sure was."

"Look at you smiling like that. Just because you were with him. It was only a one-night stand."

"That's one more than you had."

"I think it's really sad that he died."

"So do I."

"I heard that she's in a coma."

"She'll probably die, too."

"Don't say that! She's only seventeen."

"Way too young to die. But, so was he."

"Way too young."

—ᨓ—

Doris Rentschler walks slowly into the room on heels, clutch bag under one arm, sunglasses barely covering red puffy eyes. As she approaches the casket, she sucks in a sob with a high little note, and covers her mouth with a black-gloved hand. She reaches out to touch the silver box as her upper body gently quakes.

Pulling a tissue from her bag, she snaps it closed, turns, nods to a few people that she knows, and walks over to a corner where she half falls into a chair, dabbing at her nose.

—❧—

"I wonder how old Don would like watching his wife crying over him."

"If he ever had doubts Doris was diddling with him, he would be sure now."

"They should have arrested her years ago."

"For what? Showing the boys the ropes?"

"You're darn right."

"Hell, I wish I could have been so lucky."

—❧—

Sam Becker walks in next, glances at the casket, and heads over to take one of Tina Tillman's hands in both his own, speaking to her softly. Jack steps out of the shadow of a corner to stand beside her. Sam finishes with Tina, then gives Jack a hug, looking like a small bird enclosed in the arms of the tall, tattooed, and muscled thirty-four-year-old. One would never guess that Jack and James were brothers, except for the simple sharing of Tina's full lips and the large hands of some distant relative. Sam turns from the pair, and slips into a chair beside Doris. She is now slumped to one side, propped from total collapse with an elbow.

—❧—

"Jesus, he looks like shit."

"I heard he's got cancer again."

"I don't know why the hell he doesn't cut that damn ponytail off. For Christ's sake, it's not 1967."

"He's making a cabinet for the wife to keep her fancy dishes in."

"He's a hell of a woodworker."

"The wife thinks his work is going to be worth some money someday."

"I wouldn't know a damn thing about that."

"That Vietnam sure ruined a lot of people's lives."

"What do you mean?"

"He's sick from that Agent Orange they used over there."

"Oh, balls. The U.S. military wouldn't use chemicals that jeopardized their men."

"So when are you going to pull that big fat head of yours out of the sand?"

—~—

Mike Finkbeiner strolls in wearing a sports coat that looks like he's had it since he was twelve. His head tucks into the shell of his shoulders as he glances around the room. Jack nods to him, and Mike walks over to shake hands, shyly acknowledging the mother. He shows the two of them a photo he holds in one hand, encased behind glass in a thin wood frame. Afterwards, he walks over and props the framed photo beside James' portrait. The photo captures a smiling James, no daring or suspicion in his eyes, standing beside his crimson-colored GTO, a blue sky and green trees in contrast behind. Mike steps back and swipes his nose quickly with the back of his hand, then drops his chin down in a momentary reverence.

—~—

"The damn fool. He shouldn't have been out racing. Especially with that girl in the car."

"He wasn't racing."

"I heard they were out on Austin Road up to their tricks."

"Mike, the kid over there by the coffin, he told me that James didn't race that night. He said they were just driving home."

"So what the hell happened?"

"Carl Dixon pulled out in front of them from a side road."

"He's not even supposed to be driving!"

"Carl said he didn't even see the headlights."

"James was probably speeding."

"He was. He must have jerked the wheel too hard to miss him

and lost control. The car looks like a fricking accordion."

"Well, it's too bad. James was a hell of a mechanic."

—∾—

Martha Becker walks into the room a few steps ahead of Brenda Bagwell, who trails her daughter, Lily Rose, behind her by the hand. The child's eyes are wide with panic. Martha looks around the room nodding to those she knows. Brenda keeps her head down, neither glancing left nor right, and moves slowly towards the coffin. The two women and the child stand in a line in front of it.

"Where is he?"

"He's inside the box, Sweet Pea."

"How can he breathe?"

"He can't." Brenda's voice breaks and her entire body begins to shake with the rising sobs. The child, too, begins to cry. Martha steps over and sweeps Lily up into her arms.

"You don't need to breathe anymore once you die, Lily Rose," Martha says.

"Will he be in the box forever?"

"Only part of him is in the box. The most important part of him is up in heaven."

"Maybe Uncle James will see Growlie up there. Maybe they can make friends."

"I bet they already have."

Martha kisses Lily on the cheek and carries her over to pay her respects to Tina and Jack. Sam stands up and walks over to Brenda, wrapping his arm around her to pull her in close. She drops her head upon his shoulder and wipes away at her nose and her eyes.

—∾—

"That bitch should be crying."

"Don't say that."

"She already had Billy. Why did she have to have James, too?"

"Look at her. Obviously she loved James."

"She's a drama queen. She just doesn't want everyone to hate her."

"I don't hate her."

"Why not?"

"She's really nice. Billy was gone a long time. She probably thought he wasn't coming back."

"Well, you at least wait until you know he's not coming back."

"I guess she got lonely."

"I can't believe that you are defending her."

"Judge not until you have judged yourself."

"Oh, brother. Infidelity is a sin."

"All I'm saying is that we don't know the whole story."

"I know enough of the story to know that that girl there, Brenda Bagwell, is a bitch."

—∞—

Martin Becker strolls in dressed in rumpled clothes and a five o'clock shadow. Make that a five o'clock shadow times two. He walks directly up to the casket, glances from one photo to the other, and drops his chin and his eyes for a moment. Turning on one heel, he searches around the room until he spies a padded chair in a dark corner, drops into it with a sigh, and stares off to a spot three feet in front of him on the floor. Lily Rose Bagwell yells out "Grandpa!" and runs over to Martin, crawls up into his lap, wrapping her thin, long arms around his neck. Martin looks at her and weakly smiles.

—∞—

"I've never seen Martin Becker look like that. What the hell is going on?"

"Fred Simmons saw Martin's son hitchhiking along Textile Road with a backpack."

"You don't say. Isn't he a ... you know, a little funny?"

"You mean a homosexual?"

"That'd be it, yeah."

"When did Fred see him?"

"A few days back."

"I got one better than that."

"What's that?"

"Jane Schmidt saw a wrecker hauling Martin's son's Toyota into Sam's abandoned barn. The car was wrecked."

"So?"

"I didn't hear about a car accident, did you? The next day she saw Martin pulling up to the barn."

"Sounds like Jane has a lot of time on her hands."

"She always has, but like I was saying ... She pulled off down the road and got out some binoculars. Said she saw Martin carrying some boxes out of the barn into the back and set them on fire."

"What's so strange about that?"

"That don't sound strange to you?"

"Maybe a little."

"I'd like to go poke around in that fire a little bit."

"Now who's got too much time on their hands?"

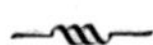

Everyone in the room turns to watch Taylor Jacobs and his wife, Dawn, walk into the room. From the facial expressions of the mourners, it's apparent that they are all shocked to see them. He has his hand hooked around her left bicep and can be seen not just guiding her, but pulling her into the room. Four feet from the coffin, Dawn breaks away and runs over to Tina, moving within inches of the woman's face.

"It's your fault for raising a boy like that. That kid seduced practically every female in this town. He had to have my daughter, too? She's only seventeen years old!"

Taylor walks quickly over to his wife, talks softly to her and begins to gently pull her away. Dawn sweeps the room with her eyes.

"What's wrong with you people? Paying respects to that man whore! Our daughter is lying in a coma! In a coma! Do you hear me?"

Dawn breaks away and heads back over to the coffin, reaching out for James' framed headshot. Jack Tillman bolts over and grabs the photo before she can get her hand on it.

"I'm sorry about what happened, lady. But it takes two to tango. And from what I've heard about your daughter, she was no saint."

"How dare you! You fucking son of a bitch!"

Dawn begins beating on Jack's chest with both fists. Martha Becker jumps up from where she sits, and moves quickly over to Dawn, encircles her shoulders with one arm and pulls her away with the other hand. She speaks softly to Dawn, as the younger woman drops her head on Martha's shoulder to cry. Martha leads her out the front door of the funeral home.

—~—

"Wow."

"This whole thing is terrible."

"It really is."

"I can't believe that she's still in a coma."

"Some people stay in those forever."

"Martha Becker is such a nice woman. That bitch, Brenda, is really lucky to have her as a grandmother."

"Stop calling her a bitch. She used to be a friend of yours."

"Barely. She never wanted to be with us. She always wanted to be with Billy and James. Billy and James."

"You're just jealous of her."

"I am not."

"You always have been."

"That's not true."

"It is, and you know it."

"You know what? You're not my friend either."

"Oh, my gosh. Look who's here."

—~—

Billy Bagwell walks in wearing jeans, a good-looking navy sports coat and a new pair of brown boots. His gait is uneven, but his stature looks strong and tall. Humbly, he heads towards the coffin, nodding shortly and silently to a few of the people gathered. Lily Rose yells out "Daddy!" and runs over to take his right hand in both of hers and smile adoringly up at him.

"Only part of Uncle James is in the box, Daddy. Most of him is in heaven."

"That's right, Peanut."

"He and Growlie are going to be friends up there."

"Probably. You just stand quietly with Daddy for a minute, okay?"

Billy's eyes grow wet as he stares at the two photos of his old friend. He drops Lily's hands and reaches into the pocket of his coat and pulls out a pair of dog tags on their chain, and places them on top of the coffin between the photos. Nodding his head, he closes his eyes.

Epilogue

October 1991

36 Light Rays

Morning

Billy glances up at his face in the rearview mirror. A slight discoloration persists at the corner of his left eye, and the tear on his upper right lip, though mostly healed, will definitely leave a scar. He will walk through the rest of his life with these reminders of his fight with James, his blood brother who, in the end, betrayed him. At this moment, he feels caught between anger towards James and an acute longing for the companionship they once shared. Up in heaven, or wherever the hell the dead go, walking on a cloud or in the lush green of paradise, or shoveling coal into raging fires, James possesses his tags. The coldness of the metal and the subtle jangling as they dance upon his chest can haunt him through eternity. Or maybe they were lost or cast aside in the preliminary journey, as the dead pass from earth to sky, reviewing their deeds, pleading amends to the higher power, whoever, whatever, that power may be.

Sitting in his pickup, he is the tenth driver in a line of twenty, waiting to get through an ailing stoplight. He has gone from living for months in a sea of sand, where insects as big as his hand crawled, to whiling away the hours in a small town, to this: Atlanta, Georgia. Once the home of one James Glover, twenty-six years old at the time of his death by enemy fire. His last breath escaping through the hole in his chest, eyes turned up to the God in heaven that he believed in. A final tear rolling down his face to drop and splatter on the plastic seat of a Humvee.

Billy searches for a house, the address of which Glover scrawled on a small triangle of paper one desert day of 120 degrees when the Marines huddled under canvas for a spot of shade.

—∿—

Billy threw down his cards in disgust. He hadn't had a winning hand in an hour. They'd been sitting there surrounded by sand for so many days that he had forgotten that green grass, flowers, and trees even exist. He stood up and squeezed himself through the lounging Marines to find himself a place in a corner. He heard Glover whoop like a banshee as he scooped up yet another winning pot, then shimmied through sitting and lying bodies to join Billy on the other side of the tent.

"You bored or what, Bagwell?" Glover asked.

"Is there a word for beyond bored?

"What you got there in your hand?"

"A picture of my daughter. The wife just sent it."

"Let me see."

Billy handed the snapshot to Glover, who examined it closely.

"She sure is a pretty little girl. Like an angel."

"Yeah."

"Did you ever notice, Bagwell, that you never see a picture of a black angel? I've got five sisters, all younger than me. The youngest, Chantel, she said to me one day, 'how come I've never seen a picture of a black angel?' I told her that there must be black angels because there are black Madonnas."

"There are?"

"Yeah, over in Europe. There's statues."

"How do you know about that, Glover?"

"I went to college for a couple of years. Took a religions course."

"Why the hell didn't you stay in college?"

"Ran out of money. My daddy died two years back, and my brother and I had to support the family. He's working and I joined up to get more education."

"I joined up to help make the world a safer place. That sure as shit isn't happening here."

"We'll see some action, Bagwell."

"You think?"

"Yeah. I had a dream. What you going to do when you get back?"

"My dad's best friend, Sam, uncle to my wife, he's a woodworker. I'd like to learn how to do that."

"They were in Nam together, right? But your daddy didn't make it."

"That's right."

"Will you do me a favor, Bagwell? I wanted to give someone the address to my family, just in case."

"Just in case? If anyone's going to make it, it's you. I've never seen such a lucky man."

"Well, okay, but just in case. I'm going to give you the address. Will you do something for me? If I don't make it, will you tell my mama and the rest of them how it happened? I don't want them wondering. I want them to know the truth."

"Sure I will. But only if you do the same for me."

James nodded his consent as he wrote out the address on a small triangle of paper, and Billy wrote his out on a slightly larger square.

—∞—

All the way from the Midwest to the East Coast Billy took small roads, avoiding the cities. He wanted to see the land, under the overcast skies, as the first weather systems of the autumn gathered force. He needed to think.

Billy's eyes ping-ponged from side to side as he drank in the images of America in the autumn. The plump orange pumpkins gathering size in the fields side by side with multi-colored gourds all surrounded by the brown skeletons of stalks nestling ears of Indian corn.

The whole nation seemed to spread beneath cloud-covered skies, holding the light out, and the voice of the multitudes in. Voices of the living, as well as the voices of the dead. They echoed against the rocks and trees, ricocheting past ears of strangers, burrowing into the ears of the known. Haunting. Begging for assessment. Inspiring retribution. The hero's journey of he who is courageous enough to travel alone.

If he hadn't lit that cigarette.

If that one tendril of smoke hadn't escaped to rise.

Glover might still be alive.

Billy stopped at one point at an orchard where crisp, fresh apples were mashed into cider. Some left whole were coated in caramel. Others were covered with a sweet sticky shell, the color of James Tillman's GTO, now rolled into a hunk of metal, glass gone, interior burned, tires folded in like the feet of a flying bird.

If Glover had let that broken radio be. He knew the three-second rule! He must have felt desperate, like his luck was running out. Did his voice, a gibberish lost in static, seal their fate?

Glover might otherwise be home with his family.

As Billy drove beneath the canopy of clouds, his heart ached for an answer. He did at one point cast his eyes upward and pleaded, even though his belief in a higher power was strained. He did at one point pound his right fist against the steering wheel out of frustration. He did, though he was ashamed occupants of passing cars might see him, begin to sob. His chest heaved and quaked, alarming ribs healing from his fight with James into a dull ache.

A ray of light cut a hole in the overcast sky and beamed down upon the road.

Billy drove through it.

The reason behind particular events was meant to remain mysterious.

He would never know for sure how the enemy knew he and Glover were hidden in the sand.

Billy stopped in one small town at a farmer's market where he bought a handmade rag doll for Lily Rose. He knew she would love the little brown pigtails tied with ribbons and small pink buttons sewn on as eyes. There was a medium-sized throw, as the woman described it, handmade in colors that he knew Brenda loved. He bought the soft, fringed thing, hoping that one day soon he could give it to Brenda without her thinking he had completely forgiven her.

He was still a long way from that, unable to even imagine making love to her.

In a box, in the back of his pickup, he loaded up pumpkins, gourds, and corn, already sure he'd be back in Willis in time to share Halloween with his Peanut.

Billy passed through the land watching every cow, every horse, every sheep, every pig, every deer half hidden among the trees, every bird lifting off into flight. Just as he embraced a new lease on life, the pain in his belly began again. When he stopped at a rest area, his piss was pink. His hands began to shake, and the clouds in the sky spread into his head. He couldn't pretend anymore or hide it. The war, short, one-sided, and rather uneventful overall to many, had left him shell-shocked and sick.

He did cast his eyes upward and shout mean words. He did beat his fist against the wheel. He did break down and sob once more.

And when a cluster of rays of light incised their way through the mass overhead and hit the road in front of him, he swerved to miss the first two. But when he realized that they may be a gift to his war-torn, ravaged heart of a being, he drove through the final five.

He did cast his eyes up in wavering faith. He did rub the edge of his hand to soothe it. He did find that the pain in his heart was unloaded.

The reason behind particular events was meant to remain mysterious.

Stepping on the gas, he headed towards Atlanta.

—ⲙ—

Traffic light after traffic light Billy sits in lines of cars, most waiting patiently, but an occasional curse breaks the day, or a series of blasting horns. People crowd the sidewalks, moving along quickly, carrying shopping bags, briefcases, munching hotdogs from a local stand.

Billy feels tense with claustrophobia. His hands sweat and his heart beats loudly as he repeatedly licks his lips. Held up at yet another stoplight, he studies a map of the city. At this point, he's three-point-four miles from Glover's family.

The architecture begins to close in like an enemy, and the signs surround him like angry eyes.

The "Georgia peaches" walk by teetering on high heels, their summer dresses covered with sweaters for the fall. They look more sophisticated than the girls in Willis. Their strides long and hard on those teetering heels, their faces pinched, lips pursed, eyes defiant. They have found their place in this man's world.

He's two-point-one miles away now from Glover's mama, who had to love her son as much or more than the Marines who used to vacate a seat for the well-respected man to sit down.

When Billy passes a city park, the contraction that's been coiled inside releases for a moment, and his eyes wander over people lunching on the benches, lying on blankets in the grass, running after balls kicked, thrown, or batted. Okay, so they are not just slaves to the concrete.

Glover's neighborhood, two miles from the city hub, one mile on the other side of the park, has bars bolted over windows, graffiti sprayed on walls, and packs of kids gathered on corners spilling out into the street. In the air, smoke rises off of barbeques, loud consistent beats vibrate the pavement, laughter tinkles through the air like bells.

Billy parallel parks his pickup between the fins of a '62 Cadillac and the front end of an '85 Chevy, painted fluorescent green. Glover's family home, located at 505 Petunia, is yellow with white trim. An old sofa and two chairs sit on the porch, and on that sofa two young girls are curled up looking at a book. In flower boxes, healthy-looking chrysanthemums add their gold and yellow to the scene. When Billy steps out of his pickup on his left leg, he shakes out his right and steps down gingerly. The leg hurts less day by day, but it will always be one inch shorter than the other.

The girls look up, as he opens the white picket gate and heads up the short walk to the porch. They jump up from their seat and run inside.

"Mama! Mama! There's a man here!"

By the time that Billy walks up the three steps to the porch, an elderly woman stands at the door, wiping her hands on her apron. The two girls stand beside her.

"Are you Mrs. Glover?" Billy asks.

The woman softly says, "Yes."

"My name is William John Bagwell. I served in the Marines with your son, James."

A look passes over the woman's face that Billy recognizes as a shadow of pain. She glances down and swallows, then draws her gaze back up.

"You're Bagwell? My Jimmy wrote a lot about you in his letters. Get back, girls." She opens the door and stands aside. "Please, come in."

The house is modest, but immaculately clean, and the smell of cooking food fills the air. Billy begins to salivate, a good sign, because he hasn't really been hungry for days.

"Would you like a glass of ice tea? Oh, and please sit down. Chantel, go get the man some tea. Do you like lemon and sugar in yours?"

"Yes, Ma'am, that sounds great," Billy answers.

The young girl skips out of the room. Billy sits down in a chair as Glover's mother sits down opposite him on a long brown sofa.

"Jimmy told me that if something happened to him, if he didn't make it home, you'd be showing up."

"He did?"

"In a letter."

Billy watches the older woman turn her face away and blink back tears. She is small with short grizzled black and gray hair. She sits delicately perched on the edge of the sofa with strong-looking hands folded in her lap. Billy can see how she must have once been as pretty as the two girls are now.

She turns her head back and says, "My name is Lydia. These are Jimmy's two youngest sisters, Sherese and Chantel. Jimmy said that you would tell us what happened. I couldn't help but notice your limp. Did you get injured, too?"

Chantel walks back into the room with a tall glass of tea and shyly hands it to Billy. She joins her mother and her sister on the sofa.

"Yes, Ma'am."

"These are the only two that are home right now. But that's okay. You can tell us, and we'll tell the rest of the family."

Billy lifts the glass and takes a long drink. "This is delicious. Thank you."

"My son received a medal for dying in that desert. He was one of only 147 allies who died in that war."

"Yes, Ma'am."

"So few to die. Why was my son one of them? I know the Lord took him because he wanted him. But, how did it happen?"

"I want you to know, Ma'am, that your son was very well-liked. In fact, I believe that he was the most well-liked man in our unit. And respected. We all respected him."

Lydia looks down at her hands that are twisting into knots. "My Jimmy was always very well liked."

"On that day, Ma'am, visibility was very low. Your son and I were sent out on a two-point mission to set up and possibly eliminate one or more of the enemy. We dug out and waited and waited. I ... I did something really foolish that day. I lit a cigarette. Your son may have told you that we were forbidden to smoke. In addition, we had problems with our radio. We kept trying to receive a message from command. The smoke of the cigarette, the radio ... something tipped off the enemy that we were there, and before we knew it, we were hit with the missiles." It was Billy's turn to glance off now and swallow hard. In his head, he could hear those missiles coming in. He could feel the earth shake and roll. He could remember his bladder release and the feeling of flying.

"William? William, maybe you're not ready to tell the story yet."

Billy turns back to the woman and the two girls. "But, I have to. I lost consciousness. When I came to, I found that I was injured. But your son ... he was lying there. My friend. He was lying there, and I could see red bubbles rising out of his chest. I crawled over and I shot him up with morphine. I ... I tried to do what I could."

"I see. You blame yourself."

"Well, yes, Ma'am, I do."

"The Lord took my son, William. No matter what you could do, he was marked. It was his time to be carried home. If it wasn't, Jimmy wouldn't have died."

"And they didn't come. They knew where we were, but they didn't come."

"You mean the Iraqis?"

"No. Our guys. I picked up Glover, your son, and threw him over my shoulder. I carried him through the sand. It was night now, and the sand had settled. There were stars out. Finally they came. But, it was too late."

"You were injured yourself, but you carried my son. Thank you."

"But, I didn't save him."

"You couldn't save him."

"He ... he died in the Humvee riding back to the safety zone. I ... I took these to give to you." Billy pulls the dog tags off over his head, stands up, and hands them to Lydia. He watches as the woman, the mother, lightly traces her son's personal info with the tips of her fingers. He sits back down as she looks up.

"Thank you, William. My son wrote that you were a good friend. I remember he wrote me that he thought of you like a brother."

Billy pulls onto the freeway and steps on the gas, heading back to his homeland, feeling like he has wings to fly. For a few hours, he will forget the sandstorms of the desert, the premature death of his brothers, the invisible and visible scars that he carries. He will remember that his daughter is his, will always be his, in that way that lights his heart. He will remember that Sam will need him in the coming months as he fights for his life again. He will remember that the people of this land deserve to hear about the overt and covert actions he observed overseas. He has a place in the world to fulfill. Though he may never run as fast as he once did, or even live long enough to see his hair gray, there must be a series of days to unfold and a reason for the pleasure and the pain to reside. The pumpkins, gourds, and corn shift gently in the bed of the truck as the eyes of the rag doll, lying beside him in the adjoining seat, stare up at him with innocence and hope.

Acknowledgements

I am living proof of the adage, "Good things come to he or she who waits," something my maternal grandmother, Margaret G. Baxter, often said. At the age of nine, I began writing, and with the encouragement of an essay contest that I won, I freed my imagination to conceive worlds I wanted to bring to life. And even though I have accomplished the publication of short prose poetry, articles, film reviews, and produced plays, the publication of this novel feels like an arrival at last. Thank you, Grandma, for pushing me so gently on, even now, from the other side.

I thank my mother, Ann F. Schultz, who has read nearly everything I have ever written, and in her unassuming way, has proofread, guided, and tirelessly supported me. I love you, Mom.

In the early stages of work on *Little Shadow*, two of my professors from California State University, Long Beach, acted as "wind beneath my wings." I thank Tyler Dilts for his support and guidance, as well as Teri Shaffer Yamada, whose kind words about the "Dark Bloom" chapter led the way.

There have been wonderful friends, through the years, who have supported me through thick and thin. They include but are not limited to: Bobbi Walsh, Donna Cole, Tamara Gulde, Kristine Pursell, and Janet Paul. I truly could not have continued to pursue my dream without you. Thank you.

Finally, I thank my publishers and editors, Marti Smiley Childs and Jeff March, for their knowledge, support, and eagle eyes.

About the Author

Author S. L. Schultz's body of work includes poetry, prose, plays, screenplays and novels. Her plays have been staged in San Francisco and Chicago, and she has published short works. She lives in Michigan where she teaches English Composition and Creative Writing in area colleges and correctional facilities.

S. L. Schultz is a graduate of California State University, Long Beach. *Little Shadow* is her first published novel, and book one of a trilogy. Visit her website at www.SLSchultz.com and follow her on Facebook.

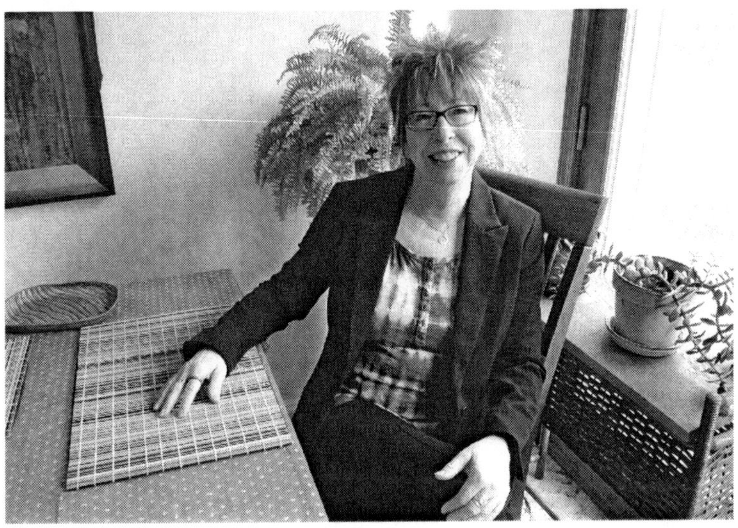

S. L. Schultz (photo by Sarah Shirk)

CPSIA information can be obtained
at www.ICGtesting.com
Printed in the USA
LVOW11s2157030418
572225LV00001B/22/P